He Loves You Not

Puck Buddies

Puck Buddies
Roommates
Bed Buddies
Baby Daddies

Stand-Alone Novels

Lost in La La Land
My Side
The Long Way Home
First Kiss
Sunder
In the Fading Light
For Love or Money
Sinderella
Beauty's Beast
The Club

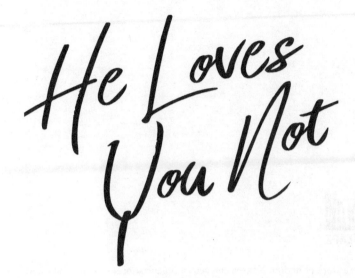

He Loves You Not

THE SERENDIPITY SERIES

TARA BROWN

SKYSCAPE

SKYSCAPE

Published by Skyscape, New York

www.apub.com

Amazon, the Amazon logo, and Skyscape are trademarks of Amazon.com, Inc., or its affiliates.

ISBN-13: 9781503903197
ISBN-10: 1503903192

Cover design by Eileen Carey

Printed in the United States of America

For Sarah, one day we will meet for a glazed raspberry bun.
Until then, thank you.

Chapter One
WRONG SIDE OF THE SUBWAY TRACKS

Lacey

"I'm here, hurry up!" Marcia's voice booming from the front door up the stairs of my family's brownstone made me smile.

"Coming!" I squealed, grabbing my sunscreen and stuffing it in my bag with everything else I might need. Marcia's ability to tan in all conditions, even under the raging midday sun on the open ocean while drinking a margarita, was the thing I envied the most about her. It was like even the sun knew she was too precious to burn. Whereas my mortal flesh would scorch under the umbrella and through my clothes . . .

Thumping down the stairs, I was met with kind brown eyes and a soft smile at the bottom where my grandma was standing in front of Marcia.

"Have fun, sweetie."

"Thanks, Grandma." I leaned in and kissed her wrinkled cheek, inhaling a little of the perfume she wore every day, even when she didn't leave the house or take her apron off.

"Is Martin back yet from his doctor's appointment?" I asked her. "I was gonna see if he wanted to come with us to a boat party later.

Friday night and end of the year and all." My younger brother had been out all day yesterday and was now at some doctor's appointment with my mom, so I hadn't seen him since school ended. Having a nurse for a mom meant the slightest sniffle was cause for alarm. His lingering cough and sore throat from the flu he'd come down with had Mom convinced he had mono. Poor guy. He probably hadn't even kissed a real girl yet but would still somehow die from the kissing disease if Mom had the diagnosis right. She and Grandma liked babying him. And he liked it too. It meant snacks delivered to his room so he didn't have to pause his video game, and crusts meticulously cut off his grilled cheese.

He milked it, and I couldn't say if given the chance, I wouldn't do the same. We just didn't get the same opportunities.

"No. They're still out." Grandma's smiled wanly, and the strange look in her eyes flashed concern. No doubt she, too, thought Martin was suffering from mono, and she was already planning her strategy to nurse him back to health with home-cooked meals and hot water bottles propped under his back.

I, on the other hand, knew he was fine. Fine enough to send spam texts about the new superhero movie coming out, like I cared.

"Too bad. Martin would have so much fun. That boat will be loaded with hotties—the perfect way for a seventeen-year-old guy to start the summer." Marcia winked, but her charming grin faded after a moment of contemplation. "Although I'm not entirely sure I could stand to watch him hit on girls."

"Or have girls hit on him." I wrinkled my nose. "Maybe we should reconsider inviting him out from now on."

Martin was equally Marcia's and my favorite person. He was funny, sarcastic, witty, and always such a homebody. He was starting senior year in September, and I wanted him to have fun, to stop missing out on the good times that being a young, connected person afforded him.

"I'll send him a text to see if he wants to meet up. See ya Sunday night, Grandma." I hugged her hard and took a cookie from the plate she was holding.

Marcia was already chewing away on one, moaning. "Your cookies are the best, Grandma. My dad hired a pastry chef from Alsace, and even his cookies aren't this good." She stepped back, shimmering in the sunlight like a Greek goddess, no doubt the result of some ridiculously expensive highlighter made from the souls of seahorses and only distributed to the wealthy elite.

"Oh, Marcia, stop. And don't text Martin to come party with you two. He's not old enough for your kind of trouble. Leave him be. He's a good boy." Grandma waved Marcia off, not taking even a sip of the flattery lingering in the air. She didn't like Marcia much; *entitled* was the way Grandma described the entire La Croix family, based strictly on the fact that they were wealthier than anyone needed to be. It wasn't like they could help being rich, the same way Grandma couldn't help being widowed, but she didn't let Marcia get away with anything as far as behavior or attitude went for that reason alone.

Marcia didn't seem offended, though. It was a weird relationship to witness. Almost like Marcia needed a firm hand sometimes and Grandma knew it.

"Have a good weekend, Grandma!" I hurried out the door, letting her close it.

"Can we please call a car?" Marcia complained as we hurried up the street away from my parents' house toward the subway station.

"No." I scowled at her, feigning disappointment. "Don't hate on the subway. I saw Keanu Reeves riding last week. If it's good enough for him, it's good enough for you."

"What does Keanu Reeves have to do with me?" She arched a perfectly shaped dark eyebrow.

"He's way more famous than you, dick." I smirked as we left Third Street and crossed Smith, hurrying for the Carroll Street station.

"He is not! I have way more followers on Instagram, firstly, and secondly, I guarantee his ass wasn't getting on the subway in the hood." She glanced around as we descended into the dim lighting that flickered as if it were sending Morse code. To her, the message would be a warning the way it was a greeting to me.

"Oh my God," I said with a groan, so tired of defending Brooklyn to everyone I knew. "Not today, Satan. It's our first Friday of summer break. You need to keep that 'tude in check."

Getting down to the subway platform was one thing; Marcia survived by holding her finger under her nose, sniffing her rose-oil moisturizer to avoid smelling the warm recycled air down there and rocking her best don't-mess-with-me expression. Actually getting her onto the subway car was always a whole other endeavor.

She was confident and cool to an outsider's perspective, but the second she got onto the train, her body tensed, she panicked, and her eyes darted both ways as if to ascertain which direction was less offensive. Her hands balled as she stared in violent jerks from the pole to the seat—pole, seat, pole, seat—and her upper lip glistened just slightly before she decided on a seat, wincing as the hard plastic squeaked under her.

I slumped beside her and shook my head, whispering, "I think it's getting worse. It took eleven seconds for you to choose. Last time was only six."

"Shut up," she whispered back, her eyes surveying the people next to us, sizing them up to determine a threat level.

She couldn't see it, but all of them were just living their lives—reading, texting, closing their eyes for the moment of rest they saw the subway as, or even staring into space and processing. They weren't out to get her with poor-people germs or gang-life plans.

Life in Brooklyn, and almost every place in New York City, was nothing like where we were going.

Where Marcia lived was a different world entirely.

She wasn't just wealthy. She was also the queen bee of our group. In fact, she was the queen bee of our school, which was saying something. NYU was filled with rich kids; being wealthy was nearly a prerequisite to attend. The tuition was higher than almost every other school in the country.

Last I checked, we were number three for getting raked over the coals for costs. But NYU was a great school with excellent academic ranks, which was why I chose it. And I didn't have to move, which cut the cost a lot for me. Considering I had only a very partial scholarship, cutting that housing cost corner meant I could still afford something resembling a life. Commuting twenty minutes each way to college and staying with my parents was the best way for me to graduate debt free. Although living at home was not ideal, I was on the path to freedom, which was more than I could say for a lot of my peers. One more year and I would be working full-time and able to afford my own place.

"Are you going to get a job with us this summer?" It was the question I asked Marcia every year, and like every year before this one, she wrinkled her nose and gasped.

"Not a chance. I don't want to work for my *dad.*" She said it like the mere idea was beneath her, which should have insulted me. But it didn't. I wasn't ashamed of working for her dad; in fact, my entire future rested on him and his company, La Croix Marketing & PR.

That was only one of his companies, actually, but it was the best in my opinion. He always sold his other ventures; the marketing and PR branch was the only one he'd insisted on maintaining himself.

Frederick La Croix was one of New York's top business developers, but unlike most, he wasn't an employee of a company. He was the man behind the company. He bought out small businesses that had an idea but not the funds to meet their potential, and after growing the companies, he would sell them. Everyone won, especially him. He was a genius, and if I was being honest, he was my man crush on most Mondays. He wasn't just a brilliant businessman; he was the cool dad who wanted to know what was trendy for my age group, thus paying attention to our needs and likes and desires. He picked our brains and spoke to us on a level that made us feel seen and respected. He was different from every other dad I'd ever met, especially my own.

And I loved nothing like I did the summers when I got to work in his office and assist in all the greatness going around. He kept the marketing and PR firm happy and stable because he used it to grow whatever company he was working to build at that moment. The days were long and grueling right before a sale, but the work changed frequently, and there was plenty of healthy competition to go around for everyone in the office.

"I can't imagine working for my father." Marcia hugged her handbag tightly. "Business seems so barbaric to me. To sell something small and easy like hand cream might not be too hard, if I had to do it, but a whole company? I don't know how he does it."

"So what's the plan, then? Travel, lie around, get manicures?" I mocked her.

"No. I don't know." She said it exasperatedly. Her dad had clearly been at her again, nagging her to find some drive and direction. It was the same song and dance he did at the beginning of every summer. Not that it ever worked. "Why does everyone care what I do for the summer?" She gave me the side-eye glare she was famous for. It killed Prince's, my favorite meme in the whole world. He really did slay the side-eye.

"Because you don't do anything over the summer except get a tan and a damaged liver." I tried to say it like I was sort of joking. It was hard. I wanted so many things for her. And seeing the potential for greatness in her being wasted again every year was annoying. "This is our last summer of fun and freedom before we have to start contributing to the world, not just taking from it. Next year when we leave college, there will be expectations. We won't be in school. We'll have to work. Will you honestly want to say you've graduated and are still living at home with your parents?" I nudged her, still trying to go easy. The lecture was a frequently revisited theme in her life. Do something. Be someone. Stop mooching.

"It's called summer break. And I do things," she argued.

This was my favorite part of the conversation.

She frowned as she continued. "Last summer I did that relief thingy with those people who needed help in Mexico. And the summer before that I handed out water bottles at that triathlon. Twice."

"Dear God." I sighed, noting her answers were getting more desperate and far between. "You know what, I give up. I won't say another word. When you decide what you wanna be when you grow up, if you ever decide to grow up, you let me know."

"Okay, good." She tried to sound like she was fed up with it all, but I knew that secretly she liked that we didn't give up on her. Her mom never grilled her about anything, and it bothered her. She would worry more if her dad stopped. She liked that he cared. And that I did too.

I didn't know if she was aware how hard it was for him to watch her skate by, though.

He was more like me.

He grew up middle class and ended up a billionaire.

When he was twenty-five and had made his first hundred million, he married a rich girl, and unfortunately Marcia's mother's influence on their daughter had been stronger than his. His hard work and dedication matched my parents', which was sad since my parents were still middle class, but they influenced me to improve myself. I saw the results of hard work. And different kinds of work.

My family lived in the city, which was a feat for a lot of young families.

We had food and warmth, and I never really wanted for anything. And even if I did want for something they couldn't provide, I worked and bought it myself.

And yes, my parents were basically treading water, never getting too far ahead, but my brother and I would both graduate from college without student loans, and for whatever reason that was more important to my parents than anything. They made sure we were both going into growth-opportunity careers, also important. They wanted more for us than they had for themselves.

Our dad was lucky his sales position was still relevant, because a lot of sales jobs had suffered through the internet revolution and the recession. Our mom's job in health care was always going to be relevant, but she had no desire for Martin or me to live like her, on our feet doing shift work for the rest of our lives.

My parents might not have become billionaires, but they had set it up so maybe Martin and I could. Best schools. Tuition paid. Live at home for free. Work only in the summer. We had it made.

"Guess who I saw yesterday?" Marcia muttered so no one else could hear us, interrupting my thoughts on how great her dad and my parents were.

"Who?" I asked, not really caring.

"You're not going to believe it," she whispered, making my stomach tighten a bit. Her sightings were always bad—something to do with scandal.

I didn't know a single person from Marcia's world who hadn't been involved in some kind of scandal, except her and me. Even her boyfriend, Monty, had a scandal. His parents, another rich family from the Upper East Side, recently sold their family's dusty old historic mansion near Central Park when Monty's grandpa died, and they bought a new penthouse in Tribeca. It was a travesty to the upper echelons of New York to see Midtown and Tribeca and SoHo become trendy, while the Upper East Side lost its sexy appeal.

Gasp!

The lives of the rich and famous.

I rolled my eyes inwardly and realized I'd missed half of what Marcia had said. "What?" I said, cutting her off.

"I know, right? So then his dad got in the limo with her, and they drove away. Maya is going to be pissed. Her mom swore it was over. But Mr. Sandu had a lot of ass in his hand for it being over."

"Gross." I cringed, catching up fairly fast even though I'd missed most of the conversation.

Maya Costa and Harry Sandu were friends of ours from high school. Learning that their parents were getting it on last year had been a massive outrage in our world. You couldn't even have a dinner party for about a month after the news leaked without someone being accused of taking sides. And both families were smack in the middle of our groups. Well, not my group. My parents didn't even know they existed.

My parents were way too busy for that shit, or for scandal in general.

"I wish I had another cookie." She smacked her lips together. "And some almond milk." She gave me a look. "You think if I sent Darren over to your house, Grandma would give him a bag of cookies for us?"

"No," I laughed. "Grandma is a spicy old lady who hates the fact that you have a driver. She'll give him cookies all right, but they won't be in a bag for us. They'll be on a plate for him and come with a glass of real milk and be served in front of the TV while she lets him have a damn break."

"A break from what? He's a driver. His entire life is a break. He sits and drives. That's not even hard work."

"I know. He's so lazy," I mocked again.

"Shut up." She held her purse tighter to her chest. "I didn't say he was lazy, but it's not like he's out digging ditches in the sun."

"No." *Not like you,* I thought to myself. I loved her, sometimes to death. As in sometimes I got so annoyed I wanted to strangle her. Lovingly. Some of my favorite conversations between Martin and me, late at night over a plate of Grandma's baking, were based on these moments of the ridiculous. And usually involved me laughing at him mocking everyone in our separate groups of friends, particularly Marcia, but always with love. She really was a handful. Although his friends were no better—rich and lacking a sense of reality because of it. "We're almost there."

I chuckled at Marcia's dislike of the subway, but then the very thing she always assumed would happen, did.

"Hey." A guy came and sat next to her, offering a cheeky grin and wandering eyes that took a stroll down the front of her top.

"Fuck off." She gave him her own version of a cheeky grin: resting bitch face and a whole lot of New York City sass.

"Don't be rude, baby. You can't sit on the train all dolled up and not expect a guy to come over and give it a try."

"Why do you guys have to push it? Did I give you a hint that I was at all interested? Was it my breathing or the way I took up this space that did it? Do I have to start filming you as I try to explain how much I seriously don't want to be hit on while you're sexualizing me and threatening my peace because you think with your dick and feel entitled to all of this?" She waved a hand up her body. "Or will you go away?"

"What?"

"Go sit over there and think about what you've done!" She pointed.

"Damn, girl." He got up and moved, going even farther than where she'd pointed.

The girl across from us laughed, nodding with approval.

"God, I love you," I muttered, always stunned by how far some people would go and Marcia's ability to put them in their place. That kind of thing never happened to me on the subway. It was like Marcia invited trouble, but even for having a privileged upbringing, she sure could pull the street side out. And that was from me. She learned to talk a certain way when she needed to. Mostly it was in Brooklyn while riding the subway, which did explain her fears. But since she was the only person it ever happened to, I tried to make her seem irrational for having them. That's what being a sibling was all about—rounding off those edges. And Martin and I were as close as she was going to get to siblings, so we took our work seriously.

"Finally." As the train halted Marcia jumped up and grabbed the pole, closing her eyes momentarily and making peace with the fact that she would have to wait a minute before using her hand sanitizer. She was way past the guy hitting on her. In her mind, the germs of the filthy subway were worse than being sexualized by a stranger.

She was the epitome for nature versus nurture as far as obsessing over cleanliness went. She had grown up in such clean conditions, she wasn't accustomed to filth. Now she was on her own in the real world, or as alone as she could be with her dad's credit card as support, and it was both crazy and amusing to watch her shirk from exposure.

We jumped off the train at the Twenty-Third Street station and hurried along the dirty platform to the stairs.

"Ahhhhhh," she sighed as we surfaced. "Fresh air!"

"Thank you." I smiled brightly, nudging her as I acknowledged her version of hardship in this friendship.

"You're welcome." She rolled her eyes. "I don't know why you can't just ride in the car like a normal person."

"Normal New Yorkers don't have drivers! My dad even leaves his work car at the office in Jersey because it's faster to take public transport."

"It's not much faster."

"On a good day, at midnight, driving's more efficient. But on a bad day, which is almost every day, taking the subway makes a huge difference. I've gotten out of the car when Darren's been driving me somewhere, because some accident happened or the roads were so backed up that I gave in and walked to your house. I've had to take my shoes off partway and walk barefoot if I was wearing heels." I folded my arms.

"Gross." She shuddered. "Barefoot in New York is like rolling around on a field of used needles." She linked her arm in mine and started the short walk to her place at the corner of Fifth Avenue and West Twenty-Sixth.

When we arrived, West, the doorman, beamed at us both. "Ladies, how is the first weekend of summer break treating you?" His knowledge of our comings and goings always surprised me. His memory and skills at observation were sorely misused working here. He should have been in the FBI or CIA. Sometimes I wondered if he was and this was an undercover gig for him, watching the rich and famous come and go.

"Excellent, thank you, West. And how is your day going?" And there was the thing I loved, absolutely loved, about Marcia. She might have talked a good game as a snob, but she legitimately cared about her people. And they knew it. She meant it when she asked and paid attention when they answered.

"Not too bad, Miss Marcia. Weather's fine, streets aren't too busy, traffic's been all right all day, which for a Friday is some kind of miracle." He chuckled. "And my wife messaged me that she's making my favorite pot roast and Yorkshires for dinner. I love her homemade gravy, the way it sinks into the pudding."

"That sounds great! You have a good weekend. Tell her I said hello." Marcia smiled wide and entered the building.

"Will do. You both have a lovely day."

"You too," we said at the same time.

In the elevator, Marcia leaned back, losing that charm. She didn't waste it on me anymore. I was like family. "What do you want for dinner?" She rubbed her stomach. "Those Yorkshires sound good. I wonder if the gravy is homemade or from a packet."

"Don't even think about asking him to have his wife send some over." I bumped her, teasingly but half seriously. She didn't have normal boundaries.

"I wouldn't," she hissed.

"Liar." I grinned as the elevator took us directly to her family's penthouse.

"Shut up." She huffed and stepped off, smiling wide again when she saw Girt, her maid. "Hello, Girt."

"Miss Marcia, Miss Lacey. How are you?"

"Excellent, thank you. TGIF, Girt. What are your plans for the weekend?" Marcia asked.

All the house staff got weekends off, even though they lived with the La Croixes. It was another cool thing about Mr. La Croix. He forced Marcia and her mom to take care of themselves at least a couple of days of the week. No cook or butler on Saturdays or Sundays.

"Oh, not much. I was thinking about hitting the farmers market and possibly taking a trip out to Sleepy Hollow with my sister. She's in the city for the week and really wants to see it. Tourists." Girt offered me a knowing smile. "And you must be starting your summer job soon?"

"Yes, ma'am, Monday. I'm pumped." I was beaming at the prospect.

"Good luck." She winked at me. "Though we know you won't need it."

"Thanks," I said as I followed the sound of Marcia's clicking heels across the foyer, which was the size of the entire main floor of my house.

Her two-story penthouse was off the charts, thousands of square feet.

Walls of windows overlooking Madison Square Park and Manhattan.

Marble floors that gleamed so brightly I could check my makeup in them.

Glitzy light fixtures that sparkled like they were made of diamonds. They probably were, now that I thought of it.

Modern decor and custom everything surrounded us at all times.

Marcia had four closets in her room. The maid, Girt, had two, one and a half more than I had at home.

Marcia's parents had his and hers master bedrooms; they didn't even share a room. I didn't ask questions about that since I didn't need answers that would scar me for life.

Even her dog had his own room, and his was bigger than my bedroom. His door had a custom sign with his name, Floof. Senor Floof. He was a Chihuahua. His name made no sense to me for a dog with short hair, so I just called him Senor.

The butler, a man named Moser, was a proper British butler, and he had some résumé. He'd worked for royals and huge icons in his day. He was older now and felt a nice, calm job here would be a great semi-retirement. I didn't see how tending to the needs of American royalty was preparing for retirement, but I also hadn't worked for true royals, so I didn't know how it could get any worse than this.

"Lacey!" Mr. La Croix welcomed me first, always.

"Mr. La Croix! How are you?" I let him embrace me and kiss my cheek.

"For the millionth time, call me Frederick or Dad, for God's sake. We're not at the office, where I also insist you call me Dad." He winked when he pulled back.

"No," I said with a laugh, refusing to call him Dad. What if I slipped up at the office by accident?

"Marcia, what are you girls doing home?" He kissed her as well. "I figured you'd be out causing a scene; it's the first Friday of summer break."

"All in good time, Daddy. We're going on a cruise of the harbor later. End-of-year parties are in full effect. We just need to prep. This thing here would wear jean shorts if I left it up to her." She pointed a thumb at me.

"As I suspected." His eyes darted from Marcia's to mine. "Grades?" He held his hand out.

"Oh, right." I pulled my phone out and logged on to NYU's dashboard, showing off my grades for the final semester.

"Holy Moses, kid!" He beamed. "Excellent work! Were your parents excited?" His eyebrows rose.

"Oh, uh." I took my phone back. "They weren't home when I got there. Mom's been taking extra shifts and forcing Martin to the doctor for imaginary diseases, and Dad was away all week." I nodded, pretending it was cool.

"I'm certain they'll be thrilled when you give them the good news."

"Yeah." I let him think that. My parents hadn't seen a report card of mine since junior year of high school. Which was fine with me. They trusted me to get my grades and attain goals on my own.

"Well, you must be excited to be starting work again on Monday." He beamed with fatherly pride. "Back at the old sweatshop."

"More than excited." I ate it up. "Is Hennie coming back too? I emailed her, but she's terrible at responding." She was the other summer temp whom I'd worked with for four years, and I adored her. Together, we adored La Croix Industries. It was like having a second family—a second family that I saw more than my own.

"She sure is. Asked me about you yesterday."

"Awesome! I can't wait. Do we have any major sales coming up?" I risked Marcia's annoyance by talking shop at the house.

"We might. I have something I'm really excited to talk to you about, actually, but I'll give you the weekend off." He chuckled. "And how about you?" He turned his attentions to his daughter, who was wrinkling her nose, something she did right before lying. Worst poker player ever. "How are your grades?"

"I passed. I'm sure I did." She didn't sound sure.

"I expect those grades emailed to me." He pointed his finger in her face but then softened and leaned in to kiss the side of her head again. "Be good. If you need Darren to pick you up at some ungodly hour, let him know ahead of time. He doesn't like getting out of bed to come traipsing after you, and he has Saturday off," he said, before lifting his phone and going back to work.

"We will," Marcia said, laughing.

"We'll take a taxi like normal people and let him sleep." I scoffed and glanced back at her, lowering my voice. "Did you pass everything?" I worried about her.

"I think so." She shrugged. "Honestly, I don't know. I haven't looked yet."

I slumped my shoulders and covered my eyes with my hand.

"You promised not to bring it up."

"I know, I'm counting backward from ten." I stopped when I got to minus four and the annoyance lifted. "Let's celebrate!" I forced a smile on my face. Because even if she was super irresponsible and some days I wanted to say "not my circus, not my monkey," the truth was, she was my monkey. And I would always be there for her.

Especially if her dad was going to kick her out when he saw this latest set of grades.

I needed to be patient with her.

Very, very patient.

And successful so I could afford her.

"Let's get dressed. You can't wear that." She plucked at my shirt. "We only have two hours before we have to be there."

She dragged me down the hall.

Her house was so weird.

There was no grandma to offer cookies and snacks, and no one to make sure we did things like eat or drink or sleep. It was like adulting, only not.

"Can we get something to eat? I don't want to party on nothing but my breakfast burrito from seven hours ago and that cookie Grandma gave me." I rubbed my belly.

"No, it'll make you look bloated. There'll be appies on the boat." She said it like that was normal. For food to be an afterthought.

The rumbling in my stomach was my own version of disagreeing. "So all that talk of roast and Yorkshires was a lie?"

"Yes," she said as she forced me to her room and pushed me toward the back of the chair as she sat at her vanity filled with all the best makeup from around the world. "We are going to be so hot tonight, even Monty won't recognize us!" she gushed. "Do my makeup that way you did it for the glitzy ball we went to. Where I looked like a fairy with all the shimmer and unicorn magic. And my hair was like—" She lifted her blonde mane and poofed it out like a bad eighties hairdo for some glam-metal rock video and gave me a horrifyingly sexy model glare. Her description and the weird pucker she was making while holding her hair was worth the entire effort it took to give her the silver and purplish hue to her eyes and cheekbones while also offering a subtle pink baby-doll pucker with extra gloss. I added a slight gray tone to her eyebrows and started blending her cheeks.

"I think you should do yours like an Egyptian princess. I have the perfect dress for it," she remarked.

"Egyptian?" I chuckled, a little scared of what that entailed and what level of sexy she was considering. Or should I say scandalous?

Thanks to Marcia, this summer was already shaping up to be a thrilling ride away from reality, and it had barely begun.

Chapter Two

THE NOT SO PRODIGAL SON

Jordan

I sat on my bed and stared out at the harbor. My parents' place in the city did have a magical view. It was a shame that coming home from Harvard wasn't the warm experience normal kids had when they got back. I'd been here for three days, and everything felt off.

My dad was grumpier than usual, but he put on a happy face whenever he saw me.

Mom was going out of her way to be overaccommodating.

And my brother had that weird glint in his eyes that suggested he knew something that I didn't.

Whatever was up, it created an air of tension that you could cut with a knife. Something was about to give, or straight-up break. Remembering I needed to transfer some money from my former trust account that was finally in my control to my Canadian friend who was investing in some marijuana company in British Columbia and getting 70 percent returns, I flipped open my laptop.

Incoming.

I stared at the text from my brother as my father's footsteps entered the room.

"Jordie!" He sounded jovial, which was weird because there was no way he was off work yet considering it was only three in the afternoon, even if it was Friday.

"Dad." I scowled, not sure why he was saying my name with such a zest for life.

"We need to talk, son." He closed the door, which, when I was a kid, meant I was in trouble. Now it meant he didn't want the house staff to overhear.

"Okay." I put down my laptop and waited for it.

"Look, I know that you don't exactly like the whole schmoozing, business-deal side of things; you're more of a straight-shooting numbers guy." He gave me that cheesy used-car salesman grin. It made my stomach hurt, because it always meant looking the other way or helping to do something I didn't want to. He switched to a woe-is-me expression as he continued, "And my situation with Grandpa hasn't always been stellar."

Underexaggeration of the year.

"But I was hoping you might help me out the next couple of weeks. I've had a real dry year. Investing has been shit."

Ironically enough, I'd been making a killing with some advice from friends; my father just wasn't motivated enough to try. An utter lack of imagination could have had something to do with that. And possibly the stubbornness that prevented him from following Grandpa's investing, something I always did. Between him and Frederick La Croix, my returns were always amazing.

"And I have a potential deal that could mean a lot of money and a lot of stability. Quite frankly, it could change the future of this business. You remember the Weitzman family?"

"No."

The bottom fell out as he revealed his hand, making my stomach hurt. "Well, they have a daughter. Amy. She's your age. Red hair."

"Okay." The name didn't ring any bells, but his hand was starting to look like setting me up the same way he and my mom had been in a business merger—marriage from hell.

"No, wait, she's younger, maybe by two years. She went to Pennbrook." He was stalling. It had to be bad. Had he already promised me to this girl? Was I getting married this weekend?

"Okay," I repeated, wishing he would just get on with it.

"Anyway, long story short, she's apparently always had a thing for you. Kinda watched you from the societal shadows at varying functions, so to speak, and"—he continued rambling while my brain screamed, *Nooooooooo!*—"since you're home for the summer, her dad and I thought you both might hit it off."

"No." I didn't have an *okay* for that. I couldn't even pretend.

"Now listen here—" He instantly changed to the man I was used to. The song-and-dance act had dropped. He stood over me, tall and trying to be intimidating, but I wasn't eleven anymore. All I had to do was stand up and stare down on him. He was stuck at five feet eleven, and I was three inches taller now.

He bristled. "You can do this family a favor for once instead of just taking, and help your old man out. I'm not asking you to marry her. Go out, get a meal, see a show, hit a nightclub. Do whatever it is you young people do. How hard is it to entertain a pretty girl so her dad feels comfortable enough to invest with me? Weeks, Jordie. Not the rest of your life. Don't be selfish about this. It's important to me," he said, bringing out the big guns.

"Dad—"

"No. Before you start making up excuses, remember that I pay for your education. I gave you the first half of your trust early, but I still have the other half. I make sure you have this beautiful life. And meanwhile all I'm asking is one favor, one small favor, so that I can continue to provide for you and this family in the comfortable way you're all used to. And when you think about it, I'm actually doing you a favor." He circled back to used-car salesman. "This is a beautiful girl we're talking about. Consider this your first test. If you can't handle this one little responsibility, how are you going to handle working for Grandpa as a partner? And your grandpa is on board with this. Is it worth the rest of your inheritance to put your family's best interests behind screwing around all summer?" And there it was, the biggest gun he had. Mentioning Grandpa and calling me worthless while disinheriting me from the second half of my trust. He was extra manipulative today.

"I'm not dating some girl because you want her dad to invest. Jesus!" I almost laughed at him. He was a caveman.

"It's a billion-dollar deal, Jordan! Do you have a billion dollars lying around to make up the difference? Cause Grandpa sure wants that money." His face flushed as he got more worked up into convincing me.

My phone vibrated, drawing my eyes down and making me fight a grin as I realized my brother, Stephen, was in the house and texting me as Dad was screaming.

Hang in there.

"A billion dollars! Think about that!" He sounded like he might have a stroke at any second, he was so amped. This was just the start. His act was amazing, and it was easier to agree than listen to him go on and on. He wouldn't stop until I did. "This is our family business, Jordie. We have to work together, everyone pulling their own weight. Right now you're not doing much to chip in."

"Fine, whatever." I gave in, like I always did. "If you can't come up with a single other intelligent idea to convince her dad you're the man to trust his money with, then I guess prostituting your own kid out is the only alternative." I sighed, defeated. If Grandpa was involved, I would end up doing it anyway; the old man was much better at presentation than Dad was. He at least would have gotten me drunk, put me in bed with her, and faked a pregnancy. He'd do a lot for a billion-dollar Klondike bar.

"Attaboy!" He ignored my jab. "Stop being such a downer, kid. The girl's a knockout, and your old man is about to show your grandpa who the boss is!"

Doubtful.

"That's my boy." He turned and left, uncaring about me and convinced he had already secured the deal.

I was alone with the prospect of how much my summer had just crashed and burned when Stephen came slinking into the room, poorly hiding the fact that he'd come by the house solely to watch this performance. "Okay, Dad's lying. Grandpa totally isn't on board, and while Amy isn't a troll—actually, she's kinda hot—she's also likely a starfish. Vapid as fuck. Like, you need to bail on this. Take the disinheritance. You can't go through with this. You won't make the summer. What kind of man would you be if you couldn't even decide for yourself where you put your dick?" He said it like he was laughing, like it might be a little funny, because this wasn't happening to him.

"You've met her?" I groaned.

"Oh, God, yes. It was awful. Had dinner a couple of times in the last two weeks before you got back. You haven't lived until you've watched her play with her phone for three hours without speaking once. I didn't even know if she was breathing the whole time. Trust me, this is not your kind of dish. She doesn't know who Chaucer is."

"Fuck you," I said with half the effort it deserved. "You don't know who Chaucer is."

"Awww, I love you, too, little buddy." He sat next to me. "But for reals. No. You can't do this. She will eat your soul. Even I wouldn't bang her with your dick."

"Awesome." And that was that. I was damned if I did and damned if I didn't. I just had to decide what flavor of screwed I wanted to be.

Chapter Three

TITANIC MISTAKES

Lacey

The party was amazing.

Packed yacht.

A light show to accompany the music.

Drinks flowing in every direction.

Trays of food circulating along with a massive buffet.

And a promise of fireworks later.

One of my best friends, Kami, had convinced her boyfriend, Miguel, a.k.a. DJ Spark, to DJ for us, and he was killing it. He was one of New York's up-and-coming celebrity DJs, which I had heard had gone to his head when it came to groupie love—something that was less than acceptable if true.

Regardless of how sleazy the DJ may or may not have been, he helped throw a fantastic end-of-year party on a two-hundred-foot yacht with 150 of our closest friends and a lot of food and booze. I personally thanked God and the caterers several times for the food.

"Oh my God, did you see who's here?" Marcia shouted at me from across the bar table we were eating at. Well, that I was eating at while she watched me in disgust.

"No, who?" I asked, before I noticed the hateful stare in her eyes. I didn't need an answer then; I knew instantly from the look. There was only one person she hated that much.

"France." She couldn't even say my ex-boyfriend's name without spewing venom, which was sad because she spoke a lot about France—not my hateful ex, but the beautiful country where I was forced to join her every year at the end of the summer for her back-to-school shopping spree. I didn't complain that she dragged me along on her private jet and we stayed at her penthouse flat, but I did refuse all her attempts to buy me things. It was bad enough that she covered flights, accommodations, transportation, food, drinks, and all the pampering we could handle. I had to draw the line at clothes and jewels. Her version of visiting France was my version of winning an all-inclusive vacation from one of the game shows my grandma watched on TV. There was no way she would have done France my way: cheap hostels and a lot of sightseeing.

She kept glaring over my shoulder. "Why would anyone invite France"—shudder—"to the end-of-year party? He's not even in college anymore. He dropped out last semester." She sounded horrified.

"I don't know." I didn't want to discuss it. He'd been my first boyfriend ever, what I'd mistaken for love. Unfortunately he turned out to be an asshat who couldn't keep his pants on and his tongue out of other girls' mouths.

"He's with someone." Marcia sounded disgusted.

"Lemme guess. Supermodel, brunette, legs up to my chin, and her vagina is longer than her skirt?" I offered without turning around. I was shoving half a gourmet sandwich into my mouth and didn't need the eye contact with the current stick insect in the middle of my gorge fest.

"Yeah, almost. Redhead this time," she sneered, before taking a sip of champagne.

"Oh, he's changing it up a little." I didn't care. My legs were likely half as long as hers, and I enjoyed carbs of every kind. I didn't need to see his flavor of the week. I'd dumped him. This girl could have him. I actually felt sorry for her. She likely had no idea what she was in for. All the wooing in the beginning really did trick you into thinking he was a sweet guy. The cheating that followed suggested otherwise. Dirtbag.

"He looks like he's getting fat." Marcia continued with her obligatory hate on my skeezy ex.

"Good," I said as I stuffed my face.

She gave me the eye, the one that said, *Put the miniburrito down.* But I didn't. I kept eating. I didn't care.

"Hello, ladies." On the other hand, Marcia had an amazing boyfriend named Monty, who slid up next to me and started eating off my plate. He was tall, tanned, muscled, stunningly beautiful to the point it almost blinded you, and the kindest man I'd ever met. His tolerance level for Marcia's bullshit should have been an indicator of lower intelligence, but he was smart on top of his good looks and outgoing personality. In fact, he was a bit nerdy. His adoration of his girlfriend was a mystery to us all, including Marcia. She had no idea how she'd landed a perfect man, but she had.

"Took me half an hour to find you, Marcia; I barely recognized you with all that makeup. You look like a unicorn going to a rave"—he turned to me—"and you like a princess from ancient Egypt. Was this supposed to be a theme party?"

"No. Someone thought we were going to be on a float later and demanded we do crazy makeup." I chuckled and tried not to stare at him.

Before he'd started dating my best friend, Monty was the highlight of all my sex fantasies.

The moment they'd made it official, I cut him from the roster, but it was hard. Sometimes, midorgasm with someone, I'd see his face in my mind out of nowhere, making me hate myself just a little. It made masturbation conflicting.

"You do kinda look like you belong on a float." He smiled, and it still made my stomach tighten, a side effect I wrestled with. Even my dad had sighed when he met Monty. And the worst part was that he was the coolest guy ever. He made all the other boyfriends and husbands and guys in general I'd ever met pale in comparison. His family was rich, but he was a hard worker and totally down to earth. He could have slacked off in everything and ridden the trust fund, but he didn't. I respected that about him. He was as close to sainthood as a guy could get at our age and in our circle of friends.

"We look hot," Marcia said to defend us, but I knew what we looked like.

"Lucky I knew Lacey at least would be near the food," he gently mocked.

"I keep telling her it's eventually going to catch up with her," Marcia said jokingly, but fooled no one.

"Whatever, we have to enjoy it now while we can still keep the weight off by working out. My mom used to be a size two." I laughed, kidding around. She only ever grew into a size four and still ate whatever she wanted. Great metabolisms ran in the family, literally. My parents ran marathons. For how my grandma cooked, and how much I ate, I should be at a weekly weigh-in monitoring body fat and calories.

"Your mom was a two?" Marcia asked, genuinely shocked.

"Yeah, she's only up a size. And she's fifty."

"Yikes." She shook her head. "My mom is still a two." She wasn't saying it to shame my mom or get into a "my mom is better than yours" argument. This was just her being factual. Again . . . sometimes I loved her to death.

"I don't know what size my mom is, but she eats cake every day. I swear, every day. She's the happiest person I know," Monty said, before stuffing one of my sandwiches in his mouth. "Anyway, you having fun?" he asked me.

"Sure am. You?"

"No. I'm sacked. I really was voting for a quiet night and possibly watching a movie. But this thing over here demanded I show my face." He winked at Marcia.

"Ugh." Marcia gave him a fiery scowl. "We can watch movies when we're old. Have fun." She sauntered off, sashaying that ass. And like he knew he should or he honestly couldn't help himself, his eyes were glued to her body.

"Monty!"

We both spun to see one of the notorious hot guys of the rich world, sort of a celebrity party boy, heading our way with his hands out wide.

I recognized him, excusing myself before I got dragged into a second or third set of introductions with Stephen Somersby. "See you later."

He was one of the infamous Somersby brothers. I didn't know them well, just by reputation.

Stephen and I had met a couple of times, but he always forgot we'd been introduced. He knew he knew me, but from where? It was annoying, but also the way it worked for someone like me—a nobody who associated with the "it" crowd. I was constantly overlooked as anything beyond a casual hookup, and that wasn't really my scene. I was okay with occasional one-night stands, just not with notorious, wealthy womanizers.

Which meant Stephen and his gross brother weren't my type. They were known as the worst snobs and the players of all players. Stephen was older than us by about five years, but still living like he was nineteen, as his presence at this party clearly indicated.

He'd recently married some amazing lady named Cynthia Whitmore. I felt a bit sorry for her. She'd seemed really nice the one time I'd met her. Marcia said she was some top lawyer who everyone thought was way too cool for Stephen. They all thought she'd bitten off more than she could chew marrying him, but Stephen's defenders—people like Monty, who was a family friend of the Somersbys—swore Cynthia had whipped Stephen into shape. The drink in Stephen's hand and the sloppy smile on his drunken face suggested that she still had her work cut out for her.

I squeezed myself into the crowd and tried to find Marcia or one of my girls.

After getting lost in the masses, I wandered along the quiet side of the boat under the stairs, pausing to take in the view of the city as the boat came around again. Sometimes, usually in the middle of a moment like this, I liked to pause and take it in. My life with Marcia could be incredibly surreal.

If I hadn't gone to the same high school, something my grandparents had insisted on paying for, and met Marcia, who brought me into her fold instantly, I knew where my life would be. I would be one of those flickering lights in the city, working in a fast-food place at night after my day job of something equally shitty. I would be hustling to save every penny so I could afford college and life. My parents helped as much as they could, covering most of my tuition at NYU every year, but it was hard for middle-of-the-road people like us.

My connection to Marcia and her family had saved me from that. My summer job with her dad was equivalent pay to two regular summer jobs, and I knew one day I would be working for him, making both my parents' incomes on my own. I was carving my path out of the middle of the road.

I was midthought about how awesome my future was going to be when a voice interrupted me. "What a gorgeous view."

"Yeah, it's stunning." I gave a side-glance toward the guy speaking and smiled politely. I knew him from somewhere, but I didn't bother trying to remember. I was five gins, half the buffet, and three flutes of champagne in, the lighting was bad, and all these dudes looked the same to me.

"I'm Jordie." He stepped closer and held a hand out. From what I could see, he was handsome. Big shoulders, thick arms, and a tight body. His jeans and T-shirt fit him well. He looked like an athlete, maybe even a pro. But I could tell he wasn't. He was rich. He had that vibe coming off him, even if he was brutally dressed down, baseball cap and all. There was no mistaking the air about him—the kind I didn't like breathing in anymore.

That wasn't always the case, once upon a time. Back when I was new to this world and didn't understand the rules and was mesmerized by the glitz and glamour.

Everyone sparkled, just like this guy, and they all seemed so set up. It was easy to admire them and want to get closer.

But then I dated one of them and got a real taste of what their lives were actually like.

One bitter aftertaste was enough, and I'd promised myself that I would never get caught up in that mistake again.

"I'm Lacey." I shook his hand, noting how big and warm it was. It was too bad he was rich.

"Have we met before?" He winced. "Sorry, that was cheesy. You just look familiar."

"I don't know." I sighed and glanced back at the harbor.

"Hard to say with all that makeup caked on." His words slowed—as if he was realizing what he was saying—and he cringed at the end. "I mean—"

"It's fine. I don't normally look like this. My friend and I were having fun getting ready." I laughed at his embarrassment. It was kind of endearing.

"I guess I'll keep that same line of humiliation going. Do you come here often?" he joked, continuing the cheese.

"No." I looked back at the party. "I mean, I go on a lot of yachts, but not like this. This party is a whole other level of pizzazz. Do you?"

"No. Not really a yacht enthusiast. Too easy." He chuckled, leaning in, smelling like something I could be tricked by, easily. He had that wind-blown, cologne, deodorant, man-sweat smell to him. You couldn't bottle it. He made it every day, fresh, and lured unsuspecting women to their knees with it. "I'm more of a sailboat kind of guy. Fewer crowds too. I don't like the whole 'hundred people on one boat' thing. Gives me the sensation that there might not be enough life jackets and the people in the lower levels would definitely not make it off the ship."

"Come on!" I started laughing. "Who makes *Titanic* jokes while they're on a boat?"

"Too soon?"

"Never," I joked back, and leaned out, smelling the salty air. "Although, as someone who would normally be part of those lower levels, I'll try not to be offended."

"Who, you?"

"Trust me, I don't fit in up here." I pointed back at the party, certain this would chase him off if he truly was one of the snobs.

"That means nothing. I never feel like I fit in up here. No one does. It's all a lie." He smiled wide, biting that lower lip like he was stopping himself from saying anything else, but then he gave in. "And those of us who see it know it doesn't matter what we become. We'll always be a bunch of frauds." He waved toward the back of the boat, where the party was raging. "Trying too hard and sacrificing what we like about ourselves to fit in. I think most people up here feel that way. They just lie and cover it up."

His words hit me somewhere deep. I was surprised that a person like him was so self-aware. Maybe he wasn't rich after all. He sounded real. It was refreshing. And not in the "I'll pretend I hate my rich life to connect with you" kind of way; he was genuinely disenchanted. An aphrodisiac for a girl like me.

"What would you be if you could be anything?" I asked. I didn't even know why, but I cared.

"Editor in chief of a publishing house or a newspaper."

"Really?" I sounded dubious.

"No, I don't know. It sounded like the right answer. Honestly, I don't know what I want to be. I love the creation inside of a novel I'm reading. I love the changes words can make or the way writers get lost in their own work, and the journey is genuine because they don't see where it's going either. The revelations you find are real. People read, and it shapes them differently. Or they escape. I have to admit that's my biggest reason to read." He took a slow, deep inhale. "But I also love the feel of the wind and the smell of the ocean. So maybe I should have said sailor." He laughed, but his heart wasn't in it.

"Maybe." I turned back to the sea, noting the way he stared and the way I let him. Too much gin and not enough sense. That's what my grandma would say. "But then you'd be leathery and worn before your time."

"That's true. And we couldn't have that. I just don't know why I have to decide now. Why I need to have it all figured out." His tone lowered, like he didn't want me to hear that last part. "So, do you go to school here?" he asked, not giving up on the conversation.

Catching a nose full of him in the wind made my heart skip a beat. Man, he smelled good. I begged the gods to let him be some moderately rich guy, the kind that didn't even count. He was hot and kinda cool in some weird, heavy sort of way.

"I do go to school here. This will be my last year." I nodded and leaned on the railing. "You?"

"Yeah. It's my final year too. I have to pretend I'm an adult and that everything I have and where I am is exactly what I want." He chuckled, but it was bitter sounding.

"You don't like where you are?" I was a bit unprepared for this conversation. And not only because I was 60 percent sure we'd never met before but also because this was a fairly intense conversation to be having on a party boat. And yet, I didn't try to end it. "Maybe you should change that," I offered.

"That's easy to say for you lower-level folk. But it's a real problem with being one of the people up here." He turned his head from the shoreline and stared at me deeply, conversing with his gaze and convincing me he was likewise staring into my soul while baring his. "We don't always get to choose. Life is easy for the rich; happiness is something else altogether. It's not part of the guarantee."

"Your first-world problems aren't going to make me feel sorry for you," I said, fully mocking him, but with a wide smile. "No one is guaranteed fun and happiness. We have to make it." I wondered about myself and that statement. Was I finding happiness in work and school and doing well? Was that real happiness? I was too tipsy to contemplate such things and pushed the questions to the back of my mind.

"And what if making happiness for yourself meant you would disappoint every person who has ever meant anything to you?" His words were a truth; I could hear it. He was being real.

"Fuck 'em."

"Fuck 'em? Is that Shakespeare?" he asked as if he were being serious.

"Burns." I laughed hard.

"I can see a Scot saying that. But what if I can't just fuck 'em? What does good old Robbie Burns say about that?" His lips toyed with a grin, maybe just the idea of one.

"Well, if that's the case, and you were born in this cage, then I guess he would say that you'll need to be extra crazy this summer. Get it out of your system before you have to start living that soulless grind." It should have rolled off my tongue easily and lightheartedly, speaking of such a whimsical idea. But instead I stared at him, a little tipsy and a lot bold, lost in his intense eyes hidden under the brim of his hat. In that moment, I knew he was right. I did know him from somewhere, but I couldn't recall and it was driving me insane. I leaned in a little closer.

"You mean I should be one of those boys of summer and spend it recklessly doing what I want?" He was mocking me or him or both of us. "Consequences be damned?"

"Yeah," I challenged, wondering if the devious sound of my voice matched my look. "What are consequences for people like you anyway? Daddy takes away one credit card and a Maserati? You should pretend you're free, fake it 'til you make it, like my dad always says. And one day you will be."

"But what if I don't want to fake it? What if I just want to be free?" He leaned in, surprising me, and possibly himself. He lightly brushed his lips against mine, lingering for a second. He reached down, took my hand, and turned away from me, drawing me along the side of the boat toward the front and opening a door. In the flash that the door was open, I saw we were going into a bathroom. A classy way for me to start my summer, but I didn't care. He hurried inside and dragged me along with him.

In the dark, his hands found my face, cupping it as he pulled me up into him and lowered his face to mine. "You're so beautiful, Lacey."

"So are you, Jordie." I wanted to get lost in this fantasy, but the second I said his name, the realization of who he was hit me like a ton of bricks. At the exact moment, someone shouted my name.

Fate was saving me. An angel of fate.

The person shouting my name did it again.

"I think someone's looking for me." I needed to get the hell out of here, and this was my moment.

"What?" he whispered, his words caressing my lips.

"Someone's calling me." I paused as I leaned away from him, close to the door, listening again. "I have to go."

"Lacey!" It was Marcia, shouting out like God had sent her.

I grabbed the door handle.

"Wait." He grabbed my arm, but it was too late; I slipped through his loose grip and opened the door, glancing back at him, trying not to glare too hard as I slammed it on his face, leaving him inside.

"Marcia!" I called, and ran for her, never more grateful to hear her voice.

"Oh my God. I thought you fell overboard!" she shouted, and hugged me. "One minute I saw you, and then you were gone."

"No, just using the ladies' room." I linked my arm in hers and glanced back as Jordan fucking Somersby, Stephen Somersby's sleazy brother, left the bathroom. He gave me a defeated stare, watching as I walked away.

He had played me perfectly.

Said everything a girl like me would want to hear.

I scolded myself for falling for it.

And he was right: we had met before, once, when he was drunk and singing karaoke with his obnoxious brother. He was Monty's man crush every Monday, but Marcia hated Stephen, so she forced Monty to spend his Somersby time away from her—away from us. They had poker nights and bromances I didn't understand. Monty was too good for them.

In the dark, his name had dinged on like a light bulb made of bitterness just as he was about to kiss me. Jordie, that was what Monty called him.

I wouldn't have kissed him again if my life depended on it. He might have been the hottest guy in the world—in the history of hot guys ever—but he was also someone Marcia said was just another France: a guy with an ugly streak despite his pretty words.

Man, guys were gross. And I felt grossed out with myself for falling for the act yet again.

Chapter Four

THE BEST-LAID PLANS

Jordan

"I'm cursed." I sat on the roof, passing the bottle to my brother.

"Oh, cursed doesn't even begin to cut it. What did she look like?" He took a long draw off the bottle and passed it back.

"An Egyptian goddess, done up in all this makeup." I laughed. "Which should have been a major turnoff, but she was cool. Different. We kissed, and for a second I just—" How did I say I had her in my grip and then she was gone, running off, leaving me crushed?

"You blew it. You always blow it. I told you being a gentleman was overrated. I certainly didn't get Cynthia by being a gentleman." He was boastful sometimes, like Dad.

"Maybe not, but you sure won't keep her by being a douche."

"No." He took another drink. "That's fair. What's your plan for finding this mystery goddess?"

"I don't know. She had so much damn makeup on, I might not recognize her again. Except that smile." I moaned into my hands. "Fuck! Why did I meet her tonight?"

"Okay, well, now you've seen the light—hallelujah!—and tasted the rainbow and all. Surely this girl is a means to ending this Amy thing Dad's saddled you with. You got a plan for that?"

"No clue. I don't understand how Dad thinks it's acceptable to use the old ways to get business now. Who does that? Do the old merger marriages even happen anymore?" I groaned and took the bottle back.

"I don't know. I don't think so. Even Grandpa probably wouldn't do that kind of shit anymore."

"Right. The way to get business is by working hard and being the best. Only an entitled asshat like Dad would ever think he could swing his name around and get what he wants."

"Did you see her tonight at the party?"

"Who?" I asked.

"Amy."

"No, was she there? I was wearing a ball cap to avoid her recognizing me."

"Yeah, that didn't work. I saw her staring at you. It was creepy."

"Great." I hadn't ever felt so disturbed by how my family was using me before, which was saying a lot.

Stephen changed the subject. "Monty said you never texted him. You need to. He misses you."

"Yeah, I will. We have a poker game on the books for the summer kickoff celebration. Should be good." I glanced at Stephen and thought hard about what I was preparing to say. "What would you do if you were in my shoes?"

"Make my own mark on the world. I would say fuck Amy. Not a chance. Especially after hooking up with a hottie on the boat. She was a sign that you should not go through with this. To not ruin your summer with some bullshit babysitting job masquerading as a girlfriend. You need to grow some balls and learn how to say no to Dad."

"I said no."

"Right, but then he beat you down and you said yes. You always do that. You'll end up married to this chick if you even let this start. Hell no."

He wasn't great at eloquently articulating his thoughts, but he had a point.

"Well, I don't want Grandpa and Dad to hate me. My future is tied to the family business just as much as yours is." I chugged back more booze in the hope of drowning that fact as well.

"Oh, you and I both know you'll never end up there permanently. I think even Grandpa knows that. Dad just doesn't have the memo yet."

"There's no memo." I gave him a side-glance. "I don't know what I want to do when I graduate. So, working there until I do is the only option I have. It doesn't exactly hurt the résumé."

"Is marrying Amy what's-her-name fine too?" he challenged, and stole back the booze.

"No. I need a stellar plan to end this. Maybe even a way to outsmart Dad so he can't blame me for it."

"Like what, fake your death?"

"That, or fake hers. Or something. I don't know. I'll start brainstorming."

"Just swear you won't let this play out. I hate it when Dad wins." He offered me the bottle again.

"Dad can't win. I won't let him. I'm twenty-two. I can't be expected to go to college, get stellar grades, work all summer for Grandpa, decide my entire future at the end of this year, and babysit literally everyone. The fate of our world cannot rest squarely my shoulders. I'm not worrying about Dad anymore. And I'm not saving him with this deal. If he can't close it with genuine effort, then he's on his own. Grandpa can't expect me to toe the family line on this."

"We're going sailing with him Monday. You can talk to him about it then."

I nodded. It wasn't exactly a plan, but it was a step in the right direction. The direction that led to me finding that gorgeous girl I'd met on the yacht, which was the only deal I was personally invested in sealing at the moment.

Chapter Five

The Last Best Weekend

Lacey

Staggering into the house after a weekend of full-on Marcia, I always smelled like a distillery and felt like I might never hear again in at least one ear. This Sunday was no different.

"You're home." Grandma walked toward me, carrying a dish towel and wiping her hands.

"Where's everyone else?" I asked, putting down my bag and trying not to blink for too long. I was wiped.

"They're on their way home now." She smiled, but there was something off. Something in her eyes and her voice and her way of wiping her hands on that towel over and over and over until I wanted to snatch it from her.

"What's wrong?"

"Oh, nothing. You want some soup?" She turned away from me, still wiping her hands.

"Grandma?" I didn't move.

"Everyone'll be home in half an hour, dear. Don't ask any more questions right now." Her voice cracked. "The soup's on the stove. Help yourself." She turned and left for her room instead of the kitchen, and my insides clenched.

I was too hungover for this, whatever this family drama was. I had plans, great plans. I was going to iron my clothes for tomorrow and get to bed early after about six Gatorades. An upset grandma and some kind of familial tension wasn't on the books for my first day back at the summer job. Likely whatever was wrong was about money. As in, my parents needed to borrow some from Grandma, again.

Groaning, I wandered into the kitchen and ladled out some of her famous broccoli-cheese soup—my favorite. She even baked the cheesy garlic fingers to go with it, made with love. Like all her food.

Since my grandpa had died a few years back, she'd come to live with us, and I always appreciated having her around. Sure, we lost the home office to her bedroom, but we gained so much more in return. She was a mother and father to me when my own were inundated with work, which was just about all the time. She cooked and tidied and ran the house, which my mother found annoying, but everyone else vetoed her into silence about it.

I spooned the soup and blew on it, cooling it off. The first bite healed at least half of the things wrong with me after a full weekend of partying and reckless endangerment to my organs.

The second bite soothed my stiff neck and shoulders—residual tension from end-of-year exams.

The third bite was a dunked piece of cheesy garlic bread. I moaned into the bowl, forgetting all my worries.

By the time Mom and Dad walked in the kitchen, Mom still in scrubs and Dad looking a little older than he had last week, I was doing amazing.

For five whole seconds, I was doing amazing.

Then I saw their eyes. Red, puffy, and swollen, like they'd been fighting again.

"Hi," I offered, trying not to be concerned. They argued about money a lot.

"Hi, sweetie." Mom hugged me. Dad looked weird, constipated or stuck in thought.

"How's it going?" I asked, kinda scared of the answer.

"Not great, kiddo. We need to talk," Dad said gravely, and sat, no greeting or hug or even a punch in the arm. I hadn't even seen him in a week.

"What about?" I gulped, feeling the burn of fear in my throat. Why were they bringing me into their problems?

"Martin."

"Where's Martin?" I asked, noting he hadn't come into the kitchen even though broccoli-cheese soup was his favorite. Was he involved in the drama? Or purposely keeping his distance from it?

"He's gone upstairs. He's resting." Mom sounded exhausted, but also like she might burst into tears any second.

"Is he all right?" I asked, no longer so sure what this was all about. Something was wrong. Really wrong. Maybe I shouldn't have eaten before they got home. I'd assumed there was something to talk about after Grandma's weird behavior, but this was on a different level than a simple financial spat.

"No." My father struggled with the conversation.

"No?" Did he just confirm that Martin wasn't okay?

My mother's shoulders shuddered as she heaved without making noises, apart from the odd sniffle.

"Martin is sick, Lacey." Dad's jaw trembled, and his eyes started to water. "We've been holding back from telling you until we had definitive news, but now we do."

"Sick?" I was lost. My hard-ass dad was crying because Martin was sick. What kind of sick made my dad cry? "What do you mean?"

"The doctors said he's going to be okay, but he's got a long road ahead of him." Mom tried to make it better before she even explained.

"What is wrong with Martin?" I demanded.

"He has cancer. Thyroid cancer. Same as Grandpa had." Dad's words turned to a grave whisper.

It took me a second to fully hear him. I repeated his sentence multiple times, but it wouldn't stick. There was no way my seventeen-year-old brother had cancer. He was fine.

"What does that mean?" I couldn't comprehend it.

"Firstly, you need to understand he's going to be okay. Your mom caught it early. His sore throat and coughing and other symptoms lasted too long. She knew something was up. He was diagnosed this week, and the doctors are already on the ball. They're going to start treatment right away, which begins with a surgery to remove the tumor."

"Tumor?" I whispered.

"Yes. But hear me, he's going to get through this." Dad's voice cracked a little, making me suspicious of whether that was the truth or whether he was saying it for my benefit. "It's just the initial shock stings."

About to ask or say something else, I realized it wasn't words that were going to shoot from my mouth. I wasn't going to make it to the bathroom, so I ran for the back door. I tripped on the last step and fell onto my knees on the grass, puking soup and bad life choices all over the yard.

My body refused to allow those words to enter, so it chased them away by expelling everything else from me.

My brother, my seventeen-year-old brother, my baby brother.

Gut-wrenching sadness rocked me, spewing my feelings and vomit everywhere.

It was a scene from *The Exorcist*.

When I was finally empty of feelings and food and fluids, I sat back on my knees and held myself. I cried, but nothing left me; dry sobs burned my eyes as my parents rushed outside after me.

I wanted to ask more questions, but I couldn't get past the lack of tears.

Mom and Dad surrounded me with arms and warmth and hugs, stroking my hair and comforting me. As if this were happening to me. I pushed them away, spinning and running for the house. I bolted up the stairs, my legs attempting to give out on every stair before I burst into my brother's room.

"They told you?" he complained, a solemn look on his face. I dove onto the bed and attacked, smothering him in pukey older-sister love. The tears hit then.

I flooded his shirt, cradling him and, in the end, myself.

"You're sick?" I couldn't seem to control myself, making it worse.

"No. Well, sort of." He grumbled again, wiggling like he wanted to get away but then eventually wrapping his arms around me. "It's not exactly like Gramps. I'm going to be fine. The doctor sounded really positive. You're not rid of me yet, and there's no way you're getting all the inheritance to yourself."

"Shut up," I snorted, wiping my face on him. "You can't leave me. I'll never make it with Mom and Dad alone."

"You have Grandma. And besides, I'd probably haunt you. Remember that time you watched *The Ring* and ended up sleeping in my bed for a month? I'd re-create some of those scenes for ya. It could be fun. Brother-sister bonding." He chuckled and adjusted us both so I was lying beside him instead of squishing him.

"For reals, you're okay?" I lifted my face and stared into his eyes, checking for deceptions.

"No, I have cancer, Lace. But I'm going to be. I seriously am not dying." His eyes held more humor than anything else. "But doing the hard things, like laundry and cleaning and chores, I mean—" He coughed like Tiny Tim. "That might be hard. I might need my big sis for that."

"Asshole!" I shoved him, laughing and hitting his arm.

"Ow, that's my cancer!" He rubbed his arm.

"Oh my God!" My stomach tensed again. "Oh my God, where?" His evil laugh revealed the truth.

"Dick!" I hit him again. "You can't joke about that."

"Yeah, whatever. I am riding this pony all the way to the stables. At this rate Grandma is going to move in with me when I leave home and do my laundry and cooking forever."

I opened my mouth to scold him some more, but our parents came into the room, climbing on the bed like we were little kids again.

We were dog piled. First Mom and then Dad and finally Grandma.

The overloving lasted awhile, everyone crying while Dad tried to be optimistic.

"We can't be sad. We caught it early. And you're young, Martin. The doctor told us you're going to be fine after surgery and might not even need radiation. So everyone in this family is going to be strong for you. This week was hard. Today we cried. But tomorrow, we look ahead and beat this thing," he said confidently.

I nodded. It was a lie, but I could lie convincingly.

Grandma lied too.

Mom didn't even bother. She shook her head and buried her snotty face in Dad's shirt.

"Guys, I'm not dying today. It's not awesome news, but it's not the worst. I could have testicular or ass cancer. Thyroid isn't so bad. Unless you're Grandpa." Martin tried to act indifferent, as he was the eternal sarcastic shit. "Anyway, Grandma, you promised me soup. Can you guys take the sniffling downstairs? And, Lace, you smell like an old dead hooker."

We all laughed.

Only Martin could bring up Grandpa dying, dead hookers, snot, and soup in the same speech and evoke feelings of camaraderie.

Our grandpa's passing had been a shock. He hadn't even been sick; he just said he had a sore throat and was dead a year later. Thyroid cancer, just like Martin now had. I remembered the doctors saying it should have been curable but, apparently, he hadn't bothered with the sore throat for a while. So, if Martin's cancer was caught early, he would likely be okay. My heart didn't care about those odds or possibilities. It was broken for what he was about to go through, and I was still in shock. I honestly didn't know what to say or do. And I was a little vexed that they'd kept this from me.

"Come on." Dad tugged at Mom and me. "He needs to eat. Poor kid's been poked and prodded all week long." He grabbed my arm and lifted me up.

"I hate you." I glared at my brother.

"You love me and you know it." He winked, and I let my dad drag me down the stairs.

When we got into the kitchen, Grandma served everyone soup.

I stepped back from my bowl. "I'm good." The smell was tainted. In fact, I might never recover from the memory. "How long have you guys known?" I needed details, not food. "Why didn't anyone tell me what was going on?"

"We've only suspected something these last couple of weeks, Lacey. You had finals and were so stressed out. We didn't want to interfere if it was nothing. I really guessed it was mono. Martin's repeated sore throat and hoarseness and the lump in his throat troubled Dr. Mercer. So he suggested, because of Grandpa's diagnosis, that we should do some more intensive testing than just strep and mono swabs." Mom finally started sounding like herself again. Dr. Mom was what Martin and I usually called her. But whenever it was one of us, she was stressed and emotional.

She continued, "I pulled some strings and got him in this week, and since I was working today, Dr. Mercer agreed to meet with us at the hospital to get the results in. It's his thyroid, but it's stage one. It's not too serious, just scary, ya know?"

"Okay." I wrapped my arms around myself and squeezed.

Mom smiled, reaching for me and rubbing my arm. "He should be back to school in September like any other year."

"I just can't believe it," I said. "Is it hereditary? Like, will we all get it?"

"It is, but the chances of you developing cancer are slim. It's a hundred-million-to-one odds or more that Martin would get this." Mom sounded exhausted but still managed to dramatically exaggerate.

"Is there anything I can do?" I wasn't sure how I could help, but I needed to make sure my family knew they had my support.

"Well—" Dad began.

"No!" Mom cut Dad off. "We can talk about the details later." She flashed a look at him, and I knew there was more to the story. I wasn't exactly sure I could handle anything else right now. At least Mom understood that.

"Okay, well, I'm gonna go shower then." I gave them all a look, like I was waiting for something else.

But they didn't say anything.

They smiled and waited for me to leave.

I turned and hurried up the stairs to the bathroom on the second floor and closed the door. I lifted the floor grate off and hung my face over the air that came blasting out, listening.

"We can't keep anything from her. She's old enough to understand and help out," Dad said.

The grate was Martin's and my secret. Every family discussion we weren't invited to was heard from this spot in the house. Tonight was the first time I didn't want to hear whatever was being said. But I needed to. If there was something I could do to help my family, especially when it came to Martin, I would.

"The sooner we tell her, the sooner she'll be able to start planning," he added. Oh, God. What did that mean?

"No, this is too stressful," Grandma said softly. "Her brother getting cancer is enough for one night; adding the fact that you're going to have to use her tuition money for his treatment costs would push her over the edge. She starts work tomorrow. Give her time to absorb one thing before throwing another at her."

My stomach convulsed, threatening to start purging again.

My tuition? They were going to use my tuition?

Martin's treatments?

My family was going to need to use my tuition money to save my brother?

How could I even complain about that, even if I wanted to? My mind tried to bitch, but there was no way I ever would. I was going to have to suck this one up. In the grand scheme of things, my brother's health was way more important than anything else.

"What if she can't afford the year and has to delay getting her degree?" Mom asked.

"We refinance the house. We could look into student loans," Dad answered.

"No!" Mom shouted, and then lowered her voice. "We agreed these kids weren't going to be like you and me, breaking our backs to afford a normal life with all our student loans. I'll talk to the bank about refinancing the house. It's only fifty grand. Worse comes to worse, she takes a year off to earn the money."

I gagged as she said all of that.

"We have to be careful. The La Croix family is counting on her graduating next year. Mr. La Croix might not be able to wait for her to take the year off to earn the money," Dad said, clearly chewing.

"And what if the medical bills are more than we expected? What do we do then, start taking out more loans?" Mom sounded worried. "Use Martin's tuition savings?"

I got up from the floor. I didn't want to hear any more of this.

Grandma was right: I didn't need to think about this tonight.

Martin had cancer.

That was more important and immediate than anything else.

There was no way I was going to feel sorry for myself. Not even a little.

Not when my parents and family were going through this.

I could figure out how to pay for my own education, and I would start doing just that tomorrow.

Tonight, I would get lost in the book recommendation I got from Martin. It was called *Swan Song* by Robert McCammon. It was about the end of the world and fitted my current mood and situation perfectly.

Chapter Six

REALITY BITES

Jordan

"And the guy on the boat hands her the rod, thinking it's going to be fun for her to reel it in." My dad laughed at his own story, far before the punch line. I had to suffer through dinner with the Weitzman family, including Amy, until I could speak to Grandpa. It felt risky since she was sitting across from me, already looking like she was being served on a silver platter especially for me.

Smiling politely, though without much interest, Amy glanced my way. Her eyes narrowed in on a detail.

My tie was crooked. I'd seen it when I was getting ready for dinner but left it. Apparently it nagged at her.

We didn't even know each other, having only met tonight, but she gave me a scowl, pointing at her neck, motioning for me to fix it.

I didn't. I pretended to be confused, as if I were that dim, not that she would realize I wasn't. She was that dim. It took me five whole minutes to realize it. We'd met, and she immediately took a selfie of us together. I'd asked her what courses she was taking in school, and she shrugged and said she didn't know. Didn't know?

It was a tragedy. Not as big of a tragedy as my being forced to pretend to date her while my dad worked on bringing her father's money into our family's investment firm. Her father had left his investment broker, taking all his money with him. He was fishing for brokers, and my dad was fishing for clients to impress my grandpa with. He said this was going to be his moment to shine, but I knew he was in trouble financially and he needed me to do this. Stephen had made a couple of comments about Mom's inheritance keeping our family afloat. Grandpa wouldn't ever let us starve, but he would let Dad make a fool of himself financially.

Something I didn't doubt Dad had done.

My dad was the grasshopper who played all summer, only summer lasted forever.

"So, here's poor Letty, holding this rod, and the fish jerks." Dad wiped his eyes, dying of laughter and barely able to tell the story about my mother. "Letty goes flying into the air." He wheezed, making everyone laugh. "I reach out as she flies by me, fully airborne, and I grab her feet, snatching her midair as she hangs over the edge of the boat. But she's dropping the rod, and the fish is right there, I can see him." He stood to hold his hands out, flexing his biceps like he was back in the moment. "So, I look at her, the rod, and her again, and I knew what I had to do." He started laughing as Mom's cheeks flared. "And that bastard right there is proof I love fishing more than my wife. Hey, Letty." He and Amy's dad, Mr. Weitzman, laughed, too hard.

Amy scowled, losing her pretty little smile for a second before regaining her composure and beaming at my dad, as if his story actually gave him bragging rights.

Mom drank a large gulp of wine, as did Amy's mother. Neither of them seemed impressed by the conversation or the amount of booze both their husbands drank.

Stephen gave me a look, the one we often exchanged during dinners with Dad. It was a special blend of "I want to punch him in the dick" and "why us, dear God, why us."

Mom didn't meet our gaze; she rarely did. She didn't want to endorse this life, but she knew no other way.

"So, have you done much marlin fishing?" Dad asked Mr. Weitzman.

Cynthia, my brother's wife, leaned in, whispering to me as she pretended to pick up her napkin. "How's it going?"

"Summer of my dreams."

Amy sat there staring at me, blank in a lot of ways.

Pretty girl.

Nice smile.

Great body.

But dumb as a bag of hammers.

I counted the hours until she would be gone and I would be alone—me and my book. I was reading Robert McCammon's *Swan Song*. My economics professor at Harvard was a huge fan of his and had recommended it to the class where I was his TA. I was enjoying the plot of the imbalanced world and the staging of the war between good and evil. And I loved postapocalyptic novels.

"So, Jordan, how much longer until you're done with school?" Mrs. Weitzman asked as she lifted a bite of lamb.

"This year's my last."

"Then you have to join the real world like a big boy," Stephen said with a grin.

"Don't worry, big brother. I won't show you up the way your wife does." I winked at him, making Cynthia giggle. She was en route to being the youngest partner at a law firm.

"Oh, I have no doubts who the family success is going to be." He lifted his drink to his wife. "May you have half the luck finding someone as amazing as her."

Mom choked on her bite of lamb, almost exactly the same way as Mrs. Weitzman.

"I'm sure Amy will show us all how it's done." Cynthia recovered for her moronic husband, but he had no regrets. He never held his tongue. Not since he'd left home and became Grandpa's favorite.

Cynthia smiled at Amy, who still appeared vacant. She was probably texting under the table and missed the insult. I didn't want to pretend to date her for the rest of the summer; one whole day was enough. I just didn't know how to broach the subject or ruin Dad's scheme, not yet.

"She really will," Amy's mom chimed in. "Amy has been taking some fashion classes on top of her regular curriculum, and she's quite good. She's working with Vera Wang this summer."

"Is Vera a friend of yours?" I asked her mother, sticking with my brother's line of torture. I liked watching all our parents squirm while we politely misbehaved.

"She is." Mrs. Weitzman's cheeks reddened. "A dear friend to anyone in the fashion community."

"Excellent." Mom lifted her glass before I could say another word. "To our children."

"Hear, hear," Dad said, lifting his glass and clinking a bit too hard. He was boorish. There wasn't another word for it. Rich, loud, rude, privileged, undereducated, and entitled. My dad's family connections gave him a pass into the world where he could be a figurehead but never wield any actual power, married to the daughter of a billionaire real estate developer and investments mastermind.

Dad had old family money, which he had tied up in my grandfather's investments. But he didn't have enough income to balance his spending. He played too hard. He traveled and entertained and showed off his wealth. He didn't work at making more money. He didn't buy things that would turn around and earn. He wasted. He made bad investments.

Something my grandfather hated almost as much as he hated being saddled with my dad.

My grandfathers coerced my parents into dating while their families were entertaining a business arrangement, not unlike my current situation. While my mom's father may have valued cash more than his own daughter, he still disliked my father. He never intended for them to marry. He dangled my mother at my father to convince Dad's family to invest. Once they did, it was too late. My mom was pregnant, and my dad became Grandpa Jack's new son-in-law. Grandpa made lemonade out of his lemons, seeing that my dad's old blue blood was worth something—connections. Grandpa Jack knew what to do with those.

At the time, the old money was going stale with the way the markets were changing, but my mother's father was the exception, a true businessman through and through. He changed with the times, making his fortunes based on new growth opportunities. He hadn't been nearly as rich as my father's family when he started out, but now he was ten times wealthier. Grandpa was ruthless in the pursuit of money. Dad thought of himself the same way.

But he wasn't.

Which was also why I got saddled with the petite redhead who sat across from me, staring vacuously.

There wasn't anything really wrong with Amy.

Her lips were shiny.

Her hair was suspended in place.

Her eyes had that cat-eye thing going on where her eyeliner winged out, like every other girl in the world. To say she followed trends was an understatement.

But she was all packaging.

Conversations with her would be one-sided, at best.

No, Dad wasn't thinking clearly on this one. Not that he ever did. My brother and I were my Grandpa's only hopes. I could get by in finances if I had to do it for a living; mostly it was common sense, so that wasn't hard, and Stephen had the shrewd business savvy. Together we would be the next generation of success in the family, which definitely skipped a line.

After dinner, I excused myself to the kitchen and sat at the counter in silence.

"You look like you're in a mood," Lucia said gruffly as she reached into the freezer and grabbed the gelato she made just for me. She slid the pint across the counter with a silver spoon.

"Dad's on schedule to having me work for Grandpa for the rest of my life with Amy as my little wife by the end of this summer." I tried not to sound like a petulant child; that was not Lucia's favorite.

"How was the roast?" She didn't even miss a beat in ignoring my whining.

"Delicious. Can you start adding drugs to my plate? Not Monday through Thursday, but definitely Friday through Sunday. I'm not making it through that marlin story again without something narcotic."

"Can I get in on that too?" Stephen sat next to me, took my spoon, and dished up a large bite and ate it all.

"The crack or the gelato?" Lucia asked.

"Boph." He struggled to say *both* as he winced through the brain freeze of too much gelato in his mouth.

"You want your own pint?" She always spoke deadpan to us, something we appreciated. The absence of emotion meant no false expression.

"Yeah, please." He nodded and swallowed the last of his bite. "Can I get a normal spoon, though?"

"No." She slid a silver spoon at him too. Her idea of a joke.

"Thanks," he grumbled, and took a bite. "So, Amy." He nudged me. "How was your first impression?"

"Yup. It's not gonna work." I dragged my spoon, getting a smaller bite now that the mention of Amy was affecting my appetite. "I checked out her Instagram when I was in the bathroom. Cynthia told me to look. I lost some intelligence."

"Yeah, it's bad. And just think, if she weren't here, you'd already have tracked down your soul mate from the boat."

"Soul mate?" Lucia's eyes widened.

"She wasn't my soul mate, dick." I nudged my brother back. "She was just kinda funny and real and not"—I pointed my silver spoon behind me toward the dining room we couldn't see—"like that."

"And sexy?"

"Maybe." I didn't want to answer that in front of Lucia. I already regretted getting drunk and telling him the fantasy bathroom story.

"I thought we agreed you were freeing yourself of this."

"We did, but I haven't had the chance to talk to Grandpa about it and come up with a backup plan." I nodded at him. "And how the hell am I supposed to get out of this while our dads are dry humping each other? Mom said they hang out three nights a week at least. All the groundwork had been laid before I even entered the picture. This was sabotage."

"It's a conundrum. Amy's dad is like a virgin who's scared to commit to just doing it. And Dad's so hard and ready to go, he's overly eager. By the end of the night, Dad will be chasing him around the billiards table with Mr. Weitzman trying to protect his virtue." Stephen held a fist in the air and slapped his forearm, earning a scowl from Lucia and me. He continued, "Why don't you tell Dad that if he wants to make the deal stick, he needs to find another way? You're out. It's sad to watch this shit."

"Sure, Steph." I still laughed at the nickname he hated. "I'll do that at the same time you tell Grandpa you agreed to be the stay-at-home daddy when you and Cynthia have kids. We can be disowned together."

"I agreed to spend the first three months at home with her, dick. It's not the same thing."

"Okay, Steph." I nudged him.

"You want some, little bro?" Stephen put his spoon down at the same moment Lucia lifted her large wooden spoon from the utensil holder.

"You boys wanna keep fighting in my kitchen?"

"No, ma'am," we said simultaneously, and looked back down at our dessert.

"That's what I thought you said." She kept the spoon out, pacing the front of the counter, opposite where we sat. "Now, Stephen, staying home those first three months with your wife and baby is honorable. Don't take shit off this spineless little sap over that." She pointed the spoon at me, making me cringe as memories of it catching my ass as a kid flashed through my mind. "You tell your grandpa that real men want to bond with their babies so that they grow up influenced by their father as equally as their mother. No bratty kids to ruin the bloodline and destroy the family business. I didn't raise whiners."

"No, ma'am," he agreed. It brought me a modicum of joy to witness our cook still beat him down, only now it was emotionally instead of physically. Though I didn't doubt her ability to still swing that spoon like a bat.

"And you." She pointed right at me again, making my entire body tense. "You need to stop searching for another girl until you get rid of this one. She might not be for you, but your mom says she likes you for whatever reason, and I didn't raise a disloyal philanderer. Now you are gonna be a man and tell your daddy you're not doing this. But I agree, first you tell your grandpa this girl is a simpleton. She has seven million selfies but no sense of herself. He'll understand. She's bad for business. You need a girlfriend who is on par with the expectations your grandpa has for you, so she can be your equal, or in his case"—she pointed the spoon at Stephen—"your superior, and help you grow. Stop being little punks. Learn to articulate so you can get what you want and make your grandpa think that's what he wants too. You know where the power in this family really is. He'll tell your dad this is a bad plan. Playing with people's hearts is sick anyway." She shook her head. "Damn."

"Yes, ma'am," we both agreed.

"Now eat your dessert and get back out there. Hiding in my kitchen all night like little babies." She turned her back to us and used the big spoon to stir whatever was in the giant pot on the stove.

Stephen smiled as he ate his gelato, kicking me under the counter. I kicked him back.

"I mean it—you wanna fight in here? I'm gonna beat some asses," Lucia growled.

In typical childish brotherly love, I ate my last bite, jumped up, shoved Stephen, and ran from the kitchen, laughing as he shouted my name and Lucia turned on him.

I almost missed having him at home, living with us. Almost.

Chapter Seven

JUST BUGGING YA

Lacey

"Lacey, can we have a quick chat?" Mom asked as I grabbed my earbuds and shoved them in my purse.

"Not now." Dad frowned at her from the table where he was texting or doing something with his phone.

"Has to be. I'm working two doubles, and that application we talked about as a solution"—Mom gave him a forced look, trying to speak words with her glare—"has to be filled out. There's a deadline."

"Mom, whatever it is, text me. I'm going to be late if I don't leave in the next fifteen minutes." I tried not to sound bratty, but being late on my first day wasn't how I rolled.

"I know, but there's something we need to talk about." She gave me the mom face, the one that suggested I couldn't weasel my way out of this. We were talking, now. "We want you to understand a few things." Her eyes darted toward the stairs, like she was talking about Martin, but I knew that wasn't the case.

We were about to talk tuition, and I really didn't want to.

"What about?" I asked, pretending I hadn't heard her last night.

"Honey, this isn't the right time. She has to go to work," Dad said, offering a look.

"Lacey—" Mom started, ignoring Dad. "It's about Martin. It's important. And you might need some time to come up with a solution."

"There's more?" My spine tingled as I contemplated that this may not be about tuition at all.

"No, well, yes. Martin's diagnosis is causing a bit of an unexpected issue," Dad said over his cup of coffee, pleading at Mom with his stare, but she didn't speak. "Since the new government made the health care changes, we're not covered like we used to be. Your mom's policy has completely changed." He winced, and Mom continued for him.

"We have to use our savings for his treatments."

And there it was.

"You need me to chip in?" I played along, knowing where this was going.

"We're so sorry, honey. We know the base amount of his first surgery, and treatments will be almost all our savings for you to go to school next year." Dad's voice cracked a bit, not like he would cry, but he was visibly upset. "We wanted to be able to help you kids through your schooling so you didn't have loans like us. But we won't have the money to cover everything, and Martin's health comes first. Grandma has already paid for all those years of private school for you two. She can't do any more."

"We're so sorry." Mom hugged me.

"Guys." I forced myself to be cool. "Martin has thyroid cancer. I'll figure out school. I don't care. I'll skip a year if I have to. I'll get a student loan. Whatever. You're right, though; there are deadlines for applications. I'll look into it today. No biggie. It's just money." I pulled back, feeling my future crashing and burning, but forcing that firm smile on my face. "Let's focus on him. When he's better, we'll worry about school."

"You're such a good kid," Mom said, then sighed into my neck. "I love you."

"I love you, too, and I want to help Martin through this. Whatever we need to do, we're a team. Let's just concentrate on the most important thing here. We'll talk more later, but for now, I have to run and get to my first big day back at the office." I pulled away and grabbed my bag, turning to leave. "Love you!" I waved and closed the door.

It was lucky I'd had the night to think about the whole financial situation. Telling me the day of my first shift was shitty, but I got why. They needed me to know sooner so I could solve it faster. They trusted me to figure this out on my own.

As I clicked along the sidewalk, I prayed the brave face I was sporting would last throughout the day. I was going to need it.

I daydreamed on the subway, running numbers. My tuition and books cost around fifty thousand a year. My scholarship covered ten thousand. Martin's surgery and treatments must be close to that, or more. I didn't know the amount but feared Mom and Dad might have to dip into our school savings. And if that happened, I had only about seven thousand dollars left from last year's spending money, which meant I needed to come up with a minimum of thirty-five thousand dollars if I was going to finish the year off debt-free.

That was a big number.

A daunting number.

My summer job might net me about fifteen thousand, so I needed to find a second job that I could do around this one.

Another challenge.

I pushed it to the back of my mind and tried to stay focused. My first day was going to be challenging enough without adding this stress.

In the elevator, I tried to smile and pretend I was fine.

"Lacey!" Hennie, my friend and fellow intern, squealed and hit the main floor running. "I missed you."

"Hennie!" I hugged her back tightly. "I missed you too."

I clung to her a little longer than I should have. But she smelled like cookies and hugged so warmly, it was nice to be held by someone like her. Especially after yesterday and this morning.

"How was the year at Harvard?" I asked.

"Good. Hectic. You?" she questioned as she struggled free from me.

"Not bad." I tried to maintain the smile on my face, but the truth was still ripping my heart out.

"Awesome, I'm glad it's over. It was hard, but I got through. You excited to be back?" She beamed.

"Yeah." I nodded, but I couldn't last another second. I needed to talk to someone or I was going to burst. "That's a lie. I just found out my little brother got diagnosed with thyroid cancer. I don't even know what to say about it. I'm honestly still in shock." Tears welled in my eyes.

"Oh my God, I'm so sorry. When did you find out?" Her face paled.

"Yesterday." I sniffled.

"Lacey. Jeez. That's rough. Isn't he, like, seventeen?"

"Yeah. Almost eighteen. He's a kid. But it's hereditary."

"Well, not to be one of those people who can't let someone wallow, but his being a kid is actually on his side. He's young and strong. And thyroid is one of those cancers people recover from. Early detection and all. One of my uncles had it. He lived, and he was a smoker."

"Yeah." I didn't bother telling her it was how my grandpa died. "Anyway, I don't really want to talk more about it. It's stressing me out hard. But if I seem off, you should know why." I changed the subject. "Are you excited to be back?" I couldn't do the brother-cancer thing all day or I would end up in the bathroom crying nonstop.

"I am. Are you?" she asked again, blushing. "I mean—"

"No, it's fine. I am. I need all the money I can get. I might have to see if there are weekend jobs or find a waitressing shift for after work."

"Oh my God, why?"

"Martin's cancer. My parents are going to have to use my tuition money, and I don't have enough in savings to front it on my own." Tears started to build again.

"Oh, no." She winced. As a person who needed financial aid, she understood how much college cost and how much of a burden the financing was for us. "What about a student loan? The deadline hasn't passed yet. I'm pretty sure the deadline is end of June; you still have a few weeks."

"I'm considering that, but I don't know if I'll get the full amount for NYU. I mean, it was fifty-something thousand last year for everything. And then I have to graduate with a massive loan, making just enough money to live on my own, not including a loan repayment."

"Right." She folded her arms over her chest, gripping her cardigan. "Well, I'm sure you'll figure this out. And if you need help, you know I'm in. I'll do anything you need. With our combined business savvy, we can come up with an out-of-the-box solution to your troubles. It'll be just like finding a way to sell Mr. La Croix's latest crazy venture to the masses."

"Thanks." I sighed, a bit defeated and still ashamed that I was even considering my problems when my brother's health was at risk. "Anyway, we better get to work. I imagine our responsibilities will be a lot heavier this summer."

"You know how he likes to add a little every year." Hennie laughed. She knew Mr. La Croix almost as well as I did. We had spent every summer since grade eleven as interns or working here in some way. She got in through school—a scholarship student with remarkable grades. And I got in through Marcia, my bestie.

"That he does."

"Good to see you again." She reached in and hugged me once more, letting me linger.

"You too." I squeezed and forced myself to let go.

Hennie was my kind of people. Nerdy, funny, smart, and down-to-earth. She was the sort of friend I enjoyed getting in some downtime with, away from Marcia and the girls. Plus, Hennie got how hard it was being average and surrounded by a bunch of rich kids. She got life. Being with her was just easy. Sometimes we didn't even talk, just sat in relaxing silence.

"See ya in a bit." I left her at the financial department and headed for the section I worked in, ready to devote myself to fetching coffees like a boss while everyone used my ideas and pretended they were theirs. Internship had its moments. At least Mr. La Croix saw it all. He knew.

When I got to the Monday-morning session we always had in the large conference room, Mr. La Croix was already at the head of the table, smiling wide. "Lacey, good morning." He beamed among his group of people, all busy preparing for the morning meeting.

I forced myself to beam back. "Good morning, Mr. La Croix. Can I get you all some coffee?" I asked the same of everyone, offering smiles and waves at familiar faces.

"No, no, come and sit." He motioned for me to take a seat across from him as everyone else got comfortable. "I wanted to talk to you this morning about a couple of ideas."

Excitement brewed in me, lifting my mood considerably. "Okay. I'm ready when you are!"

"We have a new project this year, one we're pretty excited about." Mr. La Croix was bursting with his usual giddiness, something he did every time he found a new investment opportunity. "It's a start-up by a couple of young moms in Jersey: a protein bar that helps bowel movement and provides all kinds of nutrients and actually tastes good."

"Okay." I wrinkled my nose when he said the word *bowel* and then sort of just held that expression, a little grossed out but still intrigued.

"NASA is interested." He said it like this was really amazing.

"And you want me to help with the marketing?" I was lost.

"Right. The name the women have given the product is Mom Bars."

"Oh." I tried not to grimace again.

"Exactly." He laughed, as did the handful of other people at the large table. "We're in the midst of researching some of the other products that this bar is competing with. There's a cereal called Holy Crap."

"Jeez."

"And some Bowel Buddies."

"Oh, wow." I sat back. "So you want me to come up with a new name that puts a different spin on the product?"

"No." He grinned. "Not just a name." His eyes danced and darted around the table to his other employees. "We have a few things we need you to secure on this project."

"Okay." I tried not to sound leery. Or at least as leery as I felt.

One of the ladies leaned in. "We need you to come up with a name, a marketing package, and an angle to appeal to your generation. There aren't any other millennials here, but you have a finger on the pulse of the young women who could be influential in shaping the campaign."

"You want me to manipulate my friends into eating and promoting the bars on social media?" Was I above that?

"Not in so many words . . ." Mr. La Croix laughed. "I've been trying to get Marcia into them; I even started serving them at the breakfast bar at the country club and a few hotels. But no one seems interested. NASA backing a product that keeps astronauts healthy just isn't as big of a deal as it used to be. People in my day would watch the astronaut eat it and think, 'Hey, I need that.' Nowadays, people want the endorsement of someone just like them—someone they can relate to."

"Yeah." I tried to go easy on him. "Didn't we all read that they cut funding to the space programs? And I know most of my friends, Marcia included, might not care about NASA at all. They would go for a makeup brand first."

One of the guys grabbed something from a basket. "Which is why we need you. This product needs a rebranding. Those young moms have a sound idea, and the recipe is genius." He slid a packaged bar across the table to me. "Try it."

I swallowed hard, trying not to think about Holy Crap or Bowel Buddies as I lifted the little package. "I'm not really a granola-bar kind of girl. I mean, didn't Dr. Oz say they're all like candy bars and kids shouldn't eat them?"

"Don't put that on the marketing campaign," Mr. La Croix teased, but it didn't stop the whole room from staring and waiting. A needle dropping to the floor would have echoed in the office as they paused.

I crinkled the wrapper, noting the sound of it as I peeled back one corner. A brown bar revealed itself. "Chocolate coating." I smiled, feeling like a hot spotlight was bearing down on me. I'd never eaten a single thing in my life under such scrutiny and pressure.

Forcing myself, I swallowed hard, trying to lube my tightened throat as I parted my lips and lifted the exposed corner to my mouth. I needed this. I needed it badly. Being part of the team that marketed and sold this would secure my place here, and it might also be my answer for the summer finances situation. If I succeeded, I could possibly convince Mr. La Croix that I could finish my last year of school later and stay on as a full-time employee.

Every set of eyes widened as I prepared to take the first bite, making me think I was being punked and the bar was going to taste terrible.

I closed my eyes, likely making a terribly unattractive expression as I placed it between my parted teeth and bit down.

The sweetness of the chocolate was nice. The bar was fudgy and soft. Coconut and something else, a nutty flavor I couldn't place, filled my mouth. Sweat formed on my brow and upper lip as I opened my eyes and nodded. "It's good." The chewing wasn't hard. My jaw didn't tire. I didn't lose any of my teeth or tear a gum. Best of all, it didn't taste like crap.

"You like it?" He smiled wide, sitting back and sighing. "Good! You can't taste the crickets?"

"What?" I asked, feeling the chocolate coating my teeth as Mr. La Croix handed me a water to wash it down.

"The crickets. They're ground to a flour and used as a supreme protein source. Incredibly sustainable and have the added benefit of no pollution or resource demands. They're the future, honestly."

"What!" I asked again, this time standing up and knocking my chair to the floor. "Bugs?" I shuddered, feeling a similar tightening in my throat and souring in my cheeks. It had only been one day since I'd last tasted my own bile. Was this something I would have to get used to from now on?

Turning, I bolted from the room. I crashed into the bathroom but didn't make it to a stall. I lost my stomach all over the linoleum floor.

What an amazing start to the workweek, puking my new job—the only obvious solution to my current problems and future success—all over the damn place. While some poor person would be forced to clean up this mess, I suddenly had a slew of others that a mop and bucket simply couldn't cure.

Chapter Eight

Brothers and Bugs

Lacey

"You okay?" Hennie entered my back-room closet that Mr. La Croix called my new office.

"Oh my God. What did you hear?"

"They tricked you into eating those stupid bug bars Mr. La Croix bought from those creepy yoga moms in the burbs. And you ruined the main floor washroom."

I covered my eyes, groaning. "Oh my God."

"Yeah." She sat. "Mr. La Croix was pretty concerned; he sent me to come and make sure you're okay."

"Okay?" I lifted my hands. "I puked my new project everywhere. And my new project is bug bars. What the hell am I going to do with that?"

"Don't call them *bug bars* for starters." She chuckled.

"How is this even happening?" I wiped my eyes and tried to drink a little more of the ginger ale my colleague Esme had brought me when she checked on me half an hour ago.

"Dude." Hennie cringed. "You are having the worst week. Sick brother, obviously the worst part. No tuition money. And now this." She sighed, feeling it with me. "At least Mr. La Croix trusts you enough to give you a project to spearhead."

"I guess." I burped cricket and gagged, shuddering. "Nope." I shook my head. "I can't do it. I can't. I'm going to have to tell him I'm fine with fetching coffees for the rest of my life."

"Lacey." She leaned in. "Is there a chance he's challenging you, and this is the moment that makes or breaks the start of your career here? I mean, is this really the opportunity you want to squander when you might need the full-time job for the year to save up for school?" Her words stung and yet rang out in my pounding head for a moment.

"You think?"

"I mean, if I wanted to test the ability and merit of some young summer intern before hiring her as a full-time member of my team, I would never dream of doing something this sick and cruel, but he would. That's his style."

"Oh, shit, you're probably right. He's seeing if I can go above and beyond with an impossible challenge." My stomach sank. At least, what was left of the poor thing. "How can I turn that down?"

"You can't. Not really. Especially considering the way your week's going."

"You're right. And if I impress him enough, maybe he'll let me work here while I finish my fourth year, slowly." I sat up straighter. My insides were burnt and sore, but there was no way I was going to back down from this test. "Thanks, Hennie. You definitely put things in perspective."

"Any time." She beamed. "I have to get back to work, but I'm glad you're okay."

"Me too." I smiled wider and brighter as she left, and sipped the ginger ale. I knew what I had to do. I was going to crush this project . . . like a bug.

I started by googling the cricket flour, something I discovered was actually nutritionally beneficial. It made my skin crawl, and the pictures weren't helping my constant burping, but the knowledge did help me understand the purpose of it.

Fortunately I was saved from too much cricket research by Marcia appearing like a magical genie at my office door. She leaned on the frame, looking like she was trying not to feel sorry for me.

"It was bad." I just started the conversation, assuming her dad had texted.

"What level of bad, scale of one to ten?"

"Blew past ten and landed on a clear fifteen. Or as I like to refer to it, the seventh level of hell. I puke-sprayed the entire floor."

"It's his fault. He made you eat one of those dirty bars?" She wrinkled her nose.

"He didn't tell me it was made of bugs until my mouth was full of them." I shuddered and closed my eyes, unfortunately reliving the moment and the taste and texture.

"Oh, bro." She sat and pulled out her hand sanitizer, offering me some. We both rubbed our hands with the cool liquid, filling the room with the smell. "I wouldn't even taste them. Mom made Girt take them out of the house. He can't get a single celeb to endorse them. They think they're nasty too. We all think Dad's lost his damn mind on this one."

"Not technically." I was defending him, though hating it. "The research is there. I get it."

"Research or not, I wouldn't put one of those things in my mouth if you paid me," she said. "I'm going to the spa; you in for lunch?"

"Spa for lunch?" I contemplated the time it took to get there, the time it took to get back, and the time I would spend there. "I don't get three-hour lunches."

"Daddy dearest says you can come. He called me and asked me to take you out for the afternoon. Said you needed a bit of a break. Told me he feels badly."

"Oh." I bit my lip. "Okay. Let me go see him quickly. I need to apologize and tell him I'm on board for this launch." I didn't want to walk down that hallway or see him or any of the other people in the office, not after my explosive performance. But I needed to see if this was real. I loved Marcia, but trusting her with my job was a bad idea. She'd sooner have me fired so she could have company at the spa and give me the money to make up the difference. Something that didn't sit well with me.

"Fine, but hurry up." She glanced at her phone.

My legs were a bit weak as I stood and walked to Mr. La Croix's office, trying not to notice the looks I was getting or the heat on my cheeks.

He was in a meeting with a lady, but the moment he saw me through the glass doors, he waved me in.

I poked my head in. "Sorry, Mr. La Croix—"

"Lacey. Are you okay?" He sighed. "I am so sorry. I had no idea you would freak out like that. I never would have put you on the spot if I'd known. I just didn't think you'd taste the bars if I told you. Marcia wouldn't—"

"They're delicious. And yes, the protein source is unconventional, but I understand. I've done some research, and I'll have a proposal drawn up for you."

"You still want the project?" His expression tightened.

"Yes, of course. You caught me by surprise, but I can do this." It was a lie. Mostly.

"If you believe in the product, then I'm excited to see what you come up with. We really need a hook to get those celebs and people like Marcia to endorse." His eyes glanced past me. "And now, as a way of repaying you for the horrible first day back, we would all—and by all, I mean me—love it if you took the afternoon off and spent it getting a bad taste out of your mouth."

"You sure?" I asked, glancing behind me to see Marcia tapping her watch.

"I am." His eyes narrowed as he glared at her, then darted back to me. "And I'm proud of you. Very. You're a strong and resilient girl. Well done, Lacey." He smiled. That proud, fatherly look was better than anything else at healing my wounded pride.

"Thanks." I nodded and backed out of the office. "I'll see you tomorrow, then." I turned and left, a little bit excited to hit the spa but dreading the next ten minutes. "I just have to grab my—"

"I have it." Marcia handed me my bag. "The girls are all waiting for us at the spa." She texted and talked as we headed for the end of the hall.

As we entered the elevator, I gave her a look, dreading having to give her the news, and yet needing her to know. She was part of my family, and I needed to share the pain with her. I'd wanted to call or text the moment my parents told me, but I couldn't. I didn't know how to say the words until I told Hennie. And now it was time to bring my best friend into the fold.

Chapter Nine

Gray Skies and Fancy Lies

Jordan

The ocean wind on my face cleared my head of at least 60 percent of the things I'd been stuck obsessing over for the last couple of days. Sailing with my grandpa tended to do that. He was demanding and daring, so most of the time I was distracted by the desperation of survival.

Today my thoughts were sticking with me, even through the spray of water and Grandpa shouting at us to change sails and sides of the boat.

The very last year of school ever was starting in a couple of months.

My summer working for Grandpa had started again with a bang: the yacht-racing kind of bang.

But none of that was occupying my mind at the moment.

I was consumed with the desire to break things off with the girl my parents had picked for me.

It wasn't just a matter of Amy not being my type; I also resented her because she was forced on me.

I did like the chase.

I wasn't exactly a hunter, but I enjoyed seeing something I wanted and going after it. Like the girl from the boat party, Lacey. I'd had a hard time letting that one go. There was something in her eyes, and the way she smiled while she made fun of me. It was like a kick in the balls that disguised itself as something I needed. Or maybe it was just the fact that she'd run off, leaving me wanting more.

Either way, the point was that I did want more.

"We're approaching the leeward mark!" Grandpa shouted, cutting me off from my daydreaming. "Move some asses!" he barked, sounding like a giddy schoolboy racing his paper boat on a stream, not a man midrace with twenty other boats all heading for the same tiny plot of sea. This was his favorite moment.

When I was a kid, I'd asked him if we were going to crash, and he looked me straight in the eyes and said, "We all have to die sometime, kid. No point in worrying when it's going to be. And to die sailing, what a way to go." His eyes were crazy, like they are now, and the spray of the ocean air really exacerbated his excitement.

"Grandpa!" I shouted, pointing to the side of him.

"I saw it." He grinned, even more alive now that a giant storm was coming toward us.

"Hope you got your shitting pants on," Stephen shouted at me, using his new favorite line as he nudged me, breaking Grandpa's rule on how close we were allowed to be on the boat. "Wind's going to thirty-five knots! Yeeehaaa!"

He was Grandpa's boy, through and through.

We broke without speaking, the entire crew rushing to our posts, ready for the turn that would feel like we were tipping, and then the final stretch: the finish line with the incoming storm chasing us down.

"Come on, boys!" Grandpa shouted from the helm. His wild eyes and crazy smile were lit. "If the ship goes down, we all go down!" His normal words for the final turns in the course. "Jibe!" He yelled it the same way every single time. And I never got tired of hearing it. While I didn't want to die at sea, I also loved the way his passion made my spine tingle with a modicum of fear. In reality, I knew the lifeboats would be on us in a moment, and I could swim like an Olympian.

"Ready!" we screamed in the ripping wind, scrambling, going too fast for the corner that was coming.

"Jibe ho!" he blasted at us.

I started trimming the main.

"Release!"

"Boom!"

The sea sprayed in my face as the starboard side of the boat took a sip of ocean waves.

We struggled to get to the other side, tightening the sails and bringing round the boat.

It was fast and violent and not the smartest way to hit the mark, but Grandpa liked the adventure of a well-timed jibe and the risk of someone possibly dying or drowning.

The race was ours; we knew it in the final stretch.

We shouted and celebrated far before we got past the buoy.

Stephen grabbed the champagne and popped it, spraying us all before drinking from the bottle and passing it around.

Grandpa nodded at us, looking down the boat at his crew.

I once heard someone say his crew was a bunch of lunatics. My grandpa's response was that he handpicked each and every one of us and made us the men we were.

That was the truth.

The wind was cold, even for the second to last week of May, as the rain began to pelt us.

We were soaked already, which meant we didn't care if we got wetter.

And Grandpa had on his postrace face, which Stephen always assumed was also his postsex face. I took my chance, remembering I was the man Grandpa had made me, and sauntered back to him as casually as I could with the swells and winds knocking us about. This was my moment, when he was in the throes of ecstasy.

"Great race, kid!" He wrapped an arm around my shoulders and squeezed. "Great race."

"It sure was." I watched everyone drink the champagne, like it wasn't eleven in the morning, and counted backward from ten, trying to pace myself. "Can I ask you a serious question?"

"And ruin my mood? Why would you want to do that, Jordie?" He chuckled, but there was a hint of seriousness to his tone.

"Because I've been thinking about it, and I'm pretty sure that Amy is the wrong choice for me as far as girlfriends go, pretend or not."

"Oh?" He gave me some serious side-eye.

"Well, she's not a great fit for the company. I understand Dad's trying to tie up her family's money in investments, but she's the wrong path to that money." I tried to politely imply that she had an IQ lower than a rock. "She's, uhhh, well—" I felt like a dick saying it, but it was my lifeline. "She can barely read, Grandpa. She's got no drive. She's a spoiled brat with no ambition to be anything. She's barely getting by in school, and I think her mom's paying her teachers to pass her. She doesn't even know what courses she's taking. She's not someone you could ever bring to work functions or have help you entertain clients. And God forbid she actually develops feelings for me after the deal is done and I break things off. That would be cruel." Wrong comment. Grandpa never cared about cruelty.

"I see." He bit his lip.

"Surely there's another avenue Dad could use to bait her father. Maybe I could even help." I realized I should have come up with an answer before I approached him. He was going to ask that.

"In all seriousness," he said, "I normally wouldn't give a rat's red ass who you dated in college, but this has to be handled carefully. Your dad has made some financial mistakes in the past couple of years that cost our company a lot of money. He's choosing to fix this by aligning

Amy's family with our company. Her father is a tricky man to convince, and for whatever reason, he's comfortable with you dating his daughter. Refusing the relationship could ruin the business deal. That's not how we do business here." He gave me a side-glance, and I died a little inside. "We take one for the team, kid."

"I know."

"I don't know if you do." He sighed, clearly annoyed we were having this conversation. "A man's daughter is his pride. He will not break bread with anyone who hurts his little girl." He lowered his voice. "So, what I think you should actually be after is advice on how to get dumped without being viewed as the blame in her father's eyes. How to get out of this without being the one who did it. You need her to be disinterested in you."

"Yeah, I guess I do." I grinned, not even realizing that was what I wanted until it made absolute sense.

"In my experience, Jordan, there are three things that will get you dumped: only ever calling her after ten p.m., after you've had a couple of drinks and are feeling the whiskey making you frisky; only agreeing to see her when she asks you to do something, but never asking her out; and offering her tips on how she could look better instead of complimenting her when asked how she looks." He points at me. "With women, that's a trick question; she doesn't want your opinion and only wants you to say *beautiful.* Screw that up, and she's on her way out. Everything else, a girl with the right kind of social graces will either look past or correct for you, especially if her family is in bed with yours."

"What do you mean?"

"Well, let's say you cheated. In this world, that means she can expect expensive gifts and that she's gained the upper hand. She has the control to use against you. Or say you flirt with other women. She, in turn, throws it in your face and flirts with other men. And there's always you working too much, but as punishment, she'll have an affair

and you'll end up with crabs even though you haven't strayed at all."
His last remark was a little more than I needed to know.

"Wow, you have it down to a science."

"I do. Those three things are your only ticket." He turned the boat
slightly, heading for the marina. "And don't mess that up, or it's too late.
When your mom married your dad, I was crushed. I had set up family
playdates as a ploy to get his family money invested in some deals and
to get my hands on this sweet piece of prime property they owned. I
figured if our families were friendly, we could make it happen." The
tone of the story changed as he went along. "But then she got pregnant.
She was twenty years old and knocked up by that—man." He didn't
sugarcoat his feelings, even in front of me, even about my own dad.
"And she has spent twenty-six years married to a turd. You kids are the
only reason she stays. I've offered hit men, money, houses in France, but
nothing works. She won't do it. I think she stays to punish me for being
a terrible father." He shook his head, wiping some of the sea spray off his
forehead with his weathered hand. "You know the moral of the story?"

"No." I honestly was terrified of the turn the story had taken and
that the moral was that he wanted me to grow the fuck up, and fast. I
obviously knew the old tale, pretty much from childhood, but to have
it linked to my own misery in the middle of my begging to be let off
the hook suggested there wasn't much hope for me.

"I got the land deal and the investments before she was even pregnant. She didn't cut her losses fast enough. I thought she was smarter
than that. Don't be stupid like her. But don't burn bridges either. All is
fair in love and war, but why make enemies?" He grinned wide. "And if
you want to break things off in a way your dad doesn't hate you for, then
you play it up. The moment she dumps your sorry ass, you head for
drinks and avoid other women for a few weeks. Your dad will take pity
on you. He'll see you as less of a man, one who can't keep his woman
happy, but that's the cost of a mission such as this. And Mr. Weitzman
won't care about you, since his daughter doesn't. You'll no longer be

relative to the business deal." He slapped me on the back. "Now go tie us off and get some hot waitresses down here with some refreshment. I intend to drink until the whiskey makes *me* frisky!"

"Aye, Captain." I nodded and headed for the dock, a little grossed out and lot disheartened.

"Did I mishear, or were you easing into the death of the romance between our dad and Mr. Weitzman?" Stephen grinned like a Cheshire cat from behind some rigging.

"No, figuring out a way to bite my leg off so I can escape the trap. Your turn, Steph." I winked and tossed the line to an older lady in a raincoat. "But good luck. There's a story about crabs in there you don't want to hear. Avoid that detour."

He grimaced, and I helped dock the boat and hurried to the bar to get girls and drinks and red carpets for the man and the legend that I could never live up to.

Chapter Ten

STARFISH

Lacey

"I have something terrible to tell you, but you have to promise to react rationally," I said through the pain of my massage.

"What?" Marcia sounded scared. "Is it Grandma?"

"No." I scoffed. "That old woman is going to live to be a hundred." I swallowed tears and forced the words from my lips. "It's Martin."

"What about Martin?" Worry filled our massage sanctuary as my pain became Marcia's as I told her the whole story, minus a couple of small details, like my finances.

"I can't believe this." Marcia moaned into the hole where her face was resting while the masseur dug into her, making her gasp her words. "He's seventeen. This is impossible. Did your mom have him checked by real doctors, or the ones at the hospital where she works?" The translation to that was that my family attended the peasant hospital.

"No, they're certain. Mom took him to a good doctor. They've been seeing symptoms for a bit but thought he may have had strep or mono. I told him he had the immune system of a ninety-year-old last week. Awesome." I groaned as the masseur dug into my shoulders.

"I just can't even with this. Not Martin."

"I know. It was a shitty day yesterday. And I was so hungover when the news landed. Poor Grandma. She made me one of my favorite meals, and I lost it everywhere in the backyard." I shuddered, unable to say *broccoli* for the life of me.

"Wait. You puked two days in a row? God, I wish I had that problem. I'm up like two pounds from this weekend. All that salty buffet food. You probably lost weight."

"Yeah. Maybe." I groaned as the masseur ground into my lower back, rolling the skin and making me breathe deeper to relax. Losing weight wasn't really on my mind.

"How's your stomach now?"

"Better than my brother's cancer." I sighed, not feeling sorry for myself—refusing to, in fact.

"True story." She sounded like the massage was getting a bit rough. "I still cannot believe poor Martin. Like, what are the odds?"

"Quite low. Grandpa was the only member of the family to have cancer that we know of. And he was way over fifty when he got it. I don't even know what to say. *Bad luck* isn't strong enough wording. I think there were like a billion-to-one odds he would get cancer, even if it is hereditary."

"And now the cricket project. Want me to hire someone to do the work for you so can just bask in the glory?"

A smile crested my lips. She didn't understand ethics or pride at all. "No, I just needed to wrap my head around it. No biggie. Just some cricket flour. Totally cool." I forced that last part, but it was going to become my mantra. Totally cool. That was me.

A soft chime rang in the room, signaling it was time to steam between treatments. The masseurs left the room as we got up, wrapping ourselves in fresh towels and heading to the steam room. "Where's everyone else?" We'd arrived late to the spa, so the other girls were already in treatments. We hadn't seen them yet.

"I think they're all in the steam room." Marcia opened the door, letting the steam waft out at us. "Girls?" she called as we walked in blindly.

"Hey!" they answered in unison.

"Who's all here?" Marcia disappeared into the clouds.

"All of us," Kami called out. "It's me, Carmen, and Jo. Who's with you?"

"It's just me and Lacey."

"Hey!" I smiled and waved at the steam as we got farther to the back.

It cleared more as I reached the benches and sat, burning the backs of my legs as the air tried to choke me.

"What's going on?" Marcia sat next to Carmen.

"Not much. Talking about the bomb-ass end-of-year boating." Carmen smiled. "I had a blast Friday. What about you guys?"

"Yeah, and DJ Spark slayed," Marcia said as she inhaled deeply.

"He did." Kami glanced at the floor, her lips toying with a grin. "The boy can DJ."

"He really can," I added, trying to be positive about him. I'd heard from so many people that he was a lying, cheating scumbag. As friends, we were supportive, but not entirely honest.

"Did I see you talking to Jordan Somersby?" Carmen smirked at me.

"Oh, uhhhhh. Maybe. I drank a lot." It was too hot to lie well enough to fool Marcia.

"Jordan?" Marcia's nose wrinkled when she said his name. "Somersby?"

"He had a hat on, and it was dark on the side of the boat, and I've only met him that one time. I didn't know it was him," I explained, making them all laugh.

"How could you not know who Jordan Somersby was?" Kami laughed. "God, if I could accidently get stuck between brothers, it would be a Somersby sandwich. Extra mayo."

"Ewwwww." Marcia gagged. "I hate Stephen. He's so nasty. He has banged, like, three hundred chicks. He's a whore."

"Marcia!" I gasped.

"Oh, shit, did I say that out loud?" She laughed harder. "I think the heat's getting to my head. But you know what I mean. He's seedy. And that Cynthia deserves so much more."

"The Somersby guys are major players," Jo said softly. She seemed off. Not her lively self. "Their parents were forced to get together by Captain Jack, and I heard the same about Stephen and Cynthia. She didn't want to marry him."

"No. Girl, I know them. They're Monty's closest family friends. I have been forced to hang with them more times than I care to say. Cynthia and Stephen love each other, even though he's gross. She's like a saint or angel or some shit. She's not even from a good family. At all. She's like Lacey." She pointed at me, and they all nodded, like I was the golden standard for average. And no one thought it was weird.

I barely thought it was weird. It didn't make me uncomfortable anymore that I wasn't from a pedigreed family. Marcia didn't mean it that way.

"Anyway. How old is Jordan?" Kami grinned.

"A year older than us. I heard he just started dating that weird Amy girl," Carmen blurted. "Friday night she was on the boat telling everyone. But the only girl I saw him talking to was you." She glanced at me, making my face burn even more than it was.

"Oh, right." Marcia waved it off. "My dad told me Amy's dad was looking to invest. So, of course, everyone is trying to get up her family's skirt. And hers as a throughway. This has Captain Jack written all over it."

"He has a girlfriend?" I had thoughts on the matter. Big ones. But I kept them to myself. Rich people and their cheating. And if Jordan Somersby was dating someone when he kissed me, then he was exactly the douchebag Marcia said he was. I just hated that I liked him before

I knew who he was and that I had fallen for the act. He seemed so cool. Like my own version of Monty. But Montys weren't that easy to come by, as my two-year dry spell proved.

"Speaking of cheaters, Jo thinks Theo's cheating on her," Carmen said softly, glancing at Jo. "Tell them."

"No way." I leaned toward Jo in the mist. "Why?" I knew why, but we all acted our parts and said the right thing.

"We were hanging out at his house, and his phone rang. When he answered it, he hurried up to his bedroom and closed the door. He was only up there, like, two minutes, and then he came back down. When I asked him who called, he said his bookie. He was placing bets. But I've been in the room when he places bets; he's on the phone for, like, ever. Then, I tried to check his phone when he went to the bathroom, to verify, and he changed the password."

"Maybe he lost a lot of money and he didn't want you to hear." I tried to think about it like a rational human being. "Or his mom tried to break into his phone, so he changed the password on the cloud and all his passwords changed as a result. That happened to me once."

"I don't know. I wish there were a way to be certain aside from the crazy, paranoid girlfriend move of having him followed." She sighed, leaning back. "Getting caught hiring a PI to follow him would put a dent in our relationship, as you might expect."

"When Lacey was dating France, I legit wanted to hire a PI. I knew he was cheating. Douche." Marcia rubbed a little salt in an old wound. Not intentionally—she was just one of those people. She didn't know salt could still sting, even if the wound was healed.

"France is such a loser. I still can't believe you dated him," Carmen scoffed. "He did not deserve you."

"Thanks." I tried not to sound like I was still mad at him, two years later. I was over it as far as the rest of the world knew. So over it. Never dating again. Especially not a trust-fund kid. Especially not someone like Jordan Somersby.

"It's too bad someone hasn't figured out a way to test dudes," Jo said. "An app that runs a scan and sees if they're lying sacks of shit. Theo, for instance, is an amazing liar. I've watched him with his dad. I can't tell when he's getting away with something. And I think I love him, so if this really is something stupid like bookie problems, I don't want to break things off. But if he's cheating"—Jo's tone changed—"I will rip his balls off and stuff them up his ass."

"Oh, wow," Marcia sniggered.

"A man-tester app." Carmen laughed. "We should invent it and patent that shit." We all snickered in agreement.

Mostly they laughed while I imagined us designing the app. Clearly they had different sugarplums dancing in their heads. Their version involved paying someone else to make it for them.

"I would pay top dollar to someone who tested my man. Top friggin' dollar," Kami commented in a way that made me wonder if things were okay with her and her DJ boyfriend.

Her statement dinged on a light bulb in my head. What if I could figure out a way to make this app work? I could see if Martin wanted to help—what with his nerdy, techy expertise—and we could sell it or charge a monthly fee to make more than the money I needed for school. Certain genius-level apps could sell for more than forty thousand dollars. And this was definitely genius.

I let the idea roll around in my head all afternoon, but by the time I was leaving the spa, passing the huge Post-it note wall where Marcia was putting up some stupid quote she had definitely just googled, I had already stumbled upon a major flaw of this app. There was no way to test people with phones and know if they were lying.

It was wishful thinking, and getting a second job was my best, surest option for putting money in my parents' pockets.

Just then, my phone dinged with a message from Hennie, asking if I wanted to have drinks. She was getting off work, as I should have been instead of being here in Pamperland.

"Wanna go for a drink?" I asked Marcia as she stuck the pink Post-it note to the sea of them.

"No. I have to meet Monty in, like, two hours. So I have to get ready. Who're you meeting?" She cocked an eyebrow.

"Hennie."

"Oh." She wrinkled her nose. "Your nerdy commoner friend. Cool." Her dislike of my being with other friends was amusing, if a little harsh. "Say hi for me," she offered weakly. "And text me later with snaps from Martin. I wanna see his adorable face."

"He'll love that." I laughed and kissed her cheek before pushing off and walking down the street, waving backward. "Have fun, and say hi to Monty for me."

"No, he likes you better than me," she shouted back.

"Everyone does." I laughed at my own joke, realizing I was feeling much better. The spa had rejuvenated me. I looked a little fresh-faced to be going out for drinks, but I didn't care. It was Hennie. She didn't have social expectations of me, and we wouldn't be going anywhere where people cared what we looked like. And I really could use a drink and the company of Hennie to de-stress, even though I'd just come from de-stressing.

When I got to the small pub she'd asked me to meet her at, the one a couple of blocks from our office, I smiled wide seeing her. We hadn't hung out all year, even though we'd promised we would. We said it every summer, and at the end of every spring, when we got back together at work, we realized we hadn't seen each other in all that time between.

She was a Harvard student and didn't like any of my friends. I didn't blame her. Had I been trying to befriend them now, at twenty-one, I wouldn't have liked many of them either. But I met them at thirteen; it was much easier for them to weasel their way into my heart. And her experiences in her own private school had been horridly lonely.

"Here." She slid my gin and tonic at me with an extra lime wedge. She and Marcia were the only people in the world who knew my drink. Besides Girt and maybe Moser, Marcia's household staff. Actually that wasn't true. I would bet my money that West knew it. He knew everything.

"How ya feeling?" she asked.

"Great, better. The spa was exactly what I needed. I can't believe I ended up there on my first day back." I shook my head, laughing and sitting across from her. "I'll have to remember that trick to get out of the next sales meeting. How was the rest of the day?"

"Weird. Mr. La Croix had the bathroom reno'd the second after you left." She chuckled absently.

"Oh my God." My stomach tightened. "That's why he sent me away. He didn't want me to see them cleaning up my mess." My cheeks flushed.

"I guess so. Sorry. I shouldn't have said anything. I don't blame you for the bathroom, though. I blame him and the team. They should never have done that to you. It was sick and mean."

I lifted my drink and closed my eyes, trying not to relive it. "Anyway, besides worrying about how to market the bug campaign, I also need to come up with some night-job ideas. Just in case I don't get to stay on at La Croix for the school year. I was thinking, who works nights and makes a lot of money, besides hookers?" I lifted an eyebrow. "Unless you think I'd make a good hooker."

"No." She sipped her vodka and sparkling water with a dash of cranberry juice. "No. Being a hooker is a terrible job prospect. Late nights are one thing, but getting murdered in an alley is another. Skin suit—just keep chanting *skin suit*."

"I could find an escort service and sign up. Get protection," I joked, sort of. "And if guys are dumb enough to pay someone for sex, I say women should be happy to take that money for doing none of the work.

Being a girl is easy. Starfish out, let them get busy, collect money, have a shower."

"What's *starfish out*?" She lifted an eyebrow, confirming my suspicions that she was much more innocent than me—something I sort of admired her for. She didn't have a jerk like France Miglio in her closet.

"You lie there, arms out and legs spread, on your back."

"Oh. Gross. Right. That makes sense." She toyed with the straw in her drink. "Except not all johns look like Richard Gere in *Pretty Woman*, so your night might end with heroin to try to forget the things you saw. There's a reason those girls are all drug addicts. You might be simplifying it a bit." She shuddered. "What about bartending? My cousin does it and he makes, like, five hundred a night in tips."

"Are you serious?"

"Yeah, three nights a week are nuts. He's off at four in the morning, though. That would make Friday mornings impossible. But at least you could only work Thursday, Friday, and Saturday and make two thousand between tips and wages."

"I don't know how to bartend, though. How fast could I learn this?" I glanced to where the bartender was mixing drinks and laughing with the customer he was talking to.

"He picked it up over the course of a summer. Said it was rough at first, but he figured it out. Now he's got bars asking him to work there all the time. He makes more money than my dad ever did." Her dad had been a dentist who owned his own practice, so that was saying something. To families like ours, a dentist was a respectable job and put Hennie's in the upper middle class. Compared to Marcia's friends, though, dentistry might as well have been shoe shining.

"Yeah, or I could be a night janitor," I said, changing the subject when I remembered a friend had said cleaning offices at night was good money. Plus I didn't want to talk about Hennie's dad. I knew she wouldn't want to. His tragic death was still a tense subject. I always waited for her to bring it up.

"But they work until four in the morning and not just weekends. I think you might need a different idea." Her eyes darted around the pub.

"Maybe. Anyway, enough about me. What's new with you?"

"Not much." She shrugged. "Working, school, same old story. My mom wants me to get my little sister a job at La Croix. Like that will be easy. She's addicted to her phone and hates everyone except her friends. She has no idea what a work life is." She pointed at me. "She reminds me of Marcia. Just not filthy rich."

"Yeah, you wouldn't find a girl like Marcia in a job that lasts. I love her, but no work ethic. None. I told her about the cricket thing, and she offered to pay someone to do my job for me so I didn't have to suffer." I laughed, but Hennie got a weird look in her eyes.

"Why don't you just ask her for the money?"

"Not a chance," I said, then finished my drink. "I would never ask my friends for money. Ever."

"Well, maybe the whole 'finishing fourth year slowly' thing will work out."

"Maybe." I ordered a second round for us both and contemplated all my options.

Unfortunately they weren't amazing. At all.

Chapter Eleven

SELF-RESPECT

Jordan

"Wanna watch a movie?" I asked as I held the remote to the theater system and glanced over at Amy playing on her phone. I'd invited her over late at night, like I wanted something else from her, but I wasn't my brother. "The booty call," plan A, was a bust. She didn't act like she thought this was a booty call. Almost as if she didn't understand why I would text so late. And even worse, for a girl who was allegedly interested in me, she didn't talk much. Or try to engage in any way.

I had a terrible feeling it was one of two things. Either I was her first "boyfriend" and she had no idea how to be around a guy, which would make my dad's plan extra gross, or she was being forced to date me and pretend she was interested, which made no sense. Her parents had loads of money; they didn't need my family. Unless connections were her dad's goal, weaseling into one of the old families, in which case my dad's was exactly that. His family invented blue blood.

"Movie?" I asked again when she didn't lift her face from her phone.

"Sure, whatever you want to watch," she muttered, and then made that weird selfie face she always did and took another photo, ensuring I was in the background.

"Whatever I want?" I lamented, and turned on Guy Ritchie's *Sherlock Holmes*.

The lights dimmed, and the room took over, becoming the amazing theater Stephen and I'd had custom made for us.

Massive reclining captain's chairs with footrests and cup holders, like at the movies, but with better sound and a screen that was to die for.

The movie came on, making Amy jump as she gave a deep sigh from having to lift her gaze from her phone. "I have to go to the bathroom. Don't bother pausing." She waved me off and left the room, leaving me in peace.

It was beautiful.

The opening scene was amazing.

I dug my hand into the warm buttered popcorn Lucia had told me to make myself, as she refused to do anything for me until I was single again and had regained her respect. She had worded it more directly than that. The words *little bitch* had been used as a descriptor.

But regardless of how I felt, the reality was that I couldn't be the one to break up with Amy without a plan. I didn't want to be the shame of my family, but I also didn't want this.

Hence the reason I had started to implement Grandpa's scheme. I wasn't going to call or text Amy during normal business hours, and if she tried to get in touch with me, I would be indifferent and let her make the plans. Like tonight. I ignored her texts all day and then messaged back late at night and asked if she wanted to hang. I'd expected her to say no and be annoyed.

But the girl came over and then acted like she didn't want to be here.

I chewed the popcorn aggressively, worried I was never getting rid of her, not without my dad hating me. Was being disowned the worst option?

The antithesis of mutual attraction came back a few minutes later, smiling like she was going to tell me something funny, but she didn't. Whatever she was laughing about was private.

She slumped back in the chair, making noises and clearing her throat.

I paused the movie, giving her a look, the one I gave my brother frequently.

"Sorry." She curled into herself and prepared for the movie to start again.

Sorry? Dear God. Why didn't this girl ever get angry? Why didn't she have emotions? Was she a robot?

I contemplated asking her for a blow job to prove why I'd really asked her over, but I worried she might say yes, and I'd have to close my eyes and pretend she was someone else. And I didn't really want to be touched by her. That would make it actual prostitution and the end of my morals.

"I'm gonna go," she said after a minute. "I just realized it's almost midnight." She got up and walked to the door.

"Bye." I waved dismissively and started the movie back up before she was out of the room.

When the movie ended, I got up, sighing and defeated.

I was going to have to up my jerk game after this. Grandpa was right, and I had to start doing more than just ignoring her and calling only when it could be interpreted as a booty call. I had to be disinterested to the point that she felt ignored or realized we weren't meant to be. I couldn't be too mean or ghost her, otherwise her dad would get angry that I'd disrespected her. It was a delicate balance that needed to be held.

But if I didn't end this nicely, I was going to be disowned by my father.

I wasn't sure I wanted that, not yet. It was a big decision to never see one's parents again, and I knew my dad wasn't bluffing.

Sauntering up the stairs to my wing of the house, I caught my mom on the landing. She had the same expression on her face I imagined was on mine.

"Hi, sweetie. You going to bed?"

"Yeah." I nodded.

"Did you have a nice visit with Amy?" She perked her eyes up, maybe searching a little harder than normal for the real answer.

"No. We watched a movie. She wasn't into it." I acted indifferent, or was indifferent.

I didn't know how much heart Mom had left in her. Most of the time I wanted to pull her into my arms and ask if this life was what she really wanted. To be married to a narcissist who used her as the butt of jokes. Surely there was more out there for her than this.

Instead of stepping out of my shell and risking emotional vulnerability, I did my same song and dance.

"Night, Mom." I kissed her cheek and hurried up the stairs.

Since it was only midnight, I could still get in a couple of chapters of *Swan Song*, the novel I was addicted to.

Chapter Twelve

THE DINNER DATE

Lacey

My head ached a little bit from all the gin and sliders I'd managed to get into me before going home to pass out. I should have eaten more instead of drinking my calories.

Mr. La Croix entered my little back office with a big smile and a latte. He was bringing me coffee now? Something was up. He was normally the cool dad and the friendly, hip boss, but this was a whole other ball of wax. I almost didn't trust it.

"I got you a cinnamon *dolce*." He sat at the spare chair that was really only there for Hennie. "And I wanted to say again how sorry I am for yesterday. I can't believe I did that to you. I feel terrible. Marcia read me the riot act last night when she got home. And I want to make sure—we're on good terms?"

"We're fine." I laughed nervously, hoping Marcia hadn't told her dad about my brother. I didn't need him treating me like I was delicate or special. I needed every penny I could get, but I wanted to earn them in my own right. "Thank you for the coffee. I can't believe you know what I drink."

"Hennie." He laughed. "She also looked a little under the weather, so I got her one too. You girls have some fun last night?" He sighed happily, likely reminiscing on his own bachelor days. "I remember being twenty-one; what a great time. Getting drunk on Mondays to forget my horrible day at work and all that craziness."

"Liar," I scoffed, sipping my lifesaving beverage and treating him like we were at home and not at work at all. "You were working your ass off at twenty-one and probably never got drunk all year long. You made your first seven-figure paycheck at twenty-two."

"You know me too well." He laughed harder, standing up. "It's why you're my favorite daughter."

"You're not allowed to have favorites," I teased.

"I know, but I can't help it. And since you're my favorite, I came in to remind you to drop the odd hint to your sister about setting goals and achieving them. Marcia is driving me up the wall." And there it was, the real reason for the visit.

"I'll try again when I see her tomorrow." We had another spa date; this one was set for after work, unless I managed to empty my lunch in public before then.

"Okay. And if you want off the crickets, say the word, and we find someone else," he said as he walked to the door.

"Not a chance."

"That's my girl." He beamed and walked off, backward waving at Hennie as she came staggering into my office, eyes red and London fog in hand.

"My head hurts."

"Mine too." I slid a bottle of Advil at her.

"Do you remember everything we did last night? It was a Monday. What were we thinking?"

"I don't even know. We started talking about janitors, and I was sad—" I recalled talking about starfish hookers and my new life goal to become a night worker in any lascivious capacity, but the rest was hazy.

"Oh my God, remember that crazy idea you had? Lie detector phone app to see if your guy is cheating." She snorted and slumped into her chair. We were officially the worst summer help ever. Day two and we were already hungover and slacking off.

"I wish we could figure out a way to test Theo and see if he's cheating on Jo. She's really conflicted about it. If I weren't afraid of getting caught, I would do it myself."

"Does he know you?" Hennie asked.

"Yes and no. With the right makeup on me, he could walk past me on the street and never take notice, except to check me out. He was a couple of years ahead of us at school. And being the poor girl whose grandma was paying for her to go to private school, I wasn't exactly on most people's radars. I'm sure he knows who I am as background noise, sort of like the rest of the guys see me." Not being a rich girl with an important family made me forgettable to guys who were trying to impress their fathers by bringing home girls who counted—girls like Jo and Marcia. They would want to bang me at a party, but that was about it.

"Then why don't you just hit on him and see if he takes the bait and give her the skinny? You could record it." She said it like it was an obvious solution, not understanding my place in their world. I couldn't just hit on one of their dudes to test him. They'd crucify me. I would end up being seen as a poor girl trying to ladder climb.

One day I would be someone who matters in their world by my own merit, and I would need those connections. Being friends with these people meant something to me, even if it didn't always mean the same thing to them.

"Okay, well, if you think of anything, let me know. I'm gonna go and pretend I'm working while I try to sleep sitting up with sunglasses on." Hennie shuddered as she stood.

"I'm going to pretend I'm working while I fill out my student-loan application and hope I get the amount I need."

"Go, team." Hennie slowly lifted her tea and left my office.

The morning crept by, and the application almost killed me, but by the end of the day I was happy to have it over with.

I hobbled from the office, waving goodbye to everyone at the foyer and trudging to the subway with Hennie. We rode the same train, but she got off after me in Kensington, near the park.

We didn't speak the whole ride, just sat in deathly silence until finally she slipped her sunglasses down and groaned, "This is the Mondayest Tuesday ever."

"Word." I nodded.

"My mom is gonna be home late, which means I have to make dinner." She wrinkled her nose. "I think touching food might kill me."

"My parents won't be home, either, but I have Grandma." I sighed, eternally grateful for her. "And I swear to God when I was leaving, I saw a roast on the counter thawing. You should just come to my place to eat and take your mom home a plate."

"Oh, yeah?" She worked up enough effort to smile. "I'm totally doing that. You think she's doing mashed potatoes and gravy?"

"Maybe." I chuckled. "But I wouldn't be surprised if she made fresh buns and did a beef dip."

"Oh, sweet baby Jesus, let it be beef dip."

As the train stopped, we pushed ourselves up with what might have been the last of our effort and hobbled home the block and a half to my place.

"Oh my God, I might just sleep here and be the walk-of-shame girl tomorrow morning." Hennie rubbed her eyes as we entered the house.

"Mi casa es su casa." I lifted my nose to the air and sniffed. "Beef dip."

"Thank the gods and all that is holy." She slipped her shoes off and dropped her bag on the floor.

"Oh, look, it's the walking dead," Martin scoffed as he walked to the table with his massive plate of food, straightening up when he saw Hennie. "Oh, hi."

"Martin, you remember Hennie, right?" I lifted my phone and weakly took a photo of him taking his first bite.

"What the hell, Lacey?" he asked with a mouthful.

"Marcia wanted snaps of you." I laughed and sat as I pointed at Hennie. "Grandma, you remember Hennie, right?"

"Of course, dear, how are you?" She hugged me and then Hennie.

"Dying," Hennie muttered, and sat too.

"You must have been the one out with Lacey last night." Grandma giggled and gave us both a massive plate of beef dip with perfectly colored au jus and a side of fries. "Carbs before liquor or you'll never be sicker. You have to start remembering that," she said with a laugh.

"Wow, drunk at the start of the week," Martin snorted. "What's next, day drinking?"

"Shut it." I growled the words and then ate like a wild animal, tearing and moaning at the bun and beef.

The sound of a click made me blink as I caught Martin putting his phone back down.

"What was that?" I asked with a mouthful of bun.

"Marcia will want snaps," he mimicked.

"You're dead." I pointed at him.

"Lacey!" Grandma scolded me, making Martin snicker.

"Sorry, Grandma." I glared at Martin, seeing just how far this cancer thing was going to get him. He was now Saint Martin, and I was evil Lacey, and this summer would be the end of me. But, I conceded, at least it wasn't the end of him. And even hungover, I had to admit, that was all that mattered.

Hennie and I continued to eat in silence, slowly devouring everything on the plate.

Grandma surprised us with coconut cream pie, and even though I was sweating and my body contemplated throwing up at least once during the meal, I ate every last bite. And I kept it down. My daily puking streak had to come to an end somewhere.

The sun was setting when Hennie stood in the doorway, full, sleepy, and carrying a bunch of leftovers. "Thanks so much for dinner, Mrs. Winters."

"Call me Grandma, dear. And you're very welcome." She smiled wide and hugged Hennie awkwardly. It was night and day to how she treated Marcia.

"I'll walk you to the subway."

"I'll come." Martin pulled on his shoes.

"You shouldn't be—"

"Grandma," Martin said with a sigh. "I have completely curable cancer. I'm not breakable. I need to leave the house and get some fresh air. I'm going to get friggin' cabin fever if you guys keep treading so lightly around me." He sounded like he was close to the edge, so she didn't argue. She lifted her hands like she was giving up.

"Night," Hennie said to Grandma as we walked out the front door.

"You don't have to walk me, honestly," Hennie protested as we strolled past the neighbor's house.

"It's refreshing being out of the house." Martin took a deep inhale of the city air, like he was in the mountains and the air didn't taste like exhaust.

"I bet. I couldn't handle being inside all the time. I'd go nuts."

"Yeah." He laughed and gave her a look, and I felt oddly out of place.

"I'm sorry you're sick," Hennie offered.

"Thanks. I can't believe it. I had a sore throat for like a month. And Mom kept saying it was strep or a swollen gland or mono. But, nope." He chuckled bitterly. "And I think it's worse that it's summer. At least if this happened during school, I'd have something to preoccupy myself with. But being home with Grandma twenty-four seven, when she's got nothing better to do than baby me, is making me crazy."

"Well, Grandpa did die from this same disease," I reminded him, a little harsher than I should have.

"Right, but he was old, and he smoked for, like, thirty years. It'd be safe to assume that the smoking and the cancer were related. My doctor flat out told us, even worst-case scenario, I'll be okay. I was there. I heard him. They're acting like it's a death sentence. It's not." He was exasperated. It took a lot to get him here. "It's a small surgery and a possibility of some radiation. And actually I think the radiation comes in a pill or something. It's really not a big deal."

"Well, you're their kid and grandkid, so you have to understand that they're scared," Hennie offered, sounding like another big sister. "When my dad died, my mom was afraid that she would lose me or my sister next. She's finally loosening the leash now, but for a long time I couldn't even go in the backyard by myself. I wasn't allowed to cross streets or go to friends' houses or walk anywhere alone. She kept thinking something terrible would happen to me too. My little sister, who's eighteen, about your age, still isn't allowed to do anything. It's oppressive."

Hennie's dad had died tragically, hit by a bus. The driver had a stroke and didn't stop at the crosswalk's red light. Three people died, and five others were horribly injured. Hennie was thirteen at the time. She had just started private school, so she was already out of her element. Add dead dad to that equation, and you had a recipe to be completely ostracized.

"I guess so, huh?" Martin nodded. "I just hope when this is all over, things are going to go back to normal. Being seventeen and having your grandma offer to wipe your ass for you is a little creepy." He chuckled, like this was all nothing.

"A little." Hennie smiled.

"You're lucky Mom isn't doing it." I nudged him. "Being sick and having a nurse for a mom sucks, but when you're both girls, she has no boundaries. And I've only ever had the flu and my appendix removed."

"Mom's bad. She likes to doctor people," Martin agreed. "But at least she goes to work. Grandma lingers and hovers."

"And bakes and cleans and cooks. Let's not discount the good stuff." I nudged him again, teasingly.

When we got to the crosswalk and pushed the light, Hennie glanced back. "The station is right there; you guys go back. Thank your grandma again for reviving me. Before dinner, I thought for sure I'd be spending the night."

"Her coconut cream pie is legendary for curing everything."

Martin scoffed at me. "Except cancer."

"I'll see ya tomorrow at work." Hennie winced, intentionally changing the subject.

"Less hungover." I grinned, still feeling like death, but definitely improved from all the comfort food.

"Less everything," she said with a laugh. "I got nothing done today. It was terrible. Mr. La Croix knew and didn't even care. He's too cool."

"He is the coolest. A second dad for me, so I feel like I've really let him down this week. Whatever. We'll work extra hard from now on. See ya in the morning on the train, maybe."

"Sounds good." She smiled at my brother. "Night, Martin."

"Night, Hennie." He smiled back, and I got a weird feeling in my stomach.

She looked both ways more than a normal person would and then crossed safely to the other side. She glanced back and waved several times before she finally entered the subway stairs.

But we didn't move. Martin watched her the entire time.

"What was that?" I asked when we couldn't see her anymore.

"What?" He turned, innocent of anything and everything, and yet filled with a certain something.

"What just happened?"

"Where?"

"Between you two." I pointed at the stairs and the fact that we weren't moving. "I felt like a third wheel. What are you doing?"

"I like her. She's nice. She's normal compared to your other friends. She doesn't do the diva thing or expect anything. She clears her own plate and says *thank you* and helps Grandma with the dishes. She's already passing you the salt before you can even ask for it." He mentioned so many commonplace things about Hennie, but my heart and ears translated them.

"You *like* her, like her," I gasped. I wanted to say no, and defend the fact that Hennie was mine. But there was something in his eyes that tormented me. He needed a little lift, and if Hennie lifted him, who was I to cock block that? It wasn't like she would ever be interested in him. He was almost four years younger than her, about the same age as her little sister.

"I do." He cracked a grin, but only on one side of his face. "Do you think she'd ever—?"

"You're seventeen!"

"I'll be eighteen in November."

"She's turning twenty-two in December."

"Right, but Mom's four years older than Dad." He started to get defensive.

"Martin, we're not even having this discussion. How about you worry about cancer and Mom and Grandma smothering you with too much love. Hennie is—"

"I'm going to ask her out. You need to wrap your head around that." He turned and started home. "I've already stolen her number from your phone." He cackled, and I tried not to freak out on him. This was the summer Martin got extra everything, even leniency from me.

"Stop hacking into my phone."

"No." He turned and smiled wide. "Help me with Hennie."

"No."

"You want to. You know you do." He was smug for someone who was supposed to be sick.

"If I kick you in the ass, does it affect your cancer?"

"N—yes. Everything hurts my cancer. Including your lack of regard and confidence in my capabilities to woo your friend."

"Don't woo. Just stop. Chemo. Not woo."

"I don't need chemo, hammerhead. And we'll see if Hennie is free to hang with me while I'm recovering." He winked, and I knew there would be no stopping his crush on her. It was how he was. Martin fit in well with everyone. He was smart, witty, funny, sarcastic, and handsome. He got away with everything to the point that this cancer situation was just the cherry on top.

I was too exhausted to worry about a harmless crush on an older girl. Hennie was all the things he'd said. She was kind and grounded and normal. She wouldn't date my brother, who was still in high school. But she also wouldn't break his heart. She was safe for him to like and pine for.

That didn't change the fact that I was going to have to have a heart-to-heart with her. Beg her to let him down easy.

But maybe she could wait until his treatments were over.

Seeing him now under the streetlights as they turned on, walking with a little more pep in his step and a smile on his face, I could tell having a crush wasn't such a bad thing for him. Even if it was with an older friend of mine.

"So are we going to talk about your tuition money?" He glanced at me.

"No." His word *tuition* made me ache just imagining the burden he felt.

"We have to. I need to help. I could maybe try investing or making fake IDs for high school kids. I have some friends who—"

"Martin, get better. I don't care about the money. I'll figure it out. I swear. Please don't think about this," I pleaded, stopping our walk and giving him a loving smile. "I love you, and I want you to get better so Mom and Grandma stop babying you. You're never going to become a man at this rate."

"Whatever." He said it, but the shine in his eyes suggested he wasn't going to let up, on this or Hennie.

I slipped my arm in his and walked back to the house.

"How you liking that book, by the way?"

"*Swan Song*? Yeah, it's weird. I'm completely hooked, albeit slightly confused about where it's heading."

"Just keep going," he said with a laugh.

Hearing him laugh made my tired heart a little lighter.

The stress and the money and the worry about school all faded into the background; none of it was as important as my brother. I would trade everything, all my success and chances in life, for him to be happy and healthy. It was also why I would need to come up with my own solution for the finances. Just in case he needed it.

Chapter Thirteen

MAN TESTER

Lacey

In the steam of the spa the next afternoon, I contemplated telling my friends about Martin's crush and cancer and everything that was going on in my life.

But I decided against it. That was the role Hennie filled for me. Instead I did what I normally did. Listened.

"So, back to Theo." Jo sighed deeply, bringing up the same subject again. "When I mentioned the situation to my friend from Jersey, she said she saw him last month at a club, and he was grinding with some skank."

"Oh, that's it. You need to break things off," Marcia demanded.

"I want to be sure," Jo said defensively.

"Jo, you can't possibly still love him knowing something's going on behind your back," Carmen snapped.

"Yeah, Jo. That's nuts, even if you just suspect he's cheating," I agreed.

"You guys wouldn't understand," she said morosely.

"Try us," I challenged her.

"I love him. And if this is just some stupid flirting he's doing, like you know how it is before you get married, then it's not a big deal. If it's actual cheating, yeah, I would break things off. But I want to be sure. Just in case. What if he's the one? I want to marry for love. I don't want to look back and wonder if I broke things off too soon and ruined the best thing that ever happened to me."

We all sat there, frozen and scared of this insane confession. None of us knew how to react to the truth that was now out in the steam, possibly poisoning the rest of us with too much honesty. If we told her to break things off, we weren't being supportive. If we encouraged her to stay with him until she figured it out, then we supported a bad relationship. And all of us suspected or knew he cheated. But girls had a bad habit of blaming their friends and staying with the guy.

"It's going to be okay." I promised her lies, certain he was cheating. I was a firm believer in where there was smoke, there was fire. "Take the next couple of weeks and really watch and pay attention. You'll know."

"Hire a PI anonymously, and if the PI gets caught, Theo won't know it was you behind it," Carmen suggested. "My aunt did that to my uncle and caught him red-handed. He had a clause in the marriage contract that he wouldn't get a dime of her inheritance if he ever strayed. She got her divorce, and he never got a cent from the family trust, which is where the money came from."

"I can't. It would make my parents look bad; our families do business together. Spying on their son while they were doing deals would be suspicious." She sighed. "I wish we had that guy-tester app. Or even someone to send in a hot chick and see if he takes the bait."

I was struck by an epiphany.

Had we been outside, I would have searched around myself for the apple that fell from the tree and planted the seed of genius I was experiencing. It was a dirty sort of idea, but it could work.

The details flitted about my head, joining together to form a plan. A terrible, brilliant plan.

Tara Brown

But I needed help.

I needed advice.

There was only one person whom I could turn to for that.

We left the steam, splintering off in different directions. Marcia and I went for the mud wrap while Kami and Jo went to get facials. Carmen headed for the Thai massage.

As we were wrapped in the mud and plastic, I watched for the second Marcia drifted off. She always slept during this treatment. I didn't. I spent the entire forty minutes watching her breathe deeply and twitch every now and then. Usually I brought a book or played on my phone.

But this time, the moment she was out, I got up and walked like a mummy down the hall.

I dialed my brother and hid in an alcove.

"Lacey?" He answered like he was confused.

"Yeah," I whispered, and glanced around. "I need advice."

"Okay." His tone still seemed skeptical.

"What if I created a company that fidelity-tested guys, offering this as a service for a fee? Is that morally wrong?"

"Fidelity-testing service? Who would honestly pay someone—never mind. Forget I even asked that. We both know who would pay for something so stupid. Is this hypothetical?" He laughed hopefully.

"No," I whispered, and scanned the hall again. "What would I need?"

"Honestly? I don't know. I'd need a minute to think about it."

"You have a minute."

"Okay. Uhhhhh. A website that couldn't be hacked. A system of being paid that couldn't be traced. A couple of girls who could easily blend in and not be recognized if they wore simple disguises. A way of recording every interaction as proof. An email account that's linked to the website that could send the recordings of the guy being disloyal."

"Have you given something like this much thought before?" I asked quietly, a little worried.

"Yeah, this is totally what I spend all my free time thinking about," he said sarcastically. "It's simple logic, moron."

"Can you help me make this?" I closed my eyes for a second and really contemplated if this was a good idea.

"Probably. You would make your entire year of tuition and probably mine in the next two months of summer. I would totally be down for this." He was too eager. "I legit have nothing better to do. But I have one condition."

"What?"

"Hennie. You give me your blessing to ask her out. I will knock that website outta the park."

"Fine," I hissed, and closed my eyes and forced myself into a momentary chant of *do whatever makes him happy* before I continued with the regular worries. "Are we going to burn in hell for manipulating people like this?" Second-guessing was already starting.

"No. Dude. If girls are willing to pay you for this, that's their choice, and you should take the money. And it's the guy's choice whether or not he acts like a dick. Not your problem. This is like being a PI for love. That's what you should call it. PI for Love."

"I was thinking Fidelity Tester," I whispered, and checked the hall again.

"That sounds stupid."

"You're stupid." We automatically slipped back into our brother-sister banter.

"Love Tester," he offered, ignoring the name-calling game.

"Man Tester."

"Dear God. Don't you claim to work at a marketing firm?"

"Shut up. Test Dummy." I laughed, thinking how insanely stupid this idea might be and how dumb I sounded even contemplating it.

"Winner!" He smiled. I could hear it in his tone. "Test Dummy it is. I'll set up the email account now: thetestdummyNYC at gmail dot com. The address is available; no surprise there. I guess there isn't a lineup of other creeps putting money on the name."

"Okay." I inhaled sharply. "I'll go advertise it where all the girls look, kinda random and casual, like it's on the DL." I took a second deep breath. "Thanks."

"No, no. Thank you for the chance to contribute my talents on such a positive, healthy, world-benefitting project, with the side perk being you forced to accept my adoration of Hennie. First order of business, stop the players; next up, save the whales. I'll get started now."

"Okay, doofus. I'll see you later." I hung up and held my breath for a second, noting that the mud was staring to cool a little. I had to do this now or I wouldn't ever get the gall to.

I passed a lady who smiled, understanding what it was like to have to pee after they wrapped you. The humor in her grin told me that.

But I didn't have to pee. I had something much more Machiavellian than that on my mind.

At the doorway that led to the front entry where the lounge was, I paused, peeking around the corner to see if anyone else was there.

It was empty, so I mummy sprinted across the room to the side hallway where the Post-it note wall was located. I glanced around as I quickly wrote a note, wording it in a way that might entice my friends. I cleared a spot on the wall in the middle and placed my well-worded ad.

"Trouble in love? Trouble with trust? Or just desperate to catch that man of yours in a sticky situation and have him publicly humiliated? We can help. Email thetestdummyNYC at gmail dot com for more info or check out our Instagram, thetestdummies." I read it aloud and took a photo, then sent it to my brother, hoping that insta-handle would also be available.

My heart was racing as I returned to the room.

The walk back was less suspect. I was just a girl with a mummy wrap of mud coating her body and a garbage dress. Nothing out of the ordinary about that.

But on the inside, I was a storm of second-guessing and regret.

The idea was flawless, really. I could get a camera, something tiny and discreet, and do what Hennie and Martin both suggested: wear a hot disguise, hit on the guy I was being paid to track, and post the evidence to the girl who hired me. The camera wouldn't ever point at me. I would remain anonymous.

If there was one thing the upper echelons of society hated, it was scandal. I would be paid to be discreet, and the revelations wouldn't make front-page news.

As I nestled back into my chair and watched Marcia sleep, I got more and more comfortable with my decision. I grabbed my phone and texted Martin to make sure he got the spelling correct.

The Test Dummy was brilliant. It was even a genius name. Why couldn't the bug bars be just as easy a sell?

While I was providing a service that would earn me the money I needed, I was also vigilante-style saving my friends from shitty guys their parents forced on them. At least, that was how I was choosing to justify this to myself.

Guys like Theo were crappy boyfriends because they could be, and they deserved to get caught and outed. Not just because they were doing terrible things to girls they were supposedly in love with, but also because they were bringing down the names of guys like Monty, who would never stray. Everyone sort of assumed rich guys were dirtbags, and that wasn't the case 100 percent of the time. Monty was amazing and loyal and sweet.

The ones like France and Theo deserved everything they got, and I was happy to serve them their just desserts.

For a price.

Not that the price tag would be anything to these girls. I could charge a thousand dollars a guy easily, and they wouldn't even bat an eyelash. Marcia spent more every week on different face creams and perfumes.

She bought thousand-dollar sunglasses last week, for Christ's sake.

If she knew I was stuck for school tuition, she would have paid it without asking a single question, which was precisely the reason I never told her.

I wouldn't ever ask her or anyone else for money, but I wouldn't mind earning it fair and square.

The anonymity of it all kept the transaction honest and me protected.

A small part of me, likely the common-sense side, whispered warnings of this being the worst idea I'd ever come up with. And that if I ever got caught, my link to this world would be severed. Even Marcia might not defend me and my actions. As an outsider, I wasn't allowed to take certain liberties or cause major ripples, and reporting on the sins of the rich was number one.

But the cons of the case were weak compared to the pros.

And by the time Marcia was awake, I was set in my resolve to go through with it.

Nothing was going to bring me down from this high, not even the stupid party I had to go to with Marcia tonight, even though it was a friggin' Wednesday. Who had parties on Wednesdays?

The rich.

They could afford to take work off the next day. And those of us who needed to be in their good graces couldn't afford not to show face.

Chapter Fourteen

CINDERELLA'S FIFTY BUCKS

Jordan

The party was packed, considering it was a Wednesday. I didn't understand how anyone thought this was a good idea, partying midweek. But it was summer vacation now, which meant days of the week were just a suggestion. Nothing was off the table as far as partying and socializing was concerned. If the party was good enough, Dad, Grandpa, and Stephen would work from home the next day. I would be the only one going in. And it wouldn't be the first summer where that happened every week.

Scanning the room, I sighed, thinking more about my book at home and less about the group of people I was with.

Dad was with Mr. Weitzman, parading his prize around the room. He peacocked like no other. Since the Amy thing started, I realized how hard everyone had been vying for the Weitzman fortune. And, yet again, our family was winning.

And everyone in the room knew why. Eyes landed on me, likely wondering if I was in on this, then likely assuming I was. And wasn't I?

Amy was with her friends, laughing and animated in a way she hadn't been with me. But the conversation was one I wouldn't have kept up with. She was talking about that band again, the one she was obsessed with.

"Holy shit, look at the talent over there." Stephen nudged me. "That chick is so hot."

I followed his gaze to someone we both knew too well. She was a year younger than me and a lot younger than Stephen, not to mention a complete flake. "Marcia La Croix?" She dated one of my friends, Monty, so I tried not to see her in that light. She was a knockout, but only if you didn't talk to her. I didn't know how Monty did it. The guy was either really turned on by a lack of awareness, or he was so in love he didn't notice.

"No, not spoiled little Marcia." He nodded at the girl on her left. "The girl next to her. Look at that ass."

I parted my lips to say something about him being a pervert and married, but paused because Stephen was right. The girl looked good from behind. Long dark hair to her waist that looked silky and smooth, like I could run my hands through it. Her tight dress hugged her form beautifully. Long legs, a slim waist, a perky ass. Not too tall so her high heels didn't make her an Amazon.

She turned around, glancing at something and then smiling wide. My insides tightened, and butterflies went crazy in my stomach. "Holy shit." It was her, the girl from the boat. That smile.

"Oh, wait, that's the friend of Marcia's and Monty's whose name I can never remember. What's her name? I don't think I ever realized she was this hot. Which seems impossible, right? Like, how did I miss that?" Stephen whistled softly. "Or maybe I've just been too drunk every time I see her to notice."

"Lacey." I smiled.

"Right." His eyes were glued to her, likely to that ass, as he mumbled like a pervert, "So hot."

But she was more than an ass. She was funny and sort of rude in a disinterested and yet engaged way. She was the girl who left as I was about to have my way with her. I could feel her in my hands still if I thought hard enough. Fortunately my brother kept nudging me and saying dirty words, so I didn't get too into the memories.

That dark silky hair and those bright eyes, full of humor and maybe bliss. Maybe that was what freedom and euphoria looked like. Her smile was wide, and her body, dear God. That skin-tight dress was giving me heartburn. She looked hotter tonight, less makeup and more natural beauty.

I almost took a knee seeing her again, but this wasn't the place to act on that. Not in front of my family.

"Man, if I weren't married to the second-hottest girl in the world, I'd already be peeling that dress off." Stephen glanced over at his wife, who was glaring at us both and smiling tightly. She didn't hear the conversation, but she knew her husband well enough to guess what was happening and wasn't pleased. I didn't know how Cynthia did it. She was like Monty, some kind of saint.

"You need to go grovel. Now." I nudged him back. "Before she realizes she's about to lose her status as the second-hottest woman in the world." To Stephen, the hottest woman in the world was Wonder Woman. Wonder Woman in all forms, but mostly the cartoon one. I suspected he whacked off more to cartoons than he cared to own up to, but there were things I didn't want to know about my brother, so I didn't ask.

"Yup." He slapped me on the arm. "On it." He left me alone and sauntered to his wife, kissed her cheek, and whispered something.

She smiled wide and hit him in the stomach. He feigned that it hurt, and they nuzzled into each other's cheeks.

It was weird watching my brother, of all people, be in love. I'd wanted that for him, but I never expected he would find it. And not with someone like Cynthia. She was a score. She saved her drama for

113

later, like a lady, like Stephen was supposed to. She smiled at the right people and tolerated the ones she wanted to kill, like our father. She was exactly the right kind of someone a family like ours needed, except she wasn't one of us. She was from a middle-income family and worked hard for everything she had. She was better than us. I always imagined Stephen liked that she wasn't from this world and hadn't dated half of it, the way he had.

I realized, seeing them together, that I wanted it too.

First I had to get rid of the burden I was saddled with, though.

The burden currently laughing her face off, looking lit up and happy. She and her five closest friends were discussing stalking the band across Europe all summer.

A bit defeated by the whole situation, I turned back to the bar and sipped my scotch, ignoring thoughts of Amy and Lacey and my brother.

"Can I get a water?" a woman shouted, accidentally bumping into me, spilling my scotch on my fingers. "Oh my God. I am so sorry."

I turned my gaze, hoping the unimpressed glare was adequately spread across my face. But there she was, the girl Stephen and I had just determined was the most beautiful creature in the world, standing next to me. The one I'd kissed on the boat and dragged to the bathroom. The one with blushing cheeks and a cringing face. I lightened instantly. "It's you." Clearly the fates intended for us to talk. Or had she spilled my drink on purpose?

"Sorry about the drink." The joy on her face disappeared.

"It's fine." I glanced behind me, ensuring no one saw us talking.

"No, it's not. I spilled your drink, and you guys always go for that scotch that costs a kidney per glass." She slapped her tight stomach. "I have a spare kidney. And actually my grandma on my mom's side has three kidneys, so you never know. I might have enough for two glasses."

I laughed, even though I was trying to act cool and not flirt or be too excited that we were talking again and she was funny. God, she was funny. "It's honestly fine. Why don't I buy you a drink so you don't have to give up your kidneys?" I leaned in. "And to be honest, this scotch has some serious markup on it. I've had better for less. I'd hate to see a kidney wasted on it."

"Oh, yeah?" She widened her eyes, making me tense everywhere as her lips curled up into that beautiful smile. "You'd think in a place like this, they'd give you rich folk a discount. I mean, your glitzing up the place attracts the commoners like me."

"Us rich folk? Right, the lower levels. How is it down there? I hear it's fairly relaxed. No expectations or demands." I cocked an eyebrow. Her comments on the boat about being on the lower decks made sense. She really wasn't rich. Monty had spoken of her before, only I hadn't paid attention.

"No demands? Not me," she said, clearly with a chip on her shoulder. "I have loads of expectations and demands. Unlike you rich punks, I put them on myself. Which means I get to be what I want. I get to date who I want." She jabbed right for the weak spot, like she knew what it was like being me. She leaned in closer. "And honestly, we have spines on the lower levels. Sure, we're the odd ones out at the ball, but it's worth it."

"So you're a Cinderella? The working-class beauty at the ball, and on the boat?" I accidentally let a little charm slip out and recovered with a disappointed question. "You know who I am, don't you?" Being friends with Monty meant she had to.

"Of course." She blushed and glanced down, sweeping her long black lashes as modesty and embarrassment over my compliment smothered her. "But you should know, beauty is in the eye of the beholder. And your eyes might be polluted by the drink." She recovered fast, no doubt accustomed to being hit on and for some reason not wanting to discuss the boat or the fact that we had very close friends in common.

"Then maybe I should be drinking this piss-poor scotch all the time." I swallowed hard, forgetting myself.

Tara Brown

She narrowed her gaze on me, and not in a positive way. Her gaze darted back to Amy and her friends. "Or maybe you should slow down on the drinking so you don't confuse Cinderella for your princess." She slapped down a fifty-dollar bill. "For the scotch, and if there's any change, buy your girlfriend a drink too." She turned with her water bottle and left me there, my mouth agape and stomach aching.

Stephen came over a moment later. "Tell me that hateful look she gave you at the end there wasn't you blowing it?"

"Oh, I didn't blow it." I laughed and drank the last of what was in my glass, pocketing her fifty-dollar bill and letting the bartender fill me up on the account I always had open here. "But she did." I glanced back at Amy. "Cinderella knew I had a new girlfriend and rubbed it in my face." I couldn't stop myself; I turned and searched the party for Lacey again.

When I found her, she wasn't smiling like before. She seemed less jovial, like I'd ruined some aspect of her night by hitting on her or by merely existing.

"Your pretend girlfriend is cock blocking what might be the greatest experience of your life. It's weird her name's Cinderella, though," Stephen muttered, making me laugh.

I'd already told him her name was Lacey. God, he was bad with remembering people he wasn't in business with.

"Yeah, I need to hurry up and end this. I'm dying here." I stared at Cinderella, feeling a sudden gravity in the situation. Her eyes and the way they lit up, even in rage. Her mouth and how soft it had been against my lips. Her body in that dress or in my arms in the bathroom, pressed against me. The conversation we'd had on the boat deck.

All of it was going to haunt me.

"We still on for massages tomorrow?" Stephen changed the subject but still stared at the girl. We both did. "The spa?" he prodded.

"Yeah. I could use a massage."

116

"You look like you could use a happy ending. If you want, we could go to this place—"

"You're married," I reminded him.

"Shit, right. Jesus. I can't believe I almost said that. I need to slow down on the drinks." He put his drink down and fingered his wedding band. "I still have a business card if you're interested. Best service in town."

"No." I gave him what I hoped was a disturbed glare. "Bro, I don't pay for sex."

"It's a handy, not sex, and you'd really rather suffer through it with the starfish over there?" He laughed, and I couldn't fight it. I laughed too.

Stephen and I both knew what sex with Amy would be like.

And now here I was, at a party staring at the first girl I'd been truly attracted to in ages, enough to blatantly flirt with her, but the starfish was cock blocking me.

I grabbed my drink and sipped it, stuck staring at Cinderella and wondering how to free myself fast enough to ask her out.

I could break things off with Amy right here and now, but that would be misery to deal with. Dad wasn't exaggerating when he threatened my inheritance. And risking that might be stupid. It made more sense to wait until I finished my education.

Cinderella waved goodbye to her friends and headed for the main door, struggling with the crowds. I abandoned the drink and chased after her.

"Fuck 'em," I muttered.

I had the fifty dollars I wanted to give back to her. It was a reason to talk. Maybe I could walk her home. Maybe I could explain my situation. Maybe she knew my situation and that was what disgusted her. It disgusted me.

It was a lot of maybes, and by the time I reached the door, she was already gone. I was holding the money like a glass slipper, staring out at the city street bustling with people and cars and cabs and possibilities. She could have gone any of the directions facing me, and I would guess wrong. I didn't have instincts for things like this.

I pocketed the money and decided I needed to have a conversation with Marcia La Croix. Something I didn't relish.

But it had to be done. I could ask Monty, but Marcia knew her better.

All I knew was I had to learn more about the girl with the extra kidney.

"You ready to go?" Amy asked, breaking my stare on Marcia. She must have followed me out.

"Yeah." I nodded, offering her my arm. "You know, Amy, you should consider retiring this shade of red. It doesn't suit you. Makes your skin look kind of orange." I took a random jab, hating myself instantly.

"What?" She pulled away from me as we walked down to the car and the valet pulled up. He'd fetched my car just from seeing my face. Her eyes flashed rage, but her words didn't match them. "You think so?" She swallowed her pride, and I knew in that moment we were at a stalemate. She was either desperately wanting to be my girlfriend, to the point she would take any abuse, or she had been ordered to date me. She had been similarly forced into this situation. If that was the case, this was never going to end, because neither of us wanted to ruin our parents' business dealings or our own standing with our families.

It meant I needed a new plan. I needed a faster plan. Something that would end it, with no chance of our parents thinking it could be saved. Which meant my dad would hate me forever, but if I was smart enough, my plan might salvage Grandpa's feelings for me.

No matter what, being cruel to Amy was never going to work, since she was playing the same game. And I wasn't a cruel person. Not intentionally. That said, I was willing to get really familiar with that side of myself, all for a girl who was showing me the meaning of cruel herself.

Chapter Fifteen

THE TEST DUMMY

Lacey

"I did it." As I got on the train the next day, I found Hennie and shoved my phone in her face to show her the website Martin and I had created the night before, once I got home from the rich-people gathering. He'd hidden the IP address so it was untraceable.

"Oh my God, you didn't," she gasped, snatching my phone. "This is insane."

"No, it's genius. Honestly, it's necessary. Just last night I was at a party, with that weird girl, Amy Weitzman; her boyfriend hit on me when she was five feet from us. Maybe ten. He legit called me beautiful and offered to buy me a drink." I rolled my eyes. "Douchebags." I didn't mention the fact that we'd nearly torn each other's clothes off on the harbor booze cruise. I needed to forget that had ever happened. It was hard, as was turning him down last night. He was gorgeous. Except for the baggage.

"Amy Weitzman?" Hennie's eyes widened. "She's, like, dating the drummer of Coldplay or one of those bands. He hit on you? Damn!"

"What?" I scowled. "Drummer? No, he's from here, from a wealthy family. Typical douchey rich guy. He's BFFs with Monty. His name is

Jordan—" I wrinkled my nose and snapped my fingers, forgetting his last name when I'd only said it not even a week ago. "Oh my God, it's gonna drive me nuts," I groaned. "He's got the same name as that really good cider, and he and his older brother are total man whores who always hit on everyone. I've never really met Jordan, but I always avoid the brother like the plague."

"Angry Orchard?" Hennie said.

"What?" I laughed.

"That's a cider I had once. It was good."

"Stephen and Jordan—Somersby!" I shouted, way too loud for the train. I lowered my voice. "Jordan Somersby."

"Oh, yeah. He *is* really rich. His family is one of those scary ones everyone sucks up to. They're related to, like, the Roth-what-do-you-call-its or those blue bloods, right? And his brother is a super-douche. But Jordan's not Amy's boyfriend, and he isn't a douche either."

"What?" I was lost.

"Yeah, she posts about that drummer all the time."

"But Jordan—"

"I know," Hennie gushed. "He's so hot. So hot. Those eyes and that dimple in his right cheek and the way his hair is always so perfectly styled like he has a salon in his back pocket. And his shoulders and hands. Have you ever watched him play football? He should have gone pro." She closed her eyes and moaned. "Ugh."

"How do you know him?" I chuckled and pulled my phone back. He was hot; Lord have mercy, he was hot. And he was so interesting to talk to on the boat. But he was a rich trust-fund kid, an instant disqualifier.

"Same major. He's the crush of every girl in all my classes and completely gorgeous. I've had sex fantasies about him. He hit on you?" Her cheeks flushed, but she didn't stop. "Did you flirt back? He smells so good, huh?"

"What are you talking about? He's gross. He hits on everyone; he's a Somersby."

"Stop!" she shouted. "How else can I spell it out? Not at all like his brother, and not dating anyone? Let him hit on you. I want details."

"You sure?" I scowled as dread hit me. Hard. *Oh my God.* I'd been rude to him. "How sure are you?"

"Maybe, like, ninety percent sure. Either way, I went out with some girls from class three weeks ago, and one of them is superrich and gets into every club with no issue." It was her turn to roll her eyes. "And she said Amy and the little drummer boy have had a thing for, like, a year."

"Well, now I feel terrible." I squirmed in my seat. "I was a complete dick to him for no reason."

"You were a dick to Jordan Somersby? He's, like, the nicest guy and completely normal. With all the rich douchebags out there, you pick the nice, intelligent one to pick on?" She laughed. "He writes books, like epic fantasy, for a hobby. He's a complete sci-fi and fantasy nerd. A finances geek. He's never been inappropriate with a single girl from my course. I know this because they've all tried. He's not like that. I don't think he's dated anyone in years. He was my TA all year. Totally single."

"Oh, shit." I sent a text to Marcia, double-checking. It was only seven thirty in the morning, so she wouldn't see the text for hours, but when she did, I prayed she would confirm that he was seeing Amy so I could justify my rudeness. But then again, would I want to wish that on him? She was one vapid, strange girl.

Or was their relationship like what Carmen had been saying? One of those where they didn't have a say in it. Prearranged for them. Those connections were less common now, at least, but some families still found strength in opportunistic alignments.

Feeling sick, I admitted to myself that the moment we'd gone into the bathroom on the yacht, I'd been contemplating, even if just for one drunken second, having savage sex with him. I still got hot with visions of how it was supposed to have gone. Being single for two years meant my sex life was a bit lacking. It had been a while since I'd felt the kind of heat I did when Jordan had dragged me away.

My phone screen lit up, shocking me that Marcia was awake. As I lifted it, my entire body went on pins and needles.

It wasn't Marcia. And it wasn't a text.

It was an email.

"Oh, God," I whispered, drawing Hennie's eyes to me.

"What?"

"It's the Test Dummy." I showed her.

"Oh my God, hurry up! Open it. This is such a bad idea." She gripped my arm, leaning on me.

I opened it, cringing when I saw the name. It wasn't Jo emailing me, as I'd expected. It was Kami. She wanted to check on her boyfriend, Miguel, the DJ. I almost tapped out and sent her a message declining the job. He was a celebrity of sorts. He had collaborations with huge stars. But she was my friend, and clearly more clued in than she let on. And I remembered how it felt to be cheated on. I knew that pain, and I would have wanted to know for sure long before I ever did. I had to do the job.

"Oh, God, DJ Spark, that supercute guy whose dad runs the securities company and is talking about becoming a senator, and he performs with all those celebs? Yikes." Hennie winced. "Good luck with that one."

"Right."

"Doesn't he know you really well?"

"No. I'm good friends with Kami, but he doesn't really give any of us the time of day. He's a couple of years older and went to a different school. And honestly, he's so stoned all the time that if I wear a wig and some makeup, he won't know it's me. He thinks he's better than everyone else."

"A wig." Hennie gulped. "So you're really going to do this?"

"How can I not? Kami's one of my best friends, and I have heard the rumors that she's being cheated on, and now she's caught an inkling that something's up. I'll confirm that for her, send her proof, and she'll dump him."

"Why doesn't she just dump him now if she suspects?"

"She really likes him. It's the saddest shit I've ever seen. Of all our friends in our little circle of girls, she and Jo are the only ones dating guys the rest of us dislike. But it's like they're powerless to walk away."

"They live in a messed-up world. Who else but the rich breaks up this way?" She laughed. "When I got dumped, my ex texted me, short and shitty. And then, he had his friend bring a box of my stuff to my house. The friend left it in the rain and ruined most of it."

"Harsh."

"Way harsh, but it's the way it's supposed to be. You're supposed to leave hating that person and ruining their stuff. He hated me. And once he ruined my things, I felt the same. And it helped me get over it."

"Right, but maybe the feelings were real. A large percentage of relationships in our generation are between people who don't know themselves. They're not in love. And if they are, it's superficial. They don't know how to love yet. You're an old soul."

"What's Marcia like?"

"She's like you. In her approach to love, at least." I smiled. "But she's had a good example. Her parents love each other, even in their weird way, and she and Monty are goals. He's a great guy—a die-hard nerd at heart and completely smitten with her and loyal to the death. Honestly, of all my close friends, only Jo and Kami are in unhealthy situations. Carmen is seeing a guy she won't tell her parents about. He's at school on scholarship, but he's completely cool."

"And you're the only single one?"

"Yeah." I winced. "Something that's starting to rub them all the wrong way. No one wants to bring a single girl to the couple's party. And no one wants to be the single girl at the couple's party. It's painful. I'm starting to notice I get left out a bit."

"At least you're not still dating that asshat, France," Hennie said, sneering. She was there for me a lot the summer that we broke up.

"Yeah, and he's a prime example of how the Test Dummy can work. I mean, that's how I ended up breaking things off. He got crazy drunk and hooked up with some chick. My friends were at the party, saw, took photos, and showed me. I broke up with him the next day, but it took having definitive proof to do so. He stalked me for like a month. Remember the Halloween party bullshit?"

"And this is why you're so jaded and bitter," Hennie said, laughing. "Makes sense."

"I'm not bitter. I'm educated."

"Okay." She got up and nodded, mocking me. "Let's go, crazy." She got off the train, and I followed with my phone burning a hole in my hot little hand.

It was a defining moment.

Did I email back and take the job, possibly creating chaos but also a means to pay for my final year, cashing in on the misdeeds of the guilty? Or did I walk way, head held high and moral compass intact?

The moment I got to my office and saw the picture of my dopey brother and me on my desk, I knew the answer.

What if Martin ended up needing more surgery or treatment?

What if anything went wrong?

My parents' nest egg that they used for our educations would be gone by the time school started.

No, I didn't have the luxury to second-guess this decision.

I was all-the-way committed in this one. My family was all the motivation I needed.

I sent Kami an email back, detailing what the Test Dummy required. A rough estimate of the DJ's schedule for the next two weeks. A picture of him and his full, real name. Once I had proof, I would load it onto the website where only she could view it and decide if she wanted to make it go live and possibly viral, and she would be the one to click the link and upload it to the website's main page. If the guy didn't take the bait and didn't hit on me, the fee was halved. I wouldn't collect the second payment in that case.

It was as discreet as discreet could be. A girl could take her video proof, keep it to herself, and break things off with her boyfriend quietly. But for exposure and free marketing, the website would bring more business in if spurned young women decided to post the videos publicly.

I bit my lip and sent the email, terrified of everything for half a second before my door burst open and Mr. La Croix smiled at me.

"You going to be ready to present something to us about these bug bars by Monday?"

"Sure am," I lied. Guess I knew what I would be doing this weekend unless I spent the next thirty-six hours killing it and getting inspired. Which meant no hanging with friends or pleasure reading—my absolute favorite activity.

"Excellent." He gave me a thumbs-up and left the office, leaving the door open.

I put my phone away and my head down, focusing on cricket flour and how bugs in cuisine were a culinary delicacy in other cultures. Like that of tree-hugging, hippie yoga moms.

Hours and multiple skin shivers and dry-heaving moments later, I came up with something. It wasn't great, but it would do. I would have to iron out the details still, but the concept was pretty good. Not as good as the Test Dummy, of course. If only I could bring that to the big table; it would knock people's socks off.

At the end of the day, Hennie came in, giving me a dubious look. "Hey." She slipped in and closed the door. "So, did you do it?"

"Yeah. I did. I sent her an email with the details. Price quote, a request for Miguel's personal details and whereabouts. And Martin found some awesome spy-camera pin online. Records up to six hours. It's being delivered to my house right now."

"How are you going to receive payment from your customers?" she puzzled.

Tara Brown

"I was thinking email money transfer to a secret account. Maybe offshore. Martin was looking into setting something up."

"No." She shook her head. "Those always get traced. Gift cards are the way to go."

"Gift cards? What?" I scoffed.

"Rechargeable Visa and Mastercard gift cards. They totally work, they're untraceable, and you can pay your tuition with them."

"You're a genius."

"Tell them to send four two-hundred-and-fifty-dollar Visa gift cards. You won't have to pay taxes on the money you make. Two up-front and two after delivery of the video."

"Dude." I stood up, bringing my phone and my purse. "You're so smart."

"Being corrupt isn't just about being smart. It's shrewd; I won't deny that. You ready to go home?"

"Yeah." I checked my phone and saw missed calls and texts from Marcia. "Maybe. Give me one sec." I quickly called Marcia as we walked to the elevator.

She greeted me with craziness. "Oh my God, I thought you died. Where have you been all day?"

"Working. I know you don't understand that concept, but it's something us common folk do." I laughed. "Why, what happened?"

"Okay, so I wake up to an out-of-the-blue text from you asking me about Jordan friggin' Somersby. Then I get a phone call from him this afternoon asking who you are in the grand scheme of life. What the hell did I miss?"

"Nothing. Just me being me, insulting him for being flirty while his girlfriend was right there. But Hennie says he isn't dating anyone. I just wondered if that was true. Because if he isn't, I was a complete dick to him and might have a reason to apologize."

"Well." She took a deep breath. "Not exactly. From what I hear from Monty, everyone went nuts about three weeks ago. Mr. Weitzman

126

pulled his accounts, totaling around a billion, from an investment company. Everyone has been trying to woo him, and apparently the Somersbys are using Jordan to win the family over. By way of Amy. So it's not like real dating. I mean honestly, Amy is a complete tool. Like, have you ever had a conversation with her? She doesn't even lift her face up from her phone. I watched her walk into a glass door once—didn't even stop texting, just started feeling blindly with her hands for the handle to open it. But I wouldn't say they're actually together—just trying to make their dads happy. All an act, I suppose. Like those old-school marriages."

"Jesus." I cringed. "So I was a dick to him then, wasn't I?" That didn't make me feel good.

"Well, kinda. But honestly, Monty and Stephen both think he needs to be a man and break things off with her and tell his dad no. It's pathetic. The old days of merger marriages and all that nonsense are done. Getting disinherited isn't as bad as being with someone you don't even like."

"His dad threatened to disinherit him?" Who were these people?

"His dad thinks he's the most powerful man in the world because his family is."

"Gross. So Jordan called and asked who I was?" That made me feel all kinds of funny. Especially since he was dating a girl to make money for his family. He was worse than France.

"Yeah, the weirdo called you Cinderella."

"Cinderella." I laughed, realizing I was blushing and hating it. "I see. Well, that's random."

"Not so much; you kinda are when you think about it. You're hot and poor and always at a party filled with royalty. All you need to do is lose a shoe and you're her. I tell you this all the time: you're a knockout. And his family is known for being able to spot prime real estate."

"Oh my God, stop. You know my feelings on boys with trust funds. You have the only worthy one."

"That's pretty true." She changed the subject. "What are you doing now?"

"Going home to work all night. What about you?"

"Not much. Why don't we hang out? We could do dinner." She sounded bored. She needed a job.

"I'm finishing a project for your dad, getting a big presentation ready. So I can't. But if I work hard enough tonight and tomorrow, I can probably hang tomorrow night."

"Okay." She didn't sound as excited about tomorrow.

"We can go dancing," I offered weakly, getting a warning look from Hennie. "It'll be fun."

"Okay." She perked up. "Come here after work, and I'll get a little soiree going as sort of a preclub gathering. Yay!" She went from zero to sixty, and I started massaging the spot I assumed my liver was located. Her version of a soiree was going to be intense. Too intense for me.

"I'll text you later."

"Bye!" she said in her singsong way, and hung up.

"Oh my God. I have to party again tomorrow." I sighed and stepped onto the elevator.

"No one feels sorry for you. Jordan Somersby hit on you," Hennie retorted.

"Oh my God, stop. Marcia just explained it, and he's not doing much better in my books, so let's just drop it. You coming for dinner again? Grandma made chicken potpies. I think she already made you one." It was dangerous bringing Hennie home, risking Martin flirting with her. But we all liked having her there, and I had given my consent.

"Hell yes." Hennie didn't lighten up from her worrying mood, though. But I knew once we got home and my sick brother was being all attentive and flirty, she'd be plucky again and Martin would have that silly grin on his face. If I had to sacrifice my own comfort and happiness to put it there, so be it. I was getting used to making all kinds of sacrifices for his sake lately.

Chapter Sixteen

TROUBLE IN LOVE?

Jordan

"I just got invited to Marcia's house tomorrow night." I gave my brother a look as I entered the kitchen and grabbed a homemade cookie from the cooling rack. "Marcia La Croix."

"Marcia La Croix called you?" Stephen asked over his huge bowl of cereal. It was half the box in one of Lucia's serving bowls for pasta. "Why didn't Monty call you? Befriending a guy's girl is weird and creepy. That's a dangerous mistake, trust me."

"Yeah, it's not like that. But I might have made a huge mistake regardless." I bit my lip and contemplated not telling him what I'd done. "This afternoon I called to ask about that friend of hers."

"The smoking-hot one from last night?"

"Yeah. Lacey."

"You said her name was Cinderella."

"No." I needed him to focus on how this was a bad idea, not her name.

But he didn't agree. "Awesome." He held his knuckles out for me to pound.

"You don't think it's a terrible idea to hunt her down while I'm still dealing with the Amy thing?" I tapped our knuckles, not feeling the spirit of it all. Not yet. If I were rid of Amy, I'd be doing cartwheels. Poorly.

"No, I think you need to bang that chick and then give me all the details. If you weren't my brother, I'd ask you to film the whole thing. I might still." He laughed at his own disgusting comment.

"Porn not doing it for you anymore?"

"Porn-free for a year, man. Cynthia doesn't approve."

"She has revoked your porn access." I snickered and stole his spoon, taking a huge bite of his cereal. "Not that I blame her," I said with a mouthful. "Poor Jane wouldn't even do your laundry when we were teenagers." Our maid hated Stephen. She still did, in fact.

"Jane hated me, but that had nothing to do with me whacking off in socks. She had a personal vendetta against men. Especially handsome, charming ones."

"The socks didn't help your shitty personality." I ate some more of his cereal. "And learning to do laundry was good for you." I chewed fast before I choked laughing.

"Laugh it up, chuckles. I got smart about the whole thing and started leaving the socks in your room. So you washed them, not me." He took back his cereal and his spoon, grinning wide.

"Asshole!" I backed off, shaking my head in disgust. "You're not even human, admit it. Soulless asshole."

He laughed harder, chewing and nearly choking. "I've been waiting on that one for a while."

"You're disgusting." I shuddered.

"Anyway." He coughed and cleared his throat. "We gotta go. Our massages are in, like, half an hour. On the ride over, you can tell me what you plan to do about the Amy problem."

"I don't want to talk about the Amy problem." I grabbed my wallet and phone and stalked to the door. "I'm sick of it, and it hasn't even been a week yet."

Apparently he wasn't, though.

The moment we got into the car he asked, "But what's your plan?"

"Well, last night changed a few things for me." I gave him a look. "I believed Dad when he said Amy had a crush on me, but now I'm starting to suspect her parents have given her the same bullshit spiel that she has to date me. And last night I followed Grandpa Jack's advice." I chuckled with embarrassment but continued. "I told her that the dress she was wearing looked bad on her and she needed to choose a different color."

"No!" He slapped me on the arm. "I didn't think you had it in you. Feels good, right? Sticking it to her?"

"No. It didn't. It felt terrible. It was hurtful and rude and a lie; she looked fine."

"Did she slap you?"

"That's the point I'm making. She sucked it up. Rage in the eyes, totally wanted to kick me in the balls, but didn't. She fucking took it on the chin."

"Oh, damn. Her dad has given her the speech, and our dad has given you the same. And now you're both just playing along to appease the bank accounts."

"Right."

"So you can treat this girl as badly as you want, and her family threats will make her stay with you?" His eyes sparkled with mischief.

"Yeah, but that's not my type of sport." I didn't say anything about the plans I'd been contemplating. Publicly humiliating myself so her family would refuse our relationship or something along those lines. I was going to throw myself to the wolves and risk being cut off. But I didn't want Grandpa to disown me. I loved my grandpa. But I couldn't go along with this. At this point I was even thinking about faking my own death.

"I love this, Jordie. I'm not gonna lie. Your life is amazingly entertaining. When you decided to major in finances and toe the company line instead of doing something that actually suited you, like writing or cartoon work or newspapers, I thought for sure we would never have another interesting moment from you. But here we are. Dad's pimping you out, and Grandpa's teaching you how to get dumped by a girl who will never dump you." He hadn't laughed this much around me in a long time. "This is amazing. It's going to be so boring when summer's over and you go back to Boston. I don't know how I'll get along." He cackled like a fucking witch or evil queen.

I wasn't laughing.

At all.

As the car pulled up to the spa, I climbed out, ready for a massage and the Roman steam baths. I hadn't been here in six months, and now that classes were over for the summer, I was ready to relax.

"Oh, buddy. It's going to be a rough summer." Stephen wrapped an arm around my shoulders and beamed. He was enjoying my hell a little too much.

Inside he started charming the girl at the front desk while I roamed and checked out the foyer. Bright colors caught my eye as I came to the side hallway, seeing Post-it notes covering a wall. It was just like the ones they had at school and in the subway. People were invited to tack up random posts, mostly cheesy inspirational crap they stole from googling cheesy inspirational crap.

But one caught my eye as I scanned.

Trouble in love? Trouble with trust? Or just desperate to catch that man of yours in a sticky situation and have him publicly humiliated? We can help. Email thetestdummyNYC@gmail. com for more info or check out our Instagram, thetestdummies.

I pulled my phone out and snapped a quick photo, wondering what kind of world we lived in and yet also spotting an amazing opportunity.

Maybe, if this worked, I wouldn't have to fake my own death after all. And if I handled it right, even Grandpa might give me a pat on the back for unlocking the fourth dimension in how to get dumped. I made a silent promise to myself to someday use my creative genius for the benefit of mankind.

Chapter Seventeen

Marcello

Lacey

Kami's email came back with everything I needed to trap her moron of a boyfriend.

I checked over his schedule, choosing his DJ guest appearance at a club called Bossa Nova Civic Club on Myrtle Avenue. He would be there tomorrow, Saturday night, and it was only about half an hour from my place. I could go and be home in time to watch an episode of something on Netflix.

I just had to work up the nerve to go alone and boldly hit on a guy while suggesting we go somewhere quiet, so he could take the bait. The moment he said, "Yeah, let's get a hotel or go back to my place," it'd be done. That was what I'd told myself anyway.

"Hey, kiddo. You going to Marcia's party tonight?" Mr. La Croix popped his head in my office.

"Yeah, I'm just finishing this up." I pointed to the bug bar presentation on my computer screen.

"How's that going?"

"Great." For the first time, I wasn't lying. I'd discovered something vital to the sales pitch, something that would win over celebrity endorsements. It wouldn't convince the likes of Marcia, but people like Monty would be all over it. If I was being honest, it had even won me over on the benefits of the protein. Not that I'd ever eat that shit again.

"So you'll be ready for Monday?"

"Totally." I wrinkled my nose by accident, making him laugh.

"Good to see you're still feeling the burn." He laughed harder.

"I'm not gonna lie; I have no desire to eat this, but the benefits are surprisingly enticing."

"I know." He beamed. "I've been eating a bar a day, and I'm loving it. I feel amazing and I think the anti-aging benefits are starting to kick in."

"Gross." I laughed too.

"Only gross if you think about it while you eat. Or if some jerk tells you it's bugs while you're midchew." He winked. "See you later at the house, then." He waved and walked away, greeting some other guy in the hall.

Hennie came scurrying into the office after he left. "Did you get it figured out?" She closed the door. She was far more stressed about the whole thing than I was. Which was a lot.

"Yeah. He's DJing at a club in Brooklyn."

"Near your place?"

"No, but it's a good place to go. Busy and lots of flashing lights, and once he's done his set, he'll be drinking. I'll slip in then, get him a drink, and try to get the footage of him asking me back to a hotel."

"I don't know how you're coping with this. I'm a ball of nerves, and you haven't even gone in yet." She rubbed her hands on her pants like they were sweating.

"I'm a ball of nerves, too, but at the same time I kinda wanna catch him so Kami will be free."

Tara Brown

"You're like a superhero. You need a Test Dummy costume." She was way too excited about this.

"Right, I'll have one made." I moaned. "A wig, which I hate, loads of makeup, which I don't love, and super-showy clothes, which I hate the most. With uncomfy shoes and half my ass hanging out."

"I can't imagine you dressed like that."

"That's the whole point."

"I guess so, huh. Are you still going to Marcia's tonight?" She leaned on the desk.

"I am. I don't want to, but I have to put in friend time or she gets needy. I mean, I want to hang with her—I just don't want to do the party thing again. I'm tired. I worked hard on that cricket project these last two days, and I've already gone out Monday and Wednesday this week. I don't know how they all do it. I guess not having real jobs helps."

"How'd the crickets work out?"

"Good. I found my angle. What are you doing tonight?"

"Not much." Her cheeks flushed.

"What?"

"Nothing, seriously. It's just a movie with a friend."

"A friend?" I narrowed my gaze. "Which one? Why are you being cagey—oh my God, my brother asked you out last night!" I squealed, not excited. "I fed you chicken potpie, and you cavorted with the enemy and said yes!" It slipped out.

"Grandma gave me pie, and he's not the enemy. He's adorable. I couldn't say no. He has cancer. How do you say no to someone with cancer?" She covered her eyes. "And I really like him as a friend. Which I'm trying not to process, because he's, like, eleven and I've almost graduated college."

"Dude!" I jumped up. "He's in high school!" I had given my consent; I needed to stop, but I couldn't.

136

"I know!" she shouted back, her face completely red. "But it's just a movie. And he said he wanted company. I couldn't say no. Gun to my head, I would have said yes even if he weren't sick." She gasped and covered her mouth, like her oversharing was scaring her too.

"Oh my God!" I felt a little sick and yet a little happy that she might like him back. But mostly sick. "You're almost four years older than him."

"Which wouldn't matter if he were in his first year of college, but your parents held him back because he's a November baby. And he's crazy smart and mature for his age. Which is something creepy people say, and I know that; I hear myself. If you want to hate me for it, I'll go hang out this one time and then never again."

"No." I shivered and tried not to throw up again as I recalled our bargain. "I can't cock block my brother."

"It's not like that. We're friends."

"No. It's more than that. And it's fine. He's a senior, and you're twenty-one, and it's not even four years. It's not creepy for a guy to be your age and dating a girl his age, so why is the reverse creepy? It's just weird because we're friends and he's my brother. But I get it. He's awesome, and he does have cancer." I winced. "Which is why I will ask you to go easy on him. He doesn't do anything partway. If he likes you, he really likes you. So, try to take it slow."

"I will. I swear." She seemed adamant enough.

"And you have to keep this to yourself so I don't die from TMI. Seeing my brother dating is like punishment for my soul. He's still my little bro."

"It's not a date."

"It's completely a date. To him this is a date."

"Fine, but I won't go unless I have your blessing." She sounded so tense.

I held my breath for ten seconds, really wanting to say no, but not able to bring myself to do that since I'd already given my blessing to Martin.

"Yeah. You do. That doesn't mean I'm not entitled to give you loads of shit for it." I caved. For Martin.

She leaped up and hugged me. Her fingers trembled as they dug in. "I was so worried what you'd say. You're my friend, and hos before bros and all."

"Right." I had to admit that if anyone would treat my brother with respect and kindness, it'd be Hennie. And if anyone deserved a bit of a distraction from his cancer treatments, it was Martin. I had to accept that this was going to happen, being an older sister to a cute little brother and having cute older friends. Of course one day it would happen.

I just never imagined it would be Hennie.

I let go and gave her a firm smile, the kind I faked but that looked real. I'd practiced them. "Honestly, I hope he has some fun. And I hope you do too."

"Thanks, Lacey. I owe ya one for not freaking the hell out. I think I might have if I were in your shoes."

"Let's just leave it there. I super don't want to hear any details. At all. In fact, when we talk about the fun you're having, can you lie and call him someone else?"

"Italian exchange student named Marcello?" She answered way too fast, like she'd been plotting this forever.

"Love it." I laughed and grabbed my purse. "Give him a kick in the butt for me," I said as we walked to the elevator.

"You can't kick people who have cancer. I'm not doing that," she said quietly.

"No, of course not," I agreed, also quietly.

Since it was a Friday, we always left early, per Mr. La Croix's rules. On Friday, the day ended at two instead of four thirty. It was the little things like that that made this an amazing place to work. He had others, too, like team-building week, where we spent the week away somewhere. He didn't do team-building weekends; that was our time. He paid a much higher wage than most PR and marketing firms. And he gave his employees amazing benefits, like a year off for maternity with pay, and full medical and dental coverage. Working for him was like working for a saint or living in Norway or Canada. I honestly didn't have a single complaint.

So when he asked me to jump, even for dirty bug bars, I didn't ask how high. I shot for the stars and hoped it was enough.

Marcia had no idea how amazing her dad was. Or her life.

And though I tried to help her find something to be passionate about, I told myself it was my job to love her for who she was.

The same way I loved Hennie even though she was going to spend the summer hanging with my baby brother.

No.

His name was Marcello, and he was Italian, and I didn't know him.

I needed that lie.

I continued wearing that fake-ass smile all the way to the main floor and all the way out of the building as I waved her off and started walking away.

Marcello.

His name was Marcello.

When I got to Marcia's, I couldn't help but unleash my latest woes on her.

"That's kinda gross. I'm sorry, but it is." Marcia shuddered visibly as I finished the tale of Martin and Hennie.

Martin. My baby brother. Our baby brother.

His name wasn't Marcello, and I wasn't getting past it.

"When he said he liked her, I was sort of thrown. I didn't think anything would come of it, but I also didn't think she would ever consider going out with him," I said as I moaned into the mojito Moser had made me. "This is amazing." I put all the focus on my drink and let Senor eat some of the chips in front of me.

"I just can't imagine Martin dating," Marcia muttered, glancing around the kitchen and dining area of her spacious penthouse, checking on Girt's progress with preparing for the party. The rooftop deck with its huge lounging area, dining area, and even a hot tub overlooking the city was exactly the sort of place to host fun preclub gatherings. Not to mention the massive second floor that had all the bedrooms, a theater room, and her dad's home office. Her parents wouldn't even know we were here if they stayed in their rooms. Not that her mom would be home on a Friday night at the start of summer.

"He's still in high school. What is she thinking?"

"I don't know. I can't talk about it anymore. I've puked enough to last a lifetime lately." And that was the truth about that.

I needed him to be Marcello. And I needed this party to be a distraction from the latest Martin saga.

"Who all's coming anyway?" I asked as we sat at the counter and waited for everyone to show up.

"Oh, just a few friends." Marcia got that look in her eyes, the one I dreaded. It meant she was up to something.

"Which friends?" I asked, dubious of her telling me the truth. She loved surprises. Not when people surprised her, but surprising others. And it wasn't always a surprise you wanted. Sometimes it genuinely was for her own entertainment.

"The usual suspects. Kami, Carmen, Jo. Plus Elysia and Chloe." She was purposely trying to sound nonchalant. That was always bad. "I also invited a couple of other people you might not know. Friends of friends."

"Fine, be cagey. But if this turns into some 'hook Lacey up with some creepy, spoiled douchebag' thing because you want me to marry well so I don't have to work anymore, I'm leaving." I was nervous about Kami's boyfriend being there, but I knew he'd hang with the guys around the fire and drink beers, ignoring me. I was that girl. I blended. Unless Marcia got ahold of me and forced me into clothes that showed off what she liked to refer to as *the real estate*. I preferred being the chameleon.

"Whatever. You and I both know I've stopped trying that. Your love of work and wearing those ridiculous business suits is too much, for even me, to tackle." She rolled her eyes at my raspberry suit dress, plucking at it like she always did. "There isn't a man in the world rich enough to stop you from working, or wearing this."

"Prince Harry." I smiled, toying with her while catching Girt offering me an approving and slightly seedy nod from the corner. "I'd quit working to be a philanthropist and perform all my royal duties for him. That ginger hair and his naughty smile and scruffy beard." I nodded along with my verbal fantasy. "Everyone hated him after those Vegas photos leaked and he was naked, jacking around with that blonde. But I thought it improved him. Made him even more accessible and human."

"You're disgusting. Who gets hot over naked photos of a guy with another girl? And beards are so gross."

"Normally beards are gross. But there's something about a military prince with a beard that makes me hot." I laughed at us both, her cringing face and my dirty out-loud romantic perversions. "Plus, haven't you ever wondered what a beard feels like against your—"

"Lacey!" She covered her eyes. "The germs! Plus beard hair means body hair. Gross." She gagged, like, actually heaved. "I can't." She waved her hands like tiny white flags; she was tapping out.

But all of it made me laugh harder.

Body hair was at the top of Marcia's zero-tolerance list. She was a biter, and the idea of getting hair in her teeth made her want to die.

Poor Monty had been getting half his body waxed since they started dating. His life was hard.

As if thinking Monty's name had summoned him, the elevator dinged and out he strolled, looking like a perfect specimen. "Ladies, happy Friday!" He sauntered in with lilies and a box of chocolates from Jacques's. He handed Marcia the flowers and gave her a kiss on the cheek as he placed the box of chocolates on the counter in front of where I sat, while Senor hopped off me and attacked him, jumping at his leg and demanding attention. Even the dog loved him.

I tried not to sigh as I pulled the chocolates to me. "You shouldn't have," I lied, and lifted the lid, leaning forward and smelling.

"Of course I should. Men shouldn't enter houses with empty hands." He kissed Marcia again. "Or hearts."

We both swooned, and she didn't even care when I did.

I popped a chocolate marshmallow in my mouth and closed my eyes, letting it own me. Jacques Torres was the best. His candy and cookies made me happy on a level no man had ever been able to match.

"You have to share. I'll let you smell my flowers." My moment was broken by Marcia's greedy fingers stealing a chocolate. She moaned and grabbed a second one. "One day I swear, I'm going to wake up and find out you got your wings for all this and now you've gone to heaven and none of this relationship was real." She laughed, covering her mouth.

"She's probably right," I added, placing a cherry caramel in my mouth next.

"Yes, because God dispatches angels to wealthy socialites so they can have even better lives." He didn't laugh. He pet the dog and judged us for a whole minute while we laughed harder.

My phone dinged, and I contemplated checking, but I knew the sound was an email. I'd changed it so my emails made a different ping.

The Test Dummy was getting another job.

Or maybe Kami was canceling hers altogether.

"How was the first week back to work?" Monty changed the subject as he sat, and Moser brought him a drink, offering me a quick nod to check on mine.

"Great." I slid the chocolates back at Marcia. My nerves were killing my ability to eat.

"She's lying. My father cruelly forced her to eat bugs. She got sick in front of the entire company and ruined a bathroom to the point that it needed a renovation. And she found out Martin has cancer and that her work friend, Hennie, is sort of dating him. She's our age. And Jordan Somersby tried to have a conversation with her, but she was mean to him because of that whole Amy thing he's suffering through." Marcia summed up my entire life in one breath.

"Wow." He slid his scotch at me and took my mojito. "You need more than chocolate and a mojito."

"Hence the reason we're having this little party and going out." Marcia made it sound like this was for me, but I knew she was desperate for some fun. Half her friends were back to summer intern positions. It was a better number than last summer; at least some of them were trying.

"It was an intense week," I agreed. "But the Jordan thing wasn't so bad. I was a bit of a dick to him because he flirted with me right in front of Amy, which isn't cool. You know how you types aren't great with rejection. I think I hurt his ego, but maybe he'll learn something from that. And the bug bars are turning into something. I'm spinning it." I shuddered and lifted the scotch, smelling the vanilla and trying to forget my horrific experience.

"So Frederick has you marketing them?"

"Just creating the advertising. He wants a young person's perspective on it all. You know how back in the day they just got sports stars to promote a product, and it worked? Astronauts and athletes could sell anything. Well, it no longer works like that. You need a Kardashian, and it's got to go viral on Twitter and Insta. He couldn't get a celeb to take the bait, literally."

"You girls have all the connections to get it to go viral." He glanced at Marcia.

"I'm not supporting bug bars. Jesus. I told Dad this already. Gross."

"We'll see." I laughed and lifted my glass to Monty. "To Fridays."

"Best day of the week." He clinked his glass against mine and then hers.

We all drank, and then he took her hand and kissed the back of it. She led him to the deck to make out for a moment, and I took the opportunity to check my phone.

Sure enough there was another email.

It wasn't from Kami canceling.

This was a new job.

When I saw the name of the sender, my jaw would have dropped if not for the gooey caramel still cementing it together.

Amy Weitzman wanted to hire me to catch her boyfriend, Jordan Somersby, cheating.

Seeing her name made me uncomfortable, but I knew I couldn't be choosy about jobs; that would raise eyebrows. Why would I be selective about whom I agreed to out? That could be a hint at who I was.

I needed to keep things aboveboard. Clients were clients.

But Jordan Somersby?

The guy who hit on me just days ago?

Was his hitting on me the reason she wanted to hire me?

Did she actually care about him?

Was their relationship not actually as fraudulent as everyone believed?

Or did she just want out so she could openly groove with her drummer boy?

My stomach ached as I contemplated it all.

Jordan was an issue for me. I found him incredibly attractive, and Hennie's defense of him made him less icky.

Could I find him attractive and out him at the same time, or was that a conflict of interest?

Wouldn't that be like me using the Test Dummy to ruin a relationship because I thought he was hot?

And what would it say about him if he did go for the bait? That Hennie was wrong about him. That's what it would say. It would say he was just like his brother.

But how would I bait him if he knew me?

He wasn't like DJ Dipshit; he knew my face up close and personal.

I'd have to contract someone else for moments like this.

But whom?

Deciding to worry about that detail later, I shot back the glass of scotch and typed a reply, agreeing to take the case as Moser poured me a new one and slid a bottle of water at me.

"Thanks, Moser."

"Of course." He smiled and slipped back to the bar.

I sent the email, and for one moment I felt like maybe I did the right thing. The relationship needed to end, and I could help them both with that. I was a regular altruist if there ever was one.

Of course, the moment after that thought—as I took two deep breaths, immediately regretting everything I'd just done and the reasons for doing them—he walked in. *He* being Jordan Somersby. The man I had just been hired to destroy.

Chapter Eighteen

Sexier Than Wonder Woman

Jordan

"Jordie, buddy. Marcia didn't say you were coming." Monty rushed through the doors, greeting me with open arms. I tried to focus on his face and not the one who was obviously shocked by my unexpected appearance.

I'd assumed, wrongly, that Cinderella wanted to see me again and that was why I'd been invited over. I was wrong. Horribly wrong. I could see that all over her terrible version of a poker face. She was fuming.

"Monty!" I shook his hand and half hugged. "Brother, how's it going?" Monty was the greatest guy on the face of the earth. A solid gentleman and amazing human. He was the one side of his relationship with Marcia I got. She couldn't do better in my opinion. But Monty sure as hell could have. Marcia was drop-dead gorgeous, but she was a spoiled brat. She and one of her friends once had a conversation in front of me that was so ridiculous I couldn't get a hard-on for a week. It was a tragedy to see him wasted on her arm. But they'd been together for years, and I never got the impression he was a hostage. In fact, it was he who was smitten with her.

"Good. How was the last month or so of school? I haven't seen you since Easter."

"Stressful. Finishing the degree up is daunting." I shrugged.

"Jordan!" The devil herself came sauntering in from the deck, smiling wide with eyes full of mischief. This was her doing. She wanted me here, but I didn't know why she had orchestrated this if Cinderella wasn't on board. Was this a game to her?

"Marcia, thanks for the invite. I guess I'm early." I leaned in and hugged her as well, forcing my gaze not to dart to the place it never wanted to look away from.

The beautiful and slightly sarcastic dream girl at the counter. Hate-eating chocolates and drinking scotch. Because of course she would be doing that.

"You aren't early; you're just in time. We were going to start serving appies. Everyone else should be here any second." Marcia took my hand and led me to the counter where Cinderella was shooting daggers. At both me and Marcia. One of us was dead to her. That much was brutally obvious. Painfully, actually.

Marcia smiled with fake innocence. "Jordan Somersby, this is Lacey Winters. I believe you two met the other night."

"We didn't. Not really." Lacey stood, stuffing another chocolate in her mouth, like she was shutting herself up by plugging the hole.

"We were never properly introduced." I offered her my hand, begging with my stare that she play nice on this forced date. "Jordan."

"Lacey," she said with a full mouth. She let me take her hand, but she just let it sit in mine as I shook both for us. Hers like a limp noodle. "This was the part we actually did alre—"

"What can I get you to drink?" Marcia asked me, cutting her off.

"He likes scotch. Really pretentious scotch," Lacey said, even with the chocolate coating her teeth.

"She's right." I nodded. "Scotch. And pretentious to go with my terrible attitude," I offered humbly.

"Oh my God. You always have an amazing attitude. Stop," Marcia said, praising me. She was selling me to this beautiful creature who didn't even want a sample of the product let alone a purchase.

I was so incredibly lost.

"So, how was your first week back to work?" Monty asked.

"I actually took the week off, sort of. Grandpa Jack had a sailing race for us, and Steph and I hit the spa. It's been a bit relaxed."

"Steph?" Lacey asked sharply.

"His brother's name is Stephen with a *p-h*, so we call him Steph. He loves it." Monty chuckled.

The sound of it made me smile too. "Got a massage, and we hit the steam room. It was nice. After such a long and grueling school year, I'm pretty excited to be done. How about you?" I asked Monty as the butler brought me a drink.

"It was great. My dad and uncle got me to help with a merger and let me take the lead with a couple of clients. Smaller deals, obviously, but I felt good." His eyes darted to Marcia. "Not like spending the week tanning and going to the spa with friends and getting a mani-pedi with my mom. But productive nonetheless." He gave Marcia a dig.

"You got your back waxed too," Marcia fired back coldly, making me snort into my drink.

"Yes." Monty nodded, lifting his drink. "Highlight of my week, without a doubt."

Lacey laughed and smiled up at Monty, and I thought perhaps I caught a little something there that I shouldn't have seen.

Which of course would make sense.

Monty was the full package. But he was taken by her best friend. Was it possible there was more to all this than met the eye? A bit of threesome action I wasn't aware of?

God, to be a fly on that wall.

"Shall we go outside to eat?" Marcia asked Monty.

"Let's." He led the way and had no sooner spoken than food started popping up on countertops and on the tables; a spread like this meant it was going to be some night.

But my eyes were stuck on the girl as she followed Marcia and Monty to the patio.

"So where do you work?" I asked politely as I walked alongside her.

"La Croix Marketing and PR."

"Oh, you work for Mr. La Croix. Lucky. I heard it's amazing there." Fuck me, this night was going to be brutal.

"It is. I'm very lucky he takes pity on me," she said, as if challenging me.

"She's a filthy liar," Monty said as he started serving himself up some food. "Lacey's his right hand even as an intern. Has her own office and just got assigned the lead on a new product. What intern who isn't related to the boss has this life?"

"He gave me the worst job in the world because no one else would take it. And I am practically related." She blushed and shook her head.

Seeing her blush and be humble was amazing. She was perfect. I was trying so hard to find a flaw beyond her obvious crush on Monty, though I had to admit that even I had one of those. Stephen definitely did. He always said Monty was the only guy who could tempt him onto the other team.

I needed something, beyond the thought of my brother switching teams, to focus on, but there wasn't anything. I was going to be putty in this girl's hands by the end of the night, if not take her home to my bed. "What is the project?"

"Bug bars." She cringed, lightening up and laughing a little. It was a magical sound. "Cricket flour." She actually laughed genuinely.

"Oh, I've had those at the gym. I actually didn't mind them. The whole cricket-protein thing bugged me for a moment. Pun intended."

"I got sick," she confessed, losing her humor.

"Eating them?" I was lost.

"Yeah. I was swallowing my bite when Mr. La Croix—"

"Rudely told her that they were made of crickets, and the poor girl went rushing from the room." Mr. La Croix finished the story for her, offering me his hand. "Jordie, how are you?"

"Great, sir. Thank you." I stood and shook his hand.

"How was Boston?"

"Cold. I'm happy to be home for the summer."

"You guys will all be excited when college is over. I know I was."

"Yes, sir." I nodded. I genuinely was looking forward to that. I loved finances and the simplicity of them, but they weren't exactly a passion. I wasn't a mathematician; I was more of a creative thinker. So spending all my time learning about it was exhausting.

"And I see you've met my darling other daughter, the one who will take the helm one day." His eyes sparkled with admiration and love. Naturally I glanced at Marcia, checking for some sibling rivalry, but there was none. Her face was the same. They both adored Lacey.

"Well, unless Prince Harry is still available. Then I'm afraid I won't be," she added, making Marcia and Mr. La Croix laugh. Clearly an inside joke.

"Well, maybe you can settle for someone less royal and a bit more local." Marcia draped an arm over my shoulders, as if we were this close and this joke was anywhere near the realm of appropriate.

"Anyway." Mr. La Croix shot Marcia a look. "You kids behave yourselves. Try not to get into too much trouble before it's time to go out. You know how some of you get." His eyes darted to Lacey. She pressed her lips together and nodded. He smiled. "No one needs to get sick three times in one week." He chuckled and walked inside, leaving Marcia snickering and Lacey's cheeks burning, but she nodded along like this banter was normal.

"You told him about the Sunday puking?" Her eyes flashed on Marcia.

"Yes, of course. How else was I going to ensure he felt terrible? He needed to know he was evil for doing that to you." She'd defended her friend to her father. Her friend who secretly crushed on her boyfriend and was stealing her position at the family company. What a strange group they were.

"Oh my God. He doesn't need to feel worse. He's already upset enough. He knows I don't normally have a squeamish stomach." Lacey covered her face, which nearly matched her tight pink suit dress. "Remember the sea insects we ate like peanuts in the bowl in that bar in Taiwan? He and I liked them."

"Yeah, well, it was mean, and any opportunity I get to lecture him is taken." Marcia stuffed some bread into her mouth, grinning before she started chewing.

Lacey rolled her eyes. "Anyway, I have to go get changed before everyone gets here."

"What, you aren't going clubbing in your work clothes like every other snobby New Yorker?"

"No, dick, I'm going to steal some of your clothes." Lacey flipped her friend off and headed inside, surprising me in every way. Except the sarcasm. That I knew she was fully capable of.

"So, how's Captain Jack?" Monty asked.

"Surly and gross and slutty." I spoke slowly, really putting thought into those descriptors. "His idea of grandfatherly advice comes in the form of how to avoid getting crabs."

"I love that old bastard." He grinned. "He and my Grandpa got along so well."

"I'm sorry about Old Monty. We were at the funeral, but it was so packed I never got a chance to say hi, and then I had to get back to school." I lifted my glass. "He, too, was a classic."

"To Old Monty." He clinked his glass to mine.

When Marcia left us alone, we sat down and I leaned in. "What is going on here?"

"With what?" He looked around nervously at the switch in my behavior.

"Why am I here?"

"Cause I like you?" He changed to confused.

"I met that Lacey girl a couple of nights ago, we kissed on the boat cruise, and then I stupidly hit on her a bit in front of Amy, who I honestly forgot was my 'date' at the last peacocking party. Lacey called me out on it. Which I get. But then I called Marcia to find out her story, certain I could solve my Amy issue by the end of the week and maybe ask Lacey out like a gentleman. I ask one question about the girl, and now suddenly I'm here. Having drinks with Lacey, who doesn't look like she's excited to see me, which makes me think she wasn't in on inviting me." I lowered my voice even more upon seeing his expression. "You have no idea what I'm talking about, do you?"

"Not even a little clue." He glanced back behind us. "I thought she invited you because you're one of my favorites, we never see you because Marcia hates Stephen and you two are always joined at the hip, and you've been in Boston for school for almost half a decade. Which means"—his eyes got serious again when he looked at me—"Marcia has a plan. She clearly wants to hook you and Lacey up."

"I can think of worse ways to die." I chuckled.

"Yeah, but it's weird because Marcia lumps you in with your brother's old behavior. She thinks you're a pig. She wouldn't normally hook you up with Lacey. And even if she would consider it for some uncharacteristic reason, Lacey's cool. Like, the coolest girl I know. She's smart, funny, honest, hardworking, humble, smoking hot. I mean, she's the whole package. And her little brother is her in guy form. Very rad family."

"How do you know them?"

"Her grandparents came into some money when Lacey was thirteen. They decided to pay for the kids to go to a good school. They went to Pennbrook Academy with us."

"Oh, wow, and to think I turned down Pennbrook to go to Dalton."

"Better football. I was always jealous of you." Monty sighed, still checking on the girls to ensure they weren't coming.

"Yeah, well, now I'm jealous of you. You've known her this whole time and never accidentally—"

"No, man!" Monty scoffed. "She's like a little sister. And we didn't hang out a ton until I started seeing Marcia a few years ago. She isn't that kind of girl anyway. She dated France—"

"Oh my God, that's her!" I exclaimed, probably too loudly. "Fuck! Yes. I remember her now. Halloween party like two years back at Warner's place. She was getting pissed at him, at France. He had cheated or something. She had on some crazy outfit, so I didn't recognize her."

"Right. She was Cruella De Vil. Had a wig and makeup on and a bunch of stuffed dalmatian puppies."

"They always have wigs on. I never recognize half of the Upper East Side; could be my best friend's girl, and I don't have a clue whom he's with. And not just on Halloween either. More wigs than plastic surgery clinics. I've just learned to go with it. Man! France blew that one."

"Did he ever. She actually liked the dipshit too. Hasn't dated since. Refuses to date a blue blood, in fact, so I don't know why Marcia would torture you or her." Monty sounded lost.

"She hasn't dated in two years?" We had that in common.

"No. It doesn't help that I have basically made her forbidden fruit either. Every guy in town wants her, but they know I'll hire a hit on them if they mess with her. And she's not rich, so of course no guys will actually invest their time in her. Plus she's in school, has no pressure to snap up someone rich or connected before there's no one left in the pile, and she works full-time all summer for a company that expects her to take over one day. I don't imagine she has much time for herself or anyone else."

"No."

"And the little brother I was talking about, Martin. He's sick. Just got diagnosed with cancer. Really shitty, cause it's the same variety that killed their grandpa."

"Jesus." I grimaced, heartbroken for her, and I didn't even know her.

"Like I said, her brother is a cool kid. Fortunately Marcia said he would be fine—it's treatable and shit—but the kid's only, like, seventeen."

"That's terrible."

"Don't tell her I told you. I just wanted you to know the deal in case Marcia has a plan for you two." His stare grew serious, threatening almost. "She isn't some side dish." He took his role as big brother seriously.

"I'm not a side dish kind of guy." I thought he knew me better than that, but I tried not to be insulted. "You know I haven't dated in almost two years either. I don't want commitment."

"Dear God. You live like a monk then?"

"Yeah. It's not so bad. Better than being with someone and worrying whether or not their family meets your family's expectations. Watching my brother going through his shit to get my family to agree to Cynthia was way too much effort. And I haven't felt a spark worthy of that much work in a while." My eyes darted to the doorway.

"You don't even give in every once and a while and just fuc—"

"No," I laughed. "I don't think I could do a one-night stand. Not my thing."

"Totally changing the subject, but tell me you have a plan for this Amy situation."

"I'm working on something. I mean she's not a bad person per se, but she's so incredibly narcissistic that I don't know if she's aware other people even exist. Except her friends. She's always texting and taking selfies and posting live feed of her with the beautiful people, like they're entertaining enough for that. Stephen told me she's obsessed with some drummer of some band. I heard her and her friends talking about them a lot. She's going to follow the band on tour this summer."

"Amy's going to follow a band all summer?" Marcia interrupted as she walked in on us.

"Yeah." I laughed bitterly.

"Then why don't you just break it off?" Marcia sat on Monty's lap and stole his drink.

"Because my dad is cozying up to hers, trying to make us all one big happy family so they'll invest and he can redeem himself with Grandpa Jack. I can't burn the bridge; the deal isn't even done, and it's a ten-figure payout. It's got to be handled delicately." I sounded like my grandpa. For half a second, I contemplated telling them about how I was going to us the Test Dummy to test myself, pretending to be Amy, and risk getting disinherited if I couldn't work my way out of the so-called relationship, but I decided not to. I needed to look guilty when I got caught, and Marcia was a blabber.

"You need to man up and end that. It's ridiculous, and it's killing your street cred, honestly." Marcia finished the drink. "Your dad's pimping you out. It's sad."

"All right, that feels better," Lacey interrupted, though it might have been for the best. I didn't have much to say in my own defense.

And whatever I did have was lost the moment I saw her, my spark.

She strolled out onto the deck wearing the sexiest little pale-pink dress in the history of sexy little summer dresses. It was perfect for a night of clubbing on a warm evening. And perfect for making me desperate to touch her. Her dark hair and milky skin stood out against the dress. It was almost as pale as her skin, making me uncomfortably drawn to her.

I didn't have a chance to even think about saying something polite, because the party arrived all at once.

"Everyone's here! Finally!" Marcia hurried inside, shouting and waving. "Time to party!" She was already halfway there.

Monty got up, nudging me. "Close one door before you open another." He was offering some brotherly advice—not the kind my own brother would give me. No. Stephen would see Lacey and set a challenge for me, betting me he could get her into bed before me. And he would have. And then he would discard her, because that was who he was before he fell in love. But that's not how I rolled.

My stomach ached as I stared at Lacey smiling and laughing with her friends. I longed to brush a hand along the bare skin of her back or drag my lips up her long neck.

She was beautiful.

Adding the fact that I couldn't have her made me want her even more.

Chapter Nineteen

NEVER EVER

Lacey

For everyone else at the party, the drinks flowed, even turning into shots a few times, but I managed to avoid the bar. I loaded up on food and was constantly sporting a bottle of water that was switched out by Moser. He knew me too well. He'd tried with Marcia, but she was too far gone. She wasn't having the water.

I had too much on my mind to contemplate getting drunk.

I needed to be sharp tomorrow when I took down Kami's boyfriend.

Plus, I didn't want to accidentally get drunk and end up saying something rude to Jordan again or having another bathroom rendez-vous. Not when he was my next target. I needed distance from that one. Even if he looked incredibly hot.

Marcia's plan to invite Jordan infuriated me, and he must have sensed that, because he spent the night hanging with Monty and Theo, drinking on the deck with cigars around a fire. His eyes were the only thing that dared to venture across the room to me. I caught him staring a few times.

In the light of the fire and the twinkling buildings all around him—New York's own version of a starry sky—he was obviously easy on the eyes but hard on everything else.

Hard on my morals, mostly.

He was everything I despised.

Rich, spoiled, trust-fund brat, cheater, and entitled.

"This dress is supercute." Maya, one of our school friends, plucked at the skirt, pulling me from my internal conversation.

"It's Marcia's. I had to steal it. I came here after work wearing business clothes. Because I have a job." I laughed and nudged Marcia, jumping back into the party.

"You swore you wouldn't throw it in my face anymore." She feigned a hurt look.

"I lied!" I cackled and let her attack me with hugs.

"Just love me, dammit. Accept me for who I am."

"Stop fighting it, Marcia. Even I'm working now." Maya smiled wide, interrupting us. "My mom got me in with her friend who does high-end designer work for interiors. She's, like, the best of the best and looking for her newest intern. I start on Monday." She beamed.

"Congratulations!" I dragged Marcia over to hug Maya with me.

"Yeah, I figured since my parents are splitting, I should find a career so that I can live on my own. My dad said I wasn't allowed to move out until I chose a focus. So, there it is." She laughed like she wasn't in pain, but her eyes outed her truths.

"Oh, shit." Marcia cringed.

"I'm so sorry, Maya. I didn't know."

"No one did. They told me last week. Mom's moving to the Hamptons for the summer, and Dad's going to stay in the house here. And they'll avoid each other at all costs while Mr. Sandu ends his marriage and he and Mom start their new life together." Her bitterness showed.

"Oh." I didn't bother delving any further. There was no way to pretend I didn't know they were still seeing each other. Everything was clearly out in the open. And Marcia had seen them just a week ago.

"Shit." Marcia repeated her thoughts on the whole thing.

"Complete. But I'm not going to dwell. I knew my parents were unhappy. And it's whatever. At least I'm the youngest and this doesn't really affect me. I'll get my own place and finish my last year of school and start life." She lifted her glass. "To choosing a career." She sounded perkier, but again, her eyes betrayed her.

I clinked my glass and drank a sip.

"And you'll be next," she said to Marcia like this was even an option. "I guarantee it. You'll find something you love."

"I don't know." Marcia's eyes decided to do the same thing Maya's did: convey troubled waters and high emotions. "I honest to God can't think of a single thing I'd want to do for the rest of my life. I watch my dad buy these bullshit businesses and turn them into some massive company and then sell them, and all I can think is, how did he know? How did he see the potential? All I saw was some lame shit show no one else could manage." Her eyes darted to me. "You got that from him; you got all the potential in the family."

Her words stabbed me right in the heart.

The conversation was taking a dark turn. I handed Maya my water and placed both my hands on Marcia's cheeks. "That is the dumbest thing you have ever said to me. And maybe the dumbest thing you have ever said in general." I felt tears starting to form in my eyes, which was crazy; I wasn't the crier at the party. That was Carmen. She was the one who always ended up in tears and telling everyone she loved them. And I wasn't even drunk. "You have so much inside of you that you don't see or use. Why do you think your dad and I always hound you? We see it. You're more than your mom. You're half your dad and at least a third me. So stop setting your bar so low."

"Lace—"

"No." I cut her off, refusing to let her make this a joke. Not when she'd finally opened up about her feelings. "Trying to be your dad is a waste. You're so much more than that. He's a great example of what happens when you find the thing you're good at. Nothing more. So yeah, he found it early. Lucky him. You'll find yours."

"Yeah." Maya joined the awkwardness I'd created. "You're fucking amazing, Marcia. You make everyone feel special and important and like their problems aren't the end of the world. You always cheer me up, even when shit is going downhill fast."

"You guys!" Marcia's eyes flooded. "My mascara!" She sniffed and hugged us both, pressing her glossy lips into the side of my face, oozing on me. "I love you."

"I love you more." It wasn't true. I wanted to love her more, but her ability to love was far superior to mine. It was one of the things I, well, loved about her.

"I'm gonna go fix my makeup, and when I come back, this conversation needs to change. You both better be whining that you're, like, so drunk and ready to dance," she said mockingly, and left the hug, leaving Maya and me.

"Seriously, congrats on the job." I took my water back and clinked her glass. "I'm really happy for you."

"Yeah, me too. It just fit, ya know?"

"I do." I smiled and remembered my first time helping with a PR project to create slogans and media for a small company we turned into a massive sale for Mr. La Croix.

"So, what's with you? No boyfriend?" She waggled her dark eyebrows.

"No." I laughed and glanced down. "Still repelling the right kinds of guys. On schedule to die alone. What about you?" She'd been single for a year, which was uncommon in our group, except of course for me.

"Sort of seeing a guy from Quebec, actually. He's some politician's son. I don't know."

"Like Quebec in Canada?" I hadn't seen that coming.

"Yeah. He's French Canadian and superhot and a couple of years older." She pulled out her phone and flashed a photo of a handsome man.

"Oh, snap. He is hot. How'd you meet?"

"We were at a hockey game, and the kiss cam landed on us." She laughed. "We just happened to be sitting next to each other."

"So, you met randomly in the stands?" One of New York City's socialites sitting in the stands—unheard of. Everyone had boxes.

"Yeah." She rolled her eyes. "My sister's boyfriend likes sitting in the stands and being cold and eating hot dogs. It was actually fun slumming it down there with the masses for once."

"With the peasants, you mean." I laughed.

"The peasants are crazy. It's way more loud and exciting. Anyway. He asked me to have drinks after the game. I said sure. So, we all went to this club and had a great time. At the end of the night, when I gave him my number, he texted me and said it was the best hundred bucks he ever spent, bribing the kiss cam guy to make sure it landed on us. He saw me walking in, had the ushers make sure we were sitting next to each other, and then paid the kiss cam guy."

"Oh my God." My heart melted. "That is the cutest thing I've ever heard of. He put in so much effort for the possibility of one kiss?"

"I know, right?" She beamed, glowing from the story and the love. "His name's Pierre, and his dad is some politician. I don't know Canadian stuff. But he isn't rich like us; he's closer to being like you. He's normal."

"Oh." I laughed inwardly at the *like you*. Always with the *like you*.

"Yeah, my real reason for the job and the apartment. In case my mom and dad try to pull rank and say we can't date. I already got my trust fund, so whatever. They can disinherit me if they want. I don't care anymore."

"Well, hopefully they see that their own marriage wasn't so hot, so who are they to give opinions?"

161

"Right, exactly. Anyway, we're taking it slow and seeing where it goes."

"Holy shit, look at you adulting. New job, almost done with school, getting an apartment, and with a solid boyfriend."

"I also need to look like a responsible adult so his parents don't think I'm a stupid socialite. They're not business people, but scholarly, actually." She chuckled. "He's so mature. I have to really step it up."

"Challenging. Interesting."

"It is. It's like dating someone who makes you better or wanna be better."

"Holy goals. I wish. Every guy I've met in the last year makes me want to die alone."

We both laughed. She knew. She'd seen the dating scene before.

"Well, we could be Carmen, dating someone we have to hide," I added. "The whole 'rich Juliet and poor Romeo' thing would be harder if you were hiding it."

"Yeah, I'm not hiding anything." She shook her head, darting her eyes to where Carmen was clinging to her boyfriend. "At least he really is the sweetest guy in the world, though."

"He is. Carmen's lucky." I glanced at them.

"He'll end up doing amazing things, just like her. They're both geniuses."

"Yeah, even Mr. La Croix has noticed him. That's something. I bet he gets swooped up and hired before he even grads."

"Hands down," Maya agreed. "He's already in talks with some major company."

"Okay, tell me you're sharing your dirty stories and that you're ready to get fucked up." Marcia jumped back into the conversation. She didn't have just new makeup, but also a completely different outfit. I didn't know how she did it.

"We were just talking about hockey." I grinned.

"Jesus." She wrinkled her nose. "Okay, let's do some shots before this turns into one of those parties." She linked her arms in Maya's and mine and shouted at everyone, "Shots!"

The crowd gathered as shots started lining the countertop, each glistening with the gold flakes in the bottom of the slender glass.

"To the last summer before school ends for most of us!" She lifted her drink in her hand as everyone else got one.

"And to you!" Monty smiled wide, his eyes dazzling as he looked at her.

"Fine, to me." She smirked and drank back the shot as everyone else did. I handed my shot to Kami, who gladly took it for me before Marcia noticed.

Monty came and wrapped his arms around his girlfriend, making me and the rest of the crowd turn away. I strolled out to the deck to grab food. My head was spinning just a little, even with all the water I'd drunk.

"Nice night," a familiar voice behind me said into my ear as I stuffed a massive mushroom cap into my mouth. Without choking or looking like a pig sniffing out truffles, I chewed a couple of times and swallowed like a snake, wiping my mouth as I spun around to find Jordan there. My whole body tightened.

"Yeah, should be a fun." I tried to be cool and not give away the fact that I would not be going to the club. I needed to buckle down on spending, and I really needed a good night's sleep.

"I don't think I'll be going." He walked closer, staring at me. "You have some mushroom cap." He wiped the side of my lip and licked the chunk of food off his finger, making me grimace. "What?" he laughed.

"That was disgusting." I wiped my own face, feeling the greasy spot where the cheesy lump had been.

"I suspect your face is fairly clean."

"You shouldn't. It might be dirty."

"From what?" The humor in his eyes mocked me.

"City pollution."

"If it's in the air I'm breathing, then it shouldn't make a difference if I lick it off your face."

"Shouldn't you be saving your lewd gestures for your girlfriend?" I asked, bringing us back to sobriety. His talking about licking me was making me uncomfortable. And not in the way it ought to, considering his girlfriend was paying me to get dirt on him.

"It's Friday, so that means it's been a whole week since I learned not only of her existence but also that I would be forced to date her. If this is true love in your book, then yeah, I guess we're all doomed." He laughed at the last part. It was weird.

"Wow." I didn't have a thing to add to that.

"Yes. *Wow* is about the only thing to say to something like that. Wow. Gross. How sad. Jeez, Jordan, your life is pathetic." He was losing it in front of me.

"Why don't you just refuse to take part in this?"

"You wouldn't understand."

"Because I'm from the lower levels?" I lifted my brows at the backhanded comment.

"No, yes, well—you don't have expectations placed on you at birth to date and be with the 'right' person. Your family doesn't use you as a pawn to further their placement in society. So it's impossible to understand how that feels."

"No, you're right." I laughed at him. Here he was feeling sorry for himself, like his problems were so huge. Meanwhile my brother had cancer.

"How is any of this funny?" he asked, annoyed maybe that I was laughing at him.

"Not to be a complete dick, again, but if I were in your situation, I'd just be a man about it and do what I wanted. There's nothing less attractive than seeing you rich guys play along, like your mom is carrying your balls around in her purse because you can't stand up to your family and be a success in your own right. Honestly, is being a self-made man so much worse than disappointing your horrible parents? Maybe it's just my poor white trash slipping out, but seeing a man be a man and do what he wants in life, fuck everyone else, is hot. Hotter than any Ivy League education and trust fund. It's like I told you before: fuck 'em!" I slipped past him. "Excuse me."

Shit!

I'd done it. I'd unleashed a lot of meanness again. Why did I insist on using this guy as a punching bag for all my issues?

I hurried across the deck and through the door to the elevator and pushed the button like a crazy person. I needed to get away from him. If I was going to do the Test Dummy right, I was going to have to drive a wedge between us and stop acting like we were even acquaintances. Even if he needed to hear that he was being a pussy if he couldn't just suck it up and end it with his pretend dating.

"Wait." It was spoken on my neck, he was so close.

I closed my eyes, needing to Zen the fuck out in the elevator and not be near him. "No." I didn't spin around or even give him a side-glance. I waited for the elevator and prayed Marcia wouldn't see me. She would be so pissed if she knew I was leaving. Better to ghost and text tomorrow. "Just go away," I pleaded more than anything.

"Don't go. You're right."

"I know," I scoffed, and stepped into the elevator as it dinged and the doors opened. He stepped in, too, and blocked the panel of numbers as the door closed. His face was flushed with what I assumed was anger. But then he did something weird. He reached into his pocket and pulled out a fifty-dollar bill.

"This is yours. I meant to give it back to you."

"Keep it. Put it toward buying a new pair of balls." Apparently I wasn't finding Zen after all.

"My balls are perfectly fine." He stepped closer, his eyes ablaze. He shoved the fifty dollars in my hand. "I think you need it more than I do. You can put it toward buying yourself some manners."

The elevator started to move as he said it, trapping us together.

He glared at me, hovering over me by at least six inches, even in my huge heels.

"Fuck you," I growled, throwing the fifty at him. It bounced off his chest while his eyes tried to murder me with his stare.

"Fuck me?" He laughed bitterly. "You honestly want to say *fuck me*? You're the one laughing at me and mocking me for not thinking it's so easy to walk away from my own family. Could you just walk away from yours?"

"I don't know, my family wouldn't do this to me." I took the challenge, even stepping a little closer, forcing myself to crane my neck more.

What was I doing?

Why couldn't I let this one go?

Why was I taking this so personally?

"All I do know is that you hit on me, while you're fake dating some girl." And there it was, why I was taking this personally. "So I think you're expecting the usual from me, that I'll be your side chick like the little drummer boy is with your girl? Like you so blatantly pointed out, I'm not one of you, so clearly you, who worries so much about his family, isn't going to date me and bring me home, or even ask me out. But not being from your world means I don't have to play by your rules and live some demented version of happiness. I'm free to be with whomever I want. To only date guys who think I'm worthwhile enough to ask out on a date and who would bring me home to meet their parents. And I love my life. So if the person coming into it isn't an improvement, then they're not coming in. You rich boys"—I pointed and stabbed him in the chest with my nail—"are all the same."

"Oh, really?"

"Yeah. You think you can have your cake and eat it too. You have the girl you date for your parents and the girl you date for fun and the girl you fuck because she's a wildcat in the sack. And you never have to grow up. You get to live this insane double standard for your entire lives, because you were born with a silver spoon lodged in your ass. You think I don't know who your dad is, who your brother is. I would never be the kind of girl they would approve of."

The elevator dinged, and we both turned sharply, glaring at the couple standing in front of it. I knew them, so they both smiled and then stopped themselves, stepping back from the open door when they saw our faces.

"Hey!" I greeted them fiercely as I stormed out of the elevator with Jordan's heavy footsteps hot on my heels.

"So what?" He grabbed my arm and spun me in the foyer. "You know who my piece-of-shit dad is, so you think you know me?"

"Why are you hitting on me all the time if you don't want to hook up? Clearly it's not to bring me home to Captain Jack or your gross dad or your doormat mom. I've heard people talk about your dad and your perverted brother, and I'm sorry if you've been lumped in with them as being gross and you're really not. But you are hitting on me, dragging me into bathrooms, while fake dating a girl to get her family's money. You're not really trying to be different, are you? You think Mr. La Croix hasn't spent half my life warning me about boys like you? Warning me to make something of myself that a guy would be proud to date, not fucking in yacht bathrooms when no one's looking?"

"You don't know me!" he snapped, looking like he might pull his hair out.

"I don't need to. I know your type."

"No." He shook his head, stepping closer and grabbing both my arms with his, not hard but firmly, like he wanted me to listen. "You don't. At all. When I said you were right, I was admitting that I need to be a man and tell my family to fuck themselves. I need to walk away and be an orphan and lose most of my friends and probably not see my grandpa ever again. And yeah, he's gross, but he's the only real father figure I've ever had, which might say some things about how Stephen and I turned out. And yeah, maybe your awesome family wouldn't put you in this position, but mine would. Do you have any idea what it was like coming home from college to be handed to some strange girl? You're right, I need to choose my life for me and be a self-made man and walk away from everyone I love. Sorry I didn't do it the second this card was dealt to me, sorry I didn't just walk away from my family casually, like I don't care about them even if they are ridiculous. You're right. Happy?" He was firm in his speech.

"No." I pulled free. "Stop including me in your little games. And don't hit on me until you're single."

"So you want me to hit on you?" He laughed like he might cry.

"Oh my fuc—"

"Just don't leave." He stepped back, lifting his hands in the air. "I swear to God I won't hit on you or give you any attention that you don't want. I'll be cool. You can see for yourself that I'm not a philanderer like my dad or a man whore like my brother used to be."

"Used to be? Nice try," I scoffed.

Boys like Jordan Somersby were exactly the reason why I was still single and probably would be forever. They said the right things and did the right things and swept you off your feet. But it was when you weren't looking that the sleight of hand kicked in, crushing your heart before you even knew they were holding it.

"Good night, Jordan."

"Lacey." He followed me. "You shouldn't walk home alone."

"Oh, I'm not walking," I muttered. "There's a thing you rich folk don't know about called the subway."

"Fine. I'll make sure you get there."

"Please don't."

"Let me get you a car, then."

"No, I don't want anything from you." I spat my words and continued toward the subway.

"You can't stop me from being in a public place." He followed me the block and a half to the station and down the stairs. When we got to the platform, I folded my arms over my chest and stared at the graffiti mural across from me.

"What will it take to get you to listen to me?" he finally said, not cutting the tension but adding more to it.

"Morals and a code of ethics." I gave him the side-eye I'd practiced. It wasn't as good as Marcia's, but it was close. "Stop being a giant wuss." I accidentally let it go too far again, fully mocking him.

"I'm sorry. I don't know what else to say to you to make this better. Regardless of my sharing something incredibly personal and painful with you, you've offended me in so many ways I don't think I've even processed them yet. I'm sure tomorrow I'll wake up with new bruises to my ego as some of your zingers land late on my weak mind. But you should know, I am sorry for making you think I have no integrity. You win. I'll leave you alone. Have a nice night and a nice life, and goodbye." He stepped back and left me there, alone on the platform with a couple of other girls eyeing him, watching him go.

As I stepped onto the subway, I felt worse than I had in ages. In fact, I didn't think I'd ever felt worse than this in my entire life, except of course when I found out my brother had cancer. That was always going to be my lowest of lows.

Chapter Twenty

SATAN'S MISTRESS

Jordan

"Mean as a snake. Ice running in her veins. Legit went for the jugular and the balls at the same time. Fortunately, though, I don't even have balls, according to her." I drank my beer and slumped into the chair on the deck of the yacht club, regretting everything from the night before. I wasn't even sure what I'd done to offend her so badly.

"Ouch." Monty winced.

"*Ouch* isn't the right word. She flayed me right there on the subway platform in front of a bunch of strangers. Said I had no integrity."

"I did warn you."

"I thought you were warning me against hitting on her because she was practically your sister, not because she was savage as fuck."

"No. Savage. As. Fuck." He scoffed. "She can take care of herself. She's from Brooklyn. I scare guys into thinking I'll mess with them for hitting on her and wanting some side action, but a lot of the time I'm trying to spare a guy some heartache and humiliation. She's fast and harsh and witty and smart. It's deadly."

"Yeah, I have all the bruises to show for it. She handed me my ass at the party. Chewed my head off in the elevator. Crushed me in the foyer. And then obliterated the last bits on the subway platform."

"Well, if it makes you feel better, she did much worse to France. Homeboy still can't get a date in New York. Not with a nice girl, that is. He's seeing models and pretending he's happy, but I know for a fact his dad is pissed that he's not with someone proper."

"Oh, I don't assume she's done with me." I laughed bitterly, almost crying at the end. "I am certain more is coming down the line. She probably saved the real public humiliation for later."

"Probably. But I bet you won't ever hit on another girl while you're still dating anyone else. Like Amy, for example."

"Amy who?" I gave him a look. "All kidding aside, I asked her out to a late lunch today, hoping to end this civilly. I suspect her family has the same expectations mine does. So there's no reason we can't find a mutually beneficial way to break things off without either set of parents making it weird. It's not like we'll escape seeing each other. Our dads are dating. But we could try to make this a clean break. I'm thinking if she and I are on the same page, like she wants to call this charade off as well, maybe our dads won't blame either of us."

"Bro, you might need something harder than a beer."

"Why, you got some coke lying around from high school?"

"No." Monty chuckled. "I missed you. We haven't hung out in ages."

"I know, I miss you too. Marcia hating Stephen, even married Stephen, has sort of killed the bromance time."

"It has. We let girls come between us. Anyway, what are you going to do about the whole Lacey thing? Cause if we're gonna hang out, you're going to have to patch things up with her."

"Pretty sure I won't be invited back to any parties at Marcia's house for a long time."

"Marcia loves me, so at the very least, she'll have to like you by association, and she didn't even notice Lacey was gone last night until way later, when everyone was going to the club. Marcia assumed she was drunk and got Darren to drive her home. Lacey had a weird week."

"Yeah, and I made it so much better by being a dirtbag."

"You're not a dirtbag. You made a bad choice getting up in her grill. You should have dealt with Amy before you ever went for Lacey. She's not one of us. She expects more than girls from the Upper East Side. She doesn't get the mutual affairs and joint-business-venture side of things either."

"*I* don't understand the mutual affairs and joint-business-venture side of things. And you can't tell me you and Marcia are cool with them."

"Hell no. She's my girl for real. No one touches her." Monty didn't kid around when it came to Marcia. His parents were exempt from affairs too. The worst thing they ever did was buy a new penthouse instead of keeping their old family mansion when Old Monty died.

"I'm going to lie low for a while after I break things off with Amy today. If it doesn't go well, I'll be having a very long conversation, or short depending on his mood, with my dad about where I stand with our family." I sighed, knowing how it was going to go.

"You come here, bro. You come here. You know how Mom and Dad feel about your dad. My mom hates him. She'll rename you as one of her sons. She loves you. So if shit with your dad goes bad and Captain Jack can't see that this is fucked up, even if it's a billion dollars of fucked up, then you still have family with us."

"Thanks, man."

"And no lying low. Jesus. You're home for the summer. You have done nothing wrong. Your family shit is unrealistic and insane."

"I know." I was grateful for Monty. He saw through the bullshit.

But I would need to lie low.

Last night after the incident, I went home and sent the Test Dummy my gift cards for payment to get the ball rolling and get me tested by them. So I had to assume at some point, I was going to be tested. I would fail, naturally, and if Amy and I couldn't come to a nice understanding, then she would get that video from me. I would test the waters at lunch and see if she needed that extra excuse to break up or if there was a chance that maybe we were on the same page. Maybe this could be handled mutually and strategically.

"But we're still on for the poker game tonight, right? No matter what? I'm not taking no for an answer."

"Yeah. Fine. It'll be fun to have some guy time." Another lie. I was never going to have fun again. Not until I could get past this Amy thing. "I won't be long with Amy. Maybe an hour."

"Okay. I'll pick you up at seven from your place?"

"Sure. Unless I show up with what's left of my stuff." I shrugged.

"Yeah." He narrowed his steely gaze. "I know you want to stay home and lick your wounds, but the best way to get over this is to prove to Lacey that your intentions were never creepy or underhanded. She's not a fan of underhanded."

"I gathered." I got up and finished off my beer. "I better go and face this music. Wish me luck."

"Amy isn't the one you need luck with." He laughed again and waved me off.

I walked to the car that was waiting for me and climbed into the backseat, jumping when I saw Stephen. "Holy fuck! What are you doing in here?" How did he know where I was?

"Coming to check on my baby bro. When Jenson said he was going to pick you up and take you to the Modern, I knew something was up. Is this the plan to finally get rid of Amy?"

"Yeah. I'm going to do it now. We're meeting in, like, half an hour. I'm gonna forget everything Mom and Dad and Grandpa said and just end it. Fuck 'em." I laughed bitterly. "My plan is firstly to try to get her to amicably end it, both of us friends and our dads still friends and business partners. If that doesn't work, I have another plan in the works. It will get me kicked out of the family, but I can't do this anymore. A week has been misery."

"That's the spirit." He slapped my leg. "Be a dick, and get what you want. Dad is all talk. Fuck, Grandpa Jack never would have dated someone he didn't want to. And Dad wouldn't have either. Mom might have been coerced into hanging with Dad, but he wanted her. Even with all his bullshit, I think he loves her. And in a creepy Stockholm Syndrome sort of way, I think she loves him too."

"Now you're pushing it."

"No, for reals. She doesn't leave, even though she could. She could have her own life if she wanted it. Instead she sticks it out. She goes on all those fishing trips and lives in the shadow of his life, but she never complains or tries to change things for herself."

"I don't know, man."

"Anyway, don't pussy out. Be a man. If you get disowned and kicked out, you're free." His voice cracked a tiny bit.

"Yeah, I've heard I need to man up more."

"Fuck yes, you do. It's sad seeing this shit going on. And then once you're broken up, you can tap Lacey Winters's ass and give me all the dirty details."

"You're disgusting." I shook my head. He was never going to grow up. Not even when Cynthia forced kids on him. And if I ever had something to tell, I would never spill a single thing about what went on between me and Lacey Winters. In the first place, I was a gentleman and didn't go for bragging, and in the second place, the way Lacey had treated me so far seemed to indicate that I wouldn't have anything to brag about, possibly ever. After she had treated me like her personal doormat, I didn't really want anything from her at the moment anyway, except maybe my dignity handed back to me in one piece.

Chapter Twenty-One

DEAL WITH THE DEVIL

Lacey

"Hennie, I need your help." I spoke quietly into the phone. "Can you get on the subway in, like, ten minutes, and I'll meet you there?" I'd made an executive decision about the order in which the Test Dummy guys had to be outed based on their schedules, but I didn't want Martin to know. He would not have gone for my methods.

"Um, sure. Why?" She sounded hesitant.

"Just trust me, I need help. Look pretty. If I don't make your train, get off at Fifty-Seventh Street. I'll meet you there." I stuffed the bag I was taking with me with everything I would need and prepared for the worst half hour of my life. This one was like a Band-Aid, and it just needed ripping off. I couldn't think; I needed to act.

Otherwise I was going to chicken out.

"Okay. Is this life or death?"

"Yes." I closed my eyes and tried not to feel sick about what I was going to do.

"Like, real life or death." She laughed.

"I swear, it is."

"Fine. See ya there." She hung up, and I tried not to feel terrible for roping her into this, but I didn't have a single other idea.

When the bag was packed, I headed down the stairs, meeting Grandma at the bottom.

"You're going out again?" she asked.

"Yeah, just to see Hennie for a couple of hours, and then I'll be back. When are Mom and Dad coming back home?"

"Your dad won't be back until next week, but your mom is on days off starting tomorrow. I think she's actually taking one of them off this time." She sounded drained.

"What's wrong?"

"Oh, nothing. Just make sure you're going to be back later. I'm going out with some friends for a movie, and I don't want to leave Martin alone." She was talking about him like he was five. This was going to go over really well. He loved being coddled. A lot. No wonder I hadn't seen him all morning; he was hiding in his room.

"Yeah, I'll be back." But then I would be out the door again. And now I didn't know how I would manage to leave him behind, go catch the dipshit DJ with his pants down, and then be back in time for Grandma not to realize I'd left a second time.

That was going to be a later problem. I had too many other issues right now. But if all went well, I'd have an extra two thousand dollars at the end of today and proof that Jordan was exactly the piece of shit I assumed he was. The asshole nuts didn't fall far from the asshole trees on the Upper East Side.

"See ya in a bit." I kissed her cheek and left the house.

"Bye, dear," she called after me, waving out the door. She really was the most intense of all the grandmas. Martin having cancer wasn't making her helicopter tendencies better. At all.

When I got on the train, Hennie was there as planned. I jumped on the same car as her, huffing from running to make it and sweating from wearing a hoodie—my version of incognito.

"What are you wearing? It's got to be eighty degrees outside." She grimaced at my clothes. If Hennie was judging, it was a bad choice.

"I have a job for you and I need to be hidden, thus the hoodie." I sat next to her and sighed, preparing myself mentally for the spiel I was going to have to rock, or she would say no. Rightfully so. "I have a weird proposition."

"Your propositions are always sort of weird. You have this dramatic life I can't really comprehend most days." She didn't say it hurtfully, and I tried not to take it that way.

"Duly noted. Anyway, I got asked by Amy Weitzman to test Jordan Somersby," I whispered.

"Jordan Somersby. *The* Jordan? My fantasy man?" She didn't sound excited, even if the sentence should have been one you said excitedly.

"Yes, the very one. I guess they're sort of dating. She wants him tested to see if he'll cheat. I think they both desperately want to get out of the relationship, and she needs ammo to end this or their parents won't let them. We're doing her a favor, essentially. And I guess him. I saw him last night, and he did not sound excited about being forced to date her." I laid it on extra thick.

"Wait." Hennie started to realize where this was going. "You want me to test him, don't you?"

"Yeah. It has to be you. He knows me. Like, I saw him last night. And no one else knows about the Test Dummy. They can't. So I am completely out of options."

"I don't know." She started to squirm.

"It's so easy. Amy says that he's meeting her for lunch today at the Modern. He'll arrive early and drink in the bar first, as he always does. You honestly just have to flirt and see if he flirts back, then ask if he wants to get a drink later, and he says yes, and you say, 'Okay, meet me back here in two hours.' He'll agree because of your mad skills, you'll be wearing this pin that records it all, and you'll leave. Never to see him again."

"It doesn't sound easy. And why would Jordan Somersby want to meet me? He can have anyone he wants. Not to mention he might recognize me from school."

"Not when I'm done with you." I opened the bag to let her see everything in it.

"Oh my God. I can't." She squirmed even more. "I can't."

"Remember when you said you'd be there if there was anything you could do to help me in my desperate time of need?" It might have been manipulative; I would mentally check myself later.

"Lacey." She gave me a pleading scowl. "Please don't guilt me. I can't say no to your 'my little brother has cancer' face."

"I'm begging, please. Do this five-minute favor for me, and I will owe you forever." I pouted just a little. "One time."

"Fine!" she gasped, and slumped on the subway bench, looking like she was losing out in this bargain even though I was doing all the hard work. All she had to do was ask him out. Easy. He was gorgeous and would be sitting alone. How hard would that be?

Taking my win, even if she was probably angry with me, I began recreating her.

Wanting to ingratiate myself to the upper echelons of society meant I needed a skill.

Makeup was the one my friends required the most.

Desperate to fit in, I'd become a master, following drag queen YouTube tutorials. No one blended like a drag queen.

I started with the makeup, trying to work with the jerking and swaying of the subway cars while adding a ton to what she already had going and contrasting and highlighting a lot to change her appearance. By the time I was done, she resembled Mandy Moore. I dragged out a silky brown set of extensions and started brushing and clipping them into place, giving her lush, long hair.

"When we get to the restaurant, you run to the washroom and change into the outfit I brought." I hung on to the pole and held up a garment bag with a cute summer dress. I'd seen the way Jordan had eyed mine the night before. He clearly liked summer dresses.

We got some strange looks from people, but it was New York, so whatever.

"This is insane." She grabbed the mirror from my makeup bag and gasped. "Oh my God. What did you do to me?" She touched her face lightly. "Dude." She lifted her gaze to mine. "You are really good at this."

"You like it?" I asked, a little scared from her reaction.

"It's amazing. I look like a celebrity. I look like you." She gave me a scowl. "And you look homeless?"

"Glad you're happy. Let's hurry." We got off and hauled ass to the Museum of Modern Art, then slipped into the bathroom. She took the garment bag and went in. She came back after a few minutes and passed me the bag back, clearly full of her clothes.

She held her arms out, and I smiled. "Cinderella," I said.

"I mean, I don't know." She sighed, losing her confidence. "What if he's not alone, or he doesn't want a drink, or he doesn't like me?"

"No what-ifs." I lifted the pin and put it on her dress in the seam so it was a little camouflaged. "This is how you work the camera," I whispered as I twisted it to the right once. Then I turned it back to the left. "See. Easy."

"Whatever." She looked like she might get sick but turned on her heel and stalked off. Her gait didn't match her outfit until she got to the bar. Then she stood up tall and slim and sauntered in, earning looks from multiple guys.

The one in the corner with the perfect hair and smile, the target we were there for, didn't notice her. Not until she came and sat next to him at the bar. Fortunately he didn't have anyone on either side. He smiled as she sat down while fingering the pin.

He smiled at her in a way that made my stomach ache. I prayed to all that was holy he would turn her down. He would prove he wasn't the person I thought he was. It dawned on me then that I was testing him not only for Amy, but for myself. In a perfect world, Jordan would turn down Hennie, dump Amy like a man, and then ask me out. Proper like. I'd make him sweat a little—make him work for it. And then, we'd have amazing sex, like I had been planning to in the bathroom on the boat before I was forced back to my senses. Seeing Jordan across the room, my senses were primed toward wild and passionate.

Whoa.

I was jumping in a little fast, considering he was a trust-fund dude.

But his speech the night before, that his family would disown him, had broken my heart. I'd been rude and horrid to him, and it bothered me. In the light of day now, it made me feel worse. Yes, he was dating a girl for money; it was gross. But at least he was conflicted about it.

My whole body was tense as Hennie started talking and swooning, the way she was prone to do with cute guys. She never acted this way with Martin, but I'd seen it at the office a few times. Hot guys made Hennie uncomfy.

She fidgeted with her hair, biting her lip and nodding as Jordan started asking her questions. His body language was off the charts. He turned in his chair, facing her and leaning on the bar, tilting himself so he was all hers.

I died a little inside as she batted her lashes and toyed with her hair and propositioned him so obviously.

He grinned and nodded, looking as smarmy as a guy could.

I died fully.

My whole body went numb except for the raging ache in my chest. My knees nearly buckled, but she got a glass of champagne and they toasted. He seemed really into her. He leaned forward, whispering something that made her eyes widen as she lost her charm. She met my gaze for a second and then regained her composure.

Tears were threatening me, but so was my lunch, which desperately wanted to come back up. I gagged and turned away, fleeing for the washroom so I could throw up like a normal person for once, in a toilet.

Chapter Twenty-Two

FREEDOM, FOR A COST

Jordan

The trap made my heart sore.

The girl the Test Dummy had sent was like watching amateur night at the strip club we used to go to when we were underage. But I knew that when I got that video link, it would make me look like a giant douchebag—exactly what I needed if this breakup attempt didn't go smoothly.

After that sad business was finished, I sat across from another heartless wonder, Amy, who couldn't be bothered to put her phone down. We'd sat through the usual pleasantries for an hour, and now it was time for the real talk. But she was texting a mile a minute and smiling to herself. Or whomever she was talking to.

"Amy," I said again, getting annoyed.

"Just a sec." She sent one more message and lifted her gaze, losing all that humor the moment our eyes met.

"We need to talk."

Her eyes widened like she might panic. She glanced around the fancy restaurant and began to sweat. It burst from her pores like beads, and her hand began to tremble. "Okay." She lifted her water and took a gulp.

It made me laugh. I knew what was happening, and I decided to play along. I reached across the table, taking her sweaty hand in mine and staring deeply into her eyes. "Amy, since we met I've had one question I've been dying to ask you."

Her pupils dilated, and she made a face like she might gag or cry, I wasn't sure which.

I tried to keep a straight face. "My parents, and I suspect yours as well, have an idea of where this is all going for us. And I wonder sometimes if we're on the same page."

She nodded along, desperately upset. Her eyes darted to the phone as it vibrated on the table.

"So I have to ask this question. Are you ready?"

She started to shake her head and then nodded, her eyes beginning to well.

"Will you, Amy Weitzman, please do me the incredible honor of being my ex-girlfriend?"

She looked like she was about to cry and then paused. "Ex?" Her words came out in gasps. "Ex-girlfriend?" She started breathing normally again.

"Yeah. You and I don't match up, and I know our parents are forcing us into this. I think we'd be better off just shutting this down. Ending it here and now. Before it gets too serious and they start planning the wedding."

"Oh my God." She squeezed my hand back. "Seriously? I mean, it's not you. It's me. I'm in love with this guy, and my parents hate him. And when my dad found out, he threatened to disown me. So I lied and I said I had a thing for you. You were the first person I could think of—you and your brother are notorious. Everyone knows your family." She said it like it wasn't a compliment, which was fair.

"So you want to end it as well?" I was lost.

"Of course, duh. But what are we going to tell our parents?" She pulled back, having just realized the repercussions of us cutting romantic ties. "My dad wants me to marry you. He wants a lifetime of financial security with your dad and your grandpa, it's more like. And he refuses to let me date anyone who isn't part of our world, so."

"Marry?" I choked a bit. "He said *marry*?" Her dad was worse than mine.

"Yeah. So I couldn't break things off. At all. But if you do it—"

"Whoa, no. I was thinking we need to do this together. Both of us need to keep it as peaceful as we can. I tell my parents it isn't really working, we're more like brother and sister, maybe. And you tell your parents the same thing. We like each other, but not in a romantic sense. We spent the week together, and it felt wrong."

"Ew." She wrinkled her nose.

"Okay, not brother and sister. Best friends," I offered. "We just tell our parents we're totally cool being friends and they can keep up their own charade?"

"Oh." She sat back down, losing all that excitement, and a little switch in her flipped. Her tone changed, and that stupid look on her vacant face disappeared. "I assumed you were taking one for the team and dumping me so I would be free and you would be the one in trouble. My dad could concentrate on hating you and not me."

"I was sort of hoping we could make it so that our dads can still be on good enough terms to close this deal."

"I'm not doing that. I'm not taking any of the blame." She leaned in. "I can pretend to love you for the rest of my life. We can get married." She was no longer the shy, ditzy girl she had been a week or an hour ago. "I can marry you and still have my boyfriends and trips. Who I marry means nothing to me. But I am not getting disowned because you can't man up to your own dad," she mocked.

"I see," I growled back.

"Right. So, this has to be on you. You have to be the one to ruin this and hope your dad forgives you."

"It's like that, then." I took a deep breath, hating that I would have to do this, plan B. I'd really hoped it wouldn't come to this, but I couldn't continue. It was worth throwing myself on the sword to end it. "I might have a way for you to dump me that would be legit; your parents would completely understand, and it might help me save face with my family."

"Go on. I'm listening." She sounded smarter than she ever had.

"I am expecting an email any minute with a video of me hitting on a random girl. It was made by a service called the Test Dummy. They test fidelity. I hired them under your name—"

"Whoa, wait—"

"Hear me out." I lifted my hands. "No one has to know how the video came to you; there's no receipt or anything. They sent a girl to hit on me, and I pretended like I wanted her. They recorded the whole thing, my propositioning her to go to a hotel room and everything. I did it to free us—to free both of us. It's my plan B. You can dump me with proof of my shitty behavior. Your family will be satisfied with your ending the relationship, and mine might possibly forgive me, given every male in Manhattan has been caught with his pants down. It's my best shot at possibly not being disowned. I didn't dump you or end the relationship, staying within my agreement with my father. You ended it, and with good reason. I had no control over the matter."

"That's insane."

"Yeah, well, it'd be more insane to stick this out for the rest of our lives to make our dads happy."

"Why all the charades?" she asked. "Why not just break things off with me?"

"This way, I'm a victim of the videotape, and you're a victim of me. Neither of us will really be to blame, just the circumstances."

He Loves You Not

"Damn, look at you all Sherlock Holmes and shit." She sat back. "I am impressed. I honestly thought you were a fuck boy like your brother. But you're actually smart. That is fucking devious. It's disgusting, but I think it might work." Who the hell was this girl?

It was the longest conversation we'd ever had, and I actually didn't mind being near her. She played dirty, but at least she had some personality now.

"Well, my dad is not going to want to be involved with your dad after this. So you understand you're losing the business deal, right?"

"I know." I took a deep breath, certain I was also going to be disinherited by Dad, but the important one, Grandpa Jack, could possibly understand. The entire plan B was for Grandpa Jack. Maybe he would get that I slipped up and made a mistake and got caught by someone else. It was my best shot. "I'll get the check."

"It was not very nice meeting you, Jordan." She put her hand out. "But thanks for being cool and coming up with this insane scheme."

"You're welcome?" I took her hand in mine and shook it delicately, trying so hard not to hate her or blame her for this. It had been the worst week of my life. "And I will text that video to you the moment I get it, from an unknown number. Don't show it to anyone but your mom, please. I don't need to be ruined everywhere."

"I won't, I swear. I have to go home and start preparing myself for the meltdown of the century." She got up and left as I watched her in silence.

Taking my drink in my hand, I contemplated how I was going to break the news to my dad, but the only thing I cared about was that I was free. I was single and free, and Amy was no longer my problem, and I didn't have to pretend anymore.

I lifted my phone and dialed my brother.

"Jordie, what's shaking, bro?" he answered a little too excitedly.

"It's done."

"Oh, man. You broke up with the little princess?"

"No, she's dumping me."

"How? And even better."

"No, I'm still a dead man. But Grandpa Jack might commiserate with me. I fell on my sword a little, but if this works, I'll only come out looking like a cheater who got caught, giving Amy an excuse to leave. Not a son who disobeyed his dad." I cringed but remembered his and Lacey's words. "I asked her to break things off amicably and let the dads be friends, but she didn't think that was possible. So this was the next best thing."

"Oh, well, fuck it. Congrats, man. I'm stoked for you. You wanna go out and get drunk and celebrate?"

"No, I'm going to the poker game with Monty."

"Awesome. I'll meet you guys, and we'll go out. I know a sweet spot. You are gonna need to get laid. It's been a while. We'll find you a moderately attractive chick so you don't end up like Forrest Gump after this massive sex recession."

"I don't want to have—"

"No one cares what you want. I'm already texting Monty. This is gonna be a sweet night. I'll see ya later." He hung up, leaving me hanging with my nerves and the next call I would have to make.

I learned early on that owning your bullshit to Grandpa Jack was way better than letting him find out from someone else. I closed my eyes and took a deep breath before I dialed his number and tried not to have a heart attack.

"Jordie, my dear boy." He talked like he was Hugh Hefner. "What are you doing calling me on a Saturday? You know this is Grandpa's fun day. No grandkids allowed." He chuckled, also a little too happy.

"I have some bad news." I cringed.

I might as well get it over with.

"I just had lunch with Amy, and she broke up with me. She got ahold of some video of me hitting on another woman at the bar. Someone took a recording. It was from last night."

"Caught with the cucumber out. How the hell did this happen? We talked about this. You agreed you were going to be careful for the sake of the company."

"I don't know. I saw the video and couldn't believe I'd been set up. The girl was stunning. Huge boobs." I tried to focus on the parts he would care about.

"Huge boobs, eh. Well, what can you do, my boy? Everyone has a phone nowadays and no regard for propriety. They'll record you doing anything to make noise and a buck. There's even one of me floating around out there. If you google *old man with his dick—*"

"Yeah. Everyone and their phones." I almost wished for the crabs story.

"I can't say I'm happy, kid. In fact, I'm really disappointed. But this deal was your dad's baby. I'll let him handle how to proceed with the Weitzmans. He's going to be pissed you got caught with the kielbasa out. I don't know how to fix this. Weitzman is going to pull away from your dad, and the deal's going to be ruined. It was a billion-dollar deal, Jordie. You couldn't play nice for a billion dollars?" He laughed, but the bitterness was there, riding the sound.

"I played nice, just to more than one woman," I lied. "I'm really sorry. I honestly didn't know I was being set up."

"I'm not happy, but we'll bribe or cut the right people to make the video go away. And I guess we'll have to come up with some alternate ideas to try to land that account." His casual threat disturbed me slightly, but I'd take it in exchange for having the deed done. "You've disappointed me, son. But . . . we'll figure it out. There's not much to be done. We'll discuss it Monday. Try to behave for the rest of the weekend, kid." He hung up, and I tried to swallow down the discomfort that was going to be my life.

What were my options?

No, I needed to contemplate my worst-case scenario, because I had just landed in it.

Chapter Twenty-Three

SCUMBAGS EVERYWHERE

Lacey

"And then he said he wanted me. Like, he wanted me, right then and there. He asked if I was staying at a hotel nearby. I said no, and he wrote down a hotel and a room number and said his family kept it on hand for occasions such as this. He asked if I knew who he was, and I pretended I'd never seen or heard of him. And then he put a hand on my thigh, like, really brushing it softly. It was so crazy." Hennie talked a mile a minute while I tried not to think about anything else that might make me sick.

She looked closely at me. "You okay?"

"Yeah. I just feel awful for his girlfriend. He's clearly a douchebag."

"Why, because he's unhappy in his love life and wants out? She doesn't even know him. She has a thing with that drummer dude." She sounded like maybe he was going to become a hard limit for her. As in I couldn't bash him anymore because he'd hit on her. She didn't realize it was because he was a pig and would have hit on anything. And I wasn't going to ruin that for her.

So I nodded along.

"So, you're going to hand the evidence over to Amy?" Her eyes widened, like this excited her.

"Yeah."

"Wow. I can't believe your first mark was Jordan Somersby."

"It's wasn't. I mean it was, but only because I can't get to DJ Dipshit until tonight. I figured, why not get this one out of the way while I had tabs on him?"

"Are you upset?" she asked.

"Oh, no. I mean, sort of. I just expected more from him. He's a friend of Monty's, and I don't like it when Monty hangs with guys who are a bad influence. You are who you hang with, ya know?" The lie was horrid.

"I guess so." She sighed. "Except I don't think that's true. It can't be considered cheating when your relationship isn't real. And when it comes to bad influences, look at you and Marcia; you are different as night and day, but you stick to your guns."

"I guess you're right." I shrugged and lifted my bags up, carrying everything like I was her help and she was a celebrity. She floated on her high all the way to my house.

When we got inside, Martin was walking out of the kitchen with a sandwich. He froze midbite, scowling. "Hey." He didn't look impressed. In fact, he was suspicious.

"Hey." Hennie gulped, losing some of her high. I suspected she wanted Martin to be impressed with her makeover, but it was abundantly clear he wasn't. She didn't realize that he was more than most men and not interested in her looks. "How are you feeling?"

"Fine. A little sleepy." He took another bite of sandwich and sat on the arm of the chair. "Grandma is driving me nuts." He gave me a look. "She was panicking because you weren't home yet and she had to leave to get some groceries. And she's been going on and on that tonight she has to be at the theater forty-five minutes before the movie starts, but she doesn't want me to be here without a babysitter."

"Yeah, I got the impression she's going to be weird for the next couple of weeks while this is ongoing."

"Awesome." He groaned and gave us both a nonchalant stare. "So, you still on for tonight?"

"Yeah, I'll leave here, catch me a DJ, and come back, and we'll upload the videos I got. Should be exciting."

"I don't think you should go to a club alone." He tilted his head, like he was Dad.

"I was thinking about that too. I can see if Marcia or one of the other girls wants to go. They love to club." I rolled my eyes. "Which means I'll have to disguise myself extra, make sure Marcia drinks a lot and I drink nothing, and ensure I don't get caught talking to Miguel. Which shouldn't be that hard if the club is packed."

"Just don't go by yourself. Be smart. And careful not to get caught." He nodded approvingly at me before asking Hennie, "You want a sandwich?"

"I'd love a sandwich." She smiled wide, and her face screamed, *Jordan who?* She followed him into the kitchen, and I left the garment bag and took my makeup upstairs to start the plastic surgery I would need to make myself into someone DJ Spark wouldn't recognize.

When I got into my room, I pressed my back against the door and tried taking deep breaths, but I couldn't. My ribs were killing me. It was like Jordan had stabbed me.

It was in that moment I had to own up to the fact that I liked him. A lot.

It was why I was so disappointed in him. I wanted him to be better than the average rich guy.

There was no denying I was attracted to Jordan or that I liked the fact that he called me Cinderella and asked my friend about me. He was taking chances to get to know me and showing up at parties I was at, hoping. And he apologized for being a douchebag when he wasn't even really that much of one. He was weak, which I didn't admire, but

I understood his reasons. In his world, the rules were different. And how hard would it be to walk from your own family? I couldn't imagine doing that with my own.

But deep down, none of that meant anything after today.

Jordan was a jerk. I even had proof.

I took the pin Hennie had given back on the train and uploaded the video to my phone, forcing myself to watch it.

It came on, shaking like Hennie was playing with the pin, likely to turn it on.

"Hi there." Right out of the gates Jordan oozed prowl vibes.

"Hi." Hennie sounded funny. *"Do you come here often?"*

His eyes widened, and he paused. *"I do."*

"I need a good drink recommendation. I'm celebrating." She sounded like she was smiling.

"What are you celebrating?"

"I just graduated college," she lied.

"Hey, same here." He lied too. I wasn't sure why, but I guessed that gave them something in common right off the bat.

"Why don't we share a drink?" He turned and did the facing-her thing. His smile was creepy looking, not the one he'd given me at all. I was grateful at least for that. This schmoozy side of him was icky.

"Okay. What are you having?"

"Let's get some champagne." He waved over the server. *"A bottle of your best champagne, please."* He turned back to Hennie. *"So, what did you major in?"*

"Finance."

"Interesting."

"Not so much." She laughed genuinely.

"What's your name?"

"Does it matter?" she asked, sounding like a badass ninja spy. She was better at this than I gave her credit for.

"I guess not."

"Your champagne, sir." Another man spoke.

The pop of the cork made Hennie jump and giggle. Jordan handed her a glass, and he smiled, lifting his own to "cheers" her. *"To the end."*

"To the end of school. And new beginnings," she said, reaching into the frame and clinking her glass against his. *"So, do you maybe want to continue this little celebration later?"* she asked, completely naturally. *"I have somewhere to go after this, but we could meet up in the evening."*

"Yes. I'd be into that. A couple of strangers celebrating their own successes. I have a hotel room my family keeps on hand for moments just like this. Here's the name and room number." He wrote on a piece of paper and slid it to her. *"You're very beautiful."*

"Thanks. So are you." She was getting flustered.

I ended the video there. Then I uploaded the video from my laptop onto the site. I emailed it back to Amy, praying to the gods that it never got back to her that I was behind this scam.

I felt dirty.

But I didn't even have time to pout.

I had date number two, and something told me Hennie wasn't going to be up to seducing a slimy party boy.

Chapter Twenty-Four

SHOTS!

Lacey

I did my makeup in a way that gave me extra-large almond eyes and a perfect set of huge pouty lips with a long and slender nose. I looked like an anime character, which was perfect for the DJ.

I'd left the house still feeling like shit, but as I got closer to the subway station where I was meeting Marcia, I started feeling better. I thought about going alone and getting the job done so I could curl up with a book in my bedroom, but I couldn't do it. It was safer to go with a friend. And Marcia was still amped from the night before, so she was an easy sell on a club night. It was summer after all. She would party every day if she could.

My outfit looked like a costume, but it made my mission feel real and clear.

Oddly enough, while I was riding, another email came in.

It was from a name I didn't recognize, but I would figure her guy out and test him, and by the end of the week, I'd have another thousand dollars saved up.

I felt vindicated in my head as I read the emails. The girls were desperate, needing their guys tested before serious relationships started.

And I was saving money so my brother could get the treatment he needed. And if he didn't need it, I would for sure. It wasn't like I wasn't earning the money through creative means.

It made me feel like I was providing a real service and wasn't just some crazy chick who would clearly do anything for a Klondike bar.

What I would or would not do for said bar was clearly laid out on the table. Prostitution, no. Bartender, hard pass.

Undercover man tester, hell yes.

And I felt like I was being smart about the rules.

Meeting in public places. Flirting innocently until I got the invite for more. Accepting payments through untraceable prepaid credit cards going to a PO box.

I hoped I was being smart, anyway.

Tonight would be the test. If Kami's boyfriend recognized me with all this makeup, then I wouldn't be able to approach any other acquaintances, unless Hennie wanted to be a partner.

When the train stopped, I jumped off and hurried up the stairs to where Darren was waiting with the car. I dove into the back, scaring the shit out of Marcia.

"Oh my God, who are you?"

"It's me, crazy pants." I beamed. If Marcia didn't recognize me, I was golden.

"Holy shit, your makeup and that wig!" she squealed once she realized who I was. "You look so perfect for a night of techno dance. Can you do me too?"

"Yeah, I brought my bag of tricks for just this moment." I sat across from her and opened the bag. "Are you ready to party?" I played it up like I was. I'd never told Marcia anything about why we were going clubbing, just that I was in the mood to.

Truthfully my excitement was a little dinged after the video of Jordan. But I just needed the night to get past it.

He was exactly the guy I'd feared he was.

"I am so ready." She handed me a car drink. "Moser made you a G and T for the road. He said you left last night in a huff before the club. That you and Jordan were fighting?" She narrowed her gaze. "Why did I not hear about this?"

"It's nothing. Honestly. He's a pig. He tried hitting on me again, and he's got a girlfriend. You know how I feel about this."

"He's not a pig. I heard they broke up anyway. For real this time! She claims to have caught him hitting on some girl, but we all know she was the one who had the side dish. Anyway, she dumped him."

"As she should," I scoffed.

"What?" She lifted an eyebrow.

I recovered quickly. "He hit on me and someone else, if her story checks out."

"Right, well, I guess it's official. I heard it from Brooke earlier, who said she was going to stalk Jordan and see if he wanted to hang out." She leaned in. "So if you like him the way I think you do, you need to snap him up before his family organizes another girlfriend for him."

"Marcia, if his family is picking his girlfriends and he's just sitting by letting this happen, I don't want him anyway. Brooke can have him. Just trust me, he's not the guy for me. He's gross. You remember his brother?"

"Yeah, but I was wrong. Monty said Jordan isn't like him. Stephen is nasty. And even he's better now that he's all settled and married. Jordan likes you, a lot. I could tell. And I could tell you like him too. That's why I invited him over. I hate that you're always the odd man out. I want you to find someone awesome. And if Monty says he's awesome, he is. So I'm going to give him another chance. And you should too."

"Your mom is showing." I rolled my eyes, earning a chuckle from Darren.

"Don't be a hater." She leaned in, rubbing her nose on my cheek. "Is it weird that I'm super attracted to you with this Sailor Moon look you have going on with that blonde wig?"

"No." I laughed and drank my gin. "I was thinking I looked silly hot too."

"You super look like her." She tried to selfie us, but I ducked out.

"No, dude. I look too weird." I was going to have to reconsider wearing my disguises around her so as not to risk being discovered.

"You look hot. Come on."

"Are we here?" I glanced out the window, changing the subject quickly.

"We are." Darren parked and got out to open our door.

"Thanks for being my wing woman tonight." I hugged her, seriously changing the subject. "Sorry I bailed last night; I felt pretty crappy after the whole Jordan thing. I just wanted to go out and dance tonight since I missed out."

"I'm glad you actually told me. I was wondering what the hell happened. And no one had a single clue where you went. Except Moser, of course. You know he keeps an eye on you."

"Let's just go dance and be crazy." I smiled wide, acting like this was a great idea and it was going to the best night of our lives. The dread in my stomach would be over the moment I did my job and got my proof. But there was no way I could do that until Miguel, a.k.a. DJ Dipshit, finished his set. Which meant I was going have to warm up my fun-and-flirty game for the next couple of hours.

And I did.

The music was hot, with amazing beats and breaks for the crowds to go wild over. We paused and began together, a sea of high and drunk people moving like waves with a grand master above us, using the music to make us move.

Even I had to admit that Kami's moron of a boyfriend was fantastic at what he did.

By the time he was done, Marcia was loving it. We'd found a group of people to mingle and dance with.

"I'll go get us a drink!" I shouted at Marcia, and walked to the bar, seeing Miguel shaking hands and talking to a group of guys next to it. I leaned against the bar, glancing over at him, making sure my ass popped out a bit. I played with my pin to get the recording started.

Miguel wasn't the only one who took the bait, so when a big guy standing by him slid up next to me and smiled, I shook my head and pointed at Miguel. He nodded, like of course I had my eyes set on the DJ—this was a normal occurrence. With a smug-ass saunter, Miguel made his way over to me, taking the place of the big guy and grinning.

"That was a hot set," I offered with an eyelash flutter.

"What are you drinking?"

"Shots," I lied.

"What kind of shot do you want?"

"Tequila."

"Two shots of Patrón," he shouted at the bartender.

Two shots lined up right in front of us. He licked his hand and then mine, making me want to slap him, but instead I let him sprinkle salt on it and hand me a juicy lime wedge.

"To new friends." He reached for the glasses and passed me mine, then lifted his.

I took it and clinked the glass, licking the salt, drinking the shot, and sucking the lime.

"I have a bottle of this back at my place. Any chance you wanna move the party over there?"

"Yeah." I smiled wide, but my stomach was killing me. "Is this a private party?"

"Depends on whether you're open to making more friends."

I pretended to giggle, but honestly I was about to ask him what the ever-loving fuck he was talking about. Was he asking if I was down for an orgy?

"Those guys there." He pointed, and I moved so the pin picked up the three big dudes standing next to the bar, leering at me like I was their next meal.

"Why not?" I laughed. "Lemme go tell my friends I'm leaving. Or maybe I can convince a couple of them to join the fun." I pushed off the bar and headed for the ladies' bathroom, completely ignoring my friend, who was dancing with our new group of strangers like they were her besties. I knew he'd be watching me. My stomach was aching, like the cramps were SOS signals screaming for me to run, to get out of there.

I shuddered when I thought of his hep-seedy mouth licking my hand and putting the salt there. And I'd licked it. I was gonna need a tetanus shot and a Twinrix. And maybe some mouthwash. I needed to remember to bring mouthwash next time if a full-on hazmat suit was out of the question for sexual innuendo.

I glanced at myself in the mirror, honestly not recognizing the girl looking back at me. What was I doing? Was this worth a thousand dollars?

I was actually scared of Miguel and his friends and what they were into. And I felt sick for Kami. How could her guy be so sleazy?

No, this was worth it.

It was worth saving her from this jerk. It was also worth my family's security. With that end goal firmly in mind, I remembered the whole point of this experiment and shook the slime off. I washed all the makeup off to the point that I looked a bit rough. My skin was blotchy from the hand soap and the paper towel, but I managed to get it all. I dragged the blonde wig off, letting my brown locks cascade down my back. I stuffed the wig in my oversized purse and pulled on the white blouse I'd brought, tugging it over the black tube dress and tying it up. I pulled off the earrings I was wearing and all the rings on my fingers.

Taking a second look at myself, I felt better. Not about leaving the bathroom and risking Miguel recognizing me—that still scared me—but about how I looked. I wasn't club hot or looking like I might be down for a night of fun. I was boring old me again. I did a bare minimum amount of powder, mascara, and lip gloss so I didn't look like I'd just scrubbed my face in a club bathroom, and closed the purse, heading out to the dance floor to find Marcia.

It was a sea of people I had to swim through to get to her, but when I did, I grabbed her arms and started dancing again, pretending I was drunk and fun and not possibly shitting my pants with fear or puking with disgust over my own desperation. This job was not suited for me. But it was another thousand dollars towards my tuition and it was done.

Miguel and his boys were drinking and toasting and laughing at the bar, not even looking for the girl he was confident would be coming back.

I turned away from him, certain I didn't look the same as before, and even if he suspected it was me, he wouldn't dare come talk to me. Especially not with Marcia right beside me.

Or Monty.

Wait.

Monty?

I narrowed my gaze as he met my confused look. He was smiling wide and dance walking to the music as he pushed his way through the crowd toward us.

With a certain someone hot on his heels.

Shit!

Chapter Twenty-Five

SNOW WHITE

Jordan

She wasn't happy to see me.

That might have been the understatement of the year.

But I wasn't happy to see her, either, if I was being honest.

My guys' night had been sabotaged.

Lacey's eyes narrowed and her lips pressed together as Marcia squealed and jumped on Monty and me, hugging us both.

"You came!" She kissed Monty. She attacked me next, kissing my cheek and whispering not so quietly, "You should totally tell Lacey she looks cool. Like Sailor Moon." She wasn't making much sense. Lacey didn't look cool. She looked annoyed and possibly uncomfortable and maybe even trashed, though Marcia seemed fine.

I hated that I made her feel that way, even if I also wasn't happy about the way the night had turned out. My grandpa had said the worst words possible to me, that he was "disappointed" in me. My father had left seven angry texts and five voice mails, all disowning me with a level of rage and hate I hadn't expected. I'd expected bad, but this was next level.

Even my mom had left multiple messages, asking me how I could do this to my family.

It hurt.

And instead of being home, hiding from the world, I was out.

Monty and Stephen had wanted to come here for the music, which wasn't bad, but the fact that Lacey happened to be here, too, made me think they had ulterior motives for choosing this place. Apparently no one cared that we were in friends-off mode and she hated me, as did everyone in my family except my brother. And no one cared that she had been a hurtful bitch to me either.

Hell, seeing her there, I didn't even care.

She was right. I had no self-respect.

Standing in the middle of the floor, Lacey started to look strange. She blinked slowly, swaying and shuddering. Her eyes widened and then became slits as if she was trying to focus. She turned to the right, looking at the bar, and then to the left toward the exit. Staggering, she pushed forward, past me and Monty like she didn't even know us.

People hit her with their dancing, making her stumble more.

She was drunk as hell and walking for the exit.

A guy wrapped an arm around her waist, trying to force her to dance with him. She tried to shove him off, but he didn't let go.

I sprang to life then, ignoring my brother and Monty and running for her.

"Hey." I shoved the guy. "That's my girl."

She spun around and was about to say something, possibly something to dispute me, but then she got this look of panic on her face. "Help me." She nodded and leaped for me, wrapping herself around my neck and clinging for life.

"Have her, she's fucking trashed, man!" The guy shrugged and turned back to dancing.

"I've got you." I slipped my arm under her and lifted her up onto me, holding her tightly and walking for the door. She pulled her bag up into her and clutched it, letting go of me and allowing me to carry her full weight. We got jostled and bumped and pushed until we made it out.

I exhaled in gasps as I made it to the side of the building and sat with her as she collapsed in my arms.

"I think he put something in my drink," she muttered.

"Fuck!" I pulled out my phone and texted for a ride. I sat her against the building while she passed out, leaving me holding her. If she was this out of it, maybe I should take her to a hospital.

She didn't look normal; her skin was blotchy with bits of makeup in her hairline. Her eyes were red and puffy like she'd been crying, and her lips were chapped.

She looked drunk, but maybe someone did put something in her drink.

I texted Marcia and Monty, but they didn't answer.

She was passed out in a way that scared me a little. There was no venom or fight. Just a drunk girl. Or drugged.

And that was the dilemma.

If she was drugged, did I take her to the hospital, or would that make me look like the guy who'd drugged her? Bad-publicity week had hit my family. I was out of leeway and possible-scandal hall passes.

Also, would she prefer not to look like someone who took drugs? Would Frederick rather I cared for her myself or dropped her off at his place? Or would she be pissed I brought her home for her boss, who was like a dad to her, to see her in this state? And what if she'd taken the drugs herself? Then what?

I wished she were awake to answer these questions.

When my car arrived and Jenson, our driver, got the door, I lifted her dead weight carefully and held her in my arms for the entirety of the ride. I didn't want her to feel like she was alone, and I needed to make sure she was still breathing. "She's been drugged, I think," I said to him when I saw him staring at me in the rearview mirror. "Not by me."

I almost asked him what I should do. I'd never been around some-one who'd had a drug slipped in her drink, if that was what had even happened. Who would have done such a thing?

That was a dumb question. I knew at least a handful of girls who'd said they'd been drugged at a bar. It happened. She just didn't seem like the type who let someone buy her a drink.

I couldn't go home tonight anyway. Not after my mom called and said Dad was livid. Grandpa Jack's place was out of the question. He had a standing date of sexy Saturdays, and no one needed to see that. So I took her to the only place I knew we would be fine to ride this out, and where we could possibly get help if we needed it. "Take us to the Four Seasons, please."

"Of course, sir." Jenson gave me an uncomfortable stare.

From the car I dialed a number I'd never imagined I would need to. "Four Seasons, Heinrich speaking."

"Heinrich, this is Jordan Somersby. I have a situation." I closed my eyes, knowing just the sort of pervert I looked like. "I have a friend who drank too much or took something at the bar, and I'm bringing her there to have a family doctor meet us and check her out. I'm asking you to keep this under the radar, if you know what I'm saying."

"You're bringing a dead-drunk girl here?" He sounded a little put off but careful, like he didn't want to upset me.

"She's Frederick La Croix's favorite daughter. She's taken some-thing, I don't know what. I can't very well take her to the hospital and risk everyone calling her a junkie. So yes, I'm bringing her there and having a doctor meet us," I snapped. "Can you imagine the scandal if I brought her to the hospital?"

"Of course not. You're very welcome here, sir." He sounded uncon-vinced, but he wasn't going to argue. My family and the La Croixes were not to be trifled with.

I hung up and hoped that was enough to stay the horrid thoughts he was going to have.

My reputation was having a rough week.

I had been dating a show horse for my dad, but she'd dumped me for being a fake cheater. Last night's public arguments with this girl had to have been seen by someone who recognized me, and now I was bringing her passed-out ass to a hotel.

No wonder Lacey thought so little of me and everyone else lumped me in with Stephen. I wasn't doing myself any favors.

By the time we'd parked and I'd carried her out of the car, the look on Heinrich's face, the very one he was struggling to hide, told me everything I needed to know. He definitely thought I was a pervert, hauling a dead-drunk would-be victim over my shoulder.

Fortunately the halls of the hotel were silent.

Heinrich carried Lacey's purse and followed questioningly behind me as I carried her.

"I hope your friend feels better," he managed to choke out as he closed the doors to the suite and left us alone.

"Me too," I sighed as I laid her on the bed. I walked around to the other side and pulled back the covers. I dialed a number I hadn't ever expected to need, waiting for a response.

"Hello?" the groggy person answered.

"Hey, Fitz. It's Jordan Somersby. Can you come over? I have a serious situation. Bring everything." I hated asking this at midnight, but I didn't see any other choice. Lacey couldn't go to the hospital, so I would bring the hospital to her.

"Yup. Where are you?" He didn't even hesitate. I could hear him getting up out of bed. Being a family physician for the rich and famous had to be rough.

"Four Seasons. I'll tell them to expect you at the front desk."

"Roger that. See you in fifteen." He hung up, and I dialed downstairs.

"A man named Doctor Fitzgerald Hawthorne is going to come to the front desk. Send him up straight away, please." I hung up and stared at the sleeping beauty. She'd changed princesses on me.

She was Cinderella before, and now she was Snow White, needing to be awakened. Only it wasn't a kiss that would wake her. It would be meds and fluids.

She was sweating profusely, so I removed her blouse and flung it on the floor. The tube dress was also soaked in perspiration, but it was obvious she had nothing else on underneath.

Ever the gentleman, I dragged off my sweater and T-shirt, pulling the tee over her head and arms as I slid the dress down her body, ensuring no part of her was revealed.

I nearly strained an eyeball to keep my gaze on her face as I lifted her again, noting my arms started to get tired. She didn't weigh a lot, maybe 130 pounds, but she was heavy passed out. I laid her back down on the sheets, pulled off her shoes, and wiped her face and hair delicately. I cleaned the lip gloss and mascara and cold sweat off as best as I could. Then I tugged the covers up to her shoulders.

After pulling on my thin sweater again, I started texting Monty, deleting and rewriting my text multiple times until I decided to leave it. Having people believe we hooked up was probably better than everyone worrying and rushing over here. I wanted to give her a chance to explain what the hell happened and if she wanted anyone to know about the situation.

I sauntered into the bathroom and rinsed a facecloth to wipe her down again.

My reflection almost made me laugh.

Thin sweater with no T-shirt underneath, and her lip gloss on my neck from where I'd been carrying her. Her sweat or drool on my pants from her head lying on my leg, along with the makeup from her hairline.

Excellent first night of freedom.

It might have gone down as my worst night ever.

My father hated me.

My mother was disappointed.

Grandpa Jack was also disappointed and worried about the billion-dollar deal.

My brother was in a club unsupervised.

And here I was, taking care of a girl who hated me.

A girl I wasn't sure how I felt about.

A girl who may or may not have taken drugs. Not really my type.

I wanted to dislike her, but every ounce of my being was lost in her. Even unconscious druggie her.

Deciding this was not the time to analyze how she got in this position, I took my post for the night and sat in the armchair to watch her sleep, focusing on the way the sheet that was draped over her body lifted and lowered as I waited for Fitz.

He was just slightly over twenty minutes to get there and still in his pajamas, which I admired. Not only did he not give a damn about what he was wearing, but he clearly intended to go back to bed after this ordeal, a delight I wouldn't be enjoying anytime soon. Not so long as Lacey was still Snow White in her comatose state.

"Fitz." I spoke softly as he entered. Heinrich couldn't seem to shake his dubious stare and closed the door, no doubt seeing Lacey's dress on the floor.

"She's either done drugs or been drugged. I got to the club just as it was hitting her. Took her down fast. The only thing she said was 'He put something in my drink,' and then she was out like a light. I carried her out and brought her here, and she's been like this for a bit."

"Jesus. Who is she?"

"Marcia La Croix's best friend, Lacey Winters. Frederick thinks of her as a daughter. His favorite daughter."

"Then I guess we better make sure she gets the best treatment possible." He gave me a weird look, clearly wary of the whole situation.

Fitz was a resident at NewYork-Presbyterian. He was one of Stephen's friends from high school. Sometimes, if Stephen drank too much, he got an instant feel-good IV from Fitz.

Which was what Fitz was currently hooking up to Lacey.

"If it's GHB, which I will sample her blood and check for, it needs to run its course. The IV fluids will help. Did you see what she drank?"

"No, I showed up, and she started to go downhill immediately. I don't know who drugged her or if she took it on her own. We were in Brooklyn at a club, and it was packed." I didn't say that if I'd known who did this to her, they would have already been dead. Drugging girls was disgusting, but I didn't know the truth of it all. Not yet. I would find out, though.

"She might have taken it on her own. It's a nice high if you don't take too much, or so I've heard." He said it so nonchalantly.

"She doesn't seem the sort to take drugs." I said it like I knew that. But how could I? Maybe she did. I almost chuckled when I mentally shook my head. She was much too uptight to be a rec drug user.

"This is not what I thought I was coming over for. I thought it was a quick rehydrate-Stephen mission." He yawned and stretched. "You're lucky I'm on two days off."

"I owe you big-time."

"Yes, yes you do." He said it in a low tone, checking her vitals and watching the IV.

After a moment, he took a sample of her blood. "If she isn't awake in two hours, she goes to the hospital." He glanced back at me.

"Hospital?"

"Yeah. You should have probably taken her there in the first place." He capped the blood sample off and placed it in his bag. "Bringing her here was nuts."

"I panicked. I didn't know what else to do. I mean, personally I wouldn't want the publicity of a drug issue if she took this on her own. I figured Frederick wouldn't either. He wouldn't want the scandal."

We stared, uncomfortable and unsure of what would come next. But nothing came next.

She slept for two hours.

Fitz napped while I stared, watching the rate at which the blankets lifted and lowered until finally she stirred.

She moaned a little and rolled on her back, and then, like a dead person rising from her coffin, she gasped and shot up, eyes wide and mouth open.

I jumped up, scaring her and Fitz.

"What the fuck?" She looked around the room, sweat dripping down her face. "What happened? Where're my clothes?"

"I don't know—I mean I don't know what happened to you." I was scared to get too close, and yet I wanted to hug her and maybe cry with relief a little bit.

"Where am I?" She shivered and clutched the blanket.

"The Four Seasons."

"What'd you do to me?" She glared at me, but her lower lip trembled.

"What? Nothing." What the fuck?

"Who's he?" She nodded at Fitz, who was gasping for breath as well and likely also getting his bearings.

"A doctor." I sat on the end of the bed near her feet and fought the urge to clutch my rapidly beating heart.

"I'm Fitz. You either took drugs yourself or were drugged at a bar. Jordan saved you. Brought you here, and I cared for you. That's all we know." His droll way of speaking didn't soothe her.

"Why didn't you take me to a hospital?" Her tone was accusing.

"I wasn't sure Mr. La Croix wanted that kind of scandal. In case you took the drugs yourself."

"Jesus." She looked at the IV, the bed, and me and Fitz. "Who drugged me?"

"We were hoping you could tell us that, actually," Fitz muttered, checking her vitals.

"Oh my God." She started to cry, covering her face.

"What?" I slid up the bed, pulling her into my arms. "What do you remember?"

"Miguel," she sobbed, shaking.

"Who's he?" I stroked her head and let her cry on me.

"I don't know what happened," she said, still shaking.

Fitz muttered as he took her arm and pulled the IV out gently. "Looks like you'll live. I'll give you a call when the blood sample is processed." He grabbed everything that belonged to him and walked to the door. "I'm going back to bed. I'll text tomorrow."

"Lacey." I continued to stroke her head. "Who's Miguel?" I asked again after a moment, plotting the eight hundred ways I would make this guy die before I even knew his face.

"I don't know, I can't be sure. I don't remember anything." She sniffled, not making much sense.

"You're safe now, and I promise you, nothing happened to you. I watched the drug hit you. You were glaring at me—you know, that normal hateful face you put on every time I'm around—and then you just went downhill. I carried you out of the bar right away. No one else knows what happened, and this can stay between you and me. I took care of you," I reassured her. I'd known girls who'd had something similar happen to them, and the biggest worry they'd had was what went down in the hours they lost.

I couldn't imagine how that felt.

I'd never lost time before.

But I did know that seeing Lacey this way was a flashing neon sign of how I felt for her. The anxiety and stress and worry and care were all symptoms of my feelings. She might have been the ice queen, but she was slowly melting my heart.

209

Chapter Twenty-Six

Not Enough Soap in the World

Lacey

His arms around me didn't bother me; I'd pulled him to me in the first place. And in the moment, I couldn't think of a single person I would rather have hold me. Something about him screamed safety. I didn't know what it was, but he made me feel like I would be fine, and everything would get taken care of, and nothing was a worry. I realized that in spite of his epic failure of a performance through the Test Dummy, I trusted him.

The night was a blur.

I hoped I got the recording of Miguel. That would tell me what the hell happened.

Jordan slept soundly, holding me tighter than anyone ever had. I turned, staring at him, still wearing a sweater and his boxers and sleeping over the covers with no blankets.

He might have been a lot of things, but he wasn't a scumbag. He wouldn't drug a girl or leave her in a sticky situation. Even me, the girl who had berated him savagely in front of other people. The girl who had ruined his fake relationship. I wondered whether, if he knew that, he would still have taken care of me.

Slipping from the bed, I grabbed my purse and dress from the floor and tiptoed into the bathroom. I closed the door and pulled the pin off my dress, attaching it with the cord to my cell phone, ignoring the million texts from Marcia. It was five a.m.; she wouldn't want to be disturbed now.

I loaded the video into the phone and pressed "Play," lowering the volume so I could just hear it.

The image shook, like I was fidgeting with the camera as Miguel sauntered up to me.

"That was a hot set," I said. My voice sounded funny on the recording. The music in the background was loud, but I could still hear us. Barely.

"What are you drinking?" he asked.

"Shots."

"What kind of shot do you want?"

"Tequila."

"Two shots of Patrón," he shouted as he leaned over the bar.

My stomach hurt as I watched the part where he pulled a small bottle from his sleeve; it was tiny, like an eye drops bottle. As he reached forward to grab the shots, he squeezed liquid into one of the drinks. He handed me that one as the bottle slipped back up into his sleeve. He was like a magician with that skill.

"To new friends." He lifted the glass; the look in his eyes was evil, pure evil.

I shuddered as I contemplated how many girls he'd done that to. Him and his friends.

Jesus.

I stared at my phone, a bit lost on what to do. Did I call the police? Did I send it to Kami?

What the hell was my plan?

My hands were shaking and my entire body ached, but I believed at the very least Kami needed to see what the hell was going on behind her back. What kind of person she was dating.

Not in a million years would I have imagined he would be like that. He didn't even need to be. He was young, gorgeous, rich, connected, a DJ, and dating one of the most beautiful girls on the East Coast, who was even richer and more connected.

But for him, rape was clearly not about getting laid.

I contemplated how wrong that could have gone.

How bad it might have been.

Where it would have led if not for the guy in the other room.

He, Jordan fucking Somersby, had saved me.

He'd paid attention, and he'd rushed me from the club to a hotel, where he'd had a doctor care for me. He'd spared my reputation and my virtue, so he'd saved me in more ways than one.

I didn't know how to process that. He saved my life the same day I ruined his fake relationship, and possibly his relationship with his asshat father.

Neither thing he would likely thank me for.

That was no good.

How could I continue to be cruel to him or treat him badly?

I couldn't, not without telling him I was the Test Dummy and I knew what he'd done. Which I couldn't do either.

It was a conundrum.

Deciding to be nice to him and give him the one thing I'd *never* imagined I would, a second chance, I stripped off the T-shirt I was wearing, threw it in the garbage, and pulled off my underwear, also wanting to burn those. Everything was wet and soaked in sweat.

I looked long and hard at myself in the mirror, really taking stock in the moment, before I turned and climbed into the shower, desperate to smell like L'Occitane and not Miguel's saliva.

He Loves You Not

My shower lasted longer than any shower I'd ever taken before. I sat on the bench as the hot water rained down on me, washing me clean of every possibility I forced myself to contemplate.

But no matter how much I wanted to chicken out, I told myself that this close call would save lives. If I sent it to Kami, she would see that video, lose her mind, and out him for the pervert he was, and girls everywhere would know what he'd done. I would leak it to TMZ if I had to. I would definitely leak it to the police, anonymously.

There was no way he was ever going to get away with that again.

I got out of the shower and dried off, then forwarded the video to Hennie, needing at least one person to know what had happened.

I sent a text saying I was okay. It was six a.m., but she texted back with multiple raging and shocked emojis before my phone rang.

"What the fuck?" she gasped.

"I know," I whispered.

"Why are you whispering? Does he have you hostage?"

"No. I avoided the rape train by getting rescued by none other than Jordan."

"Jordan!" she squealed. "Not our Jordan!"

"The very one." I closed my eyes.

"The one we legit just screwed over and made a fool of for the benefit of his hateful girlfriend?"

"Yeah, that one," I whispered harshly.

"Oh my God!" She didn't sound sleepy at all. "Why does God hate you?"

"I don't know," I whimpered. "But Jordan rescued me, brought me to the Four Seasons, and got me a doctor, and the doc took a sample of my blood to test for the drugs Miguel used."

"Did you send Kami the video?" She gulped. I heard it over the phone.

"I want to. She needs to know he's a rapey piece of shit."

"Don't say *rapey*. It makes rape cutesy. He's a rapist. And his friends are, too, and this needs to get leaked. Even if Kami says she doesn't want anyone to see the video, you *need* to leak it. You have to."

"Hennie, she isn't going to say she wants this covered up. Trust me. She's going to be so upset, but she'll want the world to see that shit."

"Oh, Lacey. She's your friend, so you're blind. But those girls won't want anyone to see their dirty laundry. They'll protect him like little lemmings. You need to make sure he isn't surrounded by a fortress."

"I mean, if she wants to protect him, I'll totally out him myself. I have no intention of letting this go. He drugged me so that he could rape me. I know what happened. And I have video proof of it. Fuck him. And her, if that honestly is how she responds. But I can't see it. I really can't."

"Good. You need to hand this over to the cops. This is serious. I don't think it should be protected."

"I agree." I shivered.

"Okay, but wait, you're at the Four Seasons in a hotel room with Jordan right now?"

"Yeah, he's sleeping." I lowered my voice again, realizing I was nearly shouting.

"Oh, wow. That is a crazy twenty-four hours. What are you going to do? I mean, you can't be mean to him. He rescued you."

"I know," I hissed. "I'll be nice to him. Or at least nicer than I've been up to this point."

"You better. You just set him up and screwed him over. So, I'm in your bed right now." She yawned, losing the adrenaline she was obviously rocking before.

"What?"

"Yeah, Martin asked if I wanted to hang, since you were going out to catch a creep and all. And your grandma was psychotic about him being alone. So I came over, and we watched movies 'til late. Grandma might send you some angry texts; we tried to cover for you, but she was

214

all kinds of sassy about you going out again. Grandma's a real hater of fun."

"Oh my God. I got drugged and didn't come home. Jesus. I'm a hot mess. I'm so sorry. Thanks for going over."

"No, it was great. We marathoned *The Hobbit*. I had fun. Anyway, I wanted to make sure you knew the status of Grandma's rage. I'm gonna go make coffee. I'll text you later."

"Okay. Thanks again. Bye." I hung up and stared at the door, wondering what the heck I was going to say to Jordan. *Thanks for saving my life? Thanks for being a cheater but not a pervert? Sorry I screwed you over; wish I'd trusted Monty when he claimed you were really a nice guy even though Marcia and I assumed a lot of bad shit about you?*

Cringing, I pulled on a robe and tied it tight before I opened the door and peeked into the room. He was still passed out, so I walked to the closet and got an extra blanket. I covered him with it, trying not to stare at his handsome face as he slept. It was creepy to watch someone sleep, and yet, I found myself wanting to. I spent several minutes this way, being weird, before I climbed into the bed to lie down again.

My head hurt.

My feet hurt.

My throat burned like I'd had heartburn while I was sleeping.

My stomach ached.

And for some strange reason, my right eye wouldn't stop watering.

When my head hit the pillow, my mind started working.

It ran over scenes from the pin and the club and the way I awoke.

It played with dangerous ideas like what if.

What if Jordan and the doctor weren't just taking care of me, what if they also—no. I wouldn't entertain that one.

I owed him a debt of gratitude, regardless of how I felt about the way he lived his life. As a human, he'd been pegged correctly by Monty and Marcia: Jordan was a nice man with a good heart. He was kind.

And he and Monty being friends made sense. It didn't make Monty less; it made them equals. Almost. Close to.

The pillow, the soft bed, and the sound of the cute guy who'd saved me and called me Cinderella snoring softly next to me lulled me, and eventually I lost the battle with my mind and passed out again.

This time I didn't worry about how I would wake up.

Chapter Twenty-Seven

THE MOST BEAUTIFUL GIRL IN THE WORLD

Jordan

She slept, and again I watched.

This time I didn't watch the way her chest rose and fell or worry she might die. I still worried, but it was lessened, remarkably.

I worried more about the fact that she was here, and for whatever reason, she might still hate me—well, not *whatever*, but now that her reason was nonexistent, I hoped maybe we could talk and I could explain. I could even tell her the lengths I went to, humiliating myself by pretending to hit on some random girl at a bar so that I could be free for her.

I mentally took a deep breath, realizing I was rambling in my mind.

Lacey Winters was in my bed, and there wasn't a chance I was going to screw this up.

I jumped up, ordered room service quietly from the sitting room, and showered as fast as humanly possible so she didn't wake and leave while I was in there.

While I pulled on the other hotel robe, I ordered us both new clothes and a long jacket for leaving the hotel.

I had my driver on standby to pick us up the moment the clothes arrived.

And then as the food came, I started making noises, like I had just awoken and this food was a normal hotel occurrence. I worried she might think I frequented the hotel a lot and get nervous, but her comfort was more important.

She stirred as I paid the attendant and closed the door as loudly as it would allow.

"Oh, man, I passed out." She yawned and stretched, shifting and finally sitting up. "What time is it?"

"Ten. I ordered us some breakfast. Fitz said you should try to eat and rest."

"Fitz?" She scowled.

"The doctor who was here."

"Oh, right." She tapped her finger against her lip. A storm was brewing in her eyes, but she smiled and got off the bed, fixing her robe and ensuring not even an inch of skin showed. "I want to thank you, Jordan. What you did, it was amazing, and I don't know how to ever repay you for that." She was sincere, not mean or judgmental or cruel or harsh for once.

It threw me for a loop. "You're welcome." I said it as if it was nothing, which it was. Technically. "Any man who considers himself a gentleman would have done the same thing."

"That's not true." She sat at the small table in the window.

"Coffee?" I lifted the large pot.

"Please. With cream."

I made her a coffee, an act I'd never done in my life. I'd made my own but never for another person. Except my mother. On Mother's Day.

I handed her the coffee and slid the breakfast plate in front of her.

She lifted the cup to her nose and breathed in, sighing as she took her first sip. "I can't believe last night." She sounded upset, which made sense. Someone had tried to do the worst thing possible to her.

"I need to know who." I leaned in, desperate for the answer. I had plans, not that I would tell her that.

"I don't know."

"You said a name this morning. Miguel. What did that mean?"

"Nothing." She was lying. "I don't know. I can't remember now." She was a bad liar. Why would she protect someone for this?

"I want to make sure this never happens again. He has to be held accountable."

"If I remember anything I'll tell you. I barely recall the doctor being here."

"He's a friend. I promise you, you were safe from the moment that drug hit you until this moment now."

"I'm not safe now?" She lifted an eyebrow, cracking a playful grin.

"Well—" I contemplated many jokes and innuendoes but decided against them. She likely wasn't in the mood to flirt, not after what happened. "I can't guarantee the food won't kill you." It was a bad recovery, but she made me nervous. I desperately didn't want to screw this up.

"Thank you for this, as well." She lifted her coffee and sipped.

And we were back to the awkward silence.

"So, I wanted to tell you that you were right. And I want to apologize. I have ended my relationship with Amy; it's over. You'd be proud I ruined our fathers' friendship and destroyed any chances mine would ever forgive me for this insubordination. He might never speak to me again, actually. My grandpa told me he will see me on Monday to discuss what happened, so there's a chance that he might move past this, and he's the one who matters. And Amy is free to be with her drummer. And I am—" I almost said *free to flirt with her* but paused. "Free from whoring myself out for the sake of my family anymore."

Her eyes flared, but her lips lifted into a smile. She didn't say a word. In fact, the awkward silence multiplied into something monstrous—tension.

"So I will never be that douchebag again who hits on girls while his parents are arranging his marriage." I lowered my gaze, conflicted on how this wasn't a positive thing. She'd called my integrity and honor into question. I wasn't defending myself. I'd told her she was right.

"I'm happy for you," she said after a minute, still clutching the small mug. "I should probably get going, though. I have to call everyone and let them know I'm safe." She paused in her new line of lying. "What are we telling everyone, by the way?"

"What do you want to say?" I was not giving up, but considering her situation, this was a tough dance to perform.

"I guess that we hooked up. Marcia will have tracked my phone here. She had to have seen us leave together if you were carrying me. No one saw me drunk, so I can't say that I was sick. What else is there?"

"Of course. If that's what you want to say, then it will be the story. I think you should reconsider telling me who this asshole is who drugged you, though. I'd like to deal with that."

"Thank you." Her eyebrows knit together, and her eyes softened. "You don't know what that means to me." She put the coffee down and got up, glancing at her robe. "I guess I need clothes."

"They'll be arriving momentarily. I ordered you something to throw on and a long jacket so you'd be comfortable." I got up too.

"Oh, that was nice of you," she whispered, again conflicted about something.

"Lacey." I stepped closer, taking my chance that the conflict was good and not her coming up with more reasons to hate me. "What I did the first time I met you was inexcusable. And the second time as well." I stepped closer, though not too close so as not to scare her. "I never thought about you the way you think I did. You would never be a side chick or a fling or someone I could even consider seeing only part of the time."

"Jordan—"

"Please let me finish." I tried to be firm. "The moment I saw you, I thought you were the most beautiful girl in the world. But then you challenged me and scolded me and set boundaries for not only yourself but me too. You demanded I shrug aside the person my parents had forced on me, and also respect you and myself. What I didn't realize was that I was disrespecting so many people with those simple actions. I hate that I disrespected you. And that you think I disrespected myself. I hate that you think so little of me." I took that final step, daring to lift a hand to her soft cheek and cup her face. "And I wouldn't dare ask for forgiveness, but I would ask for a chance. Please, give me a chance to prove to you who I am and how much I respect you."

Her eyes watered, and she swallowed a lump in her throat as she thought for far too long before she nodded. "Fine. I will give you one chance. You gave me a second chance at life, so I suppose that will make us even."

"Thank you." I clung to her, wanting so badly to kiss her, but I didn't. I held off, proving I was a man of my word.

I was.

Normally.

A knock at the door saved me.

"That must be the clothes." I slid my hand down her face, memorizing every piece of it, and walked to the door.

Marcia La Croix stood with her head tilted to the side and a smug look on her face.

"Hi." She grinned, moving her eyes across the room to Lacey. "You didn't answer my texts, so I had to make sure you weren't being made into a skin suit."

Lacey walked to me and slid her hand into mine, making my entire body go numb and then burst to life. "Sorry, I was busy. I should have called."

"I'll forgive you. Monty's downstairs. Let's brunch here, and you can tell us all about it." She winked.

"Fine." Lacey laughed like the horrors of the prior night had never happened. "Be down in a minute."

"Two minutes. Or I send the marines in to pry you two from this room." She shook her head and turned away, sauntering off.

As the door closed I stared down at the worried eyes searching mine.

"I'll call about those clothes again," I offered.

"I am so sorry for making you do this."

"You're not making me do anything." I smiled and went for my phone.

I contemplated thanking God as I dialed, but I decided I'd better wait for something bigger to thank him for.

Chapter Twenty-Eight
GET IN HER PANTS

Lacey

I stared at my phone for two minutes, then tried not to think as I sent the video to Kami from the Test Dummy email. I took a deep breath and told myself it was the right choice.

"The dress is a perfect fit. We need to hurry." I came out of the bathroom looking good enough, but not amazing. The clothes Jordan had surprisingly ordered me were not my new favorites, but they were better than my sweat-drenched frock from the night before. And considering I'd arrived at the hotel being carried, I was doing far better on the way out.

"My pants are too tight." He tried lunging, but the butt was fitted like skinny jeans.

"Oh, my." I started to laugh, lifting a hand to my mouth. "Yeah, those are tight." I grabbed at his sweater and pulled it down a bit, wincing. "No time to wait for different pants."

"This is ridiculous. I ordered the right size, I checked. They should fit me." He sounded desperate and looked adorable, and I was still struggling with it all.

He was so hot and sweet, and yet here I was in the hotel he'd said he was going to bring Hennie to when she'd played the role of anonymous seductress.

It was confusing.

"You can see your religion in those pants." I tried not to stare at the bulging crotch area. "But, you do look nice. They fit you well." I couldn't keep a straight face to save my life or his dignity.

"Monty's going to slaughter me." He sighed and offered an arm. "I guess my reputation hasn't got much left anyway."

Wondering if he meant since Amy dumped him, I held my breath for a moment before I took it, still hesitant in my movements around him. He had me shaken, I had to give him that. I was certain when I'd emailed Amy that my opinion of him wouldn't ever change, but everything after that moment screamed that I didn't dare judge him on his actions regarding the fake relationship. And I owed him at least the chance he'd asked for.

I wouldn't be blind going in, though; I would watch carefully, looking for clues as to who was his genuine self.

We walked to the elevator, both silent. Our awkward silence was weird. Tense.

When we got into the elevator, he glanced down at me, staring at my lips.

"They're chapped. I know." I rubbed my mouth with my free hand. "Is it really noticeable?" I didn't have moisturizer in my purse, the one thing I was missing.

"No." His eyes narrowed with humor. "I'm not staring at your lips because they're chapped, Lacey." He chuckled, still staring. My stomach dropped, and I stole my gaze back from his, glancing at the metal door making attempts to reveal our reflections. I didn't want him to see the blush on my cheeks.

He wanted to kiss me?

The door opened, saving us from another awkward moment. He led me across the foyer to the restaurant, waving when he saw Monty.

I smiled, trying really hard to be cool.

We were lying about hooking up so no one would know I was drugged, because if they did, they'd know I was the girl in the video. Thankfully no one but Hennie would ever know I was behind the Test Dummy. My face was completely hidden. Since that video was going to get released no matter what, there was a chance Jordan would put two and two together, but I could explain it away, saying I must have been standing near that girl and Miguel. Or maybe he drugged several of us.

Regardless of the outcome for me, there was also no way I could let Miguel get away with this scary shit.

Even risking my own outing, I knew I needed to bring his dirty deeds to light.

The lies and betrayal and creepiness of the night before made me question my ability to keep the Test Dummy going.

"There they are." Marcia grinned wide, her eyes full of mischief and *I told you so*. "How were the sheets? I always find them to be a bit stiff here." She cackled like an evil witch. In my head I was in high school again and dating France, and she was forcing me to disclose details I wouldn't normally.

"Anyway." Monty lifted the menu as Jordan got my chair for me and pushed it in after I sat. "It was a bit disappointing you left so early."

"You mean disappointing I left you with Stephen." Jordan chuckled and moved toward his seat.

"What are you wearing?" Monty's eyes stopped right on the bulge in Jordan's pants. It was obscene. "Are those her pants? You do know when guys say they're going to get into a girl's pants, they don't mean literally."

Jordan sighed and sat, covering himself with the cloth napkin before the server could.

"We ruined our clothes last night. I spilled drinks all over them." I bit my lip and pretended it was sexy. I hadn't asked him why he didn't want to wear his same clothes or where they'd gone. But he was adamant in wearing these.

"Wow, someone got a little crazy." Marcia snickered.

"You have no idea," Jordan muttered, humiliated in the tight pants and likely by the fact that we'd been caught up in my scandal. It was my first one. In proper society anyway.

Never before had I been the one who made ripples or waves. Even breaking things off with France was expected. Everyone knew he was a piece of shit and just didn't tell me. So, when I did figure it out and called it quits, everyone sort of shrugged and went on about their day.

But this was something else.

I'd ended up at a hotel with one of the guys every girl dreamed about.

And as much as it bothered me that I was the one in the spotlight, I was grateful that the real reason I was here stayed buried.

As we sat and laughed about Jordan's tight pants and he blushed and acted the perfect gentleman, neither revealing anything nor bringing me into this any more than he had to, I didn't mind being his public one-night stand.

"I'm gonna go to the bathroom." I stood up after we ordered.

"I'll come with." Marcia jumped at the chance to get dirt. And I never kept anything from her.

How the hell did I do this without giving her dirt?

She gripped my arm and leaned in as we strolled to the bathroom. "I want details, you scandalous ho. I cannot believe you didn't tell me where you were going or with who."

"Whom," I corrected.

"Whatever. Spill." She sounded nuts, and when I caught a glimpse of her eyes in the mirror of the bathroom, I could see she was. She gave me a look. "You have left with him two nights in a row. What is going on?"

"What do you remember?" I asked as I leaned against the counter, trying to ignore the bathroom attendant as well as she did.

"All I know is one minute you looked all cute as Sailor Moon with your long blonde wig and black tube dress and red heels. I was dancing, we were having fun. Then I saw Monty and you were there, but you looked normal. And Stephen came up and hugged me, and you were gone. And Stephen started laughing, saying he saw Jordan just sweep you up in his arms and carry you out."

"Yeah." I nodded. "That's about right."

"Why'd you change your look, or did I just imagine that? I felt weird this morning."

"The wig scratched my eyeball. I took it off, and my eye was running." I pointed to the reddish one. "So I washed my face, trying to flush my eye. And when I came out of the bathroom, Jordan was there and he wanted to talk, and we started making out." I conveniently skipped the rest.

"I can't believe he carried you from the club. That is so hot. Like a caveman carrying you off." She swooned, and I forced myself to go along with it.

"So hot."

"How was it?" She cocked an eyebrow, staring into my eyes like a snake charmer.

"He's strong. I felt safe."

"Not him carrying you." She whacked me on the arm. "The other part. In the hotel."

"Nice." I tried to lie, but it was awful. My poker face was pathetic.

"Nice?" She narrowed her gaze, ready to pry the truth from me if she had to. "Why can't you kiss and tell like normal girls?"

"Because I'm not normal. We have this conversation too much." I sighed, relieved she was possibly going to let this go. Not all the way let it go, but enough that maybe I could avoid it for a little while.

"If that bulge in his pants was a sign of how things went, I'd say more than nice." She winked at me in the mirror as she fluffed her curls a little.

Apparently not letting it go.

Our phones vibrated and pinged at the same time.

She met my gaze in the mirror again, this time not making cute smooch faces at me. A group message meant business; we'd all made each other swear that only important things and amazing gossip—or sales in my case—were ever allowed to be discussed via group chats.

My heart sank as I lifted my phone up, resting it in my hand with my PopSocket, and I winced. It was from Carmen; Kami was freaking out, and we all needed to come over ASAP.

"Oh, shit." Marcia gave me a look. "You think they broke up?"

"No." I shook my head. "This sounds worse." I said exactly what I would have said. Kami would have been sad over breaking up but not "send everyone to Carmen's house ASAP" sad. This was something bad all right. And I was going to have to work on my crappy poker face so when Kami told us, or Carmen relayed the message, I was as surprised as the rest of them. I wished for a second I'd been able to tell Marcia about the Test Dummy, but I was glad I hadn't. Her version of keeping secrets involved her eight closest friends. And this wasn't the moment I would have wanted to be outed.

"We better go." She turned and left the bathroom, texting Darren as we hurried to the table.

"We have to go. Something's up with Kami." She leaned in and kissed Monty on the cheek. Jordan stood, reaching for my hand in an awkward way. I squeezed his fingers as he stepped closer and towered over me, making me shiver with warmth. He lowered his face, brushing his lips against my cheek.

"Sorry," I whispered. "It sounds bad."

"No need to apologize." He sighed. "Can I text you later?" he asked softly, maybe so Monty and Marcia wouldn't hear.

"Yeah." I glanced back at Monty. "Text him my number, please."

"Sure." Monty gave us a conspiratorial grin.

"We gotta go." Marcia grabbed my hand and dragged me from the restaurant and from Jordan.

I couldn't think about leaving him right now. Especially considering where I was going.

Chapter Twenty-Nine
How Can This Get Worse?

Lacey

Carmen paced as we sat in the snooker room, me, Marcia, and Jo. Kami wasn't here. She was at home, not wanting to see anyone.

"Last night Miguel had a show in Brooklyn," she started to explain.

"Yeah, we were there." Marcia just outed us both. I'd almost hoped she would have forgotten where we'd been. She leaned forward. "Is he okay?"

"No." Carmen lifted an eyebrow.

"I guess, when we were at the spa, Kami saw some sign about a man-testing service, kinda like that app we were talking about. Only this service tests your man by hitting on him. If he takes the bait, they film it and send you a copy of the video."

We all wrinkled our noses. I wrinkled mine extra hard.

"Well, Kami emailed them, concerned because of the rumors she'd heard about Miguel cheating, and she thought they could help her confirm that he wouldn't." Carmen sighed, sounding grave.

I clicked the sound off for my phone as we sat there, in case Kami was emailing the Test Dummy back.

Carmen continued to pace. "So last night, he gets tested by the Test Dummy. And they sent this." She grabbed her iPad and tapped the screen, holding it so we could all see.

The video of my weird cartoon voice that only showed up on the recording, thank God, played.

We all gasped at the same part.

"Oh, fuck, did he just—"

"Yeah." Jo gave Marcia a look. "That was G, wasn't it? He was planning to date-rape that girl. Or he did. Oh my God, did he rape the test girl?"

I kept my hands tucked into balls, hiding the same black nail polish that the girl sported in the video.

"Oh my God." Marcia's eyes were wide, like she'd seen a murder, when the camera swung to the three guys. "He's a rapist? A gang rapist? He asked her to go to the hotel with his goon squad, and then they were going to rape her?" Marcia asked in a whisper. "I can't even with this."

"Yeah. So then I was telling my brother about this, and he said he'd heard whisperings that Miguel or someone in his crowd was a sick fuck who made movies of limp, helpless girls and loaded them onto sites."

The blood drained from my face; I felt it slithering inside of me.

"They bragged about it." Carmen sat on the ottoman across from the massive sectional we were on. "Kami is totally destroyed. She won't see or talk to anyone."

"Oh my God," I whispered too.

"She went to her dad right away, and he called Miguel's father, threatening him. And now the whole night is becoming a thing. The goon squad and the DJ job are done. Kami is a hot mess."

"What can we do?" I asked.

"I don't know," Carmen said with a frown. "We just need to be there for her. Be her friends and distract her. She's at her house, so maybe we should invade with movies and snacks and have a massive sleepover and not let her tell us no."

"Okay," Jo agreed.

"How did we not hear about this Test Dummy until now?" Marcia sounded skeptical. Of course, she would have known if it were a thing.

"It's hard-core underground. Everything is done on the DL, and the website is untraceable. It's routed through other countries. Or something. Anyway, lucky Kami messaged them and got him tested. God knows how far their relationship could have gone or who else he could have hurt."

"No kidding," I said, grateful I'd done it but terrified of being caught.

"Now I kinda want to try it. See if Monty's as good as he seems."

"Please." I rolled my eyes at Marcia. "You don't need that. He loves you. He's devoted." Not to mention he would know me straight out of the gates. I would never test Monty. Ever. Testing Jordan had been stressful enough. "And he would never drug a girl."

"So sleepover, then?" Jo asked, glancing at her watch. "I'll need to run home and grab a bag and talk to the parental units. Make sure they can afford to lose me from Sunday dinner." She rolled her eyes.

"Yeah, me too," Marcia agreed.

"Yeah. And I have to pack a bag for work. I'll have to leave first thing in the morning." I desperately didn't want to go along, but how could I wiggle out of it?

"Oh, dude." Marcia winced. "Tomorrow is your major presentation, isn't it? Your first time being one of the hotshots at work?"

"It is." I acted like it was nothing, but all their faces changed.

"Maybe Kami won't notice if you aren't there. I mean, with the rest of us, she'll be overloved as it is," Marcia offered.

"You think? I mean, this is her time of need." I didn't want to sound too eager.

"Yeah. You have real-world problems, unlike us." Jo laughed and nudged me. "We can't mess up your first presentation as an adult. Kami shoulda dumped his ass a long time ago."

Carmen nodded. "I think she'll be fine. She knows you love and support her. And we'll tell her extra times for you."

"Please do. Tell her I'm sorry. She deserves so much better than DJ Dipshit. And he deserves to go to jail. Jesus." I kept my voice low so it wouldn't match the video they'd just watched.

"Well, his dad will bury the video and make sure no one sees it. I'm surprised my copy hasn't been deleted. His dad's going for the Senate."

"What about the Test Dummy?" Marcia asked.

"I don't know. The way it works is that if you want the video uploaded, it will be. If not, it's deleted, and they move on. They let the buyer choose. Kami will want to kill it, no doubt. Her dad will make her so as not to cause an uproar."

"That's bullshit!" Marcia pointed at Carmen. "You know it. This needs to go to the police. It's lucky that girl was working for the Test Dummy and wasn't some random. And we don't even know if she made it home safe. Maybe he did rape her. Him and his gross friends. This is insane to bury. There are probably dozens of victims and I bet tons of proof. If they take his computer, they'd probably find all kinds of shit." She literally said everything I wanted to.

"Well, that's not how it works here, is it? Guys get off, and parents cover up for them. Just like it's always been." Carmen sighed. "If it were up to me, I'd do it. I'd blast this everywhere and humiliate him. I'd send it to TMZ or something like that."

"Yeah." I nodded. "Me too." And that made my decision to do just that easy.

There was no way this guy deserved the second chance his parents were buying him. He deserved to fry like the disgusting pervert he was.

And unlike Carmen or any of the others, my decision wasn't influenced by my parents' wishes.

I got to choose for myself.

Chapter Thirty

Felt Movement

Jordan

Hiding in my parents' basement, avoiding my dad as long as possible, Stephen, Monty, and I hung out like we were in high school again.

"Tell me again in slow motion. I think I'm missing something." Stephen tilted his whiskey glass slightly, knocking the ice to the side. "Try miming it while you talk. I like visuals better than words."

"You're an idiot. She said she'd give me a second chance to prove I'm not a completely shallow asshole who thinks of her as a one-night stand. How is this hard to comprehend?"

"The part I'm struggling with is, was this before or after you had a one-night stand with her?"

"Right." Monty pointed. "And the skinny jeans. I'm lost on the skinny jeans."

"Seriously." Stephen laughed, nodding in delight at Monty. "He reminds me of one of those new boy bands. The, uhhhhh . . ." He moved his hand like he was waving through traffic. "The Korean kids. The, uhhhhh—K-pop stars!" He got it at last. Only the reference was lost on me.

"What?"

"There are these Korean bands who sing and dance like the Backstreet Boys, only they're sort of attractive in a way that makes you question your sexuality—"

"I'm your brother!" I shouted. "Stop! Your sexuality is legitimately off-limits. You're honestly offensive."

Monty was keeling over laughing as Stephen continued. "Not like how you're making me question my sexuality now. I might have, like, felt movement when I saw your ass in those pants!"

"No. Shut it down," I demanded.

"Oh, come on, like you've never met a guy who made you question whether or not you'd—"

"I don't want to have this conversation with you. At all. Question away, but details, whether about guys or girls, are never welcome. They weren't when you had that threesome with Mindi and Robert, and they weren't when you slept with our aunt—"

"She's married to our uncle. She's not related." He laughed harder, as did Monty, who was turning red from lack of oxygen.

"You're a pervert. Everyone knows it."

"Reformed pervert." He wiped his eyes and chuckled softly as Monty wheezed and nearly took a knee.

"Whatever you need to tell yourself." I sat back, covering my groin with my sweater as best as I could. "Jesus. Everyone in Manhattan thinks I'm a pervert because I'm your brother. It's high school all over again, where I enter the class and they immediately assume I'm the pervy class clown."

"Look, did you bang her? That's all we want to know."

"*No!*" I shouted, finally losing it.

"I knew it!" Stephen slapped his hand down on his leg. "I knew you didn't. You filthy little liar. You don't look nearly happy enough to have banged her."

"I never lied."

"Well." Monty cringed. "You did let us think it."

"She asked me not to tell anyone. She was so sloppy." I regretted those words.

"What?" Monty pulled back. "What do you mean?"

"She drank too much." I didn't know why she'd wanted to keep the truth from her friends, but she'd asked me to, so I did. "Totally wasted. We went outside to talk, and she passed out. I got her in the car and took her to the hotel so she could sleep it off. I called Fitz to give her an IV so she wouldn't be hungover."

Monty scowled. "Jesus. I've never seen Lacey drink to the point of needing an IV."

"Yeah. I don't know her well enough to say what happened. God knows what they were getting into before we got there." I acted like it was no big deal.

"Marcia was pretty sober when we arrived, and she said they didn't really drink much. They had a couple. That's weird. Have you texted her again?" Monty asked.

"Not yet. I was trying to play it cool."

"Oh my God, you're such a dipshit." Stephen got up and grabbed my phone. "You text right away. She owes you. You saved her from a terrible hangover and got her to a safe place."

"She's not like that." Monty jumped up and snatched my phone and tossed it back to me.

"No. She's not." I caught it, locking the screen.

"Why'd she lie to Marcia, though?" Monty's eyes narrowed.

"I think she was embarrassed. She didn't want to look bad, I think. She woke up and had no clue what happened. She was pretty out of it."

"You took care of her, right?" His glare got harsher.

"Dude, it's Jordan," Stephen said mockingly, as if being a gentleman was something to laugh about. "He pretty much wrote, produced, and directed the tea-time video about consent."

"You say it like it's a bad thing." I pulled my middle finger out of my jeans pocket like I'd just found it in there for him.

"I just mean, you're not the sort of guy who hooks up with a girl who's drunk." He flipped me off as well.

"No, I'm not. And I don't think anyone should be." I glanced at Monty. "It's why I got her out of there. I didn't want to risk her being drunk at the bar and some other, sleazier guy taking advantage of her." Covering for her lie was making me sound like a weirdo. I knew it might, but now that I was actually saying it aloud, I heard how creepy it was.

"You should text her." Monty folded his arms. "She and Marcia are still with Kami and the girls. Some emergency meeting of the snob squad." He rolled his eyes and slumped back into the chair, then lifted his drink to his lips. "I don't know what they're doing for dinner." He lifted an eyebrow.

"I can call and ask." I cracked a grin, unlocking my phone and leaving the room.

Stephen was calling me names as the door closed behind me.

"Hello?" Lacey answered, sounding tired still.

"Hey, it's Jordan." I couldn't help but smile just hearing her voice.

"Hey." She didn't sound as happy as I was.

"What are you doing for dinner? I wanted to see if you'd like to meet up."

"Oh, uhhhhh, not much. Hanging with my family," she whispered, like she was trying to hide the fact that she was on the phone.

"Oh, you're not with Marcia and the girls?"

"No." She sighed. "I have a massive project due tomorrow, and I just couldn't handle the insanity of it all."

"Why, what happened?"

"I don't know. Shit went down between Kami and her boyfriend." She sounded weird, tense. "Can I have a rain check on dinner?" she asked, making me feel a little better. Maybe her being tired and distant had nothing to do with me, and she was just genuinely exhausted from her ordeal.

"Of course. Want to meet for a celebratory drink after work tomorrow?"

"No," she said too quickly. "Unless it's a coffee. I think I might not drink for a while."

"I love coffee." And I wanted to see her.

"Okay. Meet me on Tuesday, not tomorrow, outside my off—no, wait. Meet me at Lady M."

"By Bryant Park?" It was a random spot to meet.

"Yeah. I love those crepe cakes."

"Okay. So four thirty?"

"Four forty-five," she said shortly.

"Perfect. Have a great night."

"You too." She sighed and continued instead of saying bye. "Sorry I ran out on breakfast." She sounded better, like it was a switch.

"I forgive you." I chuckled. "Since you girls ordered, Monty and I got double of everything. It wasn't awful. Except maybe your extra-crispy bacon. It was nearly burned."

"Bacon should only be eaten extra crispy," she said, defending herself.

"No way. It ruined it. I mean, I suffered through for you and all; waste not, want not."

"Oh my God, suffered! Admit it, combined with those waffles and all that blueberry compote and whipped cream and rosemary-chicken sausage, it was outstanding." She laughed.

"It was better than outstanding. I had to undo my new skinny jeans and even Instagrammed it," I admitted, biting my lip and savoring the sound of her laughing. For the first time in a long time, I saw something I wanted, and I was willing to do anything to get it.

"You have to Instagram those pants." She giggled melodically. "I can't believe you even have Instagram."

"I do. It's mostly pictures of the sea, but there're a few meals and drinks and possibly a couple of dogs."

"Wow. Sounds like my grandma's Insta. I mean she cooked all the meals she takes pictures of, though."

"Right, so that leaves me feeling slightly less accomplished." I laughed.

"No!" she shouted, sounding jovial. Not angry or mocking me ruthlessly or near death or hungover. This was her, laughing and joking and maybe even flirting, a little. "I didn't mean to imply that you're lesser."

"You did!"

"Okay, but in your defense, my grandma is above everyone. We're all lesser."

"Okay, then." I leaned against the wall of the hallway, smiling until my cheeks hurt. "I'll accept that. I don't mind being below your grandmother."

"She's a saint." Her tone changed, just a tiny bit. "She's taking care of my brother."

I recalled the news Monty had shared about Lacey's brother, but I suspected that I shouldn't know something so intimate about her life.

"Is he younger?"

"Yeah, not by much. He's almost eighteen. A senior. He has cancer." She was genuinely giving me a second chance. She wouldn't have told me this if she weren't. This was real. Not flirty or uncomfortable talking to fill silence. This was a truth people didn't share because they wanted to; it was a burden they shared because they needed to.

"I'm so sorry, Lacey."

"It's not terminal. He's totally treatable. But he's seeing the doctor tomorrow. It's the other reason I didn't want to meet until Tuesday. I wanted to go to the hospital and see him. Be there for him. Make sure he feels okay. They're performing a minor surgery to remove the lump from his throat."

"Will your parents be there as well?" Was there something about her parents I didn't know? The way she spoke highly of her grandma but not at all about her parents made me wonder.

"Yeah, Mom will come after work; she's at a different hospital. And Dad is flying home tomorrow morning for it. He was out of town for meetings." She cleared her throat, maybe pausing. "They can't afford Martin's medical bills if they don't work extra shifts." I wished I were there, holding her. She sounded so small on the phone. So distant. "But they'll make it work. Sorry. That was such a bummer. I shouldn't have—"

"No." I clung to the small and desperate voice; it was hers. She was revealing such tiny pieces of herself, crumbs. I needed to sweep them gently into my hand and cling to them. "I'm glad you told me. I want to know you. And that includes the bad." I sauntered to the back door and opened it, walking out onto the deck. "I'm going to say the thing that every person on the earth says, but I'm going to mean it, and I want you to understand I mean it. If I can be of any help, will you please come to me? Promise you'll ask?"

"Oh, there's nothing—"

"You don't know. I'm sure right now there's nothing, but at some point if there is, I want you to ask me." I sat down and wondered where in the city she was. I wondered what her view was and how I could make her mine. My view.

"Thanks," she said after a moment. "I appreciate that."

"Tell me something else. Something you don't want to tell me. It can be anything."

"All right . . . I need advice, actually. I want to ask you a hypothetical question, and I need an honest answer."

"Shoot."

"If you knew something about someone that was bad, like they did something really terrible and it was not only illegal but horribly wrong and they did it to other people—"

"I'd tell. No questions asked, I would tell. You can't protect people who hurt others."

"But the problem is the person—"

I cut her off again. "I assume you mean they're part of the 'in' crowd and have wealthy and powerful parents?"

"Yeah." She was back to sounding small.

"Whatever you can sleep with."

"What?"

"If you can sleep with the knowledge that you did nothing because you were afraid of backlash, then let it lie. But if you know you won't be able to let it go and it'll consume you, then you have no choice: fuck 'em. If you want, I'll do it for you. If you tell me what it is, I'll out it and take all the blame." I wondered if this had something to do with her being drugged.

"No, this is something I have to do myself. But you answered my question for me."

"And you didn't answer mine." I grew worried, concerned over the question. "But whatever it is, I'll protect you."

"Thanks." She sounded unsure about that. Either not sure if I was telling the truth or not sure if it was too soon for me to say something so intense. But it felt right, in sync with the theme we had going. Brothers and cancer and grandmas and secrets about rich, elite asshats. Adding that I would protect her, like I had already since we'd met, seemed like the right thing to say.

"You tell me something you don't want to." She smiled when she spoke; I could hear it.

"I'm still wearing those stupid pants."

"What?" She burst out laughing. "Why?"

"I can't go upstairs. My dad is pissed at me, and I haven't seen him yet. I'm hiding out, actually, on the back deck right now. If I go to my room, he'll hear me from his office and come scream at me. And my brother refuses to go upstairs for me because he's a twat."

"Scream at you?"

"Yes. I've ruined his life in ending that ridiculous charade of a relationship he forced me into. I already told you, I followed your advice and manned up and stopped acting like a little bitch, as you so eloquently said it."

"I never said *little bitch.*" She was still laughing, but it sounded different, less relaxed.

"Honestly, it shouldn't have ever happened. I should have said no and meant it from the start. It's awful. But my dad will have to learn to get past it and figure out a new friend to get drunk with and seduce into his treasure tomb. And my grandpa is probably losing some major business deals over it, which I hate, but I couldn't sacrifice myself for the monetary gain." The part I didn't say was that thanks to her, I had a reason not to.

"Isn't there someone you can introduce your dad to, a new friend to distract him with?"

"There is." I nodded, staring off into space. "There's an investor my brother is wooing who would be a great replacement friend. I think Stephen is bringing him to dinner sometime this week to fill the void. And he has sons, so I should be reasonably safe from forced relations."

"Oh my God." She laughed. "You rich people. You're so crazy. Well, maybe if the investor is cool, your dad will forget you ever refused to date a girl so he could make money."

"He's an elephant. He'll never forget. And he'll never forgive. And I have to be okay with that. It was part of the dilemma I had." I made myself small for her, sharing something I really didn't want to. But like her burden, I needed someone to know.

"Your father probably will forgive you. He loves you. He's your dad."

"No," I sighed. "He doesn't love me. He loves my grandfather's power and his family's money and the life it's afforded him. And when I do things to show that he isn't the head of the family and that he doesn't

242

have control over me, he feels like I've lifted his skirt up and showed his junk to everyone."

"Your dad has no power?"

"Not really. He and my uncle are both inept. Their well-connected father made sure they both married wealthy women. But the power and responsibility were never in their hands. My grandpa will hand the reins of the company over to my brother."

"Your brother?" She didn't sound so impressed.

"He might be a known ladies' man and party hog, but he's got a real head for business."

"What about you?"

"I guess, numbers. I'm not terrible with it." I smiled. "I don't love business meetings, and I hate selling things to people. But numbers are pretty straightforward and common sense. They're exactly what you expect them to be. It's black-and-white, and the rules never change."

"What about the editor in chief or the sailor? Although I have to admit, I never would have imagined either of those being your passion."

"Well, I don't think I've put my best foot forward with you, so why would you assume anything that wasn't terrible about me? I mean, sailors are a misjudged group of people to begin with."

"Why'd you do it?" she asked, changing the subject to too many possible answers.

"What?"

"Try to kiss me in the bathroom that night on the yacht?"

"I suspect the same reason you tried to kiss me."

"I said something that spoke to your soul?" she asked, hitting me well below the belt.

"No. I thought you were the most beautiful girl in the world, and you made me laugh. And you didn't seem like you fit in. And you told me to just live and fuck 'em. And I thought maybe it was a sign I shouldn't do what my father had saddled me with."

"And then you decided the best way to win me over the second time meeting me was to hit on me right in front of your pretend girlfriend instead of breaking things off with her and finding me in an honorable way?"

"I don't know what I thought. I didn't think." I contemplated it all for a second, trying to remember what was in my head. "I just acted; I was so excited to see you. You had all that damn makeup on when we met the first time, and I was sure I wouldn't ever recognize you again. And then there you were—like, a second time you were exactly the thing I needed. And from the moment I met you, my brain split. There's before I met you and after, like seeing you standing there on that boat, staring at the city all alone, or laughing with your friends so unabashedly. You flipped a switch in me. You turned something on, not to sound corny. Something just clicked. And everything since has been crazy and chaotic and not like me at all. I don't even mind that everything is a mess, because you said you'd give me a second chance. And that's all I can think about."

She didn't say a word, making my stomach ache with curiosity. Had I shared too much? Grown too small?

Finally she said, "So if you hadn't met me, would you have continued on with Amy?"

"Maybe a little while longer," I said honestly.

"But we met, and now you've ruined your family?"

"Yeah." This was starting to feel like a trap.

"For me?"

"Uh-huh." I bit my lip and played it all back in my mind, waiting for the bottom to fall out.

"Why?"

"Because if I didn't break up with her, I couldn't ever pursue you. Not without you thinking I just wanted something basic like a one-night stand or a notch on the belt. And if I waited too long, I'd miss my chance. Someone else would ask you out, and I would spend my entire life wondering." Beyond telling her about my humiliating first time having sex, there really wasn't much left of me that she didn't know.

"I see." She said it like she didn't see at all.

"Why does this feel like you're looking for something wrong?"

"I am. I'm trying desperately to find a flaw in you, aside from the fact that you willingly let your dad prostitute you out." Her confession stung.

"A flaw? I have plenty."

"No. You don't." She sighed.

"And that makes you sad?" She was killing me.

"I don't know what it makes me, but I have to go. Call me tomorrow, if you want to."

"Okay. Have a nice night. Thanks for taking my call."

"In all honesty, I didn't recognize the number," she said, like maybe she had smiled again.

"Well, thanks for being so real and having a normal conversation."

"This was the least normal conversation I've ever had with a guy." She laughed softly. "And that is why I'm letting you call me tomorrow. Good night, Jordan."

"Good night, Lacey." I listened as she hung up. The severing of the connection was painful. And I knew I wouldn't sleep. But the hope of speaking to her tomorrow was enough to keep me going.

Even through wearing these ridiculous pants and avoiding upstairs.

Eventually I built up the courage to slip into my room, sneaking quietly and contemplating everything Lacey and I had said to each other. I was midchange from the pants, which I threw in the trash bin in the bathroom, when the light flicked on in my room.

"Jordie?" Mom's voice spoke my name too loudly.

I cringed but answered. "Yeah."

"Oh, honey. I didn't know you were home. Look—" She leaned on the bathroom door, ignoring me in my underwear standing next to the sink and holding a pair of pajama pants. "We need to talk about this

Amy thing. Her dad isn't taking our calls, and her uncle's lawyer scheduled an emergency meeting for Monday." Her dead-fish eyes flashed on mine, and for a second I thought I saw emotion.

"Not a chance. I'm not dating her. I don't even like her, and she absolutely hates me, she told me. There're plenty of ways to—"

"We all do things we don't want to, Jordie. Life is about sacrifices for your family."

"No, Mom, it's not. That might be your life, but it's not mine." I treaded lightly, not wanting to hurt her but determined not to play this game anymore. "Don't you ever wonder what it might have been like to fall in love? Real love?"

"Jordan?" Dad's voice boomed from the bedroom doorway, making us both flinch. He was drunk. "You selfish little fucker. Why can't you think about your family for once?" He staggered into my room.

"I'm selfish?" I asked, laughing bitterly as I came out of the bathroom to face him.

"Yeah, you've had a charmed fucking life, kid, and that business deal you're killing by breaking up with that girl is worth more than you." He pointed, but his hand wavered a bit. "So you're goddamned gonna fix it. Or so help me God—"

"What? She dumped me. What do you honestly think I can do about that?"

"You didn't want to date her. You did this."

Apparently my ploy to be dumped hadn't helped. At all.

"You're bullshit." Dad pointed again, stepping toward me.

I stepped forward, looking him right in the eyes, and actually down on him. I was sober, bigger, stronger, and angry in a way he didn't know I could be. My trembling hands whispered bad ideas to my brain. "What are you going to do to me? Get me a lobotomy and force Amy on me? You can't even spell *lobotomy*. And Amy wouldn't take me back if her life depended on it. She was using me to make her parents happy.

She has another boyfriend they hate." The truth, or some version of it, accidentally slipped out.

"Don't do this." Mom stepped in between us and pushed him back. "Don't do this."

"Go sleep it off." I pointed at the bedroom door.

"Don't you talk to me like that!" He pushed past Mom, knocking her into the bureau and reaching for me. I slapped his hands away and shoved him back, pushing hard on his chest. He stumbled, losing his balance. I'd never seen him this way before.

"Jordie, don't!" Mom shouted behind me, begging.

"Jordie!" Stephen and Monty shouted my name from the hallway.

I realized in that moment my arm was back and my fist was balled. I had Dad's shirt in my other hand, and I was about to give him the beating of a lifetime. I didn't even notice we'd gotten here. Or remember how. But Dad was cowering, and Mom was crying, and I was filled with rage I couldn't explain. I hated him, and I wasn't even sure why.

"Get the fuck outta my house!" He spat his words at me. "You're no son of mine."

"Been waiting my whole life to be able to say that, haven't you?" I released him, letting him fall back on my bed.

"Jordan!" My mom ran after me, grabbing my arm and spinning me. "Go to Grandpa." She kissed me on the cheek, and for the first time in a long time, I felt the presence of my mother in the embrace.

"I don't need you people." I muttered it like I was strong, but that wasn't the truth. They were breaking my heart.

And then my brother and my friend grabbed me, dragging me away.

It was not my finest moment.

Not by a long shot.

But I was finding my own way now, as nobody's son.

Chapter Thirty-One

A Matter of the "Hart"

Lacey

I fixed my skirt again and cleared my throat as I waited in the hallway.

I'd done presentations at school, but never something like this.

The boardroom wasn't packed, there weren't dozens of people, but the importance of this pitch felt like I was delivering a presidential address. In that room was Mr. La Croix and the main team, eight people all waiting for me to present the bugs in a way that would appeal to the masses.

"Hey," Hennie whispered from down the hall, interrupting my poor mental warm-up. "I came to wish you good luck."

"Thanks."

"I'll watch from here. You got this." She smiled wide.

"I got this," I whispered back, noting a bit of sweat on my upper lip.

"We're ready for you." One of the ladies from the team had opened the door and spoken softly. She winked at me, like she was wishing me good luck.

"You got this," Hennie repeated as I disappeared into the boardroom.

"Good morning." I smiled at everyone.

"Good morning, kiddo." Mr. La Croix beamed with pride. That made all of this more nerve-racking.

"All right, well, I'll get to it. As we all know, these bars are made with a prebiotic fiber, which is good for healthy stomachs, bowels, and colons. And the fat from the crickets is actually good for you, too, weirdly enough. The protein is high quality. So the food source is one of the best in the world *for* the world. It even comes with the added benefit of spermidine, which is great for anti-aging. As a result of all this awesome information, I have truly been convinced that these bars benefit not only our bodies but the world around us.

"But to convince people to eat bugs, I knew we would need to go outside the box. And ultimately, I decided not to go for the weight-loss benefits. There's enough fad food out there already. Instead, there is one thing this generation thinks about a lot, most likely thanks to Leonardo DiCaprio: the environment. Concern about the earth and our chances of surviving the waste and pillage of the planet after the industrial revolution and the tech era actually plagues most people my age. They worry a lot about the world they're inheriting.

"And the one thing these bars do that no other protein source in the world does is hit hard on the water usage farmers require in comparison to cattle or chicken farming. Even the plant-based proteins can't compete with crickets. They can be grown and harvested all year long, requiring far less from the world and giving back more than any other type of food. Farming them creates very little waste, so the footprint of these farms is almost nonexistent. If you will draw your eyes here, I have made a brief advertorial." I clicked the TV on and pressed "Play."

As the ad started, my recorded voice went on about how little water, land, and resources cricket farming required as images of third-world countries played in the background, with facts toward solving the food crisis. Mr. La Croix caught my eye and nodded.

The commercial ended with the symbol of a heart. I stood again.

"And this is the symbol we would go for. We buy land and build cricket farms called Hart Farms. From those farms, we will produce the Hart Bars. *Hart* because cricket protein will become the beating heart of efforts to end the world's food and resource crisis. Not to mention the positive effects this would have on the earth as we slowed our cattle, soy, and pork farming, making those foods gourmet, if you will. Farmers would be able to switch to cricket farming, and their overhead would virtually diminish. As the world is being saved one Hart Bar at a time, the educated and earth conscious will feel confident about supporting this product. It's common sense. From a universal 'hartbeat.'"

I finished and held my breath as they all sat there, staring.

After several moments, Mr. La Croix made the face, the one I was waiting for. He smiled and nodded. "Excellent research, Lacey. And the environmental focus will hit this one home. Well done. Hart Bars. I love it."

Everyone else started to clap.

For the first time in a week, I sighed, knowing that I had done one thing with my own "hart" and integrity intact. "Thank you."

"Excellent work, kid." He turned to the rest of the team as I hurried from the room. My palms were sweating, and my makeup was melting down my face.

"You did great!" Hennie squealed and hugged me.

"One hurdle over." I couldn't deny feeling relieved on a level I wasn't sure I'd ever felt before, but it didn't last. The next hurdle of the day was fast approaching.

"Time to see what kind of shape Martin's in before his surgery." Hennie's joyful expression faded. "You ready to go?" she asked.

"Yeah, lemme just grab my bag." I hurried to my office and grabbed my purse and phone.

We didn't talk much on the way to the hospital. Neither of us was very excited about this next part.

I was a bit lost in contemplation, replaying the presentation over and over until I was sure it had gone as well as everyone else had claimed it had. Self-doubt wasn't normally an issue for me when it came to something like product marketing—that was almost second nature—but this had been a test.

I saw it the moment I succeeded in Mr. La Croix's eyes.

And the second he'd given me that look, that one that solved a thousand problems and eased most of my heartaches, I knew at least one major thing was off my plate.

Hennie had been right; he was watching me. He was setting me up to take over.

My money troubles were one summer away from being over, and now that I'd nailed that, maybe I could talk to him about working the year and then finishing school. It suddenly didn't seem so disappointing to be doing things out of order.

Maybe it was Martin's cancer.

Maybe it was stooping so low as the Test Dummy.

Maybe it was feeling torn about a person I didn't want to like.

Maybe it was having nearly been raped.

Whatever it was, perspective had hit this week, like a train.

Martin was next, and after his procedure was finished, I would have to start making some major decisions about the Test Dummy and where I saw it going.

"So, Martin wasn't sure what was happening today. He said it was going to be a minor surgery, but he didn't know anything else." Hennie's worried tone picked at my worried bones as we hurried into the hospital.

"The doctor said he was going in to explore, and if the lump was really small, he'd remove it. We'll find out when we get there, I guess." I tried not to be a negative Nancy as we climbed the stairs to the floor my grandma and my dad and Martin were on. We found them talking to someone who appeared to be a doctor.

"Hey!" I waved and smiled.

Martin gave Hennie the look, the one that suggested she was the only person he was waiting for.

Grandma smiled, Dad waved but continued listening to the doctor, and Martin ignored my existence. All he saw was Hennie—the girl I'd personally delivered to him. I nearly rolled my eyes.

As the doctor left, Grandma got up from her chair and hugged me. "How was the presentation?"

"Oh, fine."

"Better than fine. She nailed it!" Hennie beamed with pride.

"How's it going here?" I didn't want to talk about it.

"Fine. Mom texted, all upset; she couldn't leave work on time to be here. There was a massive accident, and the ER got hit with injured people. So of course she's freaking out. Prepare for those phone calls until she can get here." Martin shrugged. "And I go into the prep area in, like, five minutes. They'll do a bunch of things to inspect me and make me feel like an alien—blah, blah, blah—and then they slice me open and haul that dirty little bastard out."

"Well, that's not exactly what the doctor said." Grandma furrowed her brow. "But close." She smiled at me. "That was nice of Mr. La Croix to let you girls leave early."

"Well." I glanced at Hennie, wrinkling my nose. We hadn't told him what we were doing, just that we needed the time off. "He's flexible."

"Very." Hennie nodded.

I hadn't wanted anyone at work to know Martin was having surgery. Mr. La Croix would have taken my project away, thinking I was already stressed enough, and given it to someone else. And I couldn't afford that. I had told Marcia, but had asked her not to tell her dad. I was almost shocked that she'd kept that promise.

"Mr. Winters?" a lady called from down the hall.

Dad turned. "Yes?"

"We're ready to take you to the presurgery room." She smiled.

"Wrong Mr. Winters." Martin laughed and hugged us all. "I'll be right back." He winked, giving Hennie the longest hug.

We all looked the same, worried faces with fake smiles.

"He'll be fine. At least he won't be able to talk when this is over. That'll be a nice change," I joked, fighting the worry I was feeling.

He laughed, and that was how he started the journey to his surgery, laughing.

I loved my brother so much.

Chapter Thirty-Two

SPERMIDINE IS NOT A THING

Lacey

Pacing the hospital was hard; waiting was misery.

I was sure I wore the floor out, the same way Grandma's hands wore out the hem of her shirt. She rolled it and folded it and stretched it. Hennie and Dad took turns getting coffees for everyone and asking if we wanted refills. Hennie had taken the latest shift, fetching another round for everyone. I wasn't sure I could handle another coffee.

It had been hours since Martin went in at one. It was now five. I'd assumed he would be in recovery by now, considering he was told the procedure could take anywhere from two to three hours.

But we'd heard nothing.

"Hey!"

I turned to see Monty, Marcia, and Jordan walking down the hall.

"Hey." I didn't know what to say or think about them being here.

"How is he?" Marcia hugged me and took a seat beside Grandma, taking her hands in hers and holding them tightly. Grandma didn't even fight her on it.

"We're waiting for news." I hugged Monty, who went and sat by Marcia.

"Hope this is okay," Jordan muttered, offering me a soft kiss on my cheek. I leaned into it, taking a deep breath of him. Our conversation last night had me reeling still, but the presentation and Martin needed to be bigger in my mind.

"It's okay," I whispered back.

"How was the presentation?" he asked as he pulled back.

"Good," I offered, a bit distracted by everything else in this moment.

"What was your angle?"

"Anti-aging at first." I almost beamed. "Turns out cricket protein is loaded with spermidine, which has major youth-boosting properties."

"If spermidine was all you needed, I feel like most of the guys around the world would have been happy to—"

"No!" Marcia cut Monty off before he got to the punch line of his joke. "What is wrong with you?"

"Right." He blushed as he and Jordan snickered. "A lot apparently."

"Anyway. Spermidine is a real thing." I scolded them with my stare. "I decided to go for resources. The world is short on them. Global warming and pollution and the food crisis are the main concerns these days. And crickets, oddly enough, are the answer to that. Sustainable. Low cost and use of resources to grow. Incredibly healthy. Our generation, myself included, is actually concerned about saving the planet, so I felt this was the real selling point. I think if we want to be able to get some young celebrity endorsement, we need that person to represent something they care about," I said, finishing my summary. "Sorry, my passion shines through once I find my angle."

"Well done." Jordan grinned. "I never doubted you."

"It sounds like you blew them away, even with all that partying you've been doing." Grandma gave me a cheeky grin.

Tara Brown

"It's the start of summer, Grandma. Everyone parties at the start and the end," I said in my defense as I took a seat and Jordan sat next to me.

"Is he out yet?" Mom came bursting into the hallway, still in scrubs and looking like she might have run the entire way even though she had been calling every fifteen minutes for three hours.

Grandma and I stood and hugged her. She was trembling when she hugged Dad.

"He's still in. But I'm sure we'll have word any minute," Grandma reassured her. "Come get off your feet."

We all shuffled in our seats so Mom and Dad and Grandma could sit together. Mom glanced at me sitting next to Jordan and raised a questioning eyebrow.

"Mom, this is Jordan. He's Monty's best friend." I realized I hadn't introduced him to anyone. I didn't honestly know how to explain his being here.

"Hello, Mrs. Winters."

"Hi. Nice to meet you. Where's Hennie?" Mom asked, brushing him off.

My stomach dropped when I realized Hennie could come back any second and she and Jordan would be in the same room. Even without her heavy makeup and clever disguise, he would no doubt realize who she was.

"She went to get coffees." I sent her a quick text. Don't come here, Jordan just showed up!

I'm in the elevator. Can you get rid of him?

I winced at her response. Yup.

"She all right?" Mom asked.

"Yeah, she's on her way back now. I just realized I haven't eaten all day. Do you guys want food?"

256

"Love some." Mom nodded. "You don't mind?"

"No, you sit. You worked almost double-shift hours on your feet. Hennie will be back any second. She's the only one Martin wants to see, let's be honest. I'll go grab snacks." I glanced at Jordan. "You wanna help?"

"Love to." He jumped up. I pulled him to the opposite side of the hall, away from the elevators.

"Stairs?" he groaned as we entered the door to the staircase.

"I like the stairs," I lied and I sent another text as we made our way down. You're in the clear.

"I hate the stairs." He grabbed my hand, stepping down in front of me and cutting me off so I couldn't move. I stood on the last step, not even close to as tall as he was. "But I like you, Lacey. A lot." He brushed my hair from my face, smoothing it at the sides. "And not just because you're the most beautiful girl in the whole world."

"Stop saying that." I gulped as his hands crept down my shoulders and arms and encircled me, hugging me to him. I leaned in, letting the scent of his neck and chest drown me in that intoxicating mixture he always smelled of.

He didn't kiss me. He hugged, like he needed it, or maybe he thought I did. I didn't know I needed it until I closed my eyes and relaxed.

We took several breaths here, holding each other in comfort. I didn't say anything, just let him hold me. And when he pulled back, I kissed him on the cheek, lingering and pressing my face against the warmth of his. "Thanks for coming."

"I told you I'd be there if you needed me." He pushed back into me, like he was savoring the embrace.

I pulled back and stared into Jordan's eyes, like this was the moment, we were going to kiss, but my phone rang.

I lifted it, saw Marcia's number, and answered right away. "Hello?"

"Come back! He's awake. He's fine. He was in recovery this whole time, they just didn't come and tell us. Assholes!"

"Oh my God. Coming." I no longer cared that Jordan might meet Hennie or that he would put two and two together. "My brother's out. He's out!" I shrieked, and spun, then ran up the stairs and burst through the door. We ran to the hall where only Monty stood.

"They went in there." He pointed at the door leading to another hallway. I let go of Jordan and shoved through, running down the hall until I passed a door with my family inside.

Everyone was standing around him, everyone but Monty and Jordan, who, thankfully, respected this intimate family moment enough to stay put.

Martin offered a slight wave, looking pale and sickly for the first time since his diagnosis.

I ran to him, nuzzling my face in his stomach and hugging tightly while he rubbed my head. There was no way I was going near the large white bandage on his throat or the tubes coming from his hands or the IV machine.

"He's going to be fine," the doctor reassured my mother. "We got it really early. There wasn't much of a mass, and I'm confident with a single dose of the radioactive iodine, he'll be back to his old self. We'll talk about that dose later, after he heals. About five weeks from now. We were able to leave some of the thyroid gland behind, so he won't need hormones. He'll be able to go home tomorrow. You can all relax now. He won't be feeling any pain, and he's completely out of the woods."

"Thank you so much." Mom hugged the doctor, making him instantly uncomfortable. Dad joined in. It was sweet, unless you looked at the doctor's face.

"Yes, he's out and he's fine," Grandma said into the phone, no doubt talking to an aunt or uncle. Our family was all waiting on bated breath for answers. "Everything was a success. Well, he can't talk, he's sore and tired, and by the looks of it he wants most of us to leave so he can rest up. Yes, totally fine."

By *most* she meant everyone but Hennie, who was holding his hand and sitting next to him on a chair.

She blushed and glanced down. I was so grateful she was here, even if it risked Jordan seeing her, which fortunately hadn't happened yet.

Martin squeezed her hand. I stood up, wiping my eyes and smiling at him.

"I hate you."

He lifted his middle finger up at me, his eyes filled with the love we never spoke of except in jest.

"Do you need anything?"

He shook his head, his eyes darting at Hennie and his eyebrows dancing.

Marcia and I both giggled.

"You're a brat." Marcia whacked his leg.

He flipped her off too.

"Promise you'll be okay?" I asked once more, to both him and Hennie.

"Totally fine, Lacey." She furrowed her brow. "I'm just glad this is over." She squeezed his hand back, making him blush.

"Okay. Do you want food?" I asked her. "More coffee or tea?"

"No," Hennie laughed. "I've had enough to last a week."

"You want us to go, don't you?" I asked Martin, trying to be loud enough that Mom could hear, though I doubted she would care. "All right, we'll leave so we're not crowding the room," I said when he nodded, giving me the *don't be a cock block* look. He was going to take all the Hennie love and adoration this cancer thing would get him.

"Grandma, you wanna come eat with us?"

"No, dear. I'm gonna stay and chaperone"—she winked at Martin, earning a scowl—"your mother and make sure she leaves." She cackled teasingly.

"Okay." I gave my brother one more look, kinda weirded out by Grandma relinquishing the reins to Hennie. "Text if you need anything." He nodded, wanting us gone. He had it bad. And by the look on Hennie's face and the grip of her hand, she felt the same. I hugged my parents, noting the difference in them both. They were lighter. Already.

And so was Hennie.

I breathed a sigh of relief at that—that Martin had his whole life ahead of him. Thanks to Mom being paranoid. Her helicopter parenting and maternal instincts toward Martin had paid off.

I waved at them as we left the room, checking a second major item off my list.

There was a feeling of bliss as we walked out.

I hadn't been a fan of the Martin-and-Hennie thing, but I didn't have to love it right now. I knew eventually I would be happy they'd found each other.

Just not yet. But maybe when he was out of high school.

But not yet.

At least I'd gotten away with Hennie and Jordan not seeing each other.

That was a problem for another day.

Chapter Thirty-Three

What Happens in the Limo, Stays in the Limo

Lacey

We walked from the hospital, the four of us, heading to Marcia's car. "Thanks for coming, you guys."

"Of course we came. Martin's family." Marcia wrapped an arm around my shoulders. "I'm just glad he's going to be okay. If you told me a month ago any of this would be happening, I would have said, 'Not a chance.' He's seventeen for God's sake. Also—" She paused, making me stop.

"What?"

"Speaking of his being seventeen and her being twenty-one. The cuteness of Hennie and Martin is a must. He adores her. And she clearly likes him. You can't hate on that. Love is love. Even when it's random like that. If your parents hadn't held Martin back, he would be starting freshman year at college this fall. There's nothing weird about a freshman and a senior dating. At all. And I can't imagine them with anyone else. I almost died in there from the adorableness."

"Fine." I relented too easily because I knew she was right. They were cute. "I know."

"Anyway, where to eat?" She lifted an eyebrow.

Monty broke in. "Honestly, I could go for something healthy. I'm feeling sluggish from all the drinking and bad eating." He rubbed his abs. "I know it's the beginning of summer, but I gotta get back into my routine."

"I hear ya," I agreed.

"I'm good for whatever." Jordan shrugged, looking a little off. "I could eat my feelings or just have a smoothie."

"Why don't we just go to my place and get salads whipped up for us?" Marcia offered.

"Actually, I'm kinda beat from this entire week. I might just go home." I was exhausted and ready for some down time.

"It's Monday." She furrowed her brow.

"Right, I mean the last seven days. Actually, longer. Since school ended, it's been insane." I glanced at Jordan and smiled. "I'll text you guys. I'm gonna take the subway." I hugged Marcia and Monty, but Jordan stepped away from them.

"I'll walk you home."

"You don't have to ride the subway with me. I'm fine."

"Oh, he doesn't have to ride?" Marcia lifted an eyebrow. "No. Hell no. If I have to do it, he has to."

"I insist." Jordan said it like he might smile, but he didn't. Something was wrong.

"Any boy who will ride the subway for you likes you. I should know." She blew a kiss and grabbed Monty's hand to pull him to the car. "I expect a rain check on everything, Lacey," she shouted back at me as Darren got out and waved.

"Fine!" I waved at him.

"See ya at home, man. Bye, Lacey!" Monty waved at us.

I turned to Jordan. "See you at home?"

"Yeah. So where is the subway here?" He changed the subject with skill, but I wasn't buying what he was selling.

"This way. Are you staying at Monty's?"

"I am." He nodded and followed me along the sidewalk. "My dad kicked me out. I am officially not his son." He laughed, but it was a broken sound, not even his bitter laugh.

He glanced down through his thick inky lashes and blushed, finally giving up the reason he was being so weird, now that Martin was out of the woods and he no longer had to be strong for me.

"Tell me," I insisted.

"Last night after you and I talked, I went upstairs to change." He closed his eyes and wrinkled his nose. "My dad confronted me. He called me selfish for ruining the business deal. He shoved me, and the next thing I knew I was holding him like I was going to punch him in the face." He opened his eyes and stared at his hands, like they weren't his. "It was crazy. And then he kicked me out and said I was no son of his. My mom told me to go to my grandpa's, but I don't want to draw him into this. It's my fault."

"I'm so sorry." I hated that his family was so insane. There was no imagining what that kind of rejection from your parents felt like. And it was worse that he'd done it because I'd told him to.

"Me too. I can't believe I almost hit him. And he was so sloppy drunk." His eyes flashed, like he was reliving a moment or two. "And now I'm crashing at Monty's. Which means it's time for me to move out of my parents' house and buy my own place."

"Buy your own place? But you're cut off."

"Oh, I have my own money. He can stop the payment of the rest of my trust if he wants to. I used what I already had to create my own investment portfolio, and—I'm fine. The point is I'm fine."

"So you'll have to buy your own place?" How weird was that?

"Yeah. And I was going to wait until you had less going on in your life, and be cooler about it all and tell you I needed help apartment shopping—"

"You want me to come apartment shopping?" My stomach started to hurt.

"Well, yes. I was thinking about saying something cheesy like I wanted a woman's perspective or a second opinion. But really, I just wanted to see your face as I picked a place to live. I wanted you to like it enough to eventually come there, and hang out. And maybe you could have sleepovers and ultimately call yourself my girlfriend."

"Oh." I didn't know what to say. We'd just had a time warp to about a year away.

"Because I don't have any skills with girls or a proper idea of how dating works."

"Right, your mom picks girls for you," I joked, hoping it lightened the mood.

"Yes. And I don't know how this will work, if I'm now coming down to the lower deck with you, to ultimately drown. Or if you're coming up to the top level to hang with me and the rest of the really terrible people."

"They're not all terrible," I offered.

"I suppose not." He didn't seem more relaxed, though. In fact, he looked crushed, and it broke my heart. Something terrible had gone on with his family and he was devastated, no matter how much he tried to act like he had everything under control. "I don't want to be that fake, polite guy with you. But I don't know how to be this guy without being too honest. And I've known you for barely any time, and this is too fast to be this real."

"That's okay." I slipped my hand into his, not sure of the protocol for a guy turning stage-four clinger or how to react when he skipped asking you out, but part of this was my fault. I squeezed his hand and offered the same comfort he'd given me on the stairs. "We had a heavy few days."

He laughed, and again it slipped out like a sob.

I understood—not exactly, but sort of. School had ended, work started up, Martin got sick, and everything went to shit. Crickets and tuition and creepy guys and illnesses and partying and sweet guys turning up on yachts. I was burned out too.

"Tell me what kind of place you were thinking about getting," I said softly as I led him down the sidewalk, gripping his hand, finally letting him hold mine like maybe this could be okay. Maybe.

"I don't know. It needs to be close to the park. Maybe work."

"So, you still work for your grandpa?"

"Yeah. When I got there this morning, he gave me a huge lecture on intertwining my personal life with business. He said he was disappointed in me, again. He told me that I would have to live with the decision I made to choose my own life over my father's demands and the costs of business." He rolled his eyes. "And then he gave me a case of scotch and cigars and said it was a housewarming gift for my new place since I was never allowed back at my dad's." He chuckled, but I swore I heard another subtle sob.

He kicked at a pebble on the sidewalk. "He said I had to move out on my own. That I'm too old to be in my parents' house anyway. He also wanted to know how it felt being so close to hitting my dad. It seemed like he'd imagined being in my shoes one too many times. He said standing up to Dad was my final test toward ultimate manhood or whatever, and I passed. I failed as my father's son and a businessman, but I passed as a man. To be honest, I have no idea what happened."

"What the hell kind of family do you have?"

"I don't even know anymore." He actually chuckled a little.

"So, your grandpa still likes you?"

"Right." He sighed.

"I'm not sure what to say." I was so confused.

"Me either. But I will say, no matter how twisted this sounds, I hate my dad being pissed at me. I don't want to be disowned."

"So now what?" I changed the subject, feeling worse and worse about his predicament by the second. "You dig in your heels, take this freedom, and sleep on Monty's sofa?"

"Not exactly." He chuckled again, losing the sadness a little. "His guest room is fairly nice. And his mom said I could stay as long as I needed. She loves me."

"Well, that's lucky.

"I know. But to add fire to everything else, my mom filed this morning." He swallowed a lump in his throat.

"Your parents are getting a divorce? Now?" I gasped. "This is too much."

"I know. She had him served this afternoon. Stephen said he lost it. I actually feel bad—well maybe not bad, but I feel like he's too dumb to know what kind of bed he's made himself."

"Will you try to patch things up with him?"

"I don't know. He's my dad, and he's dumb, and now he's going to be alone. Not right now while emotions are hot."

"Oh my God." I pulled my hand from his and wrapped my arms around him, holding him. "I'm so sorry, Jordan." On some level this was a little bit my fault. He did say this would happen if he fought back, but I hadn't really believed him. I hadn't believed any parents could be that unkind to their own child.

"It's been a weird day. Spermidine and all." He laughed again.

"Jordan." I pulled back, staring up at him. "You don't have to joke. If you want to be sad, you can be."

"I'm not exactly sad. Your brother is going to be okay. My Amy situation is over. My mom might actually start living her life for herself. My dad needs to realize he's not the center of the universe, and maybe this crushing blow will force him to reevaluate some things. You didn't cringe or run away when I mentioned apartment shopping, which means you're contemplating having sleepovers." He smiled and stared at me. "And maybe even contemplating being my girl. At the very least you'll say yes to a date."

"Let's not get too far ahead of ourselves." I forced a smile, still focusing a little on the Amy situation. "Maybe a date."

"And you killed your cricket presentation."

"Maybe don't say it like that." I wrinkled my nose.

"Right. Crushed, no. Rocked? Why is that wording so violent?" He stared intently, creating that weirdly tense moment between us again. "You're so beautiful."

"You are too." I tilted my head as he lowered his face and kissed me fiercely, until I closed my eyes and let the feel of his lips against mine, finally, erase everything else.

All the background noise of people and vehicles and our weirdly dramatic lives faded.

His breath tickled my lips as he caressed them. Then he held his mouth on mine. We froze this way, fingers trembling, lips embracing, and bodies pressed against one another. It got awkward again.

And then it was as if something switched on. His hands gripped tighter, and his tongue slipped into my mouth as our faces turned and our mouths and hands began exploring. My fingers crawled up his shoulders as his crept down my back and eventually cupped my ass, lifting my dress a little.

We went from a polite street-side kiss to me trying to climb him like a tree.

"Wait!" He broke free, holding my arms and gasping for breath. His hair was ruffled, his eyes wild, and his shirt untucked. "We shouldn't do this like this. Not here. My plac—wait, I don't have a place. Hotel?" he asked, offering a deadly grin.

I couldn't speak, but I nodded. I'd decided before I'd thought about the ramifications of what was about to happen.

He pulled his phone out and dialed. "Heinrich, it's Jordon Somersby. I need that room again. I'll be there in fifteen." He hung up and texted someone.

He grabbed my hand and pulled me in the opposite direction of the subway.

A limo pulled up, and he grabbed the door, just knowing it was for us. I stared at him for a second, making sure this was what we were doing. I needed a mental moment to reassess me and him and the fates I didn't believe in, not entirely.

"Get in." He almost growled it.

I nodded and jumped in, holding my breath as he dove into the car and slammed the door.

He didn't talk to the driver, and the partition stayed shut.

He sat there for a moment, staring at me, his chest rising and falling like he'd run a marathon.

I contemplated saying something, like maybe we should calm down or maybe we should just call it a night. But the taste of that kiss and the feel of him cupping me and pressing me into him was ringing through me. I struggled with my breath as I watched him, staring at the way he looked at me.

He was abandoned and sad and maybe a little broken, and I'd done that. I'd had a hand in it.

His broken heart tugged at mine while the kiss tugged everywhere else.

He licked his lips, and something clicked, and I attacked, climbing into his lap and wrapping my arms around him.

I kissed him hard, our mouths assaulting each other. I bit his lip as he grabbed my hips, pressing me into him, making me notice the bulge between his legs, as if I could miss it. I gasped in his mouth as he started rotating my hips, unyielding in his use of my body to massage his, forcing me to ride him and lifting my skirt. His fingers made trails of heat up and down my thighs, slipping into the sides of my underwear, as if contemplating.

I started fumbling with his belt, unable to wait, but he grabbed my hands again, pausing us. His cock was pressed against my underwear, and our mouths hovered over each other as we inhaled each other's exhales.

"We have to wait for the room. I need to fuck you on a bed. I don't want it to be like this," he whispered into my lips, his words caressing me.

"I want you to fuck me right now." I kissed him again softly. "And then again in the bed." I spoke through my ragged breathing.

The switch clicked again, and he sprang to life. He pulled my skirt up more, sliding my underwear down my thighs while I finished unbuckling his pants. I grabbed the waistband of his boxers, getting worried when I saw the outline of his erection. Licking my lips, I pulled the waistband down, eyes widening when his erection sprang from his boxers, slapping him on the abs. It went past his belly button and had girth like I'd never seen. "Uhhh."

But it didn't seem like he realized what he was packing, given the way he cupped my ass and pulled me into his lap, again kissing me hard as he placed a condom into my hand.

A little scared, I slipped a hand down there, almost measuring with my fist as I gripped him and rolled the condom on.

"Go slow for a second," I begged as I led him to the right spot, rubbing him back and forth and then easing him into me.

There was a moment I could feel the tension in the air again. It wasn't awkward; it was self-control. I started to understand him a little better. He wasn't thinking of something to say or do; he was holding back. He vibrated with it. I eased myself onto him, going up and down a few times to stretch myself in a way I'd never before stretched.

He kissed my neck, thrusting just slightly, burying himself in every way into me, his cock all the way and his mouth in my nape. I whimpered into his hair, holding his face.

He gripped me, holding my hips with his shaking fingers as I slowly started to move, catching my breath in my throat for the first few strokes. My movement gave way to permission for him to grind. And like releasing a horse from a stall, he thrust, bucking and making me ride him at the same time. I couldn't sit back, it was too much, so I wrapped my arms around him, clinging to him as our cheeks pressed against each other, speaking with breaths and gasps, getting a feel for one another.

Our lips met again, like they were lost in the confusion of this sudden assault we were both guilty of, maybe me more so than him, as our hands grounded us. He pumped into me, grunting and fucking while I clung to him, desperate to hang on.

Moaning, I started rotating my hips, riding him on my own.

The car jostled us with a sharp turn, and I cried out, losing the control I had and realizing how close I was to orgasming. Desperate for it, I slipped a hand down between us, fingering my clit as he thrust hard and fast, maintaining a rhythm I couldn't. I closed my eyes and let my head fall back as I rubbed the sensitive spot he'd already been massaging.

He held my body in place, controlling how I moved as he slapped our bodies against each other. My finger and his cock met in the middle, my clit, finishing something he'd started.

I tensed with my orgasm, pleasure filling me and forcing sounds from my mouth that I didn't normally make in the backs of cars.

I clenched and cried out as he thrust harder and faster, making me fuck the way he wanted to.

My whole body convulsed with perversely found indulgence as I used him as much as he was using me at this point. It was primal in nature and yet satisfying in a way I'd never been satisfied. Though I wasn't sure before this moment that I'd ever needed to be fucked the way he fucked me. I'd never needed to come the way I just did, gripping another human, unsure if our feet were still on the ground. It was the savage end of a savage ten days spent in agony and turmoil. This was the moment I'd anticipated in the bathroom on that boat, animalistic—no, it was better. It was better because I liked who he was. He was flawed, but he was vulnerable. And he'd shown it all to me.

He finished, with hard jerks and loud noises, gripping me and rocking.

I managed to catch my breath as he relaxed, dropping the scowl. He had an angry sex face, and for whatever reason I liked it. I ran my hands over his face and smiled.

The car stopped, and we stared at each other for half a second, wide eyed and realizing what was about to happen. The car door slamming made our eyes pop open even more. I got off of him and pulled my skirt into place as he slipped his pants up and zipped his fly with the condom still in his pants.

I started to laugh hysterically as the door opened and the light of day shone in. I couldn't imagine what was happening in his pants, but I bet it was bad.

As we stepped outside in the fresh air, as fresh as New York ever got, a hard hit of reality slammed me.

I was outside with no underwear on in the middle of a busy street in Manhattan, blushing like an idiot, and he was wetting the front of his pants.

As if the fates had it in for me, this awkward moment would of course be the one where a girl who looked exactly like Amy got out of a limo parked across the road. She turned and lowered her sunglasses, pausing and staring. Then she lifted her sunglasses and walked away before I could be sure it was her.

My heart stopped.

My mouth went dry.

Postcoitus remorse kicked in with the breeze and the random man staring at us and the fact that seeing Amy or her doppelgänger reminded me that I am the Test Dummy.

Panic and all the bitchy emotions that rode with it started to arrive, sneaking around in my head.

What-ifs plagued me.

Hennie.

Amy.

His broken heart.

Apartment shopping.

His parents' divorce.

Him finding out who I was in the grand scheme of it all.

My heart started racing as I glanced around the busy street for Amy, but she was gone. Or hiding among the trees and cars. Maybe she wasn't real, but like the ghosts of *A Christmas Carol*, she'd shown me my past sins.

The buildings around us spun.

I pushed Jordan back into the car and closed the door behind me, certainly being rude to the driver. "I have to go home." I had no excuses or other words, just that single statement that burst from me, breathy and desperate.

"What?" Jordan couldn't have sounded more shocked.

"I need to go." I leaned forward and contemplated kissing him, but my stomach twisted at the thought of the terrible person I was ever touching those divine lips again. I'd broken his heart and made him confront his dad, and his parents were getting a divorce.

Panicking in a way I never had before, and certain this was the last thing I should do but not sure what other option I had, I lied. "I'll call you later. I can't do this right now. I'm so sorry." I pulled back and jumped from the car, rushed away from him, and disappeared into the crowds.

"Lacey, wait!" he shouted, and I started to run.

And just like Cinderella, I left him shouting my name.

And not in the good way he should have been.

Chapter Thirty-Four

GHOSTING AND OTHER BASIC
THINGS TO DO

Lacey

My body spent every moment creating dreams that woke me begging for more of Jordan, but I held strong. I fought the urge to call him or answer any of his texts the first two days, regardless of how badly I wanted to. Today was the third day, and I was nowhere near as indifferent as I needed to be in order to continue ghosting him. But the reality was, I couldn't date him.

How could I?

How could I be with him and lie about what I'd done to him?

He was going to meet Hennie, that was obvious. And then what, I was the girl who ran the Test Dummy, who set him up to be ruined by his family? I was the reason his parents were getting a divorce and his dad had disowned him?

No.

Here he was talking about apartment shopping while his family life was falling apart, and I was going to, what, ask him to understand that I got my best friend from work—who was now dating my brother and whom he would absolutely meet at some point—to pretend to hit on him and record him so that his girlfriend would dump him and ruin his family?

How would I ever let him know I'd betrayed him like that, let alone make him understand?

No.

Between school, work, Martin, tuition money, my uncertainty over the Test Dummy, Miguel's video, and Jordan, something had to give.

It wasn't even a breakup. Just an end to something before it ever started.

We had limo sex and talked on the phone once.

What we had couldn't even be called a relationship.

It was a fling.

A one-night stand.

A one-week stand.

And as much as I told myself I didn't care, I was dying.

My heart, which shouldn't have been attached to him, was broken, battered, and bleeding to death. Bleeding love. Losing hope.

The Test Dummy wasn't helping.

Emails were still coming in.

I'd tested two guys the night before, one at a party in Queens and the other on campus in a library. Both had turned me down, no matter how hot I looked or how hard I came on to them. Restoring too much faith in men.

I chanted that Jordan had hit on Hennie because he was slimy.

I told myself repeatedly that he'd fucked me in a limo like a fling.

I lied to myself and said that he was barely even trying to get me back.

But the truth was painful.

He wasn't slimy. He was sad and desperate and hated his ex-girlfriend.

I'd forced him to fuck in the limo. He'd begged me to wait.

And he was currently sleeping in his car outside my office instead of going to work, double-parked but important enough, or bribing the right people with enough money, to be allowed to stay. It had been three days, and he was fully stalking me. And I couldn't face him because I wasn't strong enough to walk away again.

"Hey!" Hennie smiled weakly. "How's it going?"

"Awful." I sighed, holding up my phone. "I can't do this. Marcia just sicced the Test Dummy on Monty."

"You need to take that sign down from the spa."

"I did. I took it down days ago, but now the email address is like an urban legend." I groaned into my hands, letting the phone drop onto the desk.

"Yikes. What are you going to do?"

"I don't know. Lie and tell her he didn't hit on me and not send her the video. Maybe she'll start calling me a rip-off and bad-mouth me, and the business will die."

"You wish." She slumped into the chair across from me. "And what about Jordan?"

I winced when she said his name, feeling the burn in my chest come back.

"Ouch. I take it that is also not going awesome."

"He texted twenty times an hour yesterday for ten hours. Then he called, leaving, like, eleven messages. Now he's sleeping in the limo instead of going to work. I had to leave through the service entrance at the back of the building for lunch. Marcia is ready to kill me; Monty told her I broke Jordan's heart and am ghosting him. Which I am!" I snapped. "I don't know what to do."

"Come clean."

"I can't." I was ashamed. "I took money from people for manipulating other people."

"We took money because we provided a service. I'm not trying to church this up, but we caught people. You saved Kami from a dangerous douchebag. You did the world a favor."

"It doesn't feel that way," I admitted.

"And Martin is doing awesome."

"He is." We both smiled, but it wasn't making me feel better. Not better enough.

"Go see Marcia and come clean."

"Maybe." I contemplated it.

"No maybe, just do. I'll see ya after work." She got up and walked out.

My phone was buzzing enough that I was about to throw it against the wall. I turned it off and put it in my desk, not sure where to take this or how far I had to go before I decided enough was enough. I currently had five jobs lined up to test guys.

At this rate I would cover my tuition easily.

Maybe I could even stock Martin's tuition for next year. I could help my parents so they could go on a date night or take a day off together. If I did enough Test Dummy jobs, I could send them on a small vacation—a weekend away. But the problem was that I didn't feel emotionally invested enough to keep up. I was currently lining these gigs up for one every other night. Plus, work. I would be burned out and hated by almost every guy in Manhattan by the time this summer was over.

I told myself I would only be hated by the guys who cheated. The ones I proved were decent wouldn't have an issue with me. Except for one in particular. Jordan had failed the test but ended up being sort of decent anyway.

Deciding Hennie was probably right, I got up to go talk to Marcia. I knew she was at the spa. She'd sent me a snap of her with the mask, pretending to sleep.

It almost made me smile.

But as I left my little office, Mr. La Croix was coming down the hall, looking feisty. I pitied whomever he was going to ream out, but then his eyes met mine, and I knew he knew.

"You've got some serious explaining to do!" He spoke to me like I was one of his kids with her hand caught in the cookie jar, not his employee.

I gulped, not sure which thing he was upset about or how to smooth over whatever it was.

"I cannot believe you did this behind my back. Haven't I always loved you and treated you fairly and guided you and been a second father to you?" He was fucking angry. He paced in the hall, not even giving me the privacy of my office or his. He covered his eyes with his hands, forgetting about his glasses. "I just can't believe this, Lacey."

Heads poked from offices; people winced.

"I mean honestly, did you think Marcia wasn't going to tell me? Really?"

"I'm sorry." Fuck! Marcia knew?

"I mean, he's your brother. Which means he's my family too. How could you keep something so big from me?"

Oh, God. It was worse than him finding out about the Test Dummy.

"I've spoken with his doctors, explained the situation, who he is. His care has been transferred to a better specialist." He folded his arms, looking sick with the amount of hurt I'd caused.

"I didn't want you to think I couldn't work." My voice cracked, and he lunged at me and wrapped himself around me. I lost it there. My knees buckled, and he held me as I sobbed.

"It's okay." He rubbed my back, speaking soothingly. Switching his anger to comfort. "I've taken care of everything. I have a team assembled. We're arranging a gala fundraiser to cover any extra costs your family might run into, and the rest will be donated to the children's oncology department. Everything is going to be okay." He whispered the next part. "Marcia told me you've dropped back from the group of girls and stopped seeing Jordan. I know you're stressed. Marcia said she thinks you're working a second job at night, burning yourself out. Why wouldn't you just come to me and tell me about Martin? Or ask Jordan for help? Or ask me to help you financially?"

My pride crumpled. He knew everything.

"I know I've always tried to instill a work ethic in you, but this is too much. I wouldn't have made it to where I am if I had hurdles like yours. I had a clean ride up, which isn't how it works for everyone. That doesn't mean that you can do this all on your own. I heard your parents are working back-to-back shifts to cover expenses. It's just money, Lacey."

"They-they can't afford it all," I stammered, sending more tears down my cheeks. "I have to help."

"And so do I. This is my family too. God, even Marcia wants to be involved. She's agreed to spearhead the fundraiser." His words punched me in the stomach again. Marcia was working? "She's gathering her forces and selling plates, a thousand dollars a pop. She has donations for prizes coming in from everywhere and entertainment like you can't imagine. We're going to make all the money your family needs and donate the rest to the hospital for cancer treatments for kids like Martin." He smiled. "Family takes care of each other. You've been my daughter since you were thirteen. My protégé. My future." He hugged me again.

I had managed to catch my breath, and it was gone again.

"I love you, kid."

"I love you too." I sniffled and hugged tighter.

"Come on." He squeezed tightly. "We take care of each other." He rubbed my back as he stood. "No more secrets."

His words hit me in the gut.

No more secrets.

I had another secret, other than my brother being sick.

And I needed to deal with it before that cat got out of the bag too.

Because if this was how my other dad felt about finding out my brother was sick, he was *not* going to like finding out about the Test Dummy from someone else.

Chapter Thirty-Five

The Girl on the Train

Lacey

"I'm sorry I never warned you that I told Dad your business," Marcia said, offering a weak apology. "But yesterday I forced Martin to tell me what was going on with you because you've been distant, and he told me about the tuition and your parents working back-to-back shifts and the money problems." Marcia leaned against me as we walked to her place. "And it accidentally slipped out to Dad. And then he was so wounded that you didn't come to him."

"I know. I could tell." I sighed. "I'm just glad I don't have to keep the secret anymore."

"Me too. I miss you. All these extra shifts you're working are driving me nuts. Every time I text you, you're busy. Where are you working, anyway? I was thinking it must be driving a taxi, since you're always all over town. But you don't even know how to drive."

"No." I contemplated what I would tell her. "Running errands for people. Delivery. Bike delivery." I wanted to tell her the truth, but I was terrified. Adding the pressure of the gala fundraiser made it all worse.

What if I told them, and they were disappointed in me?

What if Jordan found out?

"It's been stressing me out so hard." I gave her a look. "Knowing that I might have to beg your dad to let me work all year, and do schooling part-time for a couple of more years when I save up the money or get the student loan, and then not be able to move out. I'm gonna be, like, forty before I can support myself."

"So what. I'm never moving out," she scoffed. "So overrated. Training new staff and decorating a new house and getting used to a new neighborhood. No thanks."

I laughed. "We don't have the same problems."

"No, we don't. I would never do to Monty what you're doing to Jordan. Monty said he's suffering, bad. Jordan doesn't get it. You just vanished. That's cruel. His dad kicked him out and refuses to see him. His mom is heartbroken and left his dad. Monty said she was so shocked at how he treated Jordan, she couldn't handle it anymore. His grandpa is even being weird. And you've been his friend through this and then just dumped him. Like it doesn't matter. That's not you."

"I'll talk to him, I swear." My insides were burning. "I just need to get past my brother and all that stuff. After the gala." I would tell everyone the truth then. And all the money would go to charity, even the money I made with the Test Dummy. I'd earn my way through school by my own wits and gumption, not deceit.

"It's in two weeks. You're honestly going to make him suffer for two weeks?"

"Look, Martin's still recovering. The gala is going to be a brutal amount of work and stress for you. I still have work full-time. Kami hasn't decided what to do about the whole Miguel thing, but no matter what, that's a whole lot of extra in our world. I don't have time for a boyfriend or even a casual thing with anyone. Especially someone who has all that shit happening in his life. Like you said, his life has fallen apart. We can't both be broken. We're no good to each other." I sounded crazy—I could see it in her eyes. She was close to backing away with her hands up.

"Fine! Jeez. But this isn't like you."

"I know!"

"As soon as that gala is done and you're back to being seminormal, you have to talk to him. If he'll even talk to you at that point. What happened with you guys anyway?"

"Honestly, nothing. We had sex once. We talked on the phone once. We rode in a limo once. We slept in a hotel once. Nothing more." I rearranged the events a little. "That's it. It wasn't like we were dating for weeks. At all. I can't do needy guys right now." I felt bad for saying that when the truth was so much worse. While we hadn't done anything beyond those things, I would have been with him if not for the whole Test Dummy secrecy thing.

I needed it to end. I just had to finish the stupid jobs I'd already gotten. Including Monty.

"You coming over?" She changed the subject.

"No, I have to go home. I have to keep working that second job for a couple of nights. I can't just quit. You have to give notice in the real world." My lying was getting better. "Two weeks."

"God, working sucks," she scoffed, turning and giving me a huge hug. "Promise you're not mad at me and doing that Lacey thing where you smile and pretend everything's fine?"

"I swear to Prada, I'm not. I'm legit not mad. At all. Just make sure Monty understands the whole Jordan thing, please. You know how I'm his fav." I grinned as I pulled back.

"No way. I'm letting you go down a couple of pegs." She winked. "Spa tomorrow morning? I already booked us in for detox wraps. I'm telling Dad you need it." She cackled and walked off, waving at me.

"You can't milk Martin's cancer so that I can go to the spa during work hours."

"I can and I will," she shouted back.

Laughing, I headed down into the subway and jumped on. But I didn't go home. I went straight for guy number one. I didn't even need a disguise. I had no clue who he was, and my pin camera wouldn't show my face. I caked on extra makeup and wore sunglasses, taking off my blouse when I got there and dragging my neckline down on my tight black dress.

The guy shot me down, didn't go for the bait at all. I couldn't help but wonder if he could sniff my emotional unavailability from a mile away.

As I sent the email to his girlfriend, telling her he checked out, I caught the train back to Brooklyn to test a guy who worked at a bar. I wanted them all done so I could be finished with the Test Dummy once and for all.

On the train, I made my makeup more gothic, noticing a little girl watching me. She seemed fascinated by the transformation. I smiled at her, but her mom gave me a deathly stare, judging me.

I got off the train at my stop and walked the four blocks to the bar. The bartender, a guy named Tony who liked girls with heavy makeup and had a pregnant girlfriend, hit on me the second I walked in.

"Hey, what's a gorgeous thing like you doing in a dump like this?" He leered at me, giving me a creepy vibe.

"You hitting on me?" I asked, cracking a grin.

"Fuck yeah, if it'll get me in that dress." He nodded his head at the booze. "What can I get you to drink, on the house?"

"Why would you want in my dress?" I didn't answer his drink question. I'd learned that lesson already.

"Cause you're fucking sexy. And I can see that little freak flag of yours waving. You looking for some cock?"

"Maybe." I made sure I got a close-up of his face as he leaned in.

"Cause I can fuck you like no one else."

"You've got a dirty mouth, you know. Maybe you should watch how you use it on unassuming women coming into your bar, God forbid expecting to be treated with respect." I got up, making my feet hate me. I'd gotten the evidence I needed in all of five minutes, and I felt more than relieved to stroll out, grossed out.

"Hey!" He ran after me on the street and spun me around. "What's with the hot and cold, doll?"

"Leave me alone."

"You came into my bar, asked me why I wanted to get in that skirt of yours, and now you're telling me to get lost?" He got closer, making my entire body go on pins and needles. "I think you like it rough and you're hoping I give it to you like that." He grabbed my arm and started dragging me to the alley.

Shit was real and I was scared.

I hit him with my bag, kicking and pulling to get free, but he was too strong.

"Stop!" I screamed as he pushed me against a wall and pinned me there.

"I'll stop when I'm done." His sneer scared the shit out of me.

I shoved him, but he backhanded me, making my face feel like it was split open and my lip bleed.

Shock set in.

My vision was hazy from the hit and the surprise.

No one had ever hit me before. I couldn't even imagine being in this situation. I suddenly realized how naive I had been, running this game without considering the risks. After the trouble I'd already gotten into at the bar and being slipped a roofie, I never expected to have another brush with misfortune. Now it was too late.

Tony's fingers fumbled with my skirt as a dark shadow covered us both. Someone shouted, and the seedy bartender was dragged off me in an instant. I was huffing and paralyzed with fear.

Someone in a hoodie was attacking the bartender. Though I couldn't see the features of the guy, he was punching and punching relentlessly.

"Stop!" I shouted, seeing the bartender go limp. The guy who'd saved me staggered back, toward me.

I turned and ran as fast as I could. Faster than I thought possible with ringing ears and hazy vision.

I hauled ass to the train and jumped on, my heart racing and tears in my eyes.

The looks I got then weren't so nice. I was a girl wearing too much makeup and revealing clothes, and I had a welt on my face that spelled trouble. No one wanted to see that girl on the train.

No one offered her anything, not even a kind word or a smile.

I'd never felt so alone or judged in all my life.

By the time I got home, Grandma was in bed. She'd left me a quiche for dinner and small note reminding me to take the garbage out.

I didn't feel like eating. I went upstairs and walked into my brother's room.

"Oh my God." He flinched.

"You should see the other guy."

"Looks like business is going well." He grimaced as he whispered. "Angry girl catch you hitting on the wrong guy?"

"Nope. The right guy tried to rape me in an alley." His eyes widened as I shook my head. "I'm fine. He might not be. Some dude walking by heard me screaming and jumped in and beat the shit out of him. I mean, like, beat him to near death."

"Lacey, oh my God. You should call the cops. You know this guy's name and where he works." He sounded psychotically angry, even with his weird raspy whisper. He was still recovering from his procedure.

"I can't draw attention to the Test Dummy. I'm starting to believe the world needs it with how many dangerous guys are out there, waiting for their moment." I climbed up onto Martin's bed and snuggled him. "That was terrifying. I really feared for my safety there."

"You didn't see who saved you?"

"No. Typical hoodie and dark hair. Honestly, I don't think I saw anything clearly. My eyes were fuzzy from the smack I got."

After a couple of minutes, he asked, "Okay, look, I love you, and I get that you're all about earning this money for school, but, dude, do you think maybe this needs to either be rethought or ended?"

"Yeah." I hid the fact that tears were flooding my eyes.

"This is dangerous. Some guy attacked you. And chances are he would do it again. You're lucky some random was there. I really think it's time for you to retire or rethink this thing. I'm not willing to be the cause of you getting beat up in back alleys, Lacey. You created the Test Dummy to help save me; now, it's time for you to take my advice and save yourself."

"I think maybe you're right." I bit my lip, sniffling. "And even worse, Kami wants the video buried. She messaged the Test Dummy this evening, saying to burn it."

"Well, I think you know what you need to do with that."

"Of course I do. But what if anyone figures out I'm the Test Dummy?"

"Well, better to be known for that than the girl who didn't warn the rest of the world that Miguel is a pervert and a rapist."

"Yup." I nodded. I'd sat on the video long enough. I'd given Kami the time to make the right choice. She hadn't, so my hand was forced.

"Let me see your face." He made me look at him. "Yikes. I want this guy dead." He sounded like an evil-villain cartoon character with his voice. It made me smile and laugh, even while crying.

I sat there, thinking about the man who'd saved me.

Had he not come when he did, I'd be having a very different conversation with my brother. And the police.

As it was, the video was going to his girlfriend, and it had the whole assault, mine and his.

I would have to watch it later and see if it was clear enough what was happening. Maybe I would have two videos for the police.

But the second video wasn't as easy as making it go viral. I would need to testify on the second one, which meant letting people know who the Test Dummy was.

The thought of that made me regret all of this.

Chapter Thirty-Six

Confessions

Lacey

My hands were shaking and sweating because I was committed.

I was in over my head.

The bruise on my cheek and the fat lip that I'd managed to cover up told me this had gone too far. At least I was good enough with makeup that no one would notice the marks. God knew I didn't need more scandal.

My stomach ached and my heart raced and my mouth went dry, but as I entered the office, I knew it was time. I needed help.

"Lacey, you're in early today," Mr. La Croix said pleasantly.

"I have something I have to show you." My words were almost a whisper I was so scared.

"Okay."

I sat at the desk and pulled up the Test Dummy website on my laptop, ready to reveal everything.

"Test Dummy! I heard all about this. This is amazing. Whoever came—wait, what's wrong?" He tilted his head.

"You have to see something Marcia and I know about. It's bad."

"Okay." He sat next to me as I pulled up the video from the admin side of the website, the one featuring Miguel. At the end, Mr. La Croix sat quietly for a second before he whispered, "Oh, fuck. Is that—?"

"Yeah."

"Oh, wow." He nodded. "Okay. Does anyone else know about this?"

"Miguel's and Kami's parents, and us girls. She showed us the video at her house."

"And they're going to bury this?" he asked, obviously keeping up with my dilemma and why I would come to him with this.

"Yeah."

"We have some decisions to make." He reached over and put his hand on mine. "I'm glad you showed me this. It's good in two ways. One, I will absolutely ensure this makes its way into the right hands to out that little shit as the pervert he is. I hate when money buys protection. And two, I've been looking into this Test Dummy website. It's genius. If we buy right before we leak this information, we can use the PR and publicity of the scandal to gain exposure for our new product."

"What?" My heart burst, and my stomach clenched as again my body contemplated a trip to the bathroom.

"Think about it. This is a genius website: the design is flawless, and the idea behind it is brilliant. I'm taking you off Hart Bars and putting you on this."

"Mr. La Croix," I gasped. "I can't possibly—with what happened to Kami, I'm personally invested."

"You did so well with the Hart Bars, I really am proud. And at this rate—"

"It's me!" I shouted as I covered my eyes. "I'm the Test Dummy." I couldn't face him and say it, so I kept my eyes closed. "I created the website with Martin." It didn't feel good admitting this aloud, not like I'd wondered if it would.

"What do you mean?" He sounded lost. "This is you?"

"Yeah," I whispered, braving a look at him.

"You made this site?"

"Well, Martin, but the Test Dummy was my idea."

"Marcia showed me this, but she didn't know who was behind it. I don't think anyone does."

"I haven't told anyone but Hennie and my brother."

"Jesus, kid. This is genius. You really went out of the box. And you've done the IT work; it's Fort Knox. Amazing stuff, you two. I should have known it was you. The marketing on the site, making it like some underground love tester, was brilliant. You are incredible."

"It's not all amazing." I pulled my makeup out of my purse and used a wipe from the bag to show him the bruise. "I got attacked by the guy I was testing yesterday, and if it weren't for Jordan finding me drugged at the bar, Miguel and his friends would have done much worse things to me."

"Lacey! Your face! You test them yourself?" His eyes darted to the screen. "Were you the girl in the video with Miguel—?"

"Jordan saved me. Miguel didn't do anything to me. Jordan didn't know I was the Test Dummy; he just thought some asshole put something in my drink. But he—Miguel—was-was going . . ."

"Oh my God. And this." He brushed my cheek.

"I know. Some guy from the street must have heard me screaming. He saved me, but it was not going well for me when this happened." I pointed at the bruising. "I got lucky a couple of times, but I can't put myself in any more precarious situations."

"Oh my God. I don't think I ever considered the lengths you had to go to make this happen. We can't risk your safety anymore. Why would you do this?"

"My tuition." I started to sob again. "I needed to cover it and maybe Martin's bills and help my pare—"

"It's okay. I get it. All you were trying to do was help Martin, but the cost was so much greater. I'm so sorry for not seeing the desperation

and need you had. Will you ever be able to forgive me for being a neg-
ligent dad?"

"Of course. I don't see it like that." Sighing, no longer scared of
his response, I clicked on the pending emails awaiting replies. "But I
have this other problem." The site had gone viral in the last two days.
I wiped my eyes.

"Holy shit!" He jumped back. "When I started looking into the
purchase, I didn't know it had grown this much. I thought it was still
really a start-up."

"It is. I don't have the infrastructure to run the company. I didn't
really expect that many people to be willing to pay top dollar for the
truth. I assumed it'd be a couple of jobs here and there—a few paranoid
girlfriends and their harmless, playboy boyfriends—but this has all gotten so out of hand since I launched the site."

"Lacey!" His eyes widened. "You can't possibly fulfill that many
requests on your own. Not to mention that we're never putting you in
harm's way again."

"I've done ten so far."

"And you have four hundred pending emails?"

"Yeah. And that number is going to triple by the end of the week
at the rate of growth I'm currently projecting."

"Not enough for one girl." He contemplated, his eyes darting to
my face. "And not safe. Can we come up with a way to make it safe,
market it, take it nationwide, and create an app, like that 'chat a fish'?"

"Yeah," I laughed. That's how he referred to all dating sites. His
response wasn't what I'd expected, and yet here we were.

"If you're interested in selling, that is, though I don't think you have
much choice at this point."

"I don't. I made a couple of huge, almost lethal, mistakes. The Test
Dummy—"

"Look, here's what we'll do. We won't tell anyone you were behind
this. I'll buy the business anonymously from you, and you will work on

it for me. And you will not test Monty. I already know Marcia sent an email asking the Test Dummy to run him. Marcia . . . I love that kid, but sometimes she can't see the forest for the trees."

"I didn't want to test him, but I worried if I started being choosy, people would wonder why."

"Right, look for patterns. Makes sense. So, you've been doing this the last couple of weeks, while working and after getting the news that your brother was sick?"

"Yeah." I sighed.

"You need to learn how to lean on me. When you come up with your next genius idea, bounce it off me. We're a team. I don't know how else to gain your confidence."

"I just worried that I would disappoint you," I confessed. "You're the only person who even checks and makes sure I'm doing the right thing. You're the only one who cares that I'm doing my best. And you're always so supportive. I don't want you to be mad at me if I screw up sometimes."

"I'm going to be angrier if you screw something up because you were too proud to ask for help. You don't think I got to where I am without help, do you?"

I nodded.

"Oh, well, that's your mistake. Not a chance. I always had tons of help. Tons of support and guidance. I had mentors who made me the man I am. I wasn't smart, but I was lucky. And you are me at that age. In fact—" He got up and walked to his desk, pulled out a slip of paper, and wrote on it. "You're more amazing than I ever was. I didn't have an idea worth even half this at your age." He handed me the scrap, which had a number on it. "I have to actually cost out what I think the business is worth and pay you that amount, but this is what I'm going to guess we're close to."

I stared at the number, confused. I lifted a finger and counted the zeroes. "No."

"You think more?"

"No," I repeated.

"Lacey, this is going to make a killing. It's evil, and it preys upon the weaknesses of jealousy and relationships, but at the same time, maybe it makes us all a little more accountable, knowing someone is watching. And look at Miguel. He's going to be outed for hurting people. Well done. Like Net Nanny for love." He sat back in his chair with his arms folded. "I am so proud of the initiative and the pride and the hard work. You had a problem, you refused to ask for handouts, so you created a unique growth opportunity by inventing a new industry and creating your own income."

The sparkle in his eyes was food for my soul.

I'd never been more disgusted, proud, scared, overwhelmed, and excited in all my life.

"I'm going to get the intellectual property copyrights going today, ensuring no one else can cut into our market. You get the IT team on an app idea. And let's all sit down for a massive company meeting to start brainstorming how to make this business safe and smart and worthwhile."

"Should I tell Marcia?"

"No." He shook his head. "You'll upset her. She'll be crushed you didn't trust her. I'll tell her it's our company and everyone who works here is sworn to secrecy on it."

"Okay."

"Okay." He smiled wide, shaking his head. "You surprised me. In a good and terrifying way. No father wants to see his daughter scared and hurt, but every father wants to see his child come up with something like this, create her own existence, and put her mark on the world. You just stamped the world, kid. Your name is on it. This is wildly original."

"Thanks." I tried to feel good about it, but I was still struggling.

"But we need to talk about Miguel and the attacker. I think some self-defense classes are in order. You and Marcia can go together. I don't want to ever see you in this position again." He lifted a hand to my cheek. "It makes me dangerously angry. I almost want to find this guy myself. Almost."

"No." I shook my head. "It was taken care of. The guy got beat to hell by some Good Samaritan."

"Okay. Well, you go on to the spa with Marcia this morning. Try to relax and come up with some ideas. We'll meet at one, spend a few hours bonking heads together, the whole team."

"Okay." I got up, my hands still shaking and my heart still racing and my mouth dry, but for different reasons than when I came into the office.

Leaving it, I was in shock.

A kind of shock I wasn't sure I would ever recover from.

I walked to the spa, right to the Post-it wall.

There among the notes were thank-yous.

They were directed at me, the Test Dummy.

Seven of them.

Seven girls had posted a note, grateful for my work.

I'd possibly saved lives, like a superhero. Of sorts.

Maybe.

Or maybe not.

I would certainly have a wider pool of responses to gauge from once this thing hit the level that La Croix Industries could take it.

Chapter Thirty-Seven

HOUSE HUNTING

Jordan

"There's a terrace up here, darling," my mom called from the upstairs. She actually sounded excited about this one, which was giving me a modicum of something resembling happiness.

I hadn't had much joy in my world since Lacey cut me out of hers. Speaking of cuts, I glanced at the cuts on my hands, healing but still swollen—little reminders of her. All that was left of our nonexistent relationship: bruises and cuts. And questions.

Like what was she doing there at that bar with that creepy guy and dressed like that?

It was like I didn't know her at all.

Which was a fair assessment. We didn't know each other that well.

And that wasn't the first time she'd acted insanely.

My mind bitterly replayed the moment she fled from the limo, the exact reason I didn't want to have sex in the fucking car like she was a fling or a one-night stand. She made such a stink about not being a one-night stand and then acted just like one. And made me one, too, whether I liked it or not. Which I didn't.

I'd felt nothing but desperation and anger. Weeks of it. Two weeks to be exact. My only reprieve had been saving her.

But it didn't save me from the pain of her abandonment.

The moment that again, like Cinderella, she left me. I desperately wanted to run into her so I could berate her with a scathing remark. I'd been practicing for days what I would say to her if I saw her again.

"Oh, and the master suite is up here. You should come see it. I think you'll like this," Mom called down.

I rounded the great room and went up the stairs. The prewar co-op was my favorite thus far, and it was on East Eighty-Sixth, between Park Avenue and Fifth, which was conveniently close to the park. I could take a leisurely stroll through the park every morning. I could even get a dog.

And with a terrace, I wouldn't worry about leaving the little guy out for the morning or afternoon on nice days.

"You could get a dog." My mother beamed, reading my mind. She had gone from Dad's little puppet to a woman reborn. She was switched back on.

I didn't ask what happened.

What changed her.

At first, I'd thought it was just knowing I was leaving and that she would have to be alone with him. But the fact that she'd already had the divorce proceedings underway suggested this had been something she thought about a lot. A scary amount, actually. Sort of how much I thought about Lacey.

For days after she'd run from the car, I texted. I called. I waited outside her work. I did everything someone in my position would do, but she was masterful in her avoidance of me.

I even saved her life, a second time.

But she didn't stick around to thank me. She ran.

I understood that a little more.

She was in shock and desperately upset and scared, as she should have been.

I was too.

I'd never hit someone like that in my life.

I saw a guy grab her, and I lost all sense. I hardly recalled it.

I saw red rage and nothing else.

Her scream still haunted me.

Along with the fact that she'd never called or texted or so much as thanked me.

It made me realize I had to accept my fate. She didn't feel the same way I did. I didn't believe it. I didn't want to, because the way everything had happened, the way she'd acted, suggested she did like me. A lot.

And then she didn't.

"This is lovely, look at the view." Mom was gushing about the place to the point that I started to wonder if she wanted it herself. Staying with Cynthia and Stephen had to be a burden. She was rich beyond belief, but she couldn't bear to be alone. "You would have an office, a guest room, a stunning master, this quiet library, and a great room to host parties with your friends."

"Do you want to stay with me?" I asked, surprising even myself.

Tears flooded her eyes. "Are you serious?" Her voice broke.

"Why don't you take the master bedroom, and then you could make this library a nice quiet area to sit and relax. And we can get a dog, and you can hang with him when I'm at work or school or whatever it is I'm going to do with my life."

"Oh, Jordie." She practically fell into my arms, sobbing on my shoulder. "I'm-I'm so sorry."

"Please don't. Please don't be sorry." My heart broke for her. She was acting like this divorce was nothing, but it was something. Something huge.

Dad was mystified, of course. Stephen was still seeing him and said he was a mess. He'd cried twice since she left. Hadn't drunk once. Was completely stupefied as to how this could happen to him. And in fact, he blamed me.

Which made sense . . . to no one else.

He still wouldn't see me. I'd tried, twice.

"I think you're right, Mom. This is it." I hugged her and kissed the top of her head. I slipped her small hand into mine and led her down the stairs. "We'll take it." I smiled at the Realtor. "Let's go write up the offer."

"These prewar buildings never have penthouse apartments come up and especially not ones that are fast possession dates like this."

"You don't have to sell it to me, Sloan. Thanks. She likes it." I smiled and led my mom to the foyer.

We rode in the car to the office and brought Sloan with us upstairs. Jack would want his shot at negotiating. He liked yelling at people.

When we got upstairs, Grandpa's face lit up from behind the glass walls of his office. He burst through the doors, hands out and smile wide. "There she is!" I imagined him and Frederick La Croix were close to being the same person, only Frederick was a gentleman. Jack was not. But when he kissed his daughter on the cheek and hugged her tightly, whispering something that made her chuckle, his heart shined through. Like he had gotten her back. Or maybe she forgave him for forcing the relationship with Dad after all those years.

"My boy!" He turned to me, hugging me as well. "How was house hunting?"

"Fruitful." I glanced back at Sloan. "We found one we like. Smaller, but it's all we need right now." I held a hand out to our Realtor. "I'm sorry for everything he says while he's in the middle of negotiating."

She smiled nervously. "Oh, I'm sure it'll be fine."

"Hah!" Jack led her to the conference room and closed the door.

"Poor woman."

"It's a good commission." I gave Mom a grin. "And she's going to earn every dime."

"And then some."

Stephen came out of his office, beaming when he saw her. "Mom!" He hugged her, staying a little longer than he used to. We all did. "Dick." He nodded at me.

"Steph."

"What's going on? You going to the gala tonight?"

"Gala?" I sighed. "Spring gala?"

"No, that was months ago. We were there. Raised funds for the Met or something." He was mocking me or the event or all of it. These social gatherings all blended together in my book.

"What's this gala?" I asked. "Another pointless excuse for the upper class to brush shoulders and trade miseries and mistresses?"

"You really haven't heard?" He frowned.

"What?" I snapped.

"Frederick La Croix is hosting a fundraiser for that girl's family. Lacey Winters. To benefit her brother's type of cancer."

"He's cured," I said sardonically.

"Yeah and they're middle class, moron. I guess she couldn't afford her last year of college because her parents had to use her tuition money to pay for his treatments. She's been working, like, a bunch of jobs. Monty said she never told La Croix, and when he offered her help, she refused to take his money. And now he's selling plates for a grand a pop, and I heard he's up to three hundred people. Whatever money doesn't go to her family goes to the kids' cancer society or some shit."

"Holy shit!" I stepped back. This was what Lacey had been going through these last couple of weeks? I was dying to see her, and she was dying from the crushing pressure of everything else crumbling in her world. My heart skipped a beat. Maybe she didn't want to start something because she was ashamed of her financial situation. Or she was working multiple jobs. Or maybe she just honestly had too much on her plate. Maybe she did like me, and that was the problem. She didn't have time for me.

"Did you buy plates?"

"Of course. Mom did. I told her to buy six. I figured you could come up with a date?" He lifted his eyebrow.

"I'll find one." I needed to find someone who wouldn't be a real date and wouldn't be offended when I spent all my time trying to get that girl to talk to me.

"Find two. We have an extra seat. Jack's bowed out. Has plans with some—thing none of us wants to know about." His eyes darted to our mom as he recovered fast.

She scowled. "I honestly don't. I don't know how the man has the strength for all this." She shook her head and walked away.

"Viagra," Stephen muttered, winking at me.

"And that's our grandpa, so hard pass on the details."

"You're such a virgin." He whacked me in the balls and walked away while I fought to not take a knee. "Monty said you aren't returning his texts or calls, by the way. Stop being a little bitch and get a social life." He flipped me off and sauntered into his office.

Even through the pain in my balls, I was focused. I needed a plan for the gala night to go my way.

As I hurried to my office, a thought kicked me in the guts.

What if she had been dressed like a whore, in a gross bar, letting some slob drool on her for money?

Lacey Winters, a hooker?

Everything in me simultaneously died and lit on fire, burning the remains of my spirit.

I trembled with rage at the idea of other men touching her, her being so broke she would do anything for money.

I needed answers. I was never going to be sane again until I had them.

Chapter Thirty-Eight
TMZ Confirmed

Lacey

Pacing in my tiny office, I contemplated the upcoming evening. Mr. La Croix had offered me a bigger workspace, but I declined him. I liked my crappy little cupboard.

"Hey!" Hennie beamed, poking her head in the office. "You excited you're about to—" She paused. "Why do you look like you're having an anxiety attack?"

"I think I am." I rubbed my sweaty hands together. "I keep thinking, like, what if Jordan comes, and he sees you and puts two and two together, and then I have to explain?" Marcia had triple checked for me that neither Stephen nor Jordan had bought plates at the fundraiser, so there was a chance I might get away with not seeing him until after. Then maybe if I was lucky, I could find the balls to come clean. Maybe. Talk about being a hypocrite. I'd ridden him so hard about being a little bitch about Amy, and here I was, also being a little bitch about my lies.

"You ghosted him weeks ago. I doubt he wants to see you at all." She said it hesitantly, like she wanted to spare my feelings, but couldn't.

"Right. I agree." It hurt, but I did. "But anxiety isn't rational."

"Dude, you sold the Test Dummy. The copyrights are in place. We have a solid plan on the services. The app is ready for sale. It's a legit business plan now, not just something you and Martin cooked up that involves testers getting raped and murdered. And Mr. La Croix has the helm, so you can't be blamed for anything that happens." Her eyes sparkled.

"What?" I scowled. "What happened?" Why did she sound weird?

"Did you check TMZ today?" She bit her lip and wiggled her eyebrows.

"Oh, shit!" I grabbed my phone and googled *TMZ* and *The Test Dummy*. The first headline almost made my knees buckle. I stumbled back into my chair and stared at the words as I read them aloud. "Son makes porn with same computer dad uses to campaign for senate." I lifted my gaze to hers. "Holy shit!"

"Right." She offered a smug grin.

"Miguel Amara, the son of Antoine and Maureen Amara, has some serious explaining to do. And backpedaling won't work this time. Sorry, rich boy. A video of the well-known musician known as DJ Spark, in which he is allegedly shown drugging a girl, has led authorities to his house, where our sources say a sting operation netted more than the police were bargaining for. The video sent to us anonymously shows Amara being fidelity tested by a company called the Test Dummy, a private corp that offers a man tester in the form of a hot girl with a secret video camera. Yikes. When did the dating waters get so murky? It's not even safe to cheat anymore, or apparently have a drink in a bar when Amara's there. We'll have more on the arrests and who else is involved."

I clicked the link to the video, and there it was, in all its glory.

"Holy shit!"

"Right!" She was pleased, but the whole thing made my stomach hurt.

I jumped up and ran past her, right to Mr. La Croix's office. He was on the phone, pacing and talking with his hands. Through the window he grinned at me, winking.

I smiled wide, knowing he'd pulled some strings to leak the story right away. I didn't expect retribution to feel so sweet.

My phone went nuts, as if on cue.

Glancing at the messages, I knew we'd made the right decision. From the messages I could tell Kami was ecstatic.

I FaceTimed Marcia and walked back to my office. Hennie was gone, so I closed the door.

"Oh my fucking God, did you see?" Marcia burst out.

"I can't believe this is real. He's caught. It's outed. And Kami sounds super pumped," I shouted with as much glee as I could muster.

"Well, do you blame her? She was being forced into silence by the Amaras. Her dad told her to play nice and not rock the boat. And now, she doesn't get any of the blame and all the reward. And she's free, completely." She glanced to the left. "I can't talk, though. As much as I am jazzed beyond belief, I'm swamped here. I'll see you at the gala."

"Okay, see ya then." I waved and hung up. It was so weird seeing Marcia work hard, or at all.

My phone kept going nuts. I threw in my obligatory comments, supporting Kami and being grateful the whole thing was out in the open. Miguel deserved everything he got.

I couldn't say much more.

I was now legally sworn to secrecy about it all.

The entire company was.

"I got my bag. You ready to go?" Hennie opened the door.

"We can't leave now if TMZ just blasted our story. We have to do damage control and make sure we're blasting the company—"

"No, Mr. La Croix just sent me this text." She flashed her phone at me.

"Get Lacey home and dressed and make sure she comes to the party on time, or else!" I read aloud, and glanced up at her. "Damn. What does *or else* mean?"

"I don't want to know. But he knows you. You're a total workaholic and a personal-attention avoider. Let's go." She shoved my bag at me and pushed me toward the elevator.

I gripped my bag, my hands still shaking and sweating like the nightmare stress ball I was as we walked to the station.

"You are so funny. He pays you six figures for the Test Dummy, and you still take the subway." She chuckled as we walked down the stairs.

"I like the subway. These are my people." When we got to the bottom of the stairs and onto the platform, I nodded at the guy pooping in the corner of the far side, away from the train guard. "Except him."

"Oh, wow." She grimaced and turned her face to mine. "Haven't seen anyone pooping down here in ages."

"Yeah. They always do it in the summer, too, when it's hot." I grabbed her hand and pulled her away from him, closer to the guard.

"So Martin was saying that every dime from tonight is going into a fund for kids like him, that your family isn't taking any of it to pay for medical bills."

"Right. The fundraiser isn't for Martin, it's for kids with cancer. He's just the poster boy for it."

"Which we both know he is loving." She laughed.

"Completely."

"So what about the medical bills?"

"Oh, man, Mr. La Croix already paid those. It's called an angel donation, and you can't do anything about it."

"What about the Test Dummy money you made?"

"Added to the fundraiser." I smiled. "And I kicked in ten percent of the sale of Test Dummy to it too."

"Holy shit!" Her eyes widened.

"And I gave Martin a huge payday for all the web design and safeguards he put into place, which ensured I never got caught."

"Dude, this summer is turning around for you. I'm not gonna lie, that first week, I really wasn't sure how you'd manage. Bugs and boys and brothers."

"It was a hard start to the season, but we made it. At least on the bugs and brothers fronts. I'm still not sure the boy problem is fixable." I hugged her. "But you helped me so much. Thanks for being there for it all."

"Even if I started dating Martin?"

"Yeah."

"Did he tell you he's graduating early?" She beamed at me as we got on the train and sat.

"No, what?"

"Yeah. He started summer courses so he could finish by January and enroll in college early. He's made sure his enrollment is moved up and everything."

"At MIT? In Boston?"

"Yup." She shrugged.

"That's kind of close to you at Harvard."

"The twenty-minute walk and separate campuses and us both being busy will be good for us."

"So you can break things off?" I realized I didn't really want that. My brother would be crushed.

"No, so he can mature on his own and we can slow things down." She smiled wide. "He's too intense, too fast. Taking it slow will be good for him. He asked me to move in with him when we're there." She rolled her eyes.

"Oh, wow." That made me feel funny.

"I told him it wasn't the sort of conversation people had after a couple weeks."

"He's that guy." I laughed. "Once he sees something he wants, he gets it. And he keeps it." I nudged her. "So if you try to escape, he might lock you in the basement."

"You don't have a basement." She wrinkled her nose and stuck her tongue out. "And even if you did, maybe I like the basement."

"For you and Marcello?" I scoffed.

"My Italian lover."

"Don't say *lover*."

"Right." She laughed. "Sorry."

I leaned against her, pretending she was dating an Italian and my brother was a little boy and my life wasn't as complicated as I seemed to make it.

The ability to create a giant pile of steamy shit out of what appeared to be a normal summer had to be a skill. I wondered if I could put it on my résumé.

Chapter Thirty-Nine

PUT THE *MOTHER* IN *SMOTHER*

Jordan

The symphony played, and the press took photos as we walked up the red carpet on the front steps of the Met.

I glanced at my mom and her friends, Iona and Lu. My three dates.

Three single socialites in their late fifties. I'd hit something resembling rock bottom.

My brother gave me a smug grin, leaning in as we entered and the music got louder and the lights dimmed. "Iona isn't so bad in bed. In case you needed a pick-me-up later."

"Jesus. Is there no limit to your debauchery?" I shuddered at the thought of them together.

"You're getting a visual, aren't you? She was on top, and those tatas are real, which I found surprising. She hasn't got a scrap of fat on her except those bad boys."

"Dude!"

"Smothered me." He made a choking gesture.

Cynthia rolled her eyes behind him, making me smile through the horrors of what I was imagining.

"You're a saint," I said to Cynthia, before I led the ladies to our table. "This is us."

"Oh, this is nice." Mom spun in a circle, giving her impressed stare to the decorations. And I had to hand it to Frederick; the venue was stunning. I wasn't one to notice decor, but this was impressive.

"I heard the boy's cancer is gone and he'll be back in school in September," Iona commented.

"I heard that too. Some nephew of Frederick's. All donations are going to the children's cancer ward," Mom added.

"That's nice." Lu smiled like she didn't really care.

I turned away from my dates as they chatted on, looking for the one person I needed to see. The one my heart ached over. I could hear her laugh and see her smile even when I didn't close my eyes. Her blunt remarks and constant sarcasm were also sorely missed.

"Drink?" Stephen came over with a flute of champagne already. "And no, I didn't get it from Miguel." He snorted.

"What?" His words hit me in the gut, reminding me of something. I'd heard that name before.

"You haven't heard? Where have you been, Mars?" He pulled out his phone and headphones and passed them to me. I slipped an earbud in my ear as he did the other. I plugged my other ear so I could hear as he started playing a video. It was of a girl talking to a guy with shaky footage. The scene was creepy as hell, worsening when I realized I recognized the voice of the girl; it was hers. My stomach dropped, and my entire body tightened as I looked at my brother. "Miguel?"

"Amara. The DJ. DJ Spark. He played at that club we went to that night you hooked up with, sorry, didn't hook up with Lacey." He laughed, slapping me in the arm.

"And that, ladies and gents, is the video uploaded by the Test Dummy, busting DJ Spark's disgusting ass as he slipped one of their testers a roofie. We have been told the young woman in question who worked for the Test

Dummy made it home safely. She didn't end up as one of the ten others who have now come forward with allegations about Mr. Amar—"

Stephen cut the reporter off by turning his phone off. "Crazy, eh?"

A thousand alarms rang out in my head, joining dots with lies and coincidences.

"The Test Dummy?" I whispered, linking things in my brain that I couldn't say aloud.

"Yeah, that's the fidelity tester. I heard quite a few guys have been caught. Fucking what's-his-name. Theo. His girl did it—caught his lying ass. He was making out with the chick from the Test Dummy, hand up the shirt and all. There's a video."

My entire body went on pins and needles.

This was what she was doing in that dress?

"You okay?"

"Yeah." I backed up, letting the earbud fall as I scanned the room.

My heart was racing.

My hands balled.

My mouth dried up.

I hurried across the massive room filled with tables and people and laughing and music.

"Martin," someone shouted, and a guy who looked just like Lacey turned. It wasn't the kid brother who made me stop, though. It was the brunette next to him. She looked different from the first time I'd seen her, but I'd recognize her anywhere.

She had saved my life, or at least helped me reclaim it from Amy, which felt as significant as having saved my life.

Or so I thought.

She was laughing and leaning on Lacey's brother. I had shown up at the hospital when he was in surgery and I never went into his room, but there was no mistaking the connection. And he was clearly with the brunette. Which meant she knew Lacey. Lacey knew the girl who tested me for the Test Dummy.

308

I nearly lost my ability to stand. I leaned on the chair next to me, watching her, processing it all.

I was just a target.

Just a mark.

Just a client.

Lacey was the Test Dummy. The brunette worked for her or with her. Or they were both employees? Or a team effort?

But the real point was that she never liked me.

It was an act that maybe she took too far. Maybe she got carried away. Maybe she didn't mean to fall for me. Maybe she didn't fall at all. Maybe it had been just me all along. My heart the only one at risk.

The girl's smile faded, and her eyes widened when she saw me staring. She shrank, recoiling and trying to back away.

Martin looked lost.

I stepped back, offering a pathetic wave before I inevitably ran into the one family member who was missing from their table. I couldn't talk to her. Not now.

Hurrying past my mom and her friends and my brother, I turned at the entrance and headed into an icy corridor to hide and think and cope with the agonizing stabbing in my chest.

Of course that was why she didn't want anyone to know she'd been drugged.

Why she pretended to hook up with me.

Why she pretended to like me.

Why she'd vanished without a trace.

"You idiot," I whispered to myself and the flowers. That was why she had almost gotten herself raped. She had put herself in danger. For a job.

Ripping my phone from my pocket, I googled the Test Dummy and stared at the sophisticated website that now existed. I searched and clicked until I finally reached the answer I was looking for. *La Croix Industries.*

That made it all worse somehow.

She was doing this for work.

I was literally a job.

A job I'd hired her to do.

I'd paid her to test me.

Or had Amy hired her first, and that was why she nearly made out with me on the boat? I was so confused about how this all fit together.

"Hey, you okay?" My brother came around the corner with Monty.

"No. How long have you known about the Test Dummy?" I asked Monty, harsher than I should have.

"What?"

"Frederick's company, the Test Dummy," I repeated.

"I never heard of it before Miguel got caught. I asked Marcia about it, and she didn't know anything."

"She's lying. Her dad owns the company."

"You sure?" Monty cocked an eyebrow.

A figure passed by us, but I didn't care who heard what. "Yeah, I'm positive. Lacey fucking Winters is the Test Dummy. A friend of hers tested me. And Lacey's the one who got drugged in that video with Miguel." I pointed at Stephen. "The night I saved her at the club, that you all thought we hooked up, she was drugged. She's the girl in that video. She tested him. I recognized her voice. And I found her drugged out. I took her to the hotel to take care of her." I laughed bitterly. "I had Fitz come and save her cause I didn't want Frederick to be embarrassed." I covered my eyes for a second. "I can't believe I helped her and fell for her and have been going out of my fucking mind for weeks because of her, and she's been blowing me off because I was nothing more than a fucking job!"

"Holy shit!" Stephen shook his head. "She tested you?"

"Well, technically, I had myself tested." I laughed harder, losing my mind. "I was desperate to give Amy a reason and the ability to break up with me. I had myself tested so I could give her ammo. That way her parents would side with her, and Grandpa would see the video and just think I was out doing what us Somersby guys do. I'd even earn his respect by seeming disrespectful. I failed the test on purpose. Lacey's friend in there is the one I met. She looks to be dating Lacey's fucking brother." I pointed inside, my voice cracking and my hold on sanity slipping. "She hit on me while recording me with some tiny camera I couldn't see. I played along, and she sent the video to me, thinking I was Amy."

"That's insane," Stephen said, sounding lost.

"You have no idea." I leaned against the wall, my insides aching and burning.

"And Lacey is the other Test Dummy? Her and her friend—"

"Who I bet works at La Croix as well!" I shouted at Monty.

"So Lacey and her friend are the faces of this operation?" Monty put his hands in his hair. "For Frederick?"

"What?" Marcia came around the corner wearing a small headset and a serious scowl.

"Nothing," Monty said, sounding angry.

"Did you just say Lacey is the Test Dummy?" She scoffed. "That's impossible."

"Yeah. Your dad owns the company, so you can kill the act." Monty was pissed. "Did you try to test me?" He stepped forward.

"Monty." She paled, answering without actually saying yes or no, which answered his question completely.

"Oh, come on! You honestly thought I might hit on someone else? You paid someone to test my fidelity, after all this time?" He was furious.

"No, I never got an answer back from the service, so technically, I didn't."

"Because it's Lacey. Of course she wouldn't think I needed to be tested. Jesus. She at least trusts me." Monty threw his hands up in the air and stormed off.

Marcia's eyes met mine. "You're lying."

"She's the girl in the Miguel video. Watch it again, pay attention." I pushed off the wall and stormed off after Monty. Misery loved company, and I needed some. I was scared to be alone with myself and my dark thoughts.

I followed his footsteps until I reached the top of the stairs and went out onto the roof.

He was standing, his breath heaving. I sat on the rooftop, staring out at the park and not saying anything.

"This is some horseshit. She fucking tested me? Me? I have never given her a reason to doubt me. And Lacey, what a liar. How could she do that to any of us? She was playing her friends. This doesn't sound right. I can't believe it's her."

"I don't know." My heart was broken. Destroyed. Obliterated.

"I'm sorry, man. I know she fucked you over hard. I thought I knew her better than that."

"I did too," I lamented. "Apparently we were both wrong."

The part that killed me the most was that I'd come to see her, feeling sorry for her hardships. I specifically came to beg her to take me back.

Lacey wasn't the dummy. I was.

Chapter Forty

HEARTBURN

Lacey

The Met was stunning.

I'd been to other galas here, but this was off the charts.

It glistened like an ice palace inside, dripping crystals and sparkles and glitter everywhere, with huge frosty plants with white flowers. The white lighting behind everything and the symphony playing made it feel magical. The corridors were walls of icy flowers and large pale trees that shone and sparkled with lights.

Marcia had knocked it out of the park.

I sighed as I entered the main area where everyone was, taking a moment to let it all soak in.

"Lacey!" Hennie rushed toward me, her eyes wide.

"Is Martin okay?" I glanced past her to where my brother was laughing with my grandma and my mom.

"It's not Martin." Her eyes watered. "He saw me," she whispered.

"Who—oh, God. Did he recog—"

"Yeah. He ran off, and I haven't seen him since. But he looked upset, like he knew exactly what was going on." She swallowed hard.

"Oh, God." I turned and headed for the hallway off to the side, hoping to find a quiet spot to make a call. I needed to find him. I needed to explain.

Jordan knew.

The bottom was falling out, and it was just as I feared.

I hurried to the bathroom, needing to find Marcia so I could tell her everything before she heard it from someone else. I texted her, asking where she was.

"Right behind you," she said.

I spun, wincing when I saw her eyes.

"Just tell me if it's true?" She sounded lost.

"Let me explain."

"No, just answer. Is it true?"

"Yeah." My voice broke.

"Did you spy on us to come up with ideas for my dad? My dad's lapdog, betraying your own friends to make a buck." She started to cry but stopped, like she was refusing the tears.

"Marcia—"

"Leave me alone. I thought we were best friends. But you and Hennie are apparently closer than you let on, huh?" She spun on her heel, leaving me there.

"No." I crumpled on the inside, but my survival instincts kicked in, and I chased her. I grabbed her arm, spinning her, and dragged her back toward the bathroom. "You need to listen to me!"

"Are you insane?" She fought, but I won. She scowled. "Let me go!"

"No!" I hauled her into the bathroom and stood in the way of the exit, staring her in the eyes. "Yes, I'm the Test Dummy. It's why I never tested Monty, because I knew he wouldn't ever cheat on you. He adores you. I tested for two of our friends, Kami and Jo, and no one else. I knew their boyfriends cheated. And Jo's was easy. I came upon Theo making out with a girl, and I emailed the video I took."

"I don't care!" she screamed.

"You do! You care, and that's why you're so pissed at me. Kami was a different story. I went to the club with you, that night."

"I know."

"And he drugged me."

"Thanks. I'm all kinds of caught up."

"No, you aren't. When he drugged me, I didn't know what to do. I was crashing fast. So I apparently stumbled into Jordan, and he took care of me."

"And then you fucked him and ghosted him like the horrible person you are."

"First of all, I didn't fuck him that night. Second of all, I had to ghost him. I tested him for Amy; he had technically been my first subject. So, when things started becoming a little more serious between us, I couldn't bring myself to keep living the lie. I was planning to tell him everything after the gala, but I guess now I won't have to." My voice broke, and tears burst from me.

"You lied to me! You and my dad."

"That's what I'm trying to tell you. Your dad wasn't involved. This wasn't his company. He's telling people it was in order to protect me."

"From what?"

"Miguel's parents." I slumped.

She didn't have a comeback for that.

"I was terrified of them, and of this exact scenario, but I couldn't let the video burn the way they wanted. I knew Kami was crushed, and I was scared. So I went to your dad out of desperation, and he protected me. He bought the Test Dummy and said it was his idea. He leaked the video because Miguel deserves to get caught for this. The guy raped girls and made movies like a sick, twisted creep."

"Why didn't you tell me?"

"Because I was ashamed." I started to lose it. "When my parents said they couldn't afford school and were working nonstop to pay for Martin's care, I didn't know what else to do. I needed extra money. And

I didn't want to ask for it." I spat my words at her as tears blinded me. "I can't be that poor girl from Brooklyn who needs a handout when things get tough. I just wanted to get tougher, to not have to have someone else do my dirty work. Through eight years of friendship, I've never asked for a dime from you or your family. I work three jobs some summers just to keep up with you guys. And this summer I was stuck." I shuddered from the heaving sobs ripping from me. "I love you, Marcia. You're my best friend in the whole world, and the fact that you think I used or betrayed you kills me." I blinked and turned away, hurrying into a crowd of girls coming into the bathroom. "Now, I have to find Jordan. Because he probably thinks something terrible right now."

"Wait!" she called after me, but I slipped to the side of the room and slid along the decorations, hiding from everyone.

I didn't want to go back out the front entrance, not looking like this. And I didn't know where the back entrance was. I needed a quiet place to text Jordan and beg him to meet me.

So I headed for the roof.

There was a bar there.

A place to sit and get a drink alone, toasting to my amazing successes and begging a guy to meet me so I could explain all the horrible things I'd done.

When I got there, it was empty. Everyone was at the gala.

I sat at the bar, sighing.

"What can I get you?" a lady asked.

"Two gin and tonics, extra lime wedges, please," Marcia said from behind me. She sat next to me. "I hate—"

"Please don't." I didn't want to hear any more. I hadn't even seen Jordan yet, and I was already at my breaking point.

"Myself. I hate myself. I'm not as smart as you or as pretty or funny. And Dad loves you more."

"Stop!" I snapped, turning to face her.

"No!" she shouted back. "It's true. He loves you more. And I think I finally get it." She blinked a tear. "It's not because you're better. It's because you need it more. Everyone loves me. Everyone welcomes me with open arms. The world loves Marcia La Croix, and if they don't, they pretend to. Being me is easy. As much as I like to complain, I see it." Her tone softened. "But they see you as my sidekick. My friend Lacey. No one realizes that it's the other way around." She sniffled.

"I love you, Marcia." I broke again.

"Let me finish. I don't think I ever thought about the fact that when you go home to your house, your parents are working nonstop. They're busy as hell. If your grandma hadn't moved in, you and Martin would be virtually on your own. But then you came to my house, and my dad saw your potential because he saw himself in you. And so he loves you a little more, adding more sunshine and water to you so you'll grow and be strong on your own. Like him." She sobbed her last sentence, leaning against me.

"I'm so sorry." I didn't know if what she said was true, at least not all of it.

"No, I'm sorry. I betrayed you just now. I never asked why you would do what you did or gave you a chance to explain."

"I'm so sorry I never told you. I wanted to, but I didn't want anyone to know. I didn't want them to think I was using my connections to get ahead. I know I'm sort of an outsider when it comes to money and power."

"You're not an outsider. You're my sister." She leaned in and hugged me hard. "And I should have listened to you about Monty. He hates me now."

"Why?" I almost laughed at how fast she turned it around to herself, but that was okay. I liked taking the focus away from myself.

"He knows I wanted to test him."

"He doesn't hate you, he couldn't. He loves you. He's just hurt." I leaned into her too. "We all are. I fucked up so bad."

"Yeah. You shoulda told me what you were doing. I coulda helped you." She sniffled and squeezed me tighter.

"I know. I almost died doing it alone." And it was the truth. The one thing I'd learned the most from this was that I needed to stop trying to solve things on my own. I wasn't very good at it; in fact I was terrible. "I got beat up."

"Oh my God." She covered her eyes. "We can't even have this conversation right now. We have to go back in." After a minute, as our drinks arrived, she said, "The gala starts in ten minutes. What do you have in your bag?" She knew I always had enough to do plastic surgery in there.

"A lot." I nodded, still sniffling. "Do you forgive me?".

"Yeah." She kissed my head. "I was so pissed you asked Hennie to be part of this operation and not me."

"I asked her because Jordan wouldn't know her. I swear, I wanted to tell you so many times."

"You owe me big-time for this. I want all the rain checks. Spa time, and only the treatments I want. When we're in *France*"—she sneered the word—"we're only eating at the places I like. And you have to give me makeovers for all my favorite looks. I want the Sailor Moon."

"Fine." I laughed and snuggled into her. Her forgiveness meant everything to me. I knew Jordan would never understand, but as long as Marcia did, I didn't care. I would try not to at least. I still owed him that explanation, though. I needed to find him.

"There you are!" Monty came rushing up, recoiling in horror when he saw our faces. "They're going to start. Your dad's looking for you." He was cold and distant, and he didn't make eye contact with me. "You look like shit."

I was no longer his fav.

I wasn't even his friend. I could see it.

"Monty." Marcia got up, giving him a terrifying smeared-makeup and puffy-faced smile. "I'm an idiot. A huge one. I'm so sorry."

"I know. You're both idiots. And assholes. And liars." He folded his arms. "And I don't want to talk about it right now. At all. So get refreshed, and get downstairs. This is a charity. Not the Marcia and Lacey shit show." He turned on his heel and left us there.

"Savage," I whispered.

"I don't think I've ever seen him this angry."

"Me either. Let me fix your face." I grabbed my bag. "We can't go back down there looking like this."

She hugged me once more, and I inhaled her. Grateful she forgave me. Or at least was pretending to until she really could.

I doubted the same could ever be said for Jordan.

Chapter Forty-One

STEPH'S PSYCHIC LINE

Jordan

"And of course, we want to thank our host for the evening, Marcia La Croix." The lady from the hospital clapped her hands as Marcia made her way up onto the stage.

"I hate to say it; she's a pain in the ass and a complete head case, but this is the best gala I've been to in ages," Monty whispered, leaning in. "The food is amazing. The drink menu is unique. Service staff are on. And the decorations are perfect. She knocked it out of the park," he muttered, sounding bitter about it all. "And the worst part is she knows it. Told her dad she found her niche."

"You love her, we both know it." I sighed, hating this night more than any night I'd lived through. In the history of nights. Worst night ever.

Lacey was sitting up with her family, looking like shit if I was being honest. Marcia wasn't doing much better. They both had clearly been crying, but they also appeared to be friends still. I couldn't imagine how Lacey talked her way out of this.

She wasn't talking her way out of it with me.

I couldn't believe this was happening. Or that I was still here.

That was Monty and Stephen's fault, talking me out of leaving. Saying that if I let this one girl ruin me, I might not ever recover. I'd end up like Grandpa Jack. Never committing to one person. Never falling in love. Never learning to compromise.

And like the angel and devil on each shoulder, they spoke, Monty certain there had to be a reason, and Stephen certain she was Satan set on ruining me.

Either way, I stayed, and now I was staring at her.

The way I always stared at her.

My guts burning.

My heart aching.

My soul empty.

My hands balled.

It was going to be a long night.

I sipped the scotch Stephen had brought to the table and tried not to look in my mom's direction. She would know something was off. She was Hawkeye lately and sober as a judge. She'd been cleansing for three days before this event to get into a gown she hadn't worn in years.

"Thank you, everyone." Marcia smiled into the mic. "I want to start by thanking you all for coming. We're so grateful to have such a supportive community. And I know all these donations will help a lot of young people recovering from cancer. Or just coping." She shone up there, the kind of person people wanted to see on a stage. "Sometimes coping is all you get. We're fortunate that our family's story has a happy ending." Her eyes lowered to where Lacey was sitting. "Martin has always been the little brother I never had. And when we found out he was sick, we knew something needed to be done to help. Seeing all these faces in the room, I can certainly say that your support has already gone a long way to help Martin and countless other kids in his shoes." Her eyes glistened as she smiled down on Martin. She grinned and whispered at him, "I hate you."

He said something that made her and the people near them laugh.

"I will hand you over to the mistress of ceremonies again while the servers ply you with liquor and sweets. I always find Daddy's wallet is a lot more accessible after a few drinks and dessert."

The crowd laughed, and she offered a slight bow as she left the stage. Servers entered the room by the dozens, each carrying trays filled with drinks or pushing carts of desserts, making everyone laugh a little more. The room erupted with talking again as people returned to socializing.

"And she didn't even suck at that." Monty was struggling with being upset.

"Why don't you go and let her grovel? Get it over with. Sit back at your table."

"No." He turned to me. "I'm not leaving you."

"We can do bros before hos another night. Go and see her."

"You sure?" He didn't sound convinced.

The music started to play again as the silent auction started back up and people left their tables to bid and chat.

"Yeah, go and bid at that table right there." Stephen pointed. "She'll see you and come up and lean in, then grab your hand and lead you off to that corner."

"That's super specific." Monty scowled.

"That's because he's done it before," Cynthia remarked, making us all laugh.

"True story." Stephen nodded. "If she doesn't come groveling, there's a chance she's going to twist this into your fault." He beamed at Cynthia. "My advice is to allow that and fall on your sword like a man. There's makeup sex and it's worth it."

Cynthia rolled her eyes at that.

Monty finished his drink and got up. "Wish me luck."

"You don't need luck, you didn't do anything wrong," I scoffed.

"That means nothing." Stephen laughed. "He needs good luck to not get blamed. Good luck, man." He lifted his drink.

"I don't get women," I muttered.

"And you won't ever if you keep paying them to date you." Stephen winked at me.

"Fuck you." I got up and decided to go circulate and bid. The sooner I did that, the sooner I could go without looking like Lacey chased me off. I didn't want to give her the satisfaction.

I was writing a bid up for a week in Aspen when I caught sight of my brother being psychic.

Marcia got up and sauntered over sheepishly to Monty. She spoke delicately to him, then took his hand in hers and led him away, going to the exact fucking corner Stephen had predicted.

I turned to see Stephen lift his drink in the air.

"Jesus." He was impressive, I had to give him that.

"Just let me past!" a voice I knew shouted from the bathroom hallway. My mind begged me not the follow. My heart ached just hearing her speak. But my inner gentleman couldn't let up.

I carried the pen and the bid book for the Aspen trip down the hall.

"Fuck you, bitch. You ruined my boy," a guy shouted. "You and your little Test Dummy game. Everyone knows it was you who took that video."

"Leave me alone. I didn't ruin him; he's a pig, and the fact that you'd dare defend someone like him doesn't surprise me at all." Lacey stood up for herself, sounding harsh. "He's a rapist."

"And you're a whore."

"Fuck you."

"Thanks, but I've done my time."

I pushed through a small crowd to find her and France, the ex, shouting at each other.

"I know what a little cock tease you can be. But it's all about head games with you. Which is why I found my fun elsewhere. Innocent virgin one minute and a complete freak in the sheets—" I didn't hear the rest. I got lost in the pounding in my ears of blood and rage. I dove forward.

"Jordan!" She shouted my name at the same time that I felt my knuckles hurt and saw this dude's face spouting blood. He hit me in the ribs, but I took the shot and punched him in the face again.

"Stephen!" she screamed somewhere in the distance.

Someone grabbed me from behind and pulled France from my arms.

It all moved in slow motion.

People shouted, I was dragged to the bathroom, and the door was slammed.

Stephen paced and shook his head as Monty came rushing in.

"What are you doing?" Stephen scolded me. "This is your second fight in, like, two weeks. And you almost hit Dad. Are you on drugs?"

"He—" I didn't have an excuse. I pointed and then lost the fight in me. I was shaking with rage and ready to kill him still, but I'd lost my reason. He'd called her names she might have deserved. He'd ridiculed her in ways she might have earned. I didn't know what she'd done to him, just me. And I was dying from it.

My knuckles bleeding again for her sake and my broken heart were proof.

The door opened, and her small face popped in, her eyes meeting mine.

I closed my eyes, certain I was dreaming.

"You can't come in here," Stephen shouted. "You've caused enough shit. Just go away. No one wants you around."

"Hey!" Monty shouted, and when I opened my eyes, she was there in front of me with an agonizing stare, and we were alone. Monty had likely dragged Stephen out by his ears.

"I'm sorry," Lacey said softly.

"For which part?" I laughed and spun around, turning the tap on to rinse my hands. "Making me crazy or humiliating me or—"

"For sending that email to Amy. I should have turned her down when I knew I liked you. And I should have told you what I was doing." Her eyes lowered. "I broke your relationship up, even if it was fake, on purpose. But more than that, I broke your trust."

"What?" That came out of nowhere. I shook my head a little, trying to see if my ears were broken from too many hits, though I didn't think France had knocked me that hard.

"I used my friend to test you on purpose. It wasn't just for Amy. I was testing you for me too. And when you hit on Hennie, even though I get why you did it, I sent it to Amy. I shouldn't have tested you in the first place. And I'm sorry."

"You liked me?" I stepped back, certain this was another game of hers.

"Yeah. Of course. I thought that was obvious. We had sex." She blushed even more and lowered her voice on *sex*.

"You were making out with guys all summer to prove they cheated."

"What?" It was her turn to look confused and take a step back.

"Theo. You made out with Theo to prove he was cheating. Hands up the shirt." Somehow my hands ended up miming it, and we both grimaced.

"I did not!" Her eyes flashed rage. "I caught him making out with some random girl, and I recorded it and sent it to my friend as proof."

"That wasn't you?" Oh, fuck.

"Of course not. So that's what you think of me, that I'm some whore because an asshole like France says it? That I would make out with guys to catch them? It went down identically to how it happened with you and Hennie. I never touched a single client." Her eyes tried to murder me with hate lasers and a glare that would haunt my dreams forever. "Except you. And I knew you were a client, and I possibly ruined you for my own gain. And I also knew my cover would be blown the second you were introduced to Hennie as my friend. You'd see her and put two and two together. I just didn't have the guts to tell you beforehand." Her voice cracked and her eyes flooded. "I didn't want you to know what I'd done to you. I couldn't bear the thought of you hating me."

"Oh, fuck." I stumbled a little.

"But I never hooked up with anyone else. I want you to know that." She blinked, and the tears streamed down her cheeks.

"But you acted like you hated me."

"I tested you and you failed. You hit on my friend, after you'd met me."

"There's something I should probably tell you now. I paid for the test, Lacey." I almost threw up. This was a giant mess.

"What do you mean?"

"I sent the email for the test, not Amy. I set myself up to offer proof as a way for Amy to be able to break things off with me so both our families were satisfied. I hit on Hennie on purpose. I knew she was the Test Dummy. She's a terrible actor."

"What!" Her eyes widened, and I saw my future. Flayed alive on the streets for all to see. This was spinning around to me, just like Stephen said it would.

She put her fingers to her temples. "I can't even believe this. Here I've been, beating myself up for hiding something from you, when you've been the master manipulator all along. Oh my God."

"Wait, what?"

"I'm such an idiot!" She turned and ran from me, through the door and along the wall with the decorations.

I chased after her, passing through the crowd where France was being tended to by some girl and surrounded by a flock of others. I was glad it was working out so well for him.

Stephen and Monty called after me, but I kept my eye on the prize.

When I got to the front door, I caught a glimpse of Lacey's dress on the red carpet.

"Lacey!" I shouted, running faster.

But she darted to the crowd of photographers taking pictures of her. They didn't let her through easily, so she slipped out of her shoes. I turned and sprinted after her. She rounded the corner of the building and headed for the east drive.

I ran for her shoes and almost picked them up, but then I realized if I spent even a second grabbing them, I'd miss her. It was the prince's biggest mistake, stopping for the shoe.

Instead I followed Cinderella into the park.

Chapter Forty-Two

THE END OF CINDERELLA

Lacey

My legs could move, since I'd worn a dress with the slit from toe to waist in the front.

When I was sure I'd lost Jordan, I stopped. My heart was racing, and my boobs actually hurt from running across the great lawn and along the reservoir.

Heaving, I tried to catch my breath, still walking along the jogging path with my arms in the air over my head.

"Lacey!" he called, startling me. I spun, disappointed when I saw him so close. There was no way I could keep running. I was pretty sure my feet were bleeding, and my body was aching from the exercise with no warm-up and not wearing the right apparel.

Somehow seeing him pained me more.

I turned and limped away as fast as I could, but his slapping shoes on the cement shouted his impending arrival.

I braced for the grab or the embrace, but he did neither. He caught up and walked alongside me, not forcing me to look at him. "Wait."

"Why?" I started to laugh, because I couldn't cry anymore. "This is the most fucked-up thing I've ever heard of." I covered my face and moaned. "You paid me to bait you, and then I ruined any chance we had at a relationship with the guilt I made myself sick from." I pulled my hands away, glaring at him. "Is this not the moment you just throw in the towel and say *fuck it*?"

"No!" He grabbed my arms, spinning me to face him. "No. This is the moment we admit we're immature and pathetic and possibly bad at communicating with others. This is the moment we admit we like each other. And we will never do anything so twisted to the other person again. Like Monty and Marcia are right now." He pointed back at the Met.

"They've been dating for years."

"And a couple of years from now, when we're still dating, we can look back on this and laugh. It's a series of unfortunate mistakes and miscommunications. You didn't do anything to hurt me intentionally, and I didn't either."

"I did!" I shouted. "I tested you, judged you, broke you up with your pretend girlfriend, and then ghosted you while your life was falling apart! All on purpose."

"Well, I forgive you," he shouted as a guy walked past us, giving Jordan a look like he wanted to tell him to run away from me. "Because I never would have hit on that girl in the bar. I'd already met you. You were wrong about me, because I was putting on an act. Had I just manned up like you said and ended that bullshit on my own, none of this would have happened. None of it." He braved stepping closer, staring down at me. "And maybe you would never have gone through with creating the Test Dummy in the first place because you would have told me about your money issues and I could have helped. I would have. I still want to." He brushed my hair from my face.

"You're insane." I didn't have a single other thing to offer. It was too soon and too fast, and he was too intense.

329

"I'm crazy about you." He took my hand in his and kissed the back of it, lingering. "I want to date and be together and win you over. Please forgive me."

The feel of his hand around mine and his lips pressed against my flesh gave way to other feelings.

"Call Heinrich and your car. We're finally going to do something right," I said before I really thought about it too much.

"Are you sure?"

"Of course I'm not sure! My feet are bleeding, and I'm wearing a five-thousand-dollar dress in Central fucking Park. Strangers are probably recording this. I feel like I'm having a heart attack." I rubbed my chest bones.

"Okay, that's a yes." He raised his eyebrows and pulled out his phone, then sent a text. He enclosed his hand around mine and pulled me, making me wince as it felt like I was walking on glass.

"Ow!" I pulled back, lifting my foot and cringing at the mess of it.

"Here." He scooped me into his arms, holding me to his chest. "Wouldn't be the first time I carried you like this to the car." He laughed.

"Oh my God. We are a mess." I wrapped my arms around his neck, holding him tight.

When we got to the street, the limo pulled up moments later.

"How does he do that?"

"He maps me constantly," he said as he bent and got the door for me before placing me inside.

"Ouch!" I gasped from the pain in my feet as I sat, my hands wanting to grab at him when he sat across from me. "Same limo?" I asked.

"The very same." He offered that smile. "Stay in your seat. I don't intend to let you make the same mistake as last time."

I contemplated getting up, but I was curious about us finally being in a bed. Maybe after a shower and some bandages were put on my feet. And a stiff drink and a nap.

He didn't speak, and the air filled up with that tension, the one I used to think was awkwardness. Now I saw. His bruised and bloody hands gripped his legs, squeezing his knees as he trembled, fighting the urge to touch me.

The ride around the park was long and quiet and tense.

We'd talked too much. To death. The truths had flooded out from every nook and cranny, blowing open both our hearts.

And now in silent reverie we would have to put the pieces back where they belonged, though once a heart was shattered, it didn't look the same. You never got those pieces back where they should have gone. That's where the changes came from. The new imperfections and cracks. They formed us, creating the person we would become together when the broken pieces healed.

As the limo stopped, my stomach ached with anxiety and excitement fluttering about in me. Jordan got out first, then lifted me up and carried me to the back door. He flashed a card and opened the door, taking me to the elevator.

He placed me on the floor once we were there, making me wince. I stood beside him, slipping my hand into his and staring at the metal doors, wondering what secrets they held for us. What expressions they hid with their brushed metal. If they'd been shiny, what would we have seen?

When the elevator dinged, we weren't in a hallway but a massive hotel room. It was furnished differently than the others. More like a house. It was the penthouse.

He lifted me and carried me across the floor to a bedroom at the back. He placed me down in the bathroom, his fingers still trembling with need and control.

He stood behind me, staring at me in the mirror. We were a sight. My hair was ruffled and pulled from the clip. My makeup had run down my cheeks. His knuckles and white shirt were bloody.

"Why are we both a hot mess every time I'm in this hotel with you?" He sighed as he unzipped me and brushed the dress down my shoulders, pooling it at my feet, leaving me completely naked except for a silver thong.

He inhaled sharply.

"Maybe we're both a hot mess, and this hotel just amplifies that." I brushed his comment off as I turned, flashing my ass in the mirror, and grabbed his bow tie, undoing it and the buttons to his shirt. I didn't want to talk about how messy we were. I dragged his jacket down with his shirt, leaving him in his undershirt. I pulled off his belt next and dropped it to the floor, making the sound of the metal hitting the marble floor echo in the silence.

I undid his pants, staring into his eyes as I let them slip down to the floor. I dragged his shirt up, pulling it off him, and then ran my fingers over his slightly hairy chest. It was a light smattering on his chest in the middle and then more on his treasure trail. At twenty-two, it was a sign of what he would have later in life. A lot. But it also made me wonder about his beard. His whiskers seemed solid, like they might be thick and spaced well enough to grow a good one.

His chest was broad and strong, not gnarled with muscle, but it could get there. He had the body type that had the potential to be incredibly thick. My hands looked tiny on his body. I ran them over his arms, squeezing the muscles. He stepped back, looking at me. Inspecting me the same way I was him. I pulled my thong off. He did his boxers. Unleashing that big, beautiful beast. I licked my lips, staring at it.

He reached forward, running a finger up my torso, stopping in a weird spot. I glanced down, smiling. "Appendix." He was touching my tiny scar.

As if the words were the moment he was needing, he sprang. He swept me into his arms, kissing me and crushing my body into his. We kissed as we walked to the shower. I cried out in his mouth as cold water rained down on us. It got warm fast, and not just from us. He lifted me into the air, holding me as he sat me on the bench. He pulled back, lifted my feet, and gently washed them. Brown dirt and old blood ran down into the drain.

"Do they look bad?"

"No. A couple of small cuts." He helped me stand and grabbed a washcloth. He soaped it up, and starting with my hands, he washed me.

It was sensual and yet something else, intimate in a trust-building sort of way.

When he got to my breasts he delicately brushed the cloth over them, flicking my stimulated nipples with light touches. I gasped, biting my lip and wishing more would happen as his hands moved to my stomach. I wanted to beg and plead with him to touch me everywhere, but the way he was moving, I didn't imagine it would do me any good. He was taking this the slow way. I'd rushed things once already.

When he got between my legs, again he was delicate with his touches. He lightly cleaned, massaging and swirling the warm water between my legs. I leaned back against the tile wall, closing my eyes as he lightly fingered the right spot. Just when he hit it, though, he would stop again.

I groaned, begging with my stare and my breath, but he ignored it. He washed my legs and feet, kneeling on the floor of the shower. His face was so close to the place I really wanted it. As I was about to beg, he did the thing I wanted. He lifted my leg to the bench, spreading me open for his inspection.

He leaned in, the water running down us both as he nuzzled his face in there, rubbing his nose against my clit. He kissed the inside of my thigh, and I realized he knew what he was doing. He was tormenting me.

I sucked my breath, whimpering as he went back, licking once, flicking my clit.

I clung to his head and pushed it into the right place, forcing him to touch me.

But he was stronger. He stood, lifting me again, dripping wet, and carried me from the running shower. He didn't get a towel or dry us off. He carried me to the bed and tossed me down, staring at me like the uncaged thing he would tame.

I spread myself, reaching for him.

He grabbed a condom, put it on, and stood staring at me. I'd never seen anything so hot in my life. A man with huge hands fondling himself, in a way that felt like I shouldn't see it. Water dripped off his beautiful body as he stared at me and made me blush. Everything else should have, but it was his stare that undid me.

He crawled onto the bed, sliding between my legs. He kissed me gently as he pushed in slowly, like I'd made him do the first time.

It took a couple of thrusts before I could relax into his movements, creating my own.

I was lost in it all, the deep kisses and the full thrusts, him invading my body in both places as his hands kneaded me, lifting and gripping.

He felt like the ocean over me, riding me and rippling over my body, writhing inside of me. I closed my eyes, arching my back and letting him fuck me sensually.

I relinquished control as his body controlled mine, moving me and pleasing me with every stroke and thrust and pump and grip.

He nibbled at my neck and sucked my nipples, inhaling them and flicking, but maintaining that rhythm inside of me. He groaned into my neck, growling almost as he gripped my ass, lifting me to meet him.

Pulling out, he sat back on his heels and placed my legs in his arms as he pulled me closer, dragging me down the bed to him. He pushed himself back in, staying upright and cupping my ass, with my legs running up his chest and my feet hooking over his shoulders. He pushed in hard, making me grunt as he filled me up.

Dragging me into the thrust, he pushed again, hitting the right spot, making another sound slip from my lips. He did it again, and again, hard and fast until I didn't stop making the sound, and my body convulsed on his. His hips pounded my ass as his cock pummeled me.

My eyes rolled into the back of my head as I orgasmed, riding the waves he was making for us.

Ecstasy overwhelmed me. I gripped the wet blankets behind me, moaning with every move he made until I finished, and even then, I whimpered as he continued to pump into me violently. When he came, his veins bulged and his angry face came back. He grunted and thrust until he looked like he might burst. He jerked and shuddered until he finally flopped on top of me, kissing my cheek.

His heaving chest and mine matched.

I watched him for a minute before I closed my eyes and contemplated what a lot of convoluted destruction we had left in our wake.

And now that the sex was done and the feet were clean, we needed to answer a lot of little details. Fill in gaps. I dreaded this part.

I hated how I'd treated him.

He spoke low, next to my ear. "So the day you got attacked by that guy outside that bar—"

"How do you know—"

"I was there." He said it in a whisper. My whole body started to shiver.

"There?" I asked softly, feeling him on top of me, tensing. "That was you?" I gasped, lifting my head and staring at him. "You were following me?"

"Yeah." He nodded, climbing off of me and lying on the bed properly. "You were working?"

"I was." I climbed up next to him and pulled the dry part of the blanket up. "The girl who messaged me was a random, so I didn't know what I was dealing with. I got the guy to hit on me, and he didn't take no for an answer." My entire body was tingling with the revelation. "You beat him up."

"Yeah, I did. I've never been so scared in all my life. I didn't understand what you were doing. Those clothes and the makeup. And that part of town. It was all so weird."

"He had a pregnant girlfriend. She had a suspicion." And I had no defense.

"I'm sorry I didn't get there faster." His eyes burned.

"I'm sorry I wasn't more honest with you, about everything."

"I get it. You're strong and independent, and you take care of yourself. And you run away from anything that could possibly interfere with your control. But you need to start understanding the word *teammate*. You don't have to do everything on your own."

"I know. I'm sorry I ran."

"Don't run away this time, Cinderella."

"I won't." I lifted my gaze to look into his dark-green eyes. "There's nowhere I'd rather be than here."

It was the truth.

And for the first time since we'd met, it was also possible for me to stay without guilt eating away at me or work needing me.

Everything was going to be okay.

His dimpled smile told me that.

My days as Cinderella were over.

It was finally time for me to be a princess to a prince.

Chapter Forty-Three

JERK-OFF SOCKS

Jordan

Everyone was here.

The housewarming costume party had been my idea. Come as your favorite superhero.

I was Kylo Ren and Lacey was Rey. She'd given me a stern look when she said she "shipped them." I didn't understand what shipping was, but I liked *Star Wars*, so that worked. I thought it was weird this was her choice since I'd mistaken these characters for brother and sister, twins. But she'd gotten pissed when I said that and insisted that I didn't really know anything about sci-fi/fantasy after all.

"How's Dad?" I asked Stephen as I munched on some nachos and watched the party.

"He has been sober for a bit. He's been running every day again. He's retiring, making Grandpa happier than anyone I've ever met. And he's in therapy."

"No shit." I was genuinely shocked.

"No shit. I think you should give him another chance to say sorry. He doesn't say it, but I can tell he wants it."

"Maybe." I nodded. "I'll give him a couple of more weeks and then see if he wants to meet for lunch." I'd agreed to reach out, but I hated it. I had already made amends with the fact that it would be me moving on. I might never get an apology. I needed to be okay with that.

"What—who's that?" Stephen asked, staring like his eyes might bug out of his Batman costume.

"Who?" I played along like it was no big deal. "Where?"

"Is that fucking Wonder Woman?" He sounded like he might die any second. He had rules about random girls wearing a Wonder Woman costume. Specific fantasies that had to be respected.

"Oh, yeah. One of Lacey's friends, I think." I nodded, staring at how amazingly that fucking costume fit the girl I'd hired. She was one of five. The costume hugged every curve and accentuated her stunning face.

"Oh my God." He twitched a little, like he might either faint or get a boner. "Batman and Wonder Woman had a thing," he whimpered like a little bitch.

"What's that?" I asked, acting the part perfectly, like I didn't know who the woman was getting food and chatting with my mom.

When she turned, he clutched my arm. "Who the hell—is that?" he whimpered.

Another Wonder Woman came out of the kitchen eating a huge corn dog. I'd made sure some of the food was kinda sexual: corn dogs, chocolate-covered bananas, taquitos. She winked at Batman—Stephen—and sauntered over to the other Wonder Woman.

A third one smiled wide and strolled over, looking amazing in her costume. "Hey, Batman." She stood next to me, acting like this was normal, and took a deep bite off her chocolate-covered banana.

His eyes narrowed. "What the fu—?"

A fourth Wonder Woman, also looking identical to Gal Gadot with Lacey's magical makeup skills, came walking over to the food.

All four of them laughed and chatted.

"Hey, honey." Cynthia came up to him. "You okay?" She felt his forehead with the back of her hand. She was Catwoman and rocking the bodysuit. "You look weird."

"Fine." He swatted her away.

His eyes locked on my girlfriend in her Rey costume as I slipped a hand around and placed it on her lower back. "You did this."

"Me?" Lacey scoffed. "No way. You look amazing in your costume, Cynthia." Lacey changed the subject.

"Thank you. You do too." Cynthia smiled along nicely as well. It was so normal to just be standing here, hanging out, like nothing was happening to my brother.

And yet it was.

He was dying.

It was just how I always pictured it.

Of course I'd always imagined there only being one I had to pay to wear the costume. It was Lacey's idea to get five.

When the fifth Wonder Woman came into the living room, Cynthia nodded at Lacey. "Let's get a drink." They left, sauntering maybe a little too.

"Sweet Jesus." Stephen watched the Wonder Women eating. "How could you do this to me? It's a sea of them eating dick-shaped food." Each one more perfect than the next. All models. All gorgeous girls in the costumes that were exact replicas sent over from California. Monty had a friend.

"Well, now, I think I might have owed you. Let me check." I pretended to think. "Yup. I did."

"This is horseshit. You know the rule," he shouted, drawing attention from the party like he was a child, which he was. A big baby.

"Maybe." I smiled coyly.

"I hate you."

"I know." I grinned; this was my moment. Twenty-two years in the making.

"Why did you do this?"

"No reason."

Wonder Woman was forbidden fruit for him. And now here he was, in his Batman suit, surrounded by the hottest Wonder Women I'd ever seen. And he was married.

"Why would you do this to—"

"Jerk-off socks." I nodded. "And many other things, but mostly jerk-off socks." I flipped him off and strolled into the kitchen to find my girl. Stephen stood in the living room, staring, and likely getting hard in his cup.

"Ladies." I nodded at Lacey, Cynthia, Marcia, and Carmen. "Monty." I nudged him.

"Hey, man, no need to shout. This is a tiny house. I think our guesthouse in Martha's Vineyard is bigger than this."

"It's all I need right now." I laughed and glanced to where my mom was chatting with her friends. "It's just me and Mom."

"And if you're lucky, you might get the odd sleepover from me." Lacey grinned.

"And that." In the time we'd been official, she'd been away in France but came home tired of hotels. But she also didn't want to sleep here if Mom was around, which I could get. It was awkward. But her living at home for one more year was also awkward. So we were stuck with quickies when Mom wasn't around.

"Hey, did you guys hear, speaking of sleepovers, that Maya's mom and Mr. Sandu moved in together?" Carmen whispered. "I saw Maya with that cute Canadian yesterday, and she said her mom seems really happy."

"Weird." Marcia's eyes narrowed, which made her look like an anime character. She had something called Sailor Moon on. Something she forced Lacey to do the makeup for.

"Why?" Monty asked.

"Because I saw Mr. Sandu at the club in the Hamptons yesterday, and he was getting tennis lessons and they looked awfully cozy."

"That guy must be snorting rails of Viagra. Who has that kind of energy?" Monty shook his head.

"Speaking of Viagra, how's the Test Dummy doing?" Carmen asked Lacey.

"I don't know," she pretended. "I just got back from France. I haven't heard."

"Shares are way up." I winked, earning a scowl from Lacey.

"Did you buy shares?" she asked as she and Marcia wrinkled their noses.

"We all did." I laughed. "When it went public, we got smart and bought. It's going to be the next 'chat a fish.'" I mocked Marcia's dad.

"Yeah, we are gonna make bank on that." Monty pounded my knuckles.

"Oh my God." Lacey rolled her eyes. "How could you?" she asked.

"How could I not? We all had to be supportive. You made that, baby!" I laughed; most of us did. Lacey didn't.

She sighed and walked out of the kitchen, leaving me hanging.

"Good luck with that one," Marcia smirked.

"What?" I asked, as if I didn't know it was still a really sore spot.

"You know what," Marcia said.

"Shit." I turned and headed up the stairs where she'd gone, to the loft where the terrace was.

"Hey, don't be mad." I pulled her out into the night air, noting how crisp it was.

"Seriously, Test Dummy?"

"No." I laughed. "Not the Test Dummy. Frederick. I always follow him. He knows his shit. When he goes public with something, it makes money. Every time." I pulled her into me. Kissed her softly. "I have a serious question for you." I loved messing with her. Her commitment phobia was amazing.

"No. I already told you I'm not moving in, I don't care how much closer to the campus you are."

"Will you—" I dropped to my knee and lifted a teal ring box.

"Don't do this. Please don't do this. You're going to make me have a heart attack. I refuse to say yes. You're going to hurt us both."

She sounded desperate, so I laughed and stood up, opening the box to reveal a dog collar.

"Since you ruined apartment shopping and made me go with my mom, I thought maybe you'd like to help me pick a dog."

"What?" She smiled wide. "Hell yes. I've always wanted a dog. I mean—it'll be your dog, but I'll totally help." Her eyes glistened with the emotion left over from the ring box. "What was the box for?"

"A joke. I stopped by Tiffany's and grabbed it to mess with you," I lied. I hated lying to her, but this one was an important lie. She'd freak out if she knew I'd bought a ring yesterday and was keeping it safe.

She thought love took huge amounts of time and effort and was built on a foundation akin to the one the Vatican was built on. She didn't understand that true love or soul mates happened when eyes met and hearts beat against each other's chests.

But I did.

From the moment I'd seen her staring at the city, all by herself in the glow from the lights, I'd known.

I had a ring and house, and soon we would have a dog. And in the year it would take for her to finally admit we were madly in love, I would be finished with school and live in New York as well, and she would sleep here instead of her parents' place, and my mom would be strong enough to find an apartment of her own. One day the ring in my pocket would be on her finger. And buying it so soon wasn't for her; it was for me.

I was playing the long game with her, trying to make magic to turn Winters into Somersby.

Frederick La Croix had bet on her once a long time ago.

And I never bet against him.

He had an uncanny ability to pick a winner every time. Some called it sorcery. He called it luck. I called it instinct.

Whatever it was, he was willing to bet his company's future on her. Just like I was already betting my heart.

I cupped her face, smiling wide and free, and whispered, not just to her but to the universe, "I adore you, Lacey."

She blinked and pressed her lips together, forbidding herself from saying anything back. She didn't have to. Her eyes said everything she didn't. "I hate you," she whispered back.

"You love me and you know it." I laughed, throwing Martin's words back at her.

"Anyway." She avoided saying it and hugged me, gripping that dog collar tightly. "What about while you're in college in Boston?"

"You and my mom can help take care of him or her. I'll come back weekends and holidays and breaks."

"I guess I could handle having an adorable part-time cuddle buddy and best friend. Marcia wouldn't get too jealous. Can we go tomorrow? I'd want a pound dog. I want to rescue some poor animal and give it a better life. Pay it forward."

"That sounds like a good idea." I kissed her forehead and slung my arm around her neck, leading her back inside where all our friends were.

"I think we should make sure it's already spayed or neutered, because otherwise we have to do the aftercare, and it's a whole thing." She rambled on about the dog as we got downstairs. "Maybe we could get one that's a couple of years older, looking for a home. That way a puppy won't get separation anxiety while you're away."

My mom's eyes darted to my pocket. She didn't miss a thing anymore. Her eyes flashed on Lacey's hands next, smiling when she saw the dog collar.

I wanted to tell my mom she didn't have to worry. I hadn't made the same mistake as her. I chose with my head and my heart at the same time. And Lacey had them both.

Epilogue

Lacey

Seeing my brother smiling and laughing on the sofa with Hennie was kinda awesome. They were adorable. It was finally the end of summer, so she was leaving very soon for school, and it would be months before they saw each other. I actually felt bad for them. Almost as bad as I felt for myself. Jordan would be leaving for school this week too. And as much as I hated the fact that I was smitten with someone in such a short amount of time, I was going to miss him like crazy. But at least we had Scruff to keep his mother and me both busy. He was a mutt from the pound. A perfect mutt. He looked a little crazy with his weird mix of Australian shepherd and labradoodle, but he was so cute and funny. He couldn't catch anything to save his life. I'd tried all week at training him but ended up with nothing but footage of me throwing snacks at him while he gave me a confused expression.

"I told you that you would have to get on board." Marcia nudged me, glancing at my brother and his official girlfriend.

"I know," I grumbled, like I didn't love it or them.

"I totally shipped them from the start." She sighed and leaned back, rubbing her belly.

"You did not." I leaned back too and also rubbed my belly. "I am so full."

"Dinner with your family is always the best. Grandma can cook."

"Grandma can cook." I winced. "I don't know how we'll make it back to your place without needing to stop and get sick along the way."

"I totally might just so I can squeeze in more dessert." She said it like it was a normal thing to do.

I laughed and gave her the look, the what-the-fuck look.

"I was joking." She lowered her voice even more. "You think they do it?"

"What? Who?" I followed her gaze to my brother. "Ewwwww. No," I groaned. "I don't want to think about that. Dude." I closed my eyes and forced images of Scruff.

"Oh my God." She lowered her voice even more. "Your grandma is walking toward me with pie."

"I saved a summer-berry pie for your father." Grandma came into the kitchen, holding it up. "Do you need a bag to carry it?" she asked Marcia.

"Bag?"

"Yeah, she does, Grandma. I'll get it." I struggled to get up with my pants undone from all the food stuffed in my stomach. "We shoulda worn leggings for dinner."

"I'm going upstairs and stealing a pair of yours right now." Marcia got up and left.

Mom and Dad laughed. They were home, at the same time. Laughing and relaxed. They didn't fight about money, not since we fixed everything.

Mom was only working her four on and taking all her four off every week now.

Dad wasn't taking any extra clients or trips. It was the most I'd ever seen them together, and they seemed to really be appreciating their time.

All in all, it was better. Money might not have saved everyone and made every problem go away. But our family was lucky enough to have problems that money could solve.

Money and surgery.

The Test Dummy sale took care of their bills and mortgage. It took care of Martin's school fund, which he didn't end up needing thanks to a full ride to MIT. He told me the money was for a house when he and Hennie got settled wherever they were going to live.

I told him he better be coming back to New York and to stop thinking about marrying girls he just met.

Martin, sporting hardly even a scar now, got up off the couch and strolled over, stretching and hitting me in the head.

Grandma smiled more, and she gave Marcia something resembling kindness. Marcia's part-time job as an event planner while finishing her degree helped with Grandma warming to her, though Marcia never noticed.

I kicked my brother in the butt.

"I'm going to Marcia's." I gave Mom a kiss and Dad a hug. I grabbed the bag for the pie and kissed Grandma.

"Okay, sweetie. Be good. And don't stay up late. You girls need sleep. Last week you were cranky from not enough sleep, and school is staring in a couple of days."

"No, Mom, it wasn't sleep deprivation, she had her period. Trust me. It was terrible. I got up to pee in the night, and she hadn't flushed properly—"

"Martin!" I hit him in the arm. "Shut up!"

"You love me and you know it." He flashed me that grin, the one I thought was an adorable baby-brother evil grin and that he probably gave Hennie when he wanted something. The thought made me shudder.

"Night!" I waved at everyone and flipped off Martin.

"Lacey!" Mom shouted as I hugged Hennie.

"See you tomorrow for shopping, right?" I pulled back, inspecting her face for truths.

"Fine." She scowled. "I hate shopping."

"It's going to be fun. Stop. You need clothes for the new semester." I grabbed the pie and put it in the bag and walked to the front door. "Let's go!" I shouted up at Marcia as she came down the stairs wearing my leggings.

"I'm coming. God." She hurried into the kitchen and got love and hugs from everyone. Martin got extra from her.

"I know which sister loves me more."

I rolled my eyes at him as she came back.

We put our shoes on and hurried out the door, cradling our bellies as we walked down the street.

"Can we call a car, please?"

"No." I gave her some side-eye. It wasn't as good as hers, but it was getting better with more practice. "You can't possibly be scared."

"I'm not scared." She tried to sound convincing. "I still hate the subway."

"Well, you really need to learn to suck it up." I walked faster for the crosswalk. A limo pulled up as I got there.

"Damn!" Marcia jumped back. "How does he do that?"

"He maps me." I sighed happily as Jordan opened the door, smiling wide. Marcia grinned, seeing Monty in the back of the car as she climbed in.

"Hi." Jordan gave me a kiss.

"Hi." I kissed him back and climbed in.

"What are you wearing?" Monty looked at Marcia.

"Look, don't fat shame me. I couldn't do my pants up. I had two helpings of dinner and pie. Look." She lifted the sweater she'd stolen from me and showed him the red line on her stomach. "It was obscene."

"Always is." I lifted my shirt and flashed my own red line and the fact that I'd undone my dress pants.

"Oh, wow." Jordan rubbed my stomach. "This is intense."

"It hurts a little."

"Maybe some hot tub?" Marcia asked.

"Yes," I agreed.

When we got over the bridge and into the city, traffic wasn't bad. We made it to her house in half an hour.

"Faster than the subway," she remarked.

"It's Friday and only six at night. Any self-respecting New Yorker wouldn't be caught dead out for at least another four hours."

"Hmm-hmm." Marcia laughed and got out of the car, clicking in her heels, sweater, and leggings to the front door. West wasn't there; he got weekends off. But the doorman smiled and let us in.

When we got to the elevator, Jordan reached down and delicately slipped my fingers into his. We held hands into the penthouse, where we were greeted by Marcia's mom and dad.

"How's it going?" I hugged both and handed her dad the pie. "From Grandma."

"Oh, come on." He opened the bag and grinned like a little boy would. "You have to tell her thank you."

"I will."

"Who's excited for school to start?" He lifted the stern dad eyebrow.

"I am. I think it's going to be a great final year for us both." I pointed at Jordan.

Jordan gave me a twinkly-eyed grin. "How's the Test Dummy doing?" Jordan asked Mr. La Croix, provoking me.

"We're selling it, didn't Lacey tell you?"

"She didn't." Jordan gave me a scowl.

"The deal wasn't finalized. I didn't want to jinx it," I said, defending myself. Or talk about it.

"You're so superstitious. You shoulda seen her, she practically spat on the contract for luck." Marcia's dad chuckled. "No, we're getting it ready to sell in the next couple weeks, actually." He glanced at me, beaming with pride. "Your first idea is going to make the company your first nine-figure sale." He patted me on the back. "Congratulations, Lacey."

"You did it." I tried to be humble, but I felt the pride a little bit. I was still a little sore over the whole thing and grateful as hell it had sold. He was right, I did almost spit on the contract for luck.

"No. We did it. And we will be doing it a lot more. I know it." Mr. La Croix hugged me again, gripping his pie almost as tightly.

"Hot tub before I cramp up," Marcia demanded, and stomped to her bedroom.

I laughed. "Best to not keep her waiting."

"Lord, no." Her mom rolled her eyes.

We hurried into bathing suits. I tried not to feel like a whale as I pulled on my bikini and my stomach wouldn't suck in.

"Oh, God." Marcia patted her slightly extended belly.

"One big poop and it's gone." I repeated what Grandma always said while laughing her face off at me.

"That's disgusting." Marcia wrinkled her nose, giggling away. She went down to the guest room, no doubt to assault Monty while he changed, so I headed out into the night alone.

The hot tub was stunning—not just the sheer size of it, but the view of Manhattan and Brooklyn was breathtaking.

I shivered as the hot water burned and soothed.

I leaned over the railing, gazing at the city lights, and sighed.

If it weren't for Grandma, Marcia, and her family, I would be one of those twinkling lights. Working while going to school and making it happen. One day I would have found a way to be here, overlooking the city from the upper decks, but it would have been a longer journey.

It still amazed me how incredible my life was, and all because of a couple of things working out a certain way.

Life was funny.

I stared out at those twinkling lights and contemplated just how surreal this moment was. And how lucky I was. Especially now that the Test Dummy was selling and I wouldn't have to think about it at the office when I went back.

That, I was grateful for.

"Oh, shit!" Jordan interrupted my silent reverie as he winced and climbed in. "Burns the cold feet."

He swam up behind me and wrapped his arms around me, kissing the side of my face. "Beautiful view. Same one I was looking at the night we met."

"No, that was from the harbor." I glanced back.

"Lacey." He laughed. "I was never looking at the city, just you." He spun me around to sit on his lap.

"You mean, you were looking even though I had sneaked up from the lower decks?"

"There were no decks. There was you and me. I didn't see anything else." He leaned in, pressing his lips against mine.

I closed my eyes and kissed him, imagining us floating there among all those bright lights, like we belonged, maybe. It took me longer to arrive at every emotion than it did him, but after a couple of months, I could say I was falling in love with him.

With him I didn't feel like Cinderella, as he always joked.

I felt like a queen, not a princess.

With him everything was possible.

He pulled back, his eyes shining with delight. "I have something to tell you."

My stomach tightened, which was not comfortable with all that food in there.

"I'm not going back to college at all this year, and I'm quitting the family business permanently."

"What?" I gasped.

Tara Brown

"I'm going to take a break from school and I'm going to figure it out from there."

"Holy shit!" My eyes widened and I hugged him tight. "Holy shit!"

"I know. I don't know what I want to do, so I'm going to spend the year working in random jobs and see if I can't find myself. And also hang out with you. I packed my bags for Boston, and everything in me said not to."

"This is huge. And crazy." I sat back, completely confused and surprised. "But I'm kinda relieved. You never seemed very passionate about numbers."

"No. I'm not." He smiled, looking more content than I'd ever seen him. "I gave my notice to my grandpa, explaining that I needed some time and space to figure out what I really want."

"Did you get disowned again?" His dad had invited Jordan and Stephen to his therapy sessions to make up, which seemed like a reasonable thing to do, but it still had me worried. Cause no matter what he said about hating his dad, the broken heart from his father's anger was there.

"No." He laughed, shaking his head. "Grandpa asked if I wanted to own a literary house or magazine or shipyard or sailing fleet. Whatever I wanted. I told him we needed to wait and see. He's so crazy."

"Not to mention his idea of a magazine is probably *Hustler*."

"Probably. Hard pass." He wrapped himself around me and kissed the side of my face as we both stared out at the city. "Anyway, I don't think I want any of that, especially not just handed over to me. I want what you have, where you start brainstorming and thinking and this sparkle hits your eyes and I can watch the creation happen inside of you. Like an apple hitting you in the head. You're so strong and sure and remarkable, and maybe I just needed to see you in action to know what I was missing."

"Maybe." I smiled, acknowledging I did exactly that. I hoped he would find that spark for himself.

While there were no guarantees in life, Jordan was betting on me. And maybe for the first time, I was betting on us both.

We had something, even if I was frightened by that.

I stared out at the twinkly lights, and I wondered where he would be if he hadn't met me, which light he would have been.

As the La Croix family had helped me change my stars, I'd helped change Jordan's.

Maybe he was right; maybe it was all fate all along.

If it was, I'd need to send her a thank-you.

Maybe I could deliver it on a Post-it note.

I snuggled into him more, closing my eyes, and for the first time in my life, I contemplated where we were going. My future had always had success in it—I didn't need a guy for that—but having one along for the ride, especially one like Jordan, felt right. Lucky for me, no more tests were needed to prove just how right.

Check out the Test Dummy website or Instagram for more fun!
  https://www.instagram.com/thetestdummies/
  http://thetestdummynyc.blogspot.ca
  Or email us at thetestdummynyc@gmail.com for a fun auto response.

ABOUT THE AUTHOR

Author photo © 2015

The internationally bestselling author of *Roommates*, the Puck Buddies series, and the Serendipity series, Tara Brown loves writing for a variety of genres. In addition to her Single Lady Spy novels, she has also published popular contemporary and paranormal romances, science fiction, thrillers, and romantic comedies. Tara especially enjoys writing dark and moody tales, often focusing on strong female characters who are more inclined to vanquish evil than perpetrate it. Tara lives with her husband, two daughters, two cats, an Irish wolfhound, and a Maremma Sheepdog. Find out more about Tara by visiting www.TaraBrownAuthor.com.